Wade Garrison

God's Coffin

by

Richard J Greene

Sequel to Wade Garrison's Promise

ISBN: 978-1-4349-8534-7 eISBN: 978-1-4349-7528-7

About the Author

Richard and his Lhasa Apso Jackson

Richard Greene was born in Denver, Colorado, in 1939, and grew up in a small two-bedroom house in Englewood, a suburb of Denver. In 1954, his parents divorced, and his father moved to Houston, Texas. Soon after that, Richard dropped out of ninth grade, worked at various jobs, including sacking groceries at a local supermarket and as an electrician's apprentice for a neighbor. He spent his summers with his dad, who owned 'The Texan' bar on the outskirts of Houston, Texas, where he got an education in life unlike his friends back in Englewood, Colorado. In August 1956, at seventeen, Richard enlisted in the United States Navy. After boot camp and Yeoman School in March 1957, he was transferred to the USS Belle Grove LSD-2 (Landing Ship Dock), serving in the South Pacific and taking part in the atomic testing at Eniwetok and Bikini Atolls in 1958.

Honorably discharged in 1960, he worked at Samsonite Luggage for a short spell and then went to work for Burlington Truck Lines as a billing clerk. The trucking industry fascinated Richard, so he attended Denver Traffic School to learn the ins and outs of the trucking industry. He worked as a dock supervisor for United Buckingham in Denver, a sales representative for Californian Motor Express in Fresno, California, and Los Angeles. Moving back to Denver, he went to work as Claims Prevention Manager for Consolidated Freightways, which included investigating road accidents of CF trucks within 100 miles of Denver. After a year with Consolidated, he was transferred from Denver to the General Claims Department in Portland, Oregon. In 1973, Richard left the Claims Department to become a supervisor in the Collection Department for Consolidated, where he remained until his retirement in December 1995 as Manager of Collections.

Still residing in Portland, Oregon, Richard and his wife Cathy spend much of their time with their children and grandchildren. Richard's other interests are golf, long walks, reading, and oil painting.

Please visit my web page, www.richardjgreene.net, or visit me on Facebook at https://www.facebook.com/richardgreene.7393.

https://twitter.com/@dickiejoe, All of my books are available on Amazon as ebook or paperback.

For Cathy

Preface

Wade Garrison rode out of Harper, Colorado, into the New Mexico Territory in 1872, believing he was riding away from a troubled past.

Now, six years later, his old friend, Sheriff Seth Bowlen, in Sisters, Colorado, is in trouble and needs help. Sheriff Bowlen sends a wire to United States Marshal Billy French in Santa Fe, who, in turn, sends Deputy Marshal Wade Garrison to help their old friend.

Innocently, Wade decides to take his wife, Sarah, and son, Emmett, with him so they can visit her family in Harper, a small town northeast of Sisters. As he and his family board the train in Santa Fe, he could not have known that a terrible storm of violence was already brewing, and this fateful decision could destroy his wife and child.

One

July 1878

Sisters, Colorado

Sheriff Seth Bowlen sat in his creaky, old chair with his feet on his wooden desk, enjoying a cup of strong, black coffee while reading the Sisters Weekly Newspaper. It was a quiet, peaceful Saturday morning, the kind of morning men like Seth Bowlen have learned to appreciate. The worn swivel chair he sat in moaned and creaked as he leaned forward to put the paper down. Picking up his coffee cup, he stood and walked to the window where he looked out at the sunny dirt street. Sam Hank's big, black dog looked dead as it lay sleeping on the ground in the sun next to the steps of the boardwalk to Hank's General Store. Watching a dust devil dance down the dirt road, Bowlen sipped his coffee, thinking it was going to be a warm one.

The town of Sisters was not unlike other small towns of the west. Its main street ran west from the Denver and Rio Grande Railway Depot, through a canyon of buildings and false storefronts. Seth let his eyes wander the sunny, dirt street that would soon be busy with Saturday morning shoppers, riders, and wagons. A few store owners were busily sweeping the boardwalks in front of their stores, which didn't seem to bother Hanks's black dog. Seth glanced at Molly's Restaurant just up the street, imagining his wife, Molly, busy inside with her impatient customers.

His cup empty, Seth turned and walked to the potbellied stove in the corner behind his desk and filled his cup. Taking a quick sip, he returned to his creaky chair and the article about the town council wanting to enlarge Sisters' city limits. The stillness Seth was enjoying was suddenly interrupted by the barking of Sam Hank's big, black dog, followed by the loud squeal of a frightened horse. Looking out the window at a man sitting on a wagon yelling obscenities at the dog, Seth smiled as the wagon and its familiar driver disappeared up the street. As silence returned to the dirt street of Sisters, he returned to the article and the paper he was reading when a single gunshot broke the silence of a peaceful Saturday morning. Looking up from the newspaper, he glanced out the window and then at the clock on the far wall that said it was only 9:15 in the morning. 'A mite early,' he thought to himself as he stood with cup in hand and walked to the window looking out into the street and boardwalks.

Two ladies across the street rushed along the boardwalk glancing back toward Jack Pritchard's Saloon. Hanks' black dog that had earlier given chase to the wagon relieved itself on the hitching rail across the street, seemingly ignoring the gunshot. Its owner, Sam Hanks, was standing on the boardwalk with a broom in hand, along with two other shop owners looking toward the saloon. After a few words passed between them, they laughed, then disappeared inside their places of business.

Seth glanced up the street toward Pritchard's Saloon as his deputy, Carl McIver, rushed out the swinging doors, across the boardwalk, down the steps, and ran down the street toward the jail.

Sheriff Bowlen sipped his coffee and watched the pudgy figure of his deputy trot along the dusty, dirt street, glancing now and again over his shoulder towards the saloon. Not anxious for the news he knew was bad, Seth turned away from the window and sat down in his squeaky chair. He put his feet on his desk, sipped his coffee, and waited for the bad news.

Deputy McIver opened the door, rushed inside, quickly closed the door, and hurried across the moaning floorboards of the wooden floor, and stopped in front of the Sheriff's desk.

Seth waited while the deputy paused to catch his breath.

Looking distraught, Carl gestured toward the door. "Pete Hoskins done killed old man Olson."

Seth looked surprised as he took his feet off of his desk. "Jacob Olson?" Seth recalled the day Pete's older brother Daniel was killed by Wade Garrison when he tried to bushwhack him across the street from that very saloon.

"Yep," replied Carl with a quick nod. "Better get over there, Seth."

Seth looked puzzled. "Why in Heaven's name would Pete kill old man Olson?"

McIver shrugged, looking puzzled as well. "Beats me, Seth."

Bowlen looked upset as he stood. "Shit fire," he said just above a whisper. "What the hell is Hoskins doing in Sisters on a Saturday morning anyways? Hell, everyone knows his pa owns most of Harper."

Carl shrugged. "Can't rightly say, Seth."

Bowlen drank the last of his coffee, gave his deputy a disgruntled look as he set the cup down. He turned to get his gun while talking over his shoulder. "Couldn't you stop it?"

Deputy Carl McIver was a short, chubby man of forty with balding, black hair, a round face in need of a shave, and brown eyes. He shrugged, looking helpless. "Shit, Seth, I was across the street, and…"

"All right, all right," interrupted Bowlen in a soft, understanding voice while buckling his gun belt. He knew the limits of his deputy, and while Carl was a good man and dependable, he was the sort of man that would stay out of harm's way as best he could. In truth, Seth found no blame in that line of reasoning. He bent to tie the strap of his holster around his right thigh and looked up at his deputy. "What'd you see?"

Excitement filled Carl's face. "When I got to them swinging doors of Pritchard's place and looked inside, Hoskins and that Booth Fox, fellah, was standing at the bar looking down at the floor. Pete had his gun out and turned to look at me as I walked in. That's when I saw old man Olson lying on the floor."

"You check Olson to see if he was dead?"

Deputy Carl shook his head. "No, I didn't, but he sure looked dead, so I thought I best come after you."

11

Sheriff Bowlen drew his .44 Colt Single Action pistol, made sure it was loaded, spun the cylinder, and slid the gun back into its holster, looking thoughtful. Not sure of what he might be walking into, he took a .12-gauge shotgun from the rack and opened its breech seeing it was empty. Seth opened his desk drawer, took out two shells from a box of shells, closed the drawer, and shoved the cartridges into the shotgun. After closing the breech, he held the shotgun out for Carl to take. "Just in case."

McIver hesitantly took the shotgun and watched as Seth grabbed his hat from the corner of his desk with one hand and put the other on Carl's shoulder, pushing him toward the door. "Let's go see what the hell happened."

Outside, Seth stopped at the edge of the boardwalk holding his gray Stetson hat in his right hand next to his thigh, waiting for Carl to close the door. Seth was an easygoing, soft-spoken man in his late forties, with a lean six-foot frame. A neatly trimmed, gray handlebar mustache sat under a slightly crooked nose hiding a thin upper lip. His head of thick, dark brown hair mixed with gray in need of the haircut he had been putting off. A scar from a knife-wielding young cowboy years ago ran from the center of his forehead, through the edge of his right eyebrow next to his nose, and across the middle of his right cheek. Although the blue eye itself hadn't been cut, the trauma left it slightly cloudy, leading people to believe he was blind in that one eye.

The warm morning sun felt soft and friendly against his face as he and Carl started down the steps, into the dusty, rut-filled street. While Seth put on his Stetson and adjusted his holster, Carl gripped the shotgun with both hands, holding it across his belly. The two men walked toward the saloon in silence, seeing several curious men began to gather along the boardwalk in front of the saloon. They were peering over the swinging doors and through the saloon windows.

Seth glanced at the side of Carl's face, seeing tiny beads of sweat beginning to form and then at Carl's hands tightly gripping the shotgun, knowing they were also sweaty. "You gonna back me in there, Carl?" Seth quietly asked as they walked toward the steps to the boardwalk.

"You know, I will," replied McIver, sounding irritated

Bowlen grinned wryly. "Wipe the sweat off your hands, Carl. Sorry for asking, and I meant no disrespect, but you've a wife and…"

12

"Same as you," interrupted the deputy, referring to the Sheriff's wife, Molly.

Seth could find no argument for that and let it go.

Reaching the boardwalk in front of the saloon, Seth glanced up at the white sign with red lettering, reading JACK PRITCHARD'S SALOON, and stopped. He turned to Carl and spoke in a low voice. "When we get inside, you do your best to get behind Booth Fox. Do it quietly, and if they start anything, you shove the barrel of that .12 gauge against the back of Booth's head and cock both hammers." He paused and looked at his deputy's sweating face. "And for Heaven's sake, don't shoot unless you have to. I don't want his brains splattered all over Pritchard's new mirror."

Seth glanced around at the crowd's faces wishing that it was his old friend, Frank Wells, walking into the saloon with him instead of Carl. "I'm in no mood to get shot by some damn drunken cowboy on what started as a quiet Saturday morning." Looking apprehensive, he turned and walked up the steps, making his way through the small crowd, telling them to step aside while ignoring their questions. When he reached the doorway, he put his hands on top of the swinging doors and paused to look into the dim saloon before he stepped inside.

Carl and his shotgun followed, bumping into Seth as he stopped to take in the scene. Bowlen ignored Carl's clumsiness and glanced around the large room of empty chairs and clean tables. A hatless Pete Hoskins was standing at the bar, looking at Seth's reflection in the large mirror behind the bar. Pete's friend, Booth Fox, and hired hand at the Hoskins's Ranch stood a few feet away from where the bar curved toward the wall.

Pete turned and stood with his back against the bar resting on his elbows, looking relaxed and friendly with his right foot resting on the brass footrest that ran the length of the dark, mahogany bar. Pete was twenty-six years old, standing five-feet-ten and lean. He was dressed in black pants, a gray shirt, and a loosely tied, faded red bandana around his neck. His wide-brimmed, black hat lay on the bar next to him, and his light brown hair was a mess. He had a three-day beard and looked like he hadn't slept in as many days. He looked at Seth with tired brown eyes, smiled wryly, and gave a quick nod. "Sheriff."

"Pete," greeted Seth, as his eyes roamed the saloon before settling on Booth Fox leaning on the bar with his elbows, hands clasped around a half mug of beer. Fox nodded hello, drank the last of his beer, then set the mug down, avoiding eye contact. Booth Fox needed a shave, had dark brown eyes, a wide mouth, white, uneven teeth, and his unruly, black, curly hair flowed from under the black Stetson he wore pushed back on his head.

Seth's eyes went from Booth to Jacob Olson's body lying on the floor, then to Pete, and then back to Booth. The sound of the swinging doors and soft words caused him to turn around. Seeing several men standing inside, he motioned them out of the saloon. "I want everyone that wasn't here when this happened to step outside." As the curious went back outside with mumbled protests, Seth walked to Jacob Olson's body, feeling sorry for Mrs. Olson and his daughter.

Carl and his shotgun had made their way to the window behind Booth Fox, giving him an unobstructed view of Fox and Pete Hoskins.

Booth turned, looked at the shotgun, and then at Carl's sweating face, smiled at Carl, and then turned back to see what Seth was doing.

Seth knelt and felt Jacob's neck for a pulse, and finding none, he put his hand over Jacob Olson's open eyes, closed them, and looked at his stained, bloody white shirt and the hole below the heart. He stood, stepped back, and studied the scene for several moments. Two half-full mugs of beer were sitting on the table where Jacob Olson and someone else had been sitting. An overturned chair lay on the floor a few feet away, apparently knocked over when Jacob stood. Olson lay on his back, his arms outstretched, a gun near his side, and his hat lying on the floor a few feet away.

Seth glanced at Hoskins, then at Fox, and finally at the bartender, Paul Leonard, standing behind the bar. He was wiping the same shot glass with a bar towel when Seth and Carl had walked in.

Paul was a short, heavyset man of thirty-something wearing a white shirt, thin string tie, and white apron over black pants. He had a high forehead of thinning, black, greasy hair and wore a black, thin mustache that sat smugly between a broad nose and thick lips. He was nervous as his eyes went from Seth to Pete, back to Seth, and then to the glass he was wiping.

Bowlen looked down at the two mugs of beer sitting on the table where Olson had been sitting. Then he looked at Paul. "Who was sitting with Olson?"

14

"Tom Lawson."

Seth glanced around the saloon. "Where is Lawson?"

Paul shrugged, "He went out back to piss before the commotion started. I guess he saw what took place and high-tailed it for home."

Deputy Carl looked at Seth. "I saw Lawson get on his horse and ride out of town just as I was coming across the street, Seth."

Bowlen couldn't blame Lawson for getting the hell out of town, but as he stared at Carl, he wondered why his deputy failed to tell him that bit of information. He turned back to the bartender. "Anyone else in here?"

"No. Place is always quiet this early."

"Wish it'd stayed that way," said Seth as he walked across the moaning boards of the floor, stopping at the bar where he looked at Leonard. "What happened?"

Paul Leonard shrugged, looking nervous. "Maybe you should ask Pete."

"I'm asking you damn it," replied an angry Seth Bowlen.

Leonard glanced at Pete and Booth Fox, and then he gestured to Pete with the hand holding the towel. "Pete and old man Olson got into an argument over something. I turned away, and then I heard a chair overturn and a gun going off." Looking embarrassed, he added, "Guess I got scared and ducked behind the bar."

Seth stared at Paul for a moment, and then he glanced at Pete and Booth Fox at the far end of the bar then Paul. "You never actually saw what happened?"

Leonard shook his head. "No, I didn't, Seth."

Bowlen looked at Carl standing behind Booth Fox in the light of the window, holding the shotgun across his stomach. Then he looked at Pete Hoskins, thinking he looked as though he'd had one hell of a night then at Pete's pistol lying on the bar. Turning, he looked at the table with the two mugs of beer, the overturned chair, and Jacob Olson. Without looking away from Olson's body, he asked, "What the hell happened here, Pete?"

Pete frowned as his sleepy eyes went from Seth to Olson's body and then back to Seth. He sighed and gestured at Fox with one hand. "Booth and I came in for a beer, and a few minutes later, Olson and Tom Lawson came in, sat down, and ordered a couple of beers. Old man Olson called to me, so I walked over to see what he wanted. That's about the time Lawson got up and walked out the back door to the outhouse. Old man Olson and me started talking, and then we began arguing." He nodded to the bartender. "Just as Paul there said we were."

Seth's questioning eyes went to Paul and then back to Pete. "Arguing about what?"

Pete sighed with a small shrug. "Doris Olson."

Surprised, Seth glanced down at Jacob Olson's body. "Why were you arguing about Jacob's daughter?"

Hoskins looked embarrassed. "He said she's with child and claims I'm the father."

Seth stared at Pete. "Are you?"

Pete shrugged, looking uneasy. "Could be, I guess, but so could several other men."

Seth shook his head, not liking the answer. "You say that to Jacob?"

Pete nodded. "That's about the time he stood knocking over his chair and went for his gun. I pulled mine and got off the first shot."

Seth turned and looked at Olson's body again, trying to imagine the scene, and then he turned to Pete. "Didn't you figure saying something like that was bound to piss Jacob Olson off?"

Hoskins looked regretful as he shrugged. "Never thought about it. It just came out."

"How long have you been seeing Doris Olson?" asked Bowlen.

Pete shrugged. "A while, I guess, but it wasn't anything serious."

Seth shook his head, looking disgusted. "Damn it to hell, Pete. Her being with child is serious."

Pete turned away, looking troubled, took a drink of beer and glanced at Booth at the end of the bar, staring into his empty beer mug.

Bowlen looked irritated as he let out a soft sigh. "Damn it all to hell, Pete."

Just then, a man outside yelled, "Pete Hoskins killed old man Olson!" followed by the usual crowd sounds of anger.

Seth turned toward the voice, knowing trouble wasn't far behind the news. Deciding to defuse the situation, he picked up Pete's pistol and told Booth to get out of town. Then he picked up Pete's hat, placed it on

16

his head, took him by the arm, and started toward the door. "I need to get you the hell out of here before this crowd gets angry."

"I ain't afraid of these assholes."

Bowlen scoffed.

"Where we going?" asked Pete.

"I'm taking you to jail. I'm sure your pa will be on his way soon as Booth tells him I've arrested you."

"You arresting me?"

"That's right, Pete."

"It was self-defense."

"We'll sort all that out." As they walked toward the door, Seth turned his head and yelled over his shoulder to Carl, who started to follow. "Stay here and make sure no one messes with anything." Then, Seth paused and turned to Paul Leonard. "You're closed for a while, Paul. Shut these big doors, and don't let no one in 'til I get back."

Seth and Pete Hoskins made their way through the crowd of mumbles and sneers, across the boardwalk, down the steps to the dirt street, and toward the sheriff's office. Once inside, Seth paused to see if they had been followed before closing the door. Then he pointed to a closed-door leading to three cells. "In there." He took the keys and keyring from a peg next to the door, opened the outer door, and gestured to the first cell. "The first one will do."

Reluctantly, Pete walked into the first cell. "It was self-defense, Sheriff."

Seth locked the cell door and looked at Pete. "We'll let a Judge determine that, Pete.

Pete sat on the cot and tossed his hat against the brick wall in anger.

"Being angry is what started this mess, Pete," said Wade. Then he stepped back, looking curious. "What the hell are you and Booth Fox doing in Sisters anyways? Your pa owns most of Harper. Couldn't you have shot someone there instead after you had your morning beer?"

Pete answered with an uncaring shrug. "How long are you gonna keep me in here?"

Seth thought about that a moment, thinking Pete looked like a young boy, defeated and helpless, and he couldn't help but feel sorry for him. Pete wasn't liked very much by most people. The only real friends he had were Booth Fox and the hands that worked on the Hoskins' ranch located to the north, not far from Harper. "Don't rightly know," replied Seth.

"Why not?"

Seth turned and walked out the door, closing it without answering, hung the keys back on the peg, and peered at Pete through the small window of the door. "Like I said, Pete, a judge, will have to make that determination." Bowlen glanced at the front door. "Right now, I'm more concerned about that crowd up at the saloon. They could turn ugly fast, and some idiot might try and put one through that thick head of yours before I can straighten this whole thing out."

"This bunch of farmers and storekeepers ain't got the guts."

Seth looked through the small window of the door, feeling irritated. "Well, that's brave of you, Son, but just in case you're wrong, I ain't aiming to get shot while standing next to you." Seth turned and walked toward the front door, stopping as he put his hand on the doorknob he turned. "I'm heading back to the saloon. I'll send Carl back to keep an eye on you. I figure your pa won't waste much time getting here."

Pete put his hands on the bars of the cell door and yelled through the small window of the outer door. "What happens then?"

"Don't rightly know at this moment, Pete. We'll have to figure that out when the time comes. Right now, I have a few things to look into." With that, he opened the front door, stepped outside, and headed for the saloon.

Two

August 1878

New Mexico Territory

Deputy United States Marshal Wade Garrison was cold and tired from lack of sleep as he lay on the hard, cold ground waiting for the sun to rise above the eastern horizon. He turned his head and looked over his shoulder at the thin, blue line separating the earth from the sky, knowing it would be light soon. The rocky cliff Wade lay on overlooked the campsite of the three men that he, Marshal Billy French, and Deputy John Turner had been trailing for three days. Fighting the urge to sleep, he hoped that Turner and French were still awake, then he looked over his right shoulder toward the hills in the east, wishing the sun would hurry. Wade was hungry, cold, and his muscles ached from the rocky surface he lay on. Wade wanted to finish this and get home to Sarah and his son, Emmett.

Fighting sleep, he looked up at the black sky full of stars whose moon had long since disappeared into the west. Then he looked back to the eastern horizon and the light, blue sky above the jagged hills, thinking it won't be long now. He couldn't see French or Turner, but he knew that Marshal Billy French was about forty yards to his right between two good-sized rocks. Deputy Turner was to his left about the same distance, hidden behind a large fir tree and scrub brush.

As the minutes passed, the sky grew lighter, and in that faint light just before sunrise, he could see the horses and bedrolls of the men they were after on the basin floor below the overhang. Taking the long glass from the pocket of his coat, he pulled it apart, took off his wide-brimmed, black hat, and looked at the camp. In the dim light, he could barely make out the sleeping figures of the three men lying on the ground covered by their blankets, and he envied their sleep. Their horses hobbled a few feet away, were saddled with their heads down.

As the sun broke over the horizon, he glanced back at the bright, orange ball feeling its warmth as it spread its light over the red, rocky surface he was laying on. He put the long glass back into his coat pocket, put his gloves and hat back on, and glanced to where French and Turner were hiding. His right hand found the Sharps rifle lying next to him, and as he cocked its hammer, he knew the sun would be at his back and in the eyes of the men below him. A coyote nearby gave out its lonely cry, and Wade could hear the horses snorting and getting nervous. Afraid they would give them away, he set the Sharps down and crawled away from the ledge toward the shallow gully and the horses.

Once in the gully, he rubbed his mare's neck while talking in a soft, calm voice to her and the other horses as the warm sun-filled the gully. Hoping the coyote had gone away, a gunshot, followed by another and then another, broke the silence. Wade hurried back to the cliff in time to see the men below mounting their horses while firing at Deputy John Turner. Wade picked up his Sharps, knelt onto his right knee, resting his left elbow on his left knee, and took aim. Billy French opened up with his Winchester, and instead of hitting the rider, Billy hit the horse. As it screamed and fell, it threw its rider, who managed to take cover behind a large boulder, firing at Billy with his pistol.

Billy kept firing his Winchester at the man behind the boulder, keeping him pinned down. Wade aimed at one of the two men riding away, but they disappeared around a sheer cliff on the other side of the meadow before he could pull the triggers. Cursing the lousy luck, Wade ran to the gully and his mare, took off her hobble, tossed it aside, and quickly tightened her cinch. He pulled the reins from the tree, swung up, and gently hit the mare's rump with the barrel of the Sharps, nudging her into a gallop out of the gully. He rode around the hill after the two men where Billy and Turner were exchanging gunfire with the man in camp.

Early morning sunshine filled the New Mexico desert as he chased after the two riders and their dust across the badlands. Knowing his mare would tire before long, he turned in the saddle and quickly dumped his saddlebags and bedroll. Then he took off his coat, tossed it in the air to lighten her load, and leaned against her neck. As if the mare knew what he wanted from her, she lowered her head and ran.

The ground they rode across became flat and open, and the mare was closing but getting tired, and her breathing labored. Reaching a small hill two hundred yards behind the two men, and knowing it was now or never, he pulled the mare up and stood tall in the saddle. He took aim through the peep sight at the front rider, pulled the first trigger, then the second. Feeling the recoil against his shoulder at the same instant, he heard the explosion of the .50 caliber cartridge. So sure of his aim, and without looking to see if he hit his target, he reloaded, aimed at the second rider, and pulled the first trigger, then the second feeling the kick of the Sharps. The rider jerked and slumped forward in the saddle, then fell. Wade reloaded then nudged the mare down the hill pausing at the first body seeing the large hole in the front of his coat. He nudged the mare and rode past the first rider's horse that had slowed and then stopped.

As he approached the second rider, he saw the man was trying to crawl away. Wade shoved his Sharps into its scabbard, took out his .45 Colt pistol, pulled up, climbed down, and dropped the reins of the mare.

The rider and managed to pull himself onto a good size rock and turn onto his back. "You got me good," he said while raising both hands showing they were empty.

Wade cautiously walked toward the man whose right shoulder of his coat was bloody and figured his shoulder bones were shattered. Keeping his gun pointed at the man, Wade walked over to him, bent down, and took the man's pistol from its holster, and tossed it a few feet away.

The man looked up at him with fear on his face. "You gonna finish me?"

Wade thought of Paul Bradley, who he left in Mexico for the vultures, and shook his head. "No, I'm taking you back to hang for that rancher you boys killed." Wade looked down at him. "Why shoot the old man? He wasn't even carrying."

The man looked regretful. "We didn't know that until it was over. He came upon us, sudden like as we were taking a few cows. Frank drew his gun and fired." He paused to wince in pain. "Got scared and left without the cattle."

"So it was all for nothing," said Wade in disgust. Knowing he wasn't going anywhere, Wade turned to get the man's horse a few feet away so he could put him on it and take him back to Billy. Hearing the click of a hammer from a pistol, he crouched as, turned, falling on his side, and fired at about the same time the other man did. Luckily the man missed, but Wade didn't. Getting up, he cautiously walked over and kicked the small pistol out of his hand. Thinking the man must have had it hidden in his coat's inside pocket, Wade bent down to feel his neck for a pulse. Finding none, he stood thinking that Sarah was damn near a widow and knew he had been lucky after being so careless from being tired.

An hour later, he rode into the outlaw's camp, with the two men draped and tied over their saddles, seeing the third man sitting on the ground holding his bloody arm. After a brief story of what happened, he, Marshal Billy French, and Deputy Turner set out for Santa Fe with their wounded prisoner and his two dead companions.

Santa Fe, New Mexico

Wade Garrison opened his eyes, looking into the blue eyes of his four-year-old son standing beside his bed, staring at him. He smiled at the boy, moved over, and held the covers back for the boy as he climbed into bed.

The boy grinned happily, and after Wade covered him, the boy asked, "When did you get back?"

Wade raised his head and looked over his shoulder at Sarah to see if she were still asleep, then he laid his head back onto his pillow and whispered, "Late, and I thought we agreed there'd be no more bed jumping."

The boy made a serious face and whispered, "The coyotes woke me, Pa, and I got scared." Young Emmett Garrison was nearing his fifth birthday and was tall for his age, as was Wade when he was a child. His hair was the same light brown color as his mother's, his face freckled, and his eyes were blue like his father's. Sarah wanted to name their first son after her grandfather, Randolph Talbert, but Wade had been stubborn about

22

naming their son after his best friend. And while Sarah could be quite stubborn herself, she understood the importance of the name Emmett, so they compromised on Emmett Randolph Garrison, a name that seemed to fit the boy.

Wade gently brushed his son's light brown hair away from his eyes and talked in a whisper. "Ain't no reason to be afraid, Son. Them coyotes are more afraid of us than we of them. You're safe here in the house, and besides, Dog wouldn't let anything get you."

The boy thought about that but for a quick moment. "But Dog's little like me. I called for you," he said, wearing a frown. "But you never came."

"Not so loud," whispered Wade. "You'll wake your ma." Then he glanced around the room, looking curious. "Where is Dog?'

"He's sleeping."

A smart dog, thought Wade.

"Did you catch the bad men?" asked Emmett, looking concerned.

"Yeah, we caught the bad men."

Emmett grinned proudly and then whispered, "Are they in jail?"

Wade turned and checked on Sarah once again. "Shhh, you'll wake your ma."

Emmett lifted his head and looked over his pa at his mother and then his pa. "No, we won't; nothing wakes her up."

Pretty close to the truth, thought Wade.

Emmett frowned. "I'm hungry."

Wade looked past Emmett to the clock on the small table next to the bed, whose ticking seemed loud in the quiet, dim bedroom. Dawn had not yet brought the full light of day with it, but the dim light provided enough light that he could see the dark hands of the clock against its white face. "Shit, it ain't even five o'clock, Emmett."

The boy frowned. "I thought 'shit' was a bad word."

Wade looked apologetic. "I shouldn't have said that but that don't change anything. It's still before five."

The boy looked puzzled. "Is that late?"

"No, it ain't late," whispered Wade, sounding a little irritated. Then he smiled at his son affectionately and sighed. "It's early, and I need a little more sleep." He helped his son snuggle down under the covers, tucking them around young Emmett's neck. "Go to sleep." The boy grinned, looking happy and content as he closed his eyes. Wade closed his eyes, trying to get comfortable with the extra body in bed. The minutes passed into sleepless frustration, while images of the two men he had killed rode through his mind. Opening his eyes to rid his mind of the two men, Wade looked into the innocent face of his sleeping son, wondering what sort of man Emmett would grow up to be. Sarah let out a soft snore, and when he turned and looked at the back of her head of light brown hair, he realized he wasn't going back to sleep. Wade sat up, carefully pushed the covers back, and got out of bed wearing his faded, red long johns. After he covered his son, now snuggled up next to his mother, Wade quietly reached for his pants lying at the foot of the bed, tiptoed across the room, and quietly opened the door. He looked back at his son and wife, sleeping, stepped out of the room, and closed the door.

After putting on his pants, he walked across the room to the kitchen, feeling the cold floor on his bare feet, wishing he had thought to bring his socks and boots with him. Feeling the chill of the morning, he walked to the wood cooking stove, built a fire, then filled the big coffee pot with water from the inside pump he installed last year. He added the coffee grounds, and while he waited for the coffee to boil, he went to his son's bedroom and opened the door. The mutt he had named Dog was lying on top of the ruffled covers, looking comfortable and not in the mood to get up. Dog was a small, yellow dog with floppy ears, black eyes, and black nose. Dog raised his head and looked up as if saying 'I ain't ready,' laid his head back down and closed his eyes. Wade slapped his hand gently against his leg and called him. Dog raised his head, looked at Wade, then slowly and reluctantly stood and stretched at what seemed a long time before he jumped off the bed and followed.

Barefooted, Wade and the dog stepped out the back door into the dim light of dawn. The neighbor's big, black, and white dog that had been asleep on their porch stood and stretched as it watched them with a disinterested stare. Dog's ears perked as he paused and growled deep in his throat at the other dog that ignored him. Wade whispered, "Hush."

Dog laid his ears back in defeat and quietly followed a barefoot Wade to the outhouse. As the two made their way back to the kitchen door, the house next door was beginning to show signs of life. Stepping onto the back porch, Wade stopped at the washbasin and the water pitcher, where he washed and dried his hands with an old towel. Stepping inside,

24

Dog hurried back to the warmth and comfort of Emmett's empty bed. Hearing the sound of boiling coffee, Wade moved the pot to the edge of the stove, away from the heat. Feeling the need to be alone a little longer, he filled one cup and walked to the window. Leaning with his shoulder against the wall next to the window, he sipped his coffee while looking out at the vast landscape dotted with small houses, barns, corrals, chicken coops, and outhouses.

Turning from the window, he glanced around the room of meager furnishings, and as he sipped his coffee, guilt for what he had not been able to provide for Sarah found him. In the stillness of the quiet room, he drank his hot coffee and remembered the day Sarah walked into the Marshal's Office in Santa Fe with her one suitcase. He was angry with her for following him from Harper, knowing he had nothing to offer but a meager living at best. Taking her out back behind the Marshal's Office away from Billy and the others, he told her to go back to Harper and her father's ranch. They argued for the better part of the day, and when the arguing was over, she stayed, and they married. Looking around at the meager furnishings once again, he had second thoughts about refusing the money offered by her parents on two separate occasions. The first was when Janice and Jasper Talbert journeyed from Harper to attend their daughter's wedding in the small adobe church in Santa Fe. The second was when Janice Talbert traveled to be with her daughter when she gave birth to Emmett.

Sarah had been born into a privileged life of expensive furniture, a large house, hands to help with the feeding of chickens, and the chopping of wood. The very things she now did herself while he was gone for days on end, hunting those that broke the law. Taking a drink of coffee, he stared at their bedroom door, marveled that she never complained, and always wore a smile, appearing quite happy and content. The years had been kind to them, and Sarah managed to save a little money here and there, and thanks to her cooking, he was not as lean as he once was, but the extra weight looked good on him.

At twenty-six and standing five-feet-ten, Wade was a handsome figure with brown hair, tanned face with white squint lines around his piercing but friendly blue eyes. The clean-shaven face and square jaw warned of his stubbornness, something the men he hunted could attest. As his gaze returned to the window, he watched the tip of the sunrise above the hills to the east, slowly making its way above the hills into the clear blue, New Mexico skies.

As if on cue, the Garrison rooster, with neck stretched sitting on top of the hen house with wings flapping, announced the arrival of a new day. Joined by several other roosters, their greeting echoed through Santa Fe, New Mexico. His troubled mind found the death of the Indian, Dark Cloud, outside a saloon, and Sherriff Frank Wells, as he lay dying on the bloody floor inside the saloon in Paso Del Rio six years ago.

A thin plume of smoke rising from the chimney of the Schmidt house took his mind off the past while envisioning the stocky Martha Schmidt busy at breakfast. He drank the last of his coffee, turned from the window, filled his cup, and then another for Sarah. Adding two spoonfuls of sugar to hers, he picked up both cups and headed for the bedroom. Managing the door without spilling, he quietly walked across the room and set Sarah's coffee cup on the table next to the bed.

She opened her sleepy eyes and smiled a warm, soft smile. "Good morning."

"Sleep well?"

She yawned and stretched, looking not quite awake. Her light brown hair was a mess, and she looked disappointed. "I thought you'd sleep in."

He smiled. "So did I." Then he pointed at their son.

"You've got to be kidding." She turned, seeing the top of the boy's light brown head sticking out from under the covers. Looking disappointed, she turned to Wade. "Looks like the talk you had with him did a lot of good."

"A coyote scared him," whispered Wade, looking skeptical.

"I doubt that." She sat up while Wade helped put her pillow between her back and the headboard before handing her the cup of coffee. She held the cup close to her face and closed her eyes, feeling the warm steam against her skin while smelling its strong aroma. She put the cup to her mouth, careful not to burn her lips, took a small sip, and smiled. "Thank you." She carefully moved to one side so she wouldn't wake her son and patted the bed next to her.

He sat down, careful not to spill his coffee, leaned back against the pillow and headboard, then put his arm around her.

She nestled against him, holding the cup with both hands, and waited for him to tell her what happened. Soon after they married, they had argued about his silence when he returned after being gone for days at a time. He argued that he didn't want to talk about it while she argued that she had to know, and in the end, it was Sarah's stubbornness that won. She drank her coffee and listened while he told her a short version of what happened, then she asked, "Do you have to work today?"

He nodded. "Yeah." Then he took a drink of coffee.

"That's not right. You were gone for three days and didn't get in until late."

He shrugged. "So did Billy and Turner."

She let it drop, feeling grateful for the few minutes she shared with him now. The room got quiet as neither felt the need for words. While they drank their coffee, listening to the familiar morning sounds of barking dogs and cows, mixing with the soft breathing of their sleeping son. Wade thought of the two men he had killed, wondering if they had families, while Sarah thought of telling Wade she was with child and of fixing breakfast.

While Wade dressed after breakfast, Sarah cleaned the table of dirty breakfast dishes, and little Emmett headed outside to play the child's game of chasing chickens. Being a smart animal, Dog watched from the safety of the back porch.

The minutes passed, and soon Sarah stuck her head out the back door. "Leave them chickens alone. Your pa's leaving; you best come say goodbye."

Sarah, having just turned twenty-four, was as pretty as she had been the day she and Wade first met. Standing just over five-feet-two, she was thin but shapely, with a small waist, rounded hips, and small breasts. Sarah still preferred wearing her long, light brown hair in a ponytail that swayed from side to side as she walked. An oval, slightly freckled face held a thin nose, full lips, and big soft brown eyes that seemed to turn darker when she was angry.

Emmett stopped chasing the chickens, turned, and ran to the porch, just as his pa walked out of the back door. The boy stopped short of the porch and looked up, eyeing the US Deputy Marshal's badge pinned to his pa's shirt, which was one of several things he secretly coveted.

Wade glanced at Dog sleeping next to the doorway and then at the boy while speaking in a stern yet gentle voice. "Mind your ma, Son, and don't tease Dog. He's smaller than you."

The boy glanced at Dog and then looked at his pa. "Yes, sir."

Wade leaned his Sharps rifle against the wall, placed the bandolier of cartridges on the wash table, and knelt to one knee, and lowered his voice to a whisper. "Your ma ain't been feeling too good of late, Son, so you need to cut her some slack and behave."

The boy looked worried. "What's wrong with her?"

Wade smiled. "I'm sure it's nothing serious." Then he stood and looked down with a firm face. "You just do as I say, and mind your ma."

"Yes, sir."

"And don't forget to give the mare fresh oats and clean water. She's had a tough time of it."

"Yes, sir."

Wade smiled at his son and ruffled the boy's hair. "Now, go on inside and help your ma." Then as his eyes met Sarah's, who was at the door, they smiled at one another as if sharing a secret.

"What time can I expect you?" she asked.

"Not sure. I guess when I get here."

She watched as he walked toward town for a few moments before she closed the door.

Deputy Jeb Rollins was sitting behind the desk, resting his feet on one corner of the desk, when Wade walked into the jailhouse. Rollins was a heavyset man in his early thirties, standing five feet six with balding, light brown hair, and a broad nose. "Morning, Wade," he said lazily as he leaned back in the chair, stretching his arms above his head.

Wade closed the door. "Jeb," he replied while his eyes found the cell holding their prisoner with his bandaged arm. As Wade walked past the cells toward Jeb, he noticed the all too familiar figure of Slim Peterson, sleeping off his usual drunken stupor. Walking to the gun rack behind the desk where Jeb was sitting, he put his Sharps in it then hung the bandolier on a nearby peg. Looking out the front window at some passerby's, he thought about Slim's devoted wife. Looking back at the sleeping figure, he wondered how she kept putting up with his constant drinking. Turning to the deputy, he asked, "Had your breakfast yet?"

28

Rollins shook his head with a yawn, looking sleepy. "About an hour ago." Then Jeb stood, picked up his hat, and walked from behind the desk. "Need to make my rounds. French ain't been in yet."

Wade glanced at the door and then at the papers on top of the desk. "Being Sunday and us getting in late, I don't expect he'll be in much before early afternoon." He tossed his hat on the desk and lifted the top of the coffee pot sitting on the short, fat potbellied stove in the corner. Finding there was still coffee inside, he touched the side of the pot and finding it warm. As he filled it, he nodded to Slim Peterson sleeping on the cot in the spare cell. "He been awake any?"

Deputy Rollins glanced at the drunk, chuckled, and shook his head. "Nah, but he's been snoring and flopping about most of the morning. Man sure snores heavy, kept me up most of the night."

"Most drunks do," replied Wade. Then he glanced at the cot next to the potbellied stove where Deputy Jeb Rollins had spent his turn at the night shift. He sipped his coffee, made a face thinking it was bitter, turned to the window, and looked out at the street and buildings beyond. "Town's quiet."

Jeb nodded in agreement. "It's been quiet all morning. S'pect, most people are still in bed or getting ready for church." Then as he walked to the door, he put on his hat while talking over his shoulder. "Be back in a bit."

Wade continued to stare out the window at a cat across the street under the boardwalk that looked like it had something, perhaps a mouse or small bird, in its mouth. The sound of the door closing took him away from the cat and its prize. He turned back to the street, seeing the cat was gone while hearing Jeb's heavy footsteps fade across the boardwalk. He thought about Deputy Todd Jewett and the night he died in Pine Springs, New Mexico.

The raspy voice of Slim Peterson broke the stillness of the jailhouse. "Can I go now, Mr. Garrison?"

Wade turned from the window to Slim Peterson standing inside his cell, grasping the bars, looking like he'd had a rough night. It was a mystery to Wade as to why everyone called Tom Peterson "Slim" because he was not slim at all. He was a short, chubby man of forty with black hair, an oval face, and dark, tired eyes. The left side of his dirty, white shirt hung out of his soiled and wrinkled gray pants, and Wade wasn't sure which Slim needed the most; a bath, a drink, or a hot meal. He thought of Slim's wife, Nora, a pretty but matronly looking woman of about forty. Nora worked hard at the café down the street and took in laundry to help make ends meet. Slim was an excellent carpenter when he was sober, but that seemed seldom to Wade, who had heard from someone that Slim was the way he was because of the war. "The cell door ain't locked, Slim. Go home."

Slim Peterson blinked several times as he pushed the cell door open and walked out on wobbly legs toward the front door.

"Your hat," reminded Wade.

Slim turned, looking confused, and then seeing his hat in the cell, walked back in, picked it up, put it on, thanked Wade, and then walked out the door.

Wade sat down in the chair behind the desk, drank the last of his coffee, put the cup down, and picked up five new posters of men wanted for one thing or another and started looking through them. Setting them down, he found a note from Billy French to Deputy John Turner, telling him it was okay to take tonight off. As Wade tossed the note back on the desk, he figured he would pull the graveyard shift.

Wade stood, walked to the window, rested his left shoulder against the sill, and, looking out at the nearly empty street, knew that Sarah was going to be upset about the night shift.

The clock in the corner chimed ten, immediately followed by Sunday morning church bells throughout the city. A woman and her young son, he knew as Jimmy, hurried along the boardwalk toward the church. As he watched them, Wade recalled the night the boy told him about the three men he had seen on the outskirts of Santa Fe.

His eyes moved up the street to the train depot just as the telegraph operator, Elmer Moore, step out of the telegraph office. Wade watched with curiosity as Elmer hurried across the boardwalk, down the steps into the dusty street, and then run toward the Marshal's Office. Elmer ran past the big front window to the door, opened it, and hurried inside.

Elmer Moore was a balding, short, plump man dressed in black pants, a white shirt with gartered sleeves, and a string tie. After closing the door, he hurried across the room, waving the mysterious envelope with his left hand. "I got a telegram for Marshal French, Mr. Garrison."

Wade sat down in the chair and leaned forward, resting his elbows on top of the desk. "He ain't in yet, Elmer."

Elmer stopped at the edge of the desk, looked at the envelope in his hand, and then at Wade. "Need to give this to the Marshal right away," he said, looking worried.

"Well, Elmer, like I done told you, he ain't here yet." Wade glanced out the window. "My guess is he and his family is in church about now." He turned back to Elmer. "But you can leave that with me, and I'll see he gets it."

Elmer's shoulders slumped in disappointment with the look of uncertainty on his face. "S'pose I could," he said thoughtfully, then begrudgingly, he slowly handed the envelope to Wade. "The man who sent it is waiting for a reply."

Wade took the envelope with the telegram and stared at it with a great deal of curiosity. "Who sent it?"

"Sheriff, by the name of Seth Bowlen."

Wade's face lit up. "Seth Bowlen?"

Elmer nodded. "Yes, sir, and he's await'n for a reply."

Wade quickly opened the envelope, took out the flimsy piece of paper, and read Elmer Moore's penciled words. "Need a United States Marshal in Sisters Colorado. STOP. Will wait for reply. STOP. Sheriff Seth Bowlen." He reread the words, looking thoughtful as his left hand unconsciously rubbed his chin and mouth, wondering why Seth would send a gram to Santa Fe asking Billy for help. This isn't like Seth Bowlen to ask for help, he told himself. Then he looked at Elmer. "Do me a favor, Elmer. Go find Jeb and tell him to come back and watch things." Then he stood, picked up his hat, and headed for the door. "I'll go find Billy."

Elmer followed him outside. "As soon as I find Deputy Rollins, I'll head back up to the telegraph office and send word that the Marshal will be answering directly."

Wade closed the door thinking about Seth Bowlen, and he never heard or answered Elmer. After the two stepped into the street, Moore hurried to find Jeb reminding Wade the Sheriff was waiting for a response. Wade looked in the direction of the church and then in the direction of Billy's house. Not sure whether Billy would be in church or at home, he decided to try his house first, thinking that would be easier than trying to get his attention during church services.

Wade pulled the gate to the white picket fence open, stepped in, and walked to the front door, He knocked on the door, and a few moments later, he heard movement inside, and then the door opened.

Billy French stared at him with a puzzled look. "Everything all right?" Billy French was a big man in his late thirties, with deep-set, brown eyes, light brown hair, a handlebar mustache, and square jaw. From his clothes, it was apparent that Billy wasn't going to church.

Wade handed him the telegram. "Elmer said Seth's waiting for a reply." Then, looking apologetic, added, "I read it before I came looking for you, to make sure it was important."

Billy took the telegram with a curious look. "Come in." Staring at the envelope, he stepped back from the door.

Wade stepped inside, took off his hat, and glanced around the tiny entryway and hall walls filled with several black silhouetted figures in frames and a few photographs. The smell of a late breakfast made its way from the kitchen at the other end of the hall.

Billy closed the door, turned, and walked into the parlor, pulling his suspenders up over his shoulders. Inside, French gestured to a small and uncomfortable looking, tanned, overstuffed chair. "Have a seat."

Wade sat down, looking uncomfortable, and waited while French opened the envelope, took out the telegram. After reading it, Billy sat down on a small, tan sofa of embroidered flowers and leaves, looking upset. He thoughtfully folded the paper, placed it back in the envelope, and looked at Wade. "Shit," he said irritably, "I can't go to Sisters. I have to be in Albuquerque in two days." Then he turned to the window. "I wonder why he didn't send for the United States Marshal up in Denver."

Wade looked puzzled. "Can't say." Then he paused and asked, "Want me to go?"

French glanced at him briefly and then turned and stared out the window, considering that. "It's not like Seth to ask for help."

"That's what I was thinking. Seth must be in trouble."

"Guess I could send you," Billy said, looking thoughtful. "You might be there a spell, though, depending on what the problem is. Seth wouldn't ask for help unless he was mixed up in something he couldn't handle."

Wade smiled. "There ain't much that Seth can't handle."

Quiet filled the tiny room, and then Billy looked at Wade. "Would your Sarah be agreeable to you being gone a couple of weeks, maybe even longer?"

Wade shrugged, thinking about her morning sickness. "I think so. She's used to it."

Billy chuckled without humor. "About as much as my missus."

Wade smiled, thinking of Sarah while looking uneasy as he stared at the wide-brimmed, black hat he slowly twirled with his fingers. "Sarah's got the morning sickness."

Billy's smile vanished. "If she's with child, you can't go to Sisters."

Wade looked up and nervously shifted in the small chair. "Might be a good thing to take her with me."

The Marshal looked doubtful. "Hell of a long trip for a woman carrying a child."

Wade shrugged. "Not really. If she is with child, she isn't far along, and it's been a while since she's been home. I'm sure her folks would like to see their daughter and grandson."

French pursed his lips in thought, stood, walked to the window, parted the lace curtains with one hand, and stared out at the dirt street beyond the white picket fence, the tiny front yard of weeds, and a lonely lilac tree. "All right," he softly said as he turned. "You go to Sisters." Then he walked toward the parlor door. "I'll put on a shirt and get my hat, and then we'll send a reply to Seth."

Wade stood, filled with anticipation of seeing his old friend. "I'll wait outside."

Arriving at the telegram office, Marshal French wrote a short message on a piece of paper and handed it to Elmer to send to Seth Bowlen in Sisters, Colorado. The telegram read: "*Sending US Deputy Wade Garrison. STOP Billy French United States Marshal STOP.'*

While Elmer tapped out the code over the telegraph lines, French and Wade walked outside, stopping at the edge of the boardwalk. Billy leaned against the porch post with a look of concern, folded his arms, and stared north toward Colorado. "I sure as hell would like to know what sort of mess has Seth ask'n for my help."

Wade stood next to him, wondering the same thing as he looked down the street at the bridge leading to the Mexican side of Santa Fe, remembering the night he went looking for Seth and Frank Wells in a Mexican cantina.

Billy turned to him. "I'm thinking you best go tell Sarah." Then he looked at the railroad tracks disappearing into the distance. "If it's on time, there's a train due in around ten tomorrow morning that will take you north to Sisters." Then he turned with a quizzical look. "Think you can be ready to leave by then?"

Wade glanced away from the tracks in the other direction toward his house, thinking of telling Sarah. "Believe so. Well," he sighed, stepping from the boardwalk, "I best go tell Sarah."

Billy watched him as he walked up the dusty street, imagining the scene between him and Sarah, and smiled, glad that it wasn't him going home to talk to his missus. Then, with a small chuckle, he stepped from the boardwalk toward the marshal's office, filled with curiosity about Seth Bowlen's problem.

Three

Sisters, Colorado

Wade opened his eyes to the sudden jerking of the train as it slowed, and the conductor bounced off of the seats while making his way toward the rear of the rail car, yelling, "Sisters!" Wade sat up, looking sleepy as he stared out the window at the familiar buildings. The sun hung low in the western sky over the Rocky Mountains, and its red-orange color covered the landscape of prairie grass, red sandy soil, and the buildings of Sisters, Colorado.

Sarah sat across from him, staring out the window, looking anxious while unconsciously biting the right side of her lower lip as she always did when nervous. Wade turned from the window, thinking she looked beautiful in her blue and white bonnet, her light brown hair lying over one shoulder of her blue dress with a lace collar. Emmett was still asleep on the seat next to her with his head on her lap.

The train jerked again as it slowed while approaching the Sisters Depot, as Wade looked at his son, wondering how he could sleep through all the jerking and noisy travelers. Familiar buildings slowly passed the window as the train slowed to a stop, bringing back the memory of his and Sheriff Seth Bowlen's first meeting and the advice Bowlen had given. *"You're not prepared for what you're about to find trailing these four men."* Now, all these years later, Wade knew that Seth Bowlen had been right about that, as he had been about a lot of other things in the weeks that followed that warning.

The train jerked, pulling Wade from the memory as it crept along the tracks, coming to a sudden stop alongside the tiny, single-story depot building.

Standing at the corner of the building was Seth Bowlen, dressed in tan pants tucked into his brown boots and a long, dark brown coat with a bulge on the right side covering his gun. He wore a gray Stetson hat, white shirt, string tie and looked very much the lawman he was. Eagerly, he searched every passenger car doorway and window as it passed.

At seeing Seth, Wade's face filled with a grin as he lowered the upper half of the window, leaned his head out, and yelled, "Seth Bowlen!"

Seth glanced here and there, searching for the owner of the voice, finding Wade's head sticking out of one of the passenger car windows. He grinned, waved, and hurried through the small crowd, gesturing toward the door of the passenger car. Wade nodded his understanding and turned to Sarah. "Better wake Emmett, Seth's await'n."

"Seth Bowlen?" she asked with excitement.

"The one and only," replied Wade with a grin full of excitement himself. Seeing that Emmett was not about to wake up, he reached down and picked up his sleeping son. While holding him in one arm and his head resting on his shoulder, Wade helped Sarah up with the other. Then, he and Emmett followed Sarah down the narrow aisle to the door, down the steps of the rail car, and onto the wooden platform of the train depot.

"Wade," Seth called out, making his way through the small crowd. With an outstretched hand, he grinned. "French sent me a telegram this morning saying you and your family would be on this here train."

They shook hands firmly. "Good to see you, Seth."

"You're a sight," Bowlen said, looking happy.

Wade turned. "This here's my wife, Sarah, and this little guy sleeping on my shoulder's our son, Emmett."

Sarah smiled and extended her hand, noticing his bad eye, and politely nodded. "Mr. Bowlen."

Seth took off his hat with one hand, gently took Sarah's hand with the other, kissed the back of her hand, and smiled warmly. "It's a pleasure to make your acquaintance, Mrs. Garrison."

36

"Call me, Sarah, please," she replied. Realizing she was staring at his cloudy eye and scar, she suddenly felt embarrassed and forced herself to look into his good eye.

Sensing her embarrassment, Seth grinned, leaned a little closer, winked, and whispered, "Don't feel embarrassed about staring at the eye, Sarah. I'm quite used to it by now."

She smiled, looking embarrassed, as well as relieved. "My husband has told me so much about you, Mr. Bowlen, including the story of how you injured your eye. But I had forgotten all about it. Do forgive me for staring, please."

"Ain't nothing to forgive, Ma'am," he said with a chuckle. "I sometimes forget about it myself until I look in the mirror, and then I find myself staring at it."

Sarah laughed softly, liking this strange-looking man, and understood her husband's affection for him.

Seth turned to Wade and stepped closer so he could have a better look at their son. "Good-looking boy." Then he winked at Sarah with his cloudy blue eye. "Looks like his mother."

Wade grinned proudly.

Sarah gently brushed Emmett's hair away from his sleeping eyes. "He may have my looks, Mr. Bowlen, but he's every bit his father."

Seth chuckled with a frown. "Then, you have my utmost sympathy, Sarah."

Sarah laughed, but Wade failed to see the humor.

Seth looked at Sarah. "Have a nice trip?"

She raised her brow, looking tired. "It was a long trip, or so it seems. The body gets tired of sitting."

Bowlen smiled. "Yes, Ma'am, I'm sure it does." Then he took her by the arm with one hand and gestured toward the depot building with the other. "I've a buggy at the side of the depot, Sarah." As they walked, he said, "My missus has your room ready. You'll be staying the night with us."

She smiled, looking pleased. "I'm looking forward to meeting your wife." Then with an uncertain look, asked, "Molly isn't it?"

He grinned with a nod. "Yes, Ma'am." Then his grin disappeared. "Why, my Molly's been cleaning all day. Drove me out of the house this morning, saying I was in the way."

Sarah looked concerned. "I hope she hasn't gone to a lot of trouble on our account?"

"Lord, no," he replied as they approached the buggy. "Ain't no trouble, Sarah. You'll have a good warm meal, a clean bed for tonight, and a fine breakfast in the morning." While he helped Sarah into the buggy, Wade put Emmett in next to her, and though half asleep, he immediately migrated to his mother's arms.

Wade turned to Seth. "My horse is on the train. I wasn't sure how long we'd be and figured I'd need her. Be any trouble, me keeping her at your place?"

"No trouble at all."

Then Wade asked, "How often does the stage run between Sisters and Harper?"

Bowlen thought for a moment. "Next stage won't be in until the day after tomorrow."

Wade looked at Sarah. "You want to wait on the stage?"

"Not particularly," she said, looking disappointed. "But what else can we do?"

"Maybe we can rent us a wagon or a buggy," replied Wade thoughtfully.

"No need for that," said Seth. "You can use our wagon."

"You sure you won't need it?"

Seth shook his head. "Seldom use it."

Wade looked appreciative. "Much obliged, Seth." Then he turned to Sarah. "We can leave right after breakfast."

Seth smiled at Sarah. "That's right. You folks can be on your way first thing."

She smiled with excitement, pulling Emmett closer. "How far is Harper from here?"

"About a half day's ride," replied Wade.

Bowlen could see the disappointment and worry on her face. "Don't worry none, Ma'am. The ride will pass quickly enough, and you'll soon be at your Pa's place safe and sound."

"I hope you're right," she said, sounding tired.

"If you'd like, Ma'am," Seth said, "I'll send word as soon as you're settled."

"That won't be necessary, Mr. Bowlen..."

"Seth," he corrected with a smile.

She smiled. "Seth," and then she settled back into the seat of the buggy, her arms around Emmett. "No sense in my mother losing sleep by fretting all night and half of tomorrow. A clean bed and a good night's rest will do us all a lot of good." Then she looked at her husband. "I'm sure that you and Wade have things to discuss."

"You're an understanding woman," Bowlen told her.

She smiled. "Being the wife of a deputy US marshal has taught me two things, Seth: patience, being one, and understanding, the other. I'm certain your wife would agree."

He smiled awkwardly. "I'm sure she would." Then he patted Wade on the back, "You best go get that mare of yours, and I'll check for your belongings at the luggage car."

"All right," replied Wade, then he looked at Sarah. "I won't be long."

Seth turned and headed for the depot as Sarah leaned close to Wade and lowered her voice while watching Seth. "I felt embarrassed about staring at his eye and scar. I hope I didn't hurt his feelings."

Wade glanced at Seth's figure as it disappeared around the depot building. "Like he said, Sarah, he's used to it." Then he grinned. "Seth Bowlen isn't a man who gets his feelings hurt all that easily." He kissed her on the cheek, turned, and walked toward the train to get his horse.

Sarah looked down at her son's sleeping, innocent face and held him close as she looked around at the city of Sisters. Wondering what sort of place it was, she recalled the story Wade had told her about the two little girls whose family's wagon had the misfortune of breaking down while on their way to California in 1840 and being killed by a small, warring band of Indians.

The buggy's sudden movement caused by Wade and Seth placing their belongings in the back of the buggy made her turn from the scenery and people of Sisters. Sarah gently stroked her son's hair as she watched Wade place his Sharps rifle between the trunk and two carpetbags, followed by his saddle. After tying his mare to the rear of the buggy, he and Seth climbed in. Seth took the reins, gently swatted the back of the black horse. The buggy jerked forward, and Seth guided the horse along the dusty street toward the Bowlen residence on the other side of Sisters.

Seth turned from the main street onto a narrow, wagon rutted, dirt street framed by houses, tall oak, and cottonwood trees. Emmett was sitting next to his mother while she looked at each house they passed, wondering about their occupants. The buggy slowed, and Seth turned from the street onto a long, dirt driveway toward a peaceful setting of a white two-story house among three large oak trees and a lilac bush next to the front porch.

Seth pointed to a figure sitting in a chair on the front porch. "That'd be my Molly," he said proudly.

Molly Bowlen stood and walked to the edge of the porch and waited.

Bringing the buggy to a stop in front of the porch, Seth called out, "Molly, you remember Wade Garrison? This here's his wife, Sarah, and that little fellah looking half asleep is their son, Emmett."

Molly Bowlen stepped from the porch, all smiles, and friendly-looking, while patiently waiting for everyone to climb down from the buggy. Molly stood five-feet-two dressed in a cream-colored housedress. She was slightly plump but not fat. Her long black and gray hair that Molly usually wore up during the day lay softly across her left shoulder. She had full lips, a slightly turned-up nose, soft brown eyes, framed by tiny crow's feet, and a smile that made you feel warm and welcome. After Sarah climbed down from the buggy, Molly smiled. "Hello, Sarah. I'm so glad to meet you finally."

Sarah smiled as the two hugged, then she thanked her for taking them in, promising they wouldn't be bothersome.

"Oh, nonsense," smiled Molly warmly. "Seth and I don't get much company. It'll be nice having a woman to talk to for a change." She glanced at Seth. "Instead of Mr. Gruff."

Sarah and Wade laughed, but Seth went about his business, ignoring the comment.

Wade climbed out of the buggy, greeted by Molly with a warm smile and an extended hand. "Hello, Mr. Garrison, it's been a spell."

He took his hat off and smiled as he took her hand. "Yes, Ma'am, quite a spell, I reckon."

Wade turned and helped young Emmett down. "Emmett, say hello to Mrs. Bowlen."

Molly Bowlen smiled at Emmett as she bent down, looking into his tired, blue eyes. "Hello, young man. You look hungry."

The boy shyly moved away, melting into his mother's dress, but Sarah gently pushed the boy toward Molly. "Emmett, where're your manners? Now shake Mrs. Bowlen's hand."

Emmett reached out the way children do when they're unsure, quickly shook her hand, and buried his face into his mother's dress.

Molly laughed and then smiled at Sarah. "The last time I saw your husband was in my restaurant. He was holding this pitiful little dog." Then she turned to Wade, looking curious. "What became of that little dog?"

"He's with some friends in Santa Fe while we're away."

"What did you name him?" asked Mrs. Bowlen.

"Dog," Wade told her.

"You never gave the dog a proper name?" she asked, looking puzzled.

He shook his head, looking stubborn. "Nope, and I never named my horse neither. I just call her Horse and the mutt, Dog. He ain't no better'n my mare."

Seth grinned. "Wade doesn't think it's proper giving animals people names."

Wade glanced from Seth to Molly, and then to Sarah, who seemed to be enjoying his dilemma. "They ain't people, so why give them people names?"

Molly's face filled with concern. "Well, I guess that'd be all right if you have just one, but wouldn't it get a mite confusing if you had more than one dog? How would they know which one you're calling?"

Seth chuckled, appreciating Molly's reasoning. It was something he was sure his friend didn't.

Sarah laughed softly. "Emmett wanted to call him Charley, but my husband wouldn't have any part of it."

Wade was still contemplating Molly's question about more than one dog, looking a little perplexed. "Don't plan on having more than one dog, Mrs. Bowlen."

Molly looked at Wade for a long moment and then turned to Sarah. "You and Emmett come inside while the men gather your belongings." She affectionately put one arm around Sarah and walked up the steps to the porch. "I hope you find the bed comfortable." Molly paused at the top step and turned to her husband. "Dinner's almost ready."

41

Seth pointed to the side of the house. "Take that horse of yours without a name back to the barn." Then he chuckled, adding, "I'll take care of these other things named Luggage."

Wade caught the joke but failed to see the humor as he unhitched his mare, picked up the saddle from the back of the buggy. He walked toward the barn, leaving Seth to enjoy his joke, hoping he got a hernia carrying their luggage inside.

During dinner, Sarah noticed Emmett kept staring at Seth's face and eye and apologized for his rudeness. Bowlen smiled and asked the boy if he had any questions, but Emmett just shook his head no, then glanced at his pa.

"Well, if you should have a question," said Seth looking serious. "Just ask."

After a pleasant dinner of pot roast, potatoes, carrots, and apple pie, Sarah put little Emmett to bed and returned to the kitchen to help Molly clean up the dinner dishes. This chore gave the two ladies a chance to visit and get better acquainted, something each had looked forward to.

Seth and Wade retired to the parlor for a glass of bourbon, where Seth could explain why he had sent that telegram to Billy French. While Bowlen walked across the room to a small table in the corner, Wade let his eyes take a quick journey around the comfortable room. Seth picked up the bottle of bourbon and turned. "Drink?"

Wade shook his head. "No, thanks. I'm tired, and a drink would probably put me right to sleep."

Bowlen pointed to one of the two dark red, stuffed chairs. "Have a seat." Then he asked, "You sure about that drink?"

Wade smiled. "I'm sure."

"Suit yourself."

Wade dropped down into a chair, getting comfortable. "Mind telling me what's going on?"

The question went unanswered as Seth poured his drink as if he hadn't heard him. He put the bottle down, picked up the glass of bourbon, and walked to the other chair across from Wade, and sat down. Seth took a quick sip and stared at the glass for a moment, the way a man does when troubled over something. Then he looked up. "You remember that young fellah you killed after you returned from Mexico five or six years ago?"

Wade thought back on that morning as the entire scene raced through his mind, still clear as it if had just happened. He remembered the names of all the men he had killed since that July, six years ago, and the list was getting longer. He looked thoughtful as he nodded. "Dan Hoskins, and if memory serves me correctly, he had a brother."

Bowlen took a sip of whiskey and placed the glass on the table. "That's right. His brother's name is Pete, and their pa is George Hoskins, the owner of a large spread about ten or twelve miles southwest of Harper."

Wade nodded. "I remember." Wade knew that George Hoskins bought the place and moved his family west from someplace back east a few months before Emmett was gunned down, and Wade left to avenge him. He watched Seth take a sip of whiskey and set the glass down on the small table next to his chair, wondering what that had to do with why Seth sent for Billy.

"Little over a month ago," began Seth, "Pete Hoskins and a friend of his by the name of Booth Fox were in Jack Pritchard's Saloon right here in Sisters having a drink. Pete and a dirt farmer by the name of Jacob Olson got into an argument over Jacob's daughter, Doris." Bowlen paused to pick up the glass, took a drink, and then continued. "The story I got from Pete was that Jacob Olson accused him of getting his daughter pregnant and wanted to know what he intended on doing about it." Seth drank the last of his whiskey, got up, and walked toward the bottle sitting on the table while he kept talking. "Pete told Jacob that any number of men in Sisters could be the father of that child."

Wade chuckled without humor at Pete's stupidity.

Seth sat down, took a sip, and continued. "Guess you can imagine how pissed Jacob got over that comment?"

Wade imagined the scene and the anger the girl's father must have felt.

"Pete's story of what happened was that old man Olson stood and went for his gun, so Pete naturally drew his and shot the old man right here." Seth pointed to his heart with the thumb of his empty hand.

Wade was puzzled. "Sounds like self-defense. Any witnesses?"

"Just Paul Leonard," answered Bowlen. "He's the bartender at Pritchard's and says he was busy at the other end of the bar when it happened and ducked when he heard the shot. Paul said that when he

43

stood, old man Olson was on the floor, and Pete was standing over the body, holding his gun." Seth paused to take a drink and then told him about Tom Lawson, who claimed he never saw anything because he was out back, relieving himself.

Still, none of this story shed light on why Seth sent for a US Marshal from Santa Fe instead of Denver. Wade was tired from the trip and becoming impatient but knew that Seth enjoyed the story he's telling more than getting to the point, so he waited.

"I arrested Pete," continued Seth, "and then wired for a judge up in Colorado Springs. The judge wired back, saying he'd be here in two days. Pete's pa showed up late that afternoon, wanting to take his son home with him." Bowlen shrugged. "He said he'd see to it that Pete would come back to see the judge when he arrived. Being it looked like a clear case of self-defense, I saw no harm in letting him go, figuring old man Hoskins would keep his word."

"I'm guessing they never showed."

Bowlen shook his head, looking irritated. "Never did!" Then he took a quick drink and leaned forward in his chair, resting his elbows on his knees, holding the glass with both hands. "Judge Dan Moore from Colorado Springs came into Sisters two days later, and neither Pete nor his pa showed up." Seth chuckled and shook his head. "The judge waited until the next train for Colorado Springs came in, and I got my ass chewed out by Judge Moore as he was walking out of my office to catch the train. The next morning, me and Carl headed for the Hoskins' place." Seth sat back, looking despondent. "When we rode up to the house, George Hoskins was sitting on the porch with his son, Pete, this fellah Booth Fox, and a couple of other men, including Reese, his foreman." Seth paused in thought. "Without getting out of his chair, the old man told us to get off his land." He looked at Wade. "I was mad as hell, but being out of my jurisdiction and there being just the two of us and six of them, we put our tails between our legs and headed back to Sisters like a couple of whipped dogs."

Wade smiled, feeling sorry for Deputy Carl during the ride back, imagining the mood that whole thing had put Seth in.

Seth took a drink and then continued. "When we got back to town, I headed up to see Judge Moore." Seth grinned. "He wasn't all that happy to see me, as you can imagine. At this point, the judge said the only real crime Pete was guilty of was not returning to Sisters, and from all the evidence, it appeared Pete acted in self-defense. And until I could prove differently, he wasn't going to waste any more of his time on Pete Hoskins."

The room got quiet as Wade watched Seth take a drink, "I've heard nothing to explain why you sent that gram to Billy asking for help?"

Bowlen sat back. "I'm coming to that."

Wade was tired and wished he'd hurry.

Seth stared into the darkness outside the window. "A couple of days later, Tom Lawson showed up in my office." Seth turned to Wade with a hardened look. "Lawson had a different story about that morning."

Knowing it would be a long story, Wade stood. "I think I need a drink; this whole thing is getting complicated."

Seth kept talking while Wade poured himself a drink. "Lawson told me that he had gone out back to the outhouse, and when he got back to the rear door, he heard arguing. He opened the door just as Jacob stood knocking over his chair, calling Pete a lying son of a bitch. Tom Lawson also swore that when Jacob stood, the only thing in his hands was his clenched fists ready to knock the shit out of Pete."

Wade and his drink were back in his chair, and now he was getting interested.

"Lawson said that as Olson stepped around the table, Pete pulled his gun and shot 'em, and as Jacob lay on the floor, Pete bent down, took Jacob's gun from his holster and laid it next to his right hand."

Wade leaned forward, looking thoughtful. "That makes it murder, not self-defense."

"Not only that," agreed Seth. "But Lawson says that Paul Leonard, the bartender, saw the whole thing."

"You question the bartender about that?"

"I did, but he denied it."

Wade looked down at his drink, thinking about the bartender. "Fear more'n likely."

"That's what I thought. I tried getting the truth out of Paul by getting angry, but he's more afraid of Pete Hoskins and Booth Fox than he is of me and my anger."

Wade's patience was growing thin. "None of this explains why you needed a United States Marshal from Santa Fe when there's one up in Denver."

Seth drank the last of his whiskey and set the glass on the table between them. "I'm coming to that."

Wade took a sip of his drink and wished he'd hurry.

Seth sat forward in his chair. "I figured we had Pete dead to rights with Tom Lawson's testimony thinking that once we went to trial, maybe Paul would change his story. I went to see Judge Moore, and he issued a warrant suggesting that I head up to Denver and have a US Marshal help me serve it." Seth stood and walked to the bottle, picked it up, contemplated another drink, then set the bottle down and returned to his chair. "I took the train up to Denver and gave the warrant to Wayne Lewis, the US Marshal." He paused. "Lewis read the warrant, then said it was no good because Judge Ethan Parker had already dismissed the charges in the shooting of Jacob Olson due to lack of evidence." He leaned forward, looking mad. "Damn it, Wade, we hadn't even charged him yet. I asked how Judge Parker could rule without the man being charged or without a proper trial and witnesses." Bowlen paused to take a sip of whiskey. "Marshal Lewis tossed the warrant on his desk in front of me, said as far as the US Marshal's office in Denver was concerned, the case was closed." Bowlen's voice held the anger he felt that day. "I argued with Lewis, telling him that I had an eyewitness saying it was murder. Lewis asked who the witness was, and after I told him, he said there wasn't anything he could do. The case was closed. I asked to see this Judge Parker, but Marshal Lewis suggested that I catch the next train back to Sisters and forget about arresting Pete Hoskins."

"Sounds like this George Hoskins is a powerful man?"

Seth looked at his empty glass and then the bottle on the table a few feet away and looked at Wade. "A lot's changed in Harper since you left. George Hoskins owns bits and pieces of Harper these days and is always looking to buy more. He bought up two of the smaller ranches north of his place and tried to push out a couple more. The way I figure it, once he's done there, he'll start on Sisters."

Wade leaned forward, resting his elbows on his knees, his hands clasped under his chin in thought. "You don't need a deputy marshal,

46

Seth; you need a damn army." Then he sat back, looking irritated. "What the hell you got yourself mixed up with?"

Bowlen looked apologetic. "It's a big mess, I agree…"

"It's more than a mess," chuckled Wade without humor.

Seth looked insistent. "I can't just sit back and let Pete Hoskins off the hook for killing two men."

Wade stared at Bowlen, considering the man before him. "No, I guess you can't." Then being curious about the marshal in Denver, Wade asked how old he was.

"Marshal Wayne Lewis is a young, egotistical little bastard around your age." Seth chuckled. "Anyways, the little bastard picked up the newspaper and began reading as though I weren't even there, so I left with my tail twixt my legs, filled with the determination that I would get Pete anyway I could."

Wade smiled, imagining how angry that must have made Seth.

"Ain't funny, Wade," he said, looking irritated.

"Weren't laughing at you," Wade said, looking apologetic. "I was thinking of how you must have wanted to kick this Lewis fellah's ass all over his office."

Bowlen scoffed with humor. "Thought occurred to me, and fifteen years ago, I would have."

Wade sat forward in his chair, looking puzzled. "I must be more tired than I thought. Did you say Hoskins killed two men?"

Seth nodded. "I'm coming to that. I stopped in Colorado Springs on my way back and saw Judge Moore. He was familiar with this Judge Ethan Parker up in Denver and said he was as crooked as a branch on an oak tree. Judge Moore said before he would issue a new warrant, he wanted to talk to my witness. I said that I'd have him in his office the next day and caught the train to Sisters." He paused to take a sip of whiskey. "I got back late, so I went directly home and turned in, thinking I'd go out and talk to Lawson the next afternoon. I was just about ready to ride out when Doc Richard's little boy came running into my office saying that Tom Lawson had been shot."

Wade felt pretty confident who did the shooting.

Seth continued. "I hurried over to the doc's to check on Tom, but I was too late." He paused, looking sorry. "His missus told me that she heard two gunshots and then horses galloping away. She ran out of the house and found Tom lying on the floor of the barn unconscious. She hitched up the wagon and brought him into town."

Wade gestured with both hands. "No one saw who did it, and Tom never said?"

Seth nodded. "You're right on both counts."

"And there," said Wade, "went your case against Pete Hoskins."

Seth nodded. "I thought so at the time, but that afternoon, I mounted up, rode out to the Lawson place, and looked around. I found several horse tracks that led me past Sam Wheeler's place. I asked Sam if he'd seen any riders, and he told me he was up in the loft of his barn when he saw Pete Hoskins, Booth Fox, and another man ride toward the Lawson place that morning."

Wade's interest suddenly grew. "This Sam Wheeler sure about what he saw?"

Bowlen nodded. "Even described the horses they rode. Said Pete was riding his Appaloosa, and Booth Fox, his gray."

"That might hold up for a warrant for the murder of Lawson," said Wade thoughtfully.

"Exactly, so I headed back up to Colorado Springs and saw the judge once again."

Wade smiled. "I bet he was getting tired of seeing you."

Seth nodded. "Judge Moore said he had no trouble issuing a warrant, but seeing as I was the town sheriff having no authority outside the city limits of Sisters, and certainly not in Harper, I needed a United States Marshal to serve it. I suggested Billy French in Santa Fe, and the judge agreed, saying once the marshal was here, he'd issue a warrant for the murder of Tom Lawson, and that's when I sent that telegram asking for Billy's help."

Wade grinned. "And got his deputy, instead."

Bowlen smiled. "I'm glad Billy sent you, Wade." Then looking determined, he said. "I aim to see that Hoskins, Fox, and the third man all put on trial for Lawson's murder."

Recalling the determination Seth had when they rode together, he knew that he would no more let this thing go than he would have stayed in Sisters six years ago, letting those four killers escape into Mexico. Wade stood and walked across the room to the window and looked up at the big yellow moon as it rose above the barn. "All we got is this Sam Wheeler

48

who says he saw Pete Hoskins, Booth Fox, and another man ride toward Lawson's place the morning he was killed."

Seth took his eyes away from the floor and looked up at Wade as he stared out the window. "The judge says that's enough to issue a warrant, and after that, it's up to a jury."

The room fell quiet for several moments while Wade considered all that Seth had told him. "Hoskins is the only man that would benefit from this Lawson's death." He turned, walked back to his chair, sat down, and looked at Seth. "It's plain the Marshal in Denver gave up the name of your witness."

Bowlen nodded, looking worried. "I've considered that."

Wade sighed as he stared into his glass. "Might be best if Billy had come to Sisters, and I went to Albuquerque," he said softly.

Seth looked at Wade, curious about what he just said.

"We could have ourselves a real mess if we ain't careful. Have you told anyone else about Sam Wheeler?"

"Just Judge Moore. But I never told him his name."

Wade looked concerned. "How about your deputy?"

"No," Bowlen said thoughtfully. "Not yet, but Carl's all right."

"Maybe so, but I'd just as soon keep him in the dark a while longer."

"All right," agreed Bowlen with a quick nod. "But, we need to tell Carl soon."

Wade drank the last of his drink, placed his empty glass on the table, and turned to Seth. "I'll serve your warrant, but first, I want to talk to this Wheeler and that damn bartender."

"We can ride out to Wheeler's tomorrow."

"No," said Wade with a quick shake of his head. "I'm taking Sarah and Emmett to her pa's place in the morning."

"Forgot about that," Seth said thoughtfully. "How long you plan on staying in Harper?"

"Not sure, a couple of days, maybe."

"All right," said Seth. "We'll ride out to Wheeler's when you get back."

With a puzzled look, Wade turned to Seth. "There's something else we need to talk about."

Looking curious, Seth sat back in his chair. "What might that be?"

49

"We've been friends ever since you, Gil, Frank, and I chased them bastards into Mexico six years ago."

The memory of a wounded Frank Wells lying on the saloon floor dying rushed into Seth's memory like a bad dream.

"Thing of it is," began Wade, "I feel a little funny coming up here from Santa Fe."

Seth looked puzzled. "Funny in what way?"

"You've been a sheriff longer than I been alive, Seth. This here's your fight, and I understand that, but you don't have any jurisdiction outside Sister's city limits. So when we ride past the city line, like it or not, I have the final say."

Bowlen thought on that a moment. "Suppose I don't agree with what we're doing?"

"We talk about it."

Seth grinned. "Fair enough." Then he stood with an outstretched hand, and as they shook hands, Bowlen said, "All I want is to get these bastards before I'm too damn old. I don't want no man saying I shirked my duty."

Wade smiled. "Well, Seth, far be it from me to keep an ornery son of a bitch like you from his destiny."

He chuckled. "Amen to that."

Wade felt the weight of the day as he looked at his pocket watch. "It's getting late, and I need to get an early start tomorrow. Sarah's a bit anxious to see her folks." Then as they walked toward the door, Wade paused. "I meant to ask. How's this Jacob Olsen's daughter?"

Seth looked sad. "A few days after her pa was killed, she tossed a rope over a rafter in the barn, climbed on a stool, and hung herself."

"Good Lord," uttered Wade.

"That's two more lives Pete Hoskins has to answer for," said Seth

Four

Harper, Colorado

The trip from Sisters to Harper was a long and difficult one for Sarah and little Emmett. The dirt road was narrow and bumpy, occasionally visited by snakes, lizards, and jackrabbits. The cloudless, blue sky stretched from horizon to horizon, giving no relief from the hot sun. Emmett was asleep lying on a blanket under a small tarp behind the wagon seat Seth had rigged for shade. Sarah sat next to Wade, fighting for control of the umbrella she held for shade against the occasional gust of wind.

They had talked about this and that to pass the time, but now she sat quietly looking out onto the vastness of the land. To the east were rolling hills, a scattering of Cottonwood trees lining a dry riverbed in the distance, and plateaus of cliffs, bringing to mind castle walls she had read about as a child. To the west, rolling hills dotted here and there with trees or vegetation, making their way to the foothills. Beyond the foothills were the rugged Rocky Mountains that stretched from north to south as far as the eye could see. The higher peaks still boasted their white snow caps that seemed to touch the clear, blue sky.

As Sarah looked from the eastern plains to the mountains, the vastness of it was breathtaking. She remembered sitting in the window seat of her bedroom while growing up watching the mountains from season to season. Wade pointed out two eagles soaring high above them, floating on warm air currents. Sarah lowered her umbrella and watched the two circling with an occasional screech mixed with the grinding sounds of the wheels on the sandy soil. Such a desolate place, she thought, raising her umbrella to block the sun's warms rays. But still, Sarah marveled at its beauty. Feeling thirsty, she turned to her husband. "Care for some water?"

Wade had spoken very little the past hour except to point out the two eagles, seemingly deep in thought about something, and it was good to hear her voice. He turned from the straight, narrow road he had been watching and smiled. "Please."

She folded her umbrella, set it on the seat beside her, picked up the canteen from the floorboard of the wagon, pulled the cork, and handed it to him. After he took a quick drink, she had some water, replaced the cork, returned the canteen to the floorboard, and opened her umbrella. She had been curious about the trip, and Wade had only told her that Seth needed some help but never told her what kind of help. With nothing else to talk about, she asked about his and Seth Bowlen's talk the night before, which had given her husband a restless night. Which, in turn, gave her a restless night.

Wade was reluctant at first, but her persistence brought a short story of why Billy sent him to help Seth. When he finished, she thought about the story while listening to the monotonous sound, buzzing of grasshoppers, an occasional magpie, and horses hooves mixing with the wagon's wheels on the hard sandy Colorado soil. She looked along the single, lonely road ahead of them, disappearing into the horizon wishing Harper would come into view. The small blanket Molly had given her to sit on seemed thin. Her butt was getting sore, her back hurt from sitting, and her arms were getting tired of holding the umbrella. She wished Wade would hurry but quickly realized that was being foolish. To get her mind off her aches and pains, she thought of what she would say to her mother and father while imagining the joy of them seeing their only grandson.

The hours slowly passed, and Sarah was looking eastward, having exhausted all things to talk about with her husband when Wade's voice broke the stillness. "There's Harper."

She stiffened in her seat, making herself taller while looking north along the thin line of road they traveled. "Where?"

"There," he replied with a point of a finger.

She looked again, still seeing nothing at first, but then she saw the tiny dots that were the buildings of the town. Excitement quickly replaced the ride's boredom, and she soon forgot about her sore butt and back and thought about seeing her mother and father. Thinking Emmett would have a clean bed to sleep in, a room of his own, and she a nice warm bath before bed. As she looked at the town with anticipation and excitement, she suddenly thought of the ride back, and the smile left her face as she turned to look behind them at the long, thin line. "I hate to think about the ride back."

"Don't think about it," he said as he put his right arm around her. "Enjoy the time with your mom and dad. You may be here for two to four weeks."

She smiled. "Really?"

Emmett woke up, looking a little disoriented as he crawled out from under the tarp. "When are we gonna be there?"

Wade took his arm from around Sarah and looked back at Emmett. "Put your hat on, Son. You'll fry your brains and catch sunstroke."

"Yes, sir." The boy bent down, picked up a narrow brimmed hat, and put it on. "It's hot, Pa. When are we gonna get there?"

"Soon."

Sarah turned and smiled at their son. "If you come up here, you can see the town of Harper."

The boy grinned, stood on the trunk, and climbed over the rear of the seat. Sitting between them and he looked up at his pa. "What sort of place is Harper?"

Wade considered his question. "Like most towns."

"It's a nice place," corrected Sarah thinking the boy needed more of an answer than that. "You'll like it."

"Just another town," said Wade.

She gave Wade one of her looks as silence returned to the wagon while everyone turned their attention to the tiny dots of buildings in the distance that slowly came closer. Soon they could see the windows and doors, and Wade could make out the telegraph lines heading west that weren't there when he left for Santa Fe six years ago. As they rode toward Harper, each anticipated what lay ahead.

The town of Harper had grown during the past six years boasting several new buildings, yet Wade thought it hadn't changed all that much. He guided the tired team up the main street that was a little longer now with

53

the addition of the new buildings. Sarah pointed out this place or that to Emmett or the new buildings to her husband, commenting on how much the town had grown.

Wade drove the team along the busy, dirt street past the Blue Sky Saloon where Emmett Spears had been gunned down, past Mason's General Store, where he and Sarah first met, and the restaurant where he and Emmett Spears would eat on Saturday nights when they had extra money. As they rode past the sheriff's office, Wade stared at the white lettering, "SHERIFF'S OFFICE," painted on the window and wondered if Sheriff Harry Block was still around. Knowing the team was tired and figuring Sarah could use a rest as well, he guided the team to a stop in front of the Harper Hotel.

Sarah looked puzzled. "Why are we stopping?"

"The horses need rest. We'll get a room, so's you and Emmett can rest. I'll put the team up at the livery and have a look around while you rest. Then after you freshen up, we'll head out to the Double J."

Sarah looked disappointed. "I don't need to rest, Wade. We're so close to home." She turned and looked at Wade. "Let's keep going."

"It's an hour ride to your pa's place. Maybe you don't need to rest, but these horses belong to Seth, and they're hot and tired."

She looked at the horses, knowing he was right. The team was tired, and in truth, so was she. A nice bed would ease the pain in her back and butt. "All right, but just for a while."

"That's settled then." He jumped down from the wagon seat onto the boardwalk and helped his wife and son into the hotel. After getting them settled in a room, he drove the buggy up the street.

Guiding the horses to the livery's open doors, he noticed the name on the sign above them read, LEVI WAGNER PROP, and wondered what became of George Hatton. An old buggy sat in the weeds next to the left side of the livery and an empty corral on the right. Pulling back on the reins, he stopped next to the empty corral. Met by the smell of fresh hay and horse manure, he set the break with his left foot and called out. "Hello!"

A few moments later, Wade recognized a gray-bearded man as Levi Wagner walking into the bright sunlight. Looking older than Wade remembered, he was slightly bent over at the waist. He carried a pitchfork and was wearing a floppy hat that his gray hair seemed to fight with. His face was tanned, wrinkled, and leathery. A wide belt held up his black, soiled pants cinched too tight, leaving tiny folds in the material that gathered at the waist. Wade couldn't help but notice his pants were a little short, and he could see the man's bare ankles wearing what appeared to be old military shoes.

"What can I do for you?" Levi Wagner asked.

"Where's old George?"

Wagner rested the pitchfork against one of the open doors, thinking the man looked familiar, but he couldn't quite place him. "George passed on a couple of years back." Then he motioned with the thumb of one hand. "He's buried in the cemetery south of town with the rest of them that ain't living."

Wade glanced toward the cemetery. "Sorry to hear that." Then he turned, asking, "How'd he die?"

"Old age, I figure. Just never woke up one morning."

Wade considered that for a moment remembering back when Levi worked for George. Thinking the old man probably did not recognize him, he asked, "You own the place now?"

The old man turned his head, spit tobacco juice onto the ground, wiped the residue from his mouth, nodded once, and answered with a surly voice. "Name's above the door."

Wade chuckled, remembering Levi was always outspoken, tied the reins around the brake, and climbed down. "Team's tired, Mister Wagner. You got room for them in your livery for a couple of hours?"

Levi eyed the horses curiously. "Reckon so."

"It's been a long, hot ride from Sisters. They could use a rest, some food and water, and maybe a good rub down."

The old man looked at the horses and then at Wade. "Guess I can manage, but it'll cost you."

"How much?"

Levi spat and looked up at Wade. "Four bits a horse in advance, and if you like, I'll even check their shoes."

Wade reached into his pocket, pulled out some money, and handed the correct amount to Levi.

The old man took the money, pocketed it, and turned toward the horses while talking over his shoulder. "You sure look familiar."

"Name's Wade Garrison, Mister Wagner. I used to work for Tolliver Grimes."

Wagner turned and stared at him for several moments, trying to place the name and the face, while his memory worked hard at separating them from all the others locked inside his head.

Wade took off his black, wide-brimmed hat and combed his hair with the fingers of his right hand. "Me and Emmett Spears used to work out at the Circle T, and Saturday nights, we'd get drunk and play a little poker." He gestured toward the barn. "More than once, we were busted and drunk when you would let us sleep it off in there." He grinned at Levi. "You always took care of our horses and gave us some coffee the next morning."

The old man stared at him for another moment, letting his mind sift through the ages of memories, then a smile slowly separated his lips, showing his stained, yellow teeth. "I'll be damned." He held out his hand. "I remember you now." He and Wade shook hands. "You lit out after them four men that killed that friend of yours." Then his right hand went to his chin, scratching his beard thoughtfully. "What was his name again?"

"Emmett," Wade said, thinking he had just told him his name. "Emmett Spears."

"That's right, Emmett Spears." Levi took off his hat with one hand and scratched his head with the other. "Seems to me the last time I saw you, you were riding south with a packhorse carrying some little shit of a dog."

Wade chuckled. "I reckon that's about right."

"Whatever happened to that little fellah?"

Wade gestured to the south. "He's in Santa Fe with some friends for a spell."

"That's good," grinned Wagner. "He sure was a cute little dog." The grin was suddenly replaced by a serious face. "Seems I recall Sarah Talbert went looking for you not long after you left with that little shit dog. She ever find the two of you?"

Suddenly, Wade was explaining more than he had in a long time. He forced a small smile. "Me and Sarah got married some years back. We live in Santa Fe, and we have a son."

Levi's face filled with a grin. "Well, don't that beat all."

Looking proud, Wade gestured back toward the hotel. "She and our son are resting at the hotel. As I said, it's been a long, hot ride from Sisters, and as soon as the horses are rested, we're heading out to the Double J." Wade suddenly wondered why he was explaining everything to Levi.

"Come to visit, have ya?"

"Looks that way," replied Wade wanting to get away from Levi and the smell of the livery.

Not completely satisfied with the answer, the old man turned and walked to the nearest horse, looked at its teeth, and patted him gently on the neck. "Nice animal." Then he walked to the other horse, and held its bridle in one hand, and stroked its neck with the other. "So's this one." Then he looked at Wade over the backs of the horses. "We'll leave the wagon where she is, won't be in the way any. We'll put your stock in a couple of stalls, and I'll see to it they have plenty of oats and water." Then Levi began unhitching the horses while he talked. "You say you have a son?"

"That's right."

"What's his name?"

"Emmett."

Levi stopped and stood upright between the horses, looking over one's neck. "So you named your son after that friend of your'n that got himself shot?"

Wade nodded proudly. "I did."

The old man gave a quick jerk of the head, bent down, and disappeared behind the horse to finish. "I seem to recall hearing that you trailed them, four men, clean into Mexico, and then became a Marshal down in Santa Fe."

Wade thought word sure gets around. "That's true enough." Then he looked past the horses and wagon down the dusty street, seeing the sheriff's sign hanging on the post of the boardwalk. "Harry Block, still sheriff?"

Wagner stood, spit, wiped his mouth with the dirty sleeve of his faded underwear, and looked down the street toward town. "Yep." Then he stepped back and led the two horses away from the tongue of the wagon toward the big, open doors. "But I think old Harry's getting tired of it all. Like me, he's getting along in years, and both our days are numbered."

As Levi and the team disappeared into the livery, Wade turned and looked back down the street of Harper, past the sheriff's office, and Blue Sky Saloon to the Harper Hotel, where his wife and son were resting. Then he turned, walked to the livery door, and looked inside just as Levi put the second horse in its stall. "I'm heading down to the hotel. I'll be back in a couple of hours."

"I'll be here," replied Wagner without looking up from what he was doing.

Five

Double J Ranch

As the wagon topped the hill overlooking a house, barn, corral, and other outbuildings of the Double J Ranch, excitement flowed through Sarah as she put one arm around her son, pulling him closer. Wade looked at her happy, smiling face, knowing she was excited to see her mother and father. She hadn't seen her father since their wedding in Santa Fe and her mother since the birth of Emmett when she came to Santa Fe to help out for the first two months.

Sarah stared at the scene while Wade drove the wagon down the hill, through the open gate, and under the archway. She looked up at the carved, wooden, and weathered figures of two J's that stood for Jasper and Janice Talbert. Turning her attention to the two-story structure, Sarah had grown up in memories of happy times rushed at her. It was strange, but the six years she had been gone felt as though she were returning from a ride into town. Her eyes found the window of her bedroom on the second story floor, and memories of sitting on the window seat of that window watching the sun disappear behind the Rocky Mountains and other happy moments came to her.

She thought of the nights she and her best friend, Hattie Dougherty, talked of silly girl things long into the night. Her eyes went from the window to the side yard with its large oak and cottonwood trees, recalling picnics, parties, and Fourth of July celebrations. The sweet memories gave way to the sadness of Hattie's death while giving birth to

Emmett Spears's child, only to have the baby die within a few days. Pushing the sadness away, she turned her attention to the large front porch with white, wooden chairs and white, wooden swing suspended from the porch ceiling with a small chain. She smiled, recalling the evenings she and Wade had sat on that swing when he courted her, knowing that her mother was sitting but a few feet away in the parlor sewing next to an open window. Those tender memories gave way to the harsher ones of her sitting alone in the swing, waiting for Wade after he rode out of Harper in search of the men that had killed Emmett Spears.

The front door opened, and a figure stepped out of the house onto the front porch, walked to its edge, and raised one hand to shade her eyes from the late afternoon sun.

Sarah raised herself off the seat and waved against Wade's protests, fearing she may fall.

"There's your grandmother," she told Emmett as she sat back down and placed her arm around him, only to stand again and wave while calling out, "Ma!"

Mrs. Talbert waved, then hurried to the open front doorway, and poked her head inside, yelling to her husband that their daughter was home. She hurried across the porch, down the steps, and across the yard, stopping at the edge of the driveway. There she waited impatiently for her daughter and grandson. Janice Talbert was a small woman with light brown and gray hair, brown eyes, and a gray housedress with a white apron. She waited with a big smile while wringing her hands over her heart.

Wade had scarcely stopped the wagon when Sarah climbed down, almost falling, and as she laughed half in fear from the near mishap and half with excitement, she ran into her mother's arms. Wade set the brake with his foot, wrapped the reins around it, sat back, and put his arm around his son. Together, they watched Sarah and her mother, laughing and crying at the same time, both asking questions that neither answered.

Emmett looked up at his Pa. "Why are ma and that lady crying?"

"That lady is your grandmother Emmett, and they're crying because they're happy, Son."

"I don't understand."

Wade sighed. "I'm sure you don't, boy." Then he smiled. "Womenfolk cry when they're happy, same as they do when they're sad. I ain't never figured out why." As they watched the two women, he smiled. "Guess that's the Good Lord and the women's little secret."

"What secrets do us men have with the Lord?" Emmett asked, looking curious.

Wade quickly considered the question. "Not many, Son." He stood, stepped down from the wagon, and helped his son down. Hearing the sound of a door closing, Wade turned, seeing Mr. Talbert hurrying across the porch and down the steps into the yard.

"Who's that?" asked Emmett.

Wade took his son's hand. "That be your Grandpa Talbert, son. Your ma's, pa." Then they walked toward Sarah and her mother, hearing only a little of what they were saying to one another. Wade took off his wide-brimmed Texas Flat Hat, feeling awkward as he smiled. "Mrs. Talbert, I hope you're feeling as good as you look."

Janice stepped back from her daughter with tears in her eyes. Brushing them away, looking as happy as a mother could, she said, "Thank you for bringing Sarah back home to us, Wade."

Before Wade could reply, Mr. Talbert called out, "Sarah." Jasper Talbert was a big man with dark eyes, white hair, and a beard. Wade remembered that whenever he would visit Sarah, her pa was always watching him. He had a broad nose and wide mouth and was wearing his familiar black pants and white shirt.

Sarah rushed into her father's arms, and they held one another for a long moment. To Wade's surprise, he noticed tears in Jasper's eye as he gently pushed his daughter to arm's length to look at her. "You're a sight for these tired old eyes, Daughter." Looking embarrassed, he turned away and quickly wiped his eyes. "Got some dust in my eyes."

Knowing he lied, Sarah smiled as tears ran down her cheeks. "I've missed you, Pa." Then she turned to her mother. "You too, Ma." She stepped back and put her hand on her son's shoulder, blurting out nervously, "This here's your grandson, Emmett Randolph Garrison."

Jasper and Janice Talbert made a fuss over the boy the way grandparents often argue over who he resembled. Janice commented on how big the boy was, and after a few more minutes of making a fuss over their grandson, Jasper shook Wade's hand and motioned toward the house. "Let's all go inside and get out of the sun." He put one arm around Sarah, and the other around her mother walked toward the front porch. Wade took Emmett's hand and glanced around as they followed them into the house.

It was early morning when Wade opened his eyes from a sound sleep and looked out the bedroom window at the Rocky Mountains in the west listening to Sarah's soft breathing. She turned in her sleep, putting her warm body next to his, placed one arm around him, and held him tight as if she were trying to keep him from leaving. An occasional light snore from her brought a small smile to his lips. Not wanting to disturb her restful sleep, he stared out the window, watching as the sun's light in the east slowly made its journey down the mountains in the west.

A door closed in the hallway beyond their bedroom door, and he envisioned Mrs. Talbert heading downstairs to start the fire in the big kitchen stove for the morning meal. Or maybe it was Mr. Talbert heading out for the morning chores before breakfast. Turning his attention back to the window and the mountains, his memory crossed the miles to Mexico, the vultures, and Paul Bradley, causing him to move slightly.

Though his movement was slight, Sarah woke and looked at him. "Are you alright?"

Turning his head, he looked into Sarah's brown eyes and smiled. "Yes. I'm sorry. I didn't mean to wake you."

"I could feel your body getting tense, and you jerked slightly. Did you have one of your dreams?"

"No," he lied, and then he smiled.

"Are you sure you weren't dreaming of those men again?"

"I wasn't sleeping. I've been awake for a while, watching the sun on the mountains out the window.

She always knew when he was lying, and while he hadn't had bad dreams lately, she suspected they had returned, or he was thinking about the men he and Seth Bowlen had tracked into Mexico. He had talked very little about it over the years, and she could only wonder at his nightmares and deep silent moods he sometimes fell into during the evenings. Knowing he didn't want to talk about it, she changed the subject. "What are your plans for today?"

"I have to get back to Sisters. I want to stop by the Circle T first, though, and say hello to Mr. Grimes and the others."

"Can't Seth wait a day?"

He sighed, made a determined face, and shook his head. "Seth's expecting me."

Sarah looked sternly at him. "Seth Bowlen can wait a day. You can ride over and visit with Mr. Grimes after breakfast and then spend the rest of the day and evening with my family. After all, you haven't seen them in years. You can ride back to Sisters in the morning."

Recognizing a lost argument and knowing she was right, he tossed the covers back and sat on the edge of the bed. "All right," he said softly. "I'll head back in the morning."

Wearing the smile of victory, she rose up and walked the short distance across the bed on her knees, put her arms around him, and leaned against his back. A rooster outside yelled at the day, and Jasper's barking, black dog, mixed with the sounds of horses, cows, and other ranch, sounds familiar to her. She could feel the warmth of his naked body through her nightgown, kissed the side of his face, and nibbled on the lobe of his ear. "Are you sure you want to get up?"

When Sarah and Wade walked down the stairs into the dining room for a breakfast of ham, eggs, and potatoes, they found that Jasper Talbert had already eaten and was out in the barn. After a breakfast filled with secret smiles and coffee, Wade kissed Sarah on the cheek, excused himself, and walked out to the barn.

Mr. Talbert was on his knees in one of the stalls examining a beautiful black stallion's front legs.

"Something wrong with the horse?" asked Wade.

Jasper never looked up as he stood wiping his hands on an old cloth wearing an uncertain look, then he patted the horse on the shoulder. "Had a slight limp yesterday, and the leg seems a little swollen." Then he looked at Wade with a frown. "I'm sure it's nothing, but I intend on keeping him inside for a day or two so's I can rub the leg down good with some liniment." Finished with wiping his hands, he tossed the cloth onto a narrow shelf at the head of the stall. He took his wide-brimmed, gray hat off a hook, put it on, and walked out of the stall. "Glad you and Sarah were able to come for a visit, Wade."

"Well, sir, Sarah's missed both you and Mrs. Talbert. She talks about the two of you all the time."

Jasper looked pleased. "Any chance the three of you will ever move back to this part of the country?"

Wade thought on that a moment, knowing Mr. Talbert wouldn't like the answer. "Can't say for sure, Mr. Talbert." Feeling a little nervous, he gestured with both hands. "Me and Sarah, well, we kind of put our roots down in Santa Fe." He was right; Jasper wasn't too happy at the answer.

"Roots can be taken up and placed elsewhere," said Jasper. "It just takes a little doing."

Not wanting to discuss the topic, Wade asked, "Any chance of me borrowing a horse so's I can ride over to the Grimes place for a quick visit?"

Jasper nodded. "I think we can manage that." Then, as he walked past Wade, he talked over his shoulder. "Let's go out to the corral and see what we got." Then with a big grin, he looked at Wade. "Let's see if we can find one that won't buck you off before you get to the Circle T."

Wade chuckled amusingly as he followed, wondering how much of that was wishful thinking by Jasper Talbert.

At the corral gate, Talbert stopped and turned toward the house and mountains beyond. "Don't suppose you need me to tell you that I was mad as hell with you for quite a spell."

Wade felt awkward. "You mean about Sarah following me to Santa Fe?"

Jasper continued to stare into the distance. "You could have stayed here."

Wade didn't want to talk about the past with Mr. Talbert. What was done was done. "Yes, sir, I suppose I could have, but..." he let the sentence die, not wanting to give his reasons.

"I suppose you couldn't," replied Jasper softly, trying to understand.

Awkwardness filled the air as the sounds of horses and cows joined a slight breeze bringing all the smells of the ranch to them as they stood in silence.

"You're a proud man," said Jasper. "And I respect that, and I meant no disrespect when we offered you money after you and our Sarah married. It was meant with the best of intentions."

"I know that Mr. Talbert and the thought was highly appreciated. It's just..."

"Sarah's our only daughter," interrupted Jasper. "And we only wanted to make sure she was well taken care of." Then he shrugged, looking apologetic. "I never thought you couldn't take care of my Sarah. It's just that sometimes, a little extra makes a big difference." Then, with both hands, he gestured around the ranch. "This will all be Sarah's one day." Then he quickly corrected himself. "And yours and my grandson's." He paused, stepped away from the corral fence, and gestured with one hand at the land. "Took most of my life to build this place, and I don't want to see it sold off and disappear, becoming part of something that belongs to someone else."

Wade thought of George Hoskins.

Jasper turned. "All I'm asking is you consider that, and think about one day coming back and working this place, so I'll die knowing it won't be lost."

Not knowing what to say, Wade looked away at the land and mountains in the distance, feeling regretful for wanting to do what he liked, which was being a lawman.

Mr. Talbert put his hand on Wade's shoulder. "Would you do that for me, Son? Just think about it. That's all I'm asking."

Wade looked at him and smiled. "I'll think on it, sir. I'll think about it real hard, but I can't make no promises."

Jasper smiled and extended his right hand, hoping his daughter would have a hand in the process. "Fair enough." They shook hands firmly, then Mr. Talbert glanced toward the house. "No sense letting the woman know we had this little talk."

Wade grinned. "No, sir."

Jasper smiled and nodded with a wink. "Let's saddle you a horse."

Six

Circle T Ranch

The ride to the Circle T Ranch filled Wade's mind with memories of herding cattle, looking for strays, and other fond memories of his days at the ranch with his friend, Emmett Spears. Arriving midmorning, the hooves of Wade's borrowed horse mixed with the squawking of chickens as they darted this way and that in front of his horse.

Stu Parks walked out of the barn, leading a horse toward the corral, and upon seeing the rider, he stopped, not recognizing Wade at first. "Can I help you?"

Wade thought Stu had filled out some and was no longer the baby faced, blonde, blue-eyed, skinny kid from back east. He had gained a few pounds, his hair was a little darker, and the once hairless face now had a handsome handlebar mustache. A new tan Stetson had replaced the old floppy hat everyone made fun of.

Recognizing Wade, Stu's face filled with a grin. "Why, if it ain't Wade Garrison."

Wade grinned as he pulled up and relaxed in the saddle with his hands resting on the saddle horn. "Howdy, Stu."

Stu looked up as he wiped his hand on his red, faded shirt before offering it. "Damn, Wade, it sure is good to see you."

As they shook hands, Wade recalled how Stu wanted to tag along after the men who had killed Emmett and the disappointment on his face when Wade told him no. "Looks like you've put on a few pounds."

Stu looked embarrassed. "Yeah, I guess I have put on a few since we last saw one another." The brown mare he was leading nudged him in the back, almost knocking his hat off. He turned, gave her a dirty look, and then looked up at Wade. "What brings ya back to the Circle T? I heard you married Sarah Talbert and were marshaling down in Santa Fe."

Not wanting to go into details, he told Stu that he had brought his wife and son to see her family.

"I'd heard you named you're firstborn after Emmett Spears."

"Thought it only proper."

Stu nodded thoughtfully. "I imagine he'd be right proud."

Wade glanced toward the oak tree where the white picket fence surrounded the small cemetery several yards north of the big house. He turned back to Stu. "Mr. Grimes about?"

Stu nodded. "Yep. He was out by the corral earlier with apples for his son Charles and Emmett's horses."

Wade looked surprised. "He's still doing that?"

Parks grinned with a quick nod. "Every morning."

Wade smiled with affection thinking about Mr. Grimes. "How is the old man?"

"Still grouchy," grinned Stu as he glanced toward the big house.

Wade chuckled. "Well, I guess I best get up and see him." Wade sat tall in the saddle and looked around at the place in fond memory. "The other's out herding?"

Stu nodded. "Rode out after breakfast. Mr. Grimes wants to take a hundred or so head into Denver for selling. Says they's getting too fat."

"Be careful he doesn't sell you," joked Wade as he turned his mare. "Tell the boys I asked after 'em."

"I'll do that, Wade. Sure was good to see you." Stu watched Wade ride toward the big house, then he turned and walked his horse into the corral.

Approaching the big, two-story house and a roofed porch that ran the width of the house, Wade noticed that both had recently been painted a fresh coat of white, and the trim a green instead of the red it was before he left. Stopping at the hitching rail at the base of the steps leading up to the porch, he looked up at the window of Charles Grimes' bedroom. Recalling the night he slept in the room after his return from Mexico, Wade got down and tied the horse to the hitching rail. Glancing around, in memory, he walked up the steps across the porch and knocked on the door. When it opened, he was looking into the expressionless eyes and face of Bertha, Tolliver's long-time Indian housekeeper.

She hadn't changed much, he thought. She was still heavy, her plump face framed in black and gray pigtails hanging over her shoulders, past the sides of her large breasts. She was barefoot as she had always been, dressed in a deep, red skirt, a man's blue shirt. She had on the same necklace made of bear claws and a beaded headband.

They stared at one another for a moment, and then Wade smiled. "Hello, Bertha."

She stepped back, staring into his eyes without expression while he stepped inside, then she closed the door. "Wait here," she said as she walked barefoot toward Tolliver's office, where she disappeared into the study. Wade looked around the familiar room of fine furniture, area rugs, and paintings as the muffled sounds of Tolliver Grimes' deep voice came from the closed door of the study. The door opened, and Tolliver stepped into the living room looking excited, followed by an expressionless Bertha.

Mr. Grimes still cut a handsome figure, standing just over six feet on a big frame. His full head of white hair and beard framed a handsome, rugged face carrying the lines of hot summers and cold winters, including a couple of scars he never talked about. Dressed in brown pants and a tan shirt, with sleeves buttoned at the wrist, he grinned like a child as his slightly bowed legs rushed him across the room.

Wade grinned and extended his right hand, which Mr. Grimes quickly pushed away, giving him a hug instead of a handshake, catching him by surprise.

Tolliver gripped Wade's shoulders with his big, strong hands as he stepped back and looked at him. "Good to see ya, boy. How the hell you been?" Before Wade could answer, Grimes walked toward the liquor cabinet. "Join me in a drink."

"Happy to sir."

"Sit down, son," he said, gesturing to a brown overstuffed chair. He poured two drinks while talking over his shoulder. "Where's that family of yours?"

"They're over at Talbert's place. Brought them both up for a visit while I take care of a few things."

"I see," replied Grimes as he turned with two glasses, giving one to Wade and then raising his glass in a toast. "Good to see ya, boy." He took a quick sip, smacked his lips, made a sour face, and sat down on the sofa.

Wade took a sip of whiskey. "How are things, Mr. Grimes?"

Tolliver got comfortable, took another sip, and then looked irritated. "Told you a long time ago, son. It's Tolliver. You and I are long past that Mister bullshit."

Wade grinned. "Yes, sir."

"You still marshaling down in Santa Fe?"

"Yes, sir."

Tolliver gestured with an empty hand. "How come you ain't wearing your badge?"

"I decided to keep it in my pocket while I'm in Harper. Fewer questions, that way."

"I see," replied Grimes. "And what questions is it that you're you afraid of?"

"People just naturally ask a lot of questions when you ride into town wearing a badge."

"I suppose that's true," he said thoughtfully. "You still packing that Sharps I gave you?"

"Yes, sir," replied Wade. "But now she has one of them new telescope sites."

Tolliver looked interested. "I saw a fella give an exhibition using one of them telescope sights on a Sharps when I was up in Denver a few months back. He hit a target plum center at 1100 yards, six out of six."

Wade looked impressed. "I ain't that good, but the scope has added some distance as well as accuracy."

"Got it with you?" asked Tolliver, looking excited. "I'd like to have a look."

Wade looked regretful. "I left it with Sheriff Bowlen over in Sisters."

Grimes had a curious look on his face. "Seth Bowlen?"

Wade spent the next half hour sipping his whiskey and telling him about Seth Bowlen, Pete Hoskins, and Pete's pa, George Hoskins. When he finished, Grimes sat forward, staring into Wade's eyes. "George Hoskins is a son of a bitch who's trying to buy up most of the town and the smaller ranches and homesteads." Grimes paused and looked at his empty glass sitting on the table next to the sofa. "I heard he has a judge or two indebted to him up in Denver and a marshal who's afraid of the judges." He sighed, nodded, and then stood. "You ready?" he asked, referring to another drink.

"No, thanks." Wade held up his glass that still held a small amount. "Still have some."

Tolliver grunted. "Don't recall you being a slow drinker."

Wade grinned. "Well, it's a might early, and being married changed a few things in my life."

Grimes chuckled. "That usually happens." He walked to the liquor cabinet while talking. "After you left for Santa Fe a few years back, I heard the story about you and his son." Tolliver picked up the bottle and started to pour a drink, hesitated, then he set the bottle back down, having changed his mind. He turned. "Dan Hoskins was George Hoskins' eldest boy, and he took the boy's death hard."

Wade had always felt bad about killing Dan Hoskins, but he had no choice, remembering the night he tried to bushwhack him in Sisters. "Didn't leave me much choice in the matter." He drank the last of his drink and set the empty glass on the table next to his chair.

Grimes walked back to the sofa, thinking of the death of his son, Charles, as he sat down and stared at the floor in sad memory. "A man lives through his sons." A slow moment passed, and then he looked up. "I heard George Hoskins blamed his younger son, Pete, more than you. When they brought Dan home and carried him into the house, the old man could be heard yelling at Pete for not getting him out of town." Tolliver looked sad. "People say that incident changed the old man, making him hard, bitter, and determined to have more of everything." Grimes paused, looking thoughtful. "My guess is he's trying to replace the loss of his son. One day he'll learn, you can't replace a son with objects or anything else. Once they're gone, they're gone for good."

Wade felt sorry for Mr. Grimes and felt remorse for George Hoskins for killing his son. "Why blame Pete for the foolishness of his older brother?"

Grimes shrugged. "That's a question you'll have to ask George Hoskins. I'd heard once that Dan was the bully and a tad foolish, as well as crazy. Pete's more levelheaded and calculating, but he always rode

Dan's coattails." Grimes frowned. "When Dan got killed, the old man shut Pete out. Naturally, the boy began acting like Dan trying to impress his Pa, causing trouble here and there. So, what happened over in Sisters ain't exactly a surprise."

The tall clock in the far corner tolled noon, and as the chimes filled the silent room, Wade was thinking of how a killing destroys more than one life.

Tolliver thought of his son and then of Emmett Spears, who was like a son to him. Then he thought of Wade and found himself wishing he had never left. Pushing such foolishness aside, he stood and looked at Wade with a small smile. "That whiskey made me hungry. Can I offer you some lunch so's we can visit a while longer, and maybe talk of more pleasant things, like that son of yours?"

Wade stood. "I'd like that."

Mr. Grimes grinned, looking happy as he put one hand on Wade's shoulder. As they walked toward the dining room, he yelled, "Bertha, we have a guest for lunch!"

Seven

Double J Ranch

Sarah stood on the front porch in the early morning hours dressed in her robe, watching Wade as he drove the wagon under the archway, out of the dark shadows of the valley floor and into the sun at the top of the hill. He stopped the wagon, turned, and waved. Sarah rose to her tiptoes and waved, wishing he didn't have to leave, and then watched as he and the wagon disappeared over the hill.

Staring at the empty road, the loneliness she always felt whenever he left for long periods came back, and she dreaded the coming days and nights away from him. Wrapping herself in her arms, she wiped the tears from her eyes and thought of the night before when he held her. Knowing why Wade was sent to Sisters, she also knew the dangers he faced, and she feared for him. But that was nothing new for Sarah because whenever he left to trail after an outlaw or walk into a saloon filled with drunks, she was always afraid. She would worry until he walked through the door of their home, smiled at her, and asked what was for dinner. Taking one last look at the empty road at the top of the hill, she closed the door, leaned against it, and wiped her eyes.

Janice Talbert was standing in the kitchen doorway, holding a pot in one hand, a towel in the other, watching her daughter. She stepped from the doorway, knowing the fears her daughter held. "What troubles you, Sarah?"

Sarah wiped her face as she stepped away from the door and forced a smile. She walked to the staircase, sat down on the steps, and wiped the tears from her cheeks. "I'm like a lost child every time he leaves." Shaking her head with a small, worried smile, she looked up at her mother. "It's always the same when he leaves like this. I worry myself sick until he comes home."

Mrs. Talbert wanted to hold her daughter and comfort her, telling her everything would be all right. But experience told her that would not take away her daughter's fears or loneliness, so she gestured to the kitchen behind her. "Help me get the dishes on the table. That boy of yours is gonna be hungry when he wakes up, and your pa will be in from the barn soon." Then she turned and walked toward the kitchen. "Best, keep busy. Worrying only makes things worse. You have a child to think about."

Sarah glanced at the front door, got up, and followed her mother, knowing she spoke the truth. Worry only prolongs the misery fear holds, but she knew that she would go on worrying until her husband returned, and like a wife, wished he had taken the time to eat a good breakfast.

Harper, Colorado

Harper was beginning to show life when Wade drove the team to Levi's Livery. Wade climbed down, and after making small talk with Levi, he asked if he could leave the wagon while he got something to eat. Levi had no objections, so Wade left the wagon and horses and walked away, saying he would return in an hour.

There were a few men on horseback, a wagon or two, and several pedestrians along the dusty street of Harper. Several shopkeepers were sweeping the night dust off the boardwalk in front of their stores. The smell of hot food rushed at him from Pauline's Café down the street, and he thought about breakfast. His journey to Pauline's and breakfast was interrupted when he looked at the sign above the boardwalk to the sheriff's office. Deciding his stomach could wait, he stepped up onto the boardwalk, thinking it might be a good idea to drop in on Sheriff Harry Block. He opened the door, stepped inside, finding an unfamiliar looking man sitting behind the sheriff's desk with his feet on one corner of it reading a newspaper.

The man lowered the newspaper and gave him a close look. "Something I can do for you?"

Wade noticed the badge on his shirt. "I'm looking for Sheriff Harry Block."

The man had a used wooden match in his mouth he moved from side to side across his thick lips with the use of his tongue. His long, black hair was slicked back around his ears to his neck and past the collar of his faded brown shirt. He was clean-shaven with dark brown eyes, and although he was sitting down, Wade could tell he was a little on the chubby side.

"He ain't in," the man said as he tossed the newspaper onto the desk and tilted his head a bit, eyeing Wade from head to toe. "I'm Lee Jones, his deputy," he said as if that held some importance. The deputy folded his hands across his protruding belly, moved the matchstick to the other side of his mouth with his tongue, and waited.

Wade thought of the deputy in New Mexico that he busted in the mouth five years ago. He didn't like this man very much, either. "Know where I can find the sheriff?"

Deputy Lee Jones stared at him for a long, silent moment. "Sure do. What's the problem?"

"Personal matter."

Jones frowned, not liking the stranger's attitude. "Well, like I done told you, I'm the deputy, so whatever it is, you can talk to me about it."

"And like I said, Deputy, it's a personal matter." Wade smiled. "Or maybe you don't understand what that means."

Deputy Jones took the match out of his mouth and stared at Wade for a moment, then nodded toward the window. "Across the street at the Cafe." Then he picked up the newspaper, leaned back in his chair, and started reading as if Wade had already left.

Deciding not to waste a 'Thanks' on the asshole, Wade turned and headed out the door for Pauline's Restaurant. He found the sheriff sitting in the corner next to the window, eating what looked like ham and eggs while reading the newspaper. As he approached the table, Wade thought Block hadn't changed much. "Sheriff Block?"

Sheriff Harry Block was in his mid-sixties and considered old for a lawman, but Harper was a peaceful place, so it was a good town for a

74

lawman past his prime. Harry Block was relatively short, around five-feet-five, and heavyset, dressed in a tan wool suit and a white shirt with a string tie. He had a high forehead of thinning gray hair that he combed straight back and questioning brown eyes. Wade remembered they could be piercing when Harry was angry. A small, neatly trimmed mustache occupied his upper lip, and his tanned, rough face was full of acne. He looked up from the newspaper and smiled, looking curious. "That's right."

Wade gestured to a chair. "Mind if I sit down?"

Block folded the paper, laid it on the table, and motioned to the empty chair with one hand. As he picked up his cup with the other, he eyed Wade as he sat down. "What's on your mind?"

Wade took off his hat and set it on the edge of the table. "You may not remember me, Sheriff, but my name is…"

"I know who ya are," interrupted Block. "You're that Wade Garrison fellah that went after the four men who killed that friend of yours over at the Blue Sky Saloon."

Wade settled in his chair, wondering what sort of mood Harry Block was in.

Harry picked up his fork and knife and began cutting a piece of ham. "Seems to my recollection, you weren't too happy with me for not chasing after them fellahs."

Wade smiled, looking apologetic. "I was a mite anxious, I admit…"

"That you were," interrupted the sheriff as he put the fork with ham into his mouth and began to chew and talk at the same time. "No matter, though, son. It seems I heard you got all four but got Frank Wells and some Indian killed in the process."

Wade felt guilty enough over Frank and Dark Cloud and didn't need reminding of their deaths.

The sheriff finished chewing and swallowed. "Frank was a damn good lawman, and death's just a step away from all of us, so I ain't blaming you."

"Wasn't aware you two knew one another."

Block started on another piece of ham. "I ran across him and Seth Bowlen from time to time." He shoved the food into his mouth and looked at Wade. "I seem to recall hearing you're a deputy marshal in Santa Fe."

He looked at the absence of a badge. "Guess you ain't doing that no more."

Wade's appetite increased as he watched the yellow yolk of the egg Block cut into spread over his plate. Wishing someone would ask what he wanted to eat, he glanced around the restaurant for a waitress. "I'm still a deputy for Marshall Billy French, have been these past six years."

Block shoved another fork of food into his mouth, looking quizzical. "Forget your badge?"

Wade glanced out the window, thinking Harry asked a lot of questions. "No."

A young, redheaded girl dressed in a gray dress and white apron asked if he wanted something to eat. He looked up at her green eyes and pretty face, thinking her hair needed a comb, then he looked at Block's plate. "I'll have what he's having and a cup of coffee if you wouldn't mind, Miss."

She smiled. "Why would I mind? I'll bring your coffee." Then she looked at Block. "Another coffee, Sheriff?"

"Please, Carla. Thank you."

Wade watched her as she turned and walked away, thinking he didn't remember her from before.

"Carla English," Block said in a low voice as if reading Wade's mind.

Wade turned, looking confused. "What?"

"Her name is Carla English. Her ma and pa own this place."

Looking surprised, Wade asked, "I thought Ennis Carney owned it."

The sheriff nodded as he chewed the ham he just put in his mouth. "He did, but he sold out a couple of years back. The English family moved here from Des Moines, Iowa." Then Block smiled. "I know that cause I'm nosey, and I'm also the sheriff, and you ain't explained why you ain't boasting that badge of yours." He smiled. "Or what it is that brought you to my table. I know it ain't just to pass the time of day with an old man by interrupting his peaceful breakfast."

Wade quickly recalled how grumpy Sheriff Block could be. "I just thought it best not to wear my badge."

"And why is that Mr. Garrison?"

"I figured I could walk around town without being stared at."

Block chewed while considering that. "Suppose that might be so."

"I'd like to ask you a few questions, Sheriff, if that'd be all right."

The sheriff stared at him for a long moment, then looked down at his plate and scooped up some eggs with his fork. "I'm the one that usually asks the questions, Mr. Garrison." Then he put another fork of food into his mouth. "What's on your mind?"

Wade glanced around as he leaned forward, placing his elbows on the table, and spoke in a soft voice. "What can you tell me about George Hoskins?"

Sheriff Block stopped chewing and sat back in his chair, pushing the food from between his teeth and cheeks with his tongue as he stared at Wade. After a quick look around, he leaned forward and spoke above a whisper. "Strange sort of question over breakfast."

The waitress appeared at the table with a cup and saucer, placed them on the table, and smiled at Wade as she poured coffee into the cup. Finished, she poured the sheriff another cup of coffee and left.

Block chuckled. "Girls once smiled at me like that." Then the smile was replaced by disappointment. "But it's been a while."

Wade took a sip of hot coffee. "Since we gotta talk about something over breakfast, it may as well be George Hoskins."

Harry Block scowled as he picked up his cup. "We don't have to talk about anything, Mr. Garrison." Block sipped his coffee and looked at Wade over the rim of his cup, wondering why a United States Deputy Marshal was curious about George Hoskins. He set the cup down in the saucer. "Exactly what sort of information are you after, Mr. Garrison? I'd call you Marshal, but you're hiding that fact from the rest of the world."

Wade chuckled softly, thinking the old man still had his wits about him. "For starters, I'm curious how much of Harper Hoskins owns?"

Sheriff Block's face filled with anger as he stared at Wade while leaning forward, pointing at him with the fork he held in his right hand. He was about to say something Wade knew was not going to be pleasant when the waitress approached with Wade's breakfast.

"Here's your food, sir."

Wade glanced up and smiled at her. "Thanks." He sat back, staring at the sheriff while she placed the plate of ham and eggs in front of him, put a fork and knife next to his plate, and handed him a white cloth napkin.

The sheriff sat back in his chair, looking angry as he stared at Wade, waiting for the waitress to leave. After she walked away, he leaned forward, resting one forearm on the edge of the table, pointing his fork at Wade. He spoke in a low voice. "You ask'n if George Hoskins owns me, boy?"

Wade looked at Harry Block, wondering how the hell he drew that assumption. "That ain't what I was asking, Harry."

"It's Sheriff," corrected Block angrily.

Wade picked up his napkin, placed it over his lap, picked up his fork, and looked at Harry. "That ain't what I was asking, Sheriff, and I apologize if I came across that way."

Harry let out a soft sigh and sat back in his chair, figuring he'd misjudged the man across from him. "My apologies if I got a little ahead in our conversation by jumping to some conclusions I shouldn't. But just so's we're clear on that," Harry paused with an unyielding expression, "I ain't owned by no man."

Wade pushed a fork of eggs and ham into his mouth and looked into Block's hardened, brown eyes. "Never thought otherwise, Sheriff." He returned his eyes to his plate and cut another piece of ham.

Sheriff Block watched him for a moment letting his expression soften. "It's Harry."

Wade started to shove a fork of food into his mouth but paused and looked at Block. "Maybe I should just call you Sheriff Harry. Then if you get mad, we won't have to decide what I should call you."

Harry chuckled and then began to laugh as he pushed his nearly empty plate toward the center of the table.

Wade grinned as he took a bite of food.

"Might not be a bad idea, Mr. Garrison," said Harry. Then, with another chuckle, he leaned on the table with his left elbow, picked up his coffee cup, and took a drink. Sheriff Block put his cup down and looked at Wade. "As far as the rest of the town," he said as he glanced around the café. "Hoskins owns the Harper Café up the street, and a new three-story hotel around the corner aptly named The Hoskins Hotel, and I understand he tried to buy the Sundowner Saloon, but old Charlie won't sell."

Wade glanced out the window while he chewed his food. "Town's grown since I left."

"That's true," Block said sadly.

Wade stabbed a piece of ham with his fork. "You don't sound too happy about that."

"I ain't." Harry looked upset. "A bigger town just brings bigger problems." He picked up his cup and took another sip of coffee. "Hoskins is also on the board of the bank, and his name is on the window of the land office."

Wade stopped chewing, thinking that was convenient. "Where's the city council stand in all this?"

Block looked disgusted and let out a soft sigh. "They're all getting rich. I've two deputies the council made me hire that'd I run out of town quicker than a steer could take a shit, so you figure it out."

Things were looking a lot more complicated than Seth had let on, thought Wade. Or maybe he didn't know, which Wade believed was probably closer to the truth. Wade took a drink of coffee and glanced out the window. "I met Deputy Lee Jones earlier." He frowned. "Can't say I care much for the man."

Sheriff Block's face filled with a sour expression. "He's a sorry piece of crap, and so is my other deputy, Booth Fox. Both of 'em used to work for Hoskins."

Wade stopped chewing the food he had just put into his mouth, recalling the name Booth Fox from the shooting Seth told him about. "Maybe they still do."

Harry chuckled without humor. "I'm sure they do."

Suddenly, Wade's appetite was gone, so he placed his fork on his plate and pushed both away, thinking that he and Seth needed to have another talk. He had wanted to stay in town a little longer and visit some of the people he had known, but now he thought he had better head back to Sisters. He drank the last of his coffee and reached into his pocket for some money. "Guess I best be going, Harry."

"Breakfast is on me, Marshal," said Sheriff Block.

Looking surprised, Wade thanked him, stood, and picked up his hat. "Thanks, Sheriff, and I appreciate the talk."

"I'll walk ya to your horse." Harry Block put some money on the table, pushed his chair back, stood, and picked up his brown Stetson hat.

"I have a wagon up at the livery."

As Block walked past Wade toward the door, he looked at him with a puzzled expression.

Wade grinned. "Belongs to Sheriff Bowlen. He lent it to me so's I could bring my wife and son for a visit with her folks."

"That's right," replied Block looking thoughtful. "You married the Talbert girl. Nice family. Too bad, there ain't more like 'em in the county."

Wade agreed in silence as they walked out of the restaurant and headed up the street toward the livery. As they walked, Wade noticed Deputy Jones standing inside the jailhouse, watching them through the big window with the word Sheriff painted in white lettering.

Levi Wagner met them with a smile of stained teeth, and after saying "Hello" to Sheriff Block, he told Wade that both horses had been fed and watered.

Wade asked what he owed. Levi told him, and after Wade paid, they harnessed the two horses and started leading them outside to the wagon. As Wade passed a stall, he noticed a roan colored horse. "Nice looking horse!"

"Belongs to Deputy Jones," replied Levi.

Sheriff Harry Block looked at the horse. "Too nice a horse flesh for that idiot."

Levi chuckled as he followed Wade out the livery door into the warm, morning sun where he looked up at the clear blue sky. "Gonna be a hot one."

Wade looked up, hoping he was wrong but knew it would be a long, hot ride back to Sisters. "Afraid you're right, Levi."

Block leaned his back against one of the livery doors, took a pouch of tobacco and paper out of his pocket, and proceeded to make a cigarette. The smell of horse dung and the contradiction of fresh straw mixed with straw soaked with horse urine filled the air of the dusty livery behind him. When he finished with the cigarette, he took a match from his pocket, struck in on the livery door, and put it to the cigarette. Small billows of white smoke rose above his head, and then he took a deep drag and exhaled the white smoke. As he watched Wade and Levi hook the team to the wagon, he wondered what a Deputy Marshal from Santa Fe was doing in Harper. He knew it wasn't just to bring his wife and son for a visit.

Wade buckled the last strap, patted the horse, and turned back to the dusty street they had walked up. His eyes settled on Deputy Lee Jones and another man sitting in chairs outside the jailhouse watching them. He turned and walked around the wagon, checking the horse's harnesses. "That man sitting with your deputy Lee Jones wouldn't happen to be Booth Fox, would it Sheriff?"

A thin trail of smoke rose from the cigarette between the sheriff's lips as he glanced down the street at his deputies. "It is." He took a long drag, then dropped the cigarette to the ground, and stepped on it with the toe of his boot, and smiled. "I'm sure they're wondering who it is I'm talking to." Then he stepped away from the door, looking tired. "Maybe I should retire and leave the town to those two idiots, along with Hoskins and the rest of his men."

Wade tightened the final cinch and looked at Harry Block, staring down the town's street where he had been sheriff for more than twenty years. He knew the sheriff was nearing the day when a man can no longer be the sheriff people expect him to be. "It's not so easy to walk away, is it?" Wade thought about the promise he made to Jasper Talbert.

"No," replied Harry, looking sad. "It ain't, but I'm getting awful tired of answering questions from them two shit heads, and both are just itching to be sheriff." Then he chuckled sarcastically. "If'n I did quit, maybe they'd kill one another over who gets the job."

Levi chuckled as he stepped from behind the wagon and stared down the street. "I'd like to see that."

Wade glanced at the two deputies and then looked at Block. "And if you did retire, Sherriff, what then?"

He smiled. "I married a very frugal young lady forty years ago. Thanks to her, we have a little saved." He smiled with a determined nod. "We'd manage." Then he turned with an extended hand. "Have a safe trip, Mr. Garrison, and give Bowlen my regards."

Wade grasped it firmly. "I'll surely do that, Sheriff."

"Harry," corrected Block as he looked down the street of Harper and then at Wade. "I'm not sure what it is you and Sheriff Bowlen has going, but I heard about the killings over in Sisters, and if it's about Pete Hoskins, be careful. Booth Fox isn't my deputy by accident."

Wade looked at the two men sitting on the porch and then at Harry, who smiled, turned, and walked down the street toward his office and deputies Lee Jones and Booth Fox.

Levi was standing next to Wade. "Harry Block's a fine man." Then he spits and wiped his mouth on the sleeve of his dirty, red underwear. "But them other two are trouble."

Wade climbed up onto the wagon seat, settled in, then pulled his badge from his pants pocket and pinned it to his shirt.

Levi looked up with surprise wondering why he just now put it on.

Wade picked up the reins to the horses and looked down at the old man. "Thanks for everything, Levi."

"Anytime, Marshal."

Wade guided the wagon down the street past the jailhouse just as Sheriff Block walked up the steps to the boardwalk.

Hearing the wagon, Block stopped at the top step, turned, put his hand on the porch post, and watched Wade as he drove past. Noticing the badge on his shirt, he gave Wade an approving smile and nodded.

Deputy Jones got up from his chair and stared at Wade as he drove past. "I never noticed him wearing a badge before. Who is he?"

"A Deputy United States Marshal."

Deputy Booth Fox stood from the chair he had been sitting in with his feet propped against another porch post, "What'd he want?"

Sheriff Block smiled without looking at either. "Never really said."

Fox glanced at Harry Block. "What's his name?"

"Wade Garrison." Then he turned and walked inside.

Eight

Sisters, Colorado

The sun was almost gone when Wade drove the team and wagon past the Bowlen house toward the barn, thankful the long ride from Harper was over. He pulled the team up next to the barn, parked the wagon, and set the brake with his left foot, wondering which was the most tired, him or the two horses. His back ached, his butt was numb and sore from the hard wagon seat, and as Wade climbed down feeling years older than he was. Holding the small of his back with both hands, he turned his upper torso, stretching his upper body in an attempt to loosen his tired, aching muscles. Feeling no better, he unhitched the team and was leading them toward the barn when Seth stepped out the back door of the house and hollered, "Hold up, Wade! I'll give you a hand with them horses!"

Wade and the horses were inside the barn by the time Seth caught up and, taking one of the horses, asked, "How was the trip?"

"Hot."

Seth looked at Wade, figuring his mood was not all that friendly from the long trip. "Get Sarah and that boy all settled in?"

Wade said he had, then hung the harness over a hook on the wall, stepped out of the stall, yawned, and stretched once again. "How's Molly?"

"Fine. She's inside fixing dinner. I hope you're hungry."

"Not as much as I am tired," replied Wade.

Wade made a final stop at the washbasin at the back door to wash the day off his hands and face before going inside. He found Molly dressed in a tan, striped dress and apron, busy over the stove. He smiled with a tired look. "Hello, Molly."

She looked up and smiled. "Get Sarah and the boy settled in with her parents?"

He nodded. "I did."

She paused in her cooking. "You have a nice family Wade."

He smiled proudly. "Thanks, Molly."

"I bet you're hungry."

Seth walked in from the other room. "Come in here, and I'll buy you a drink."

Wade smiled at Molly. "Yes, Ma'am, I am hungry," Then, as he walked past her, getting a whiff of dinner, he said, "Smells mighty good, Molly."

She smiled appreciatively. "Well, thank you. It ain't nothing special."

"Sure smells special." Then he turned to follow Seth into the other room.

Molly turned back to the stove. "Dinner will be ready soon."

In the parlor, a tired Wade dropped into the same red chair he sat in a few nights ago. While his eyes took a quick trip around the familiar room, he waited for Seth to pour the drinks. His quick journey was interrupted by Seth, handing him a whiskey. As he took it, he thanked Seth and noticed he was wearing a new, blue-gray shirt. "Been shopping while I was gone?"

Seth was puzzled by the question.

Wade grinned as he gestured to the shirt. "New shirt?"

Seth looked down, smiled sheepishly, and pointed toward the kitchen. "Present from Molly."

Wade sipped his drink, glanced toward the kitchen, and then at Seth with a curious look. "Is it your birthday?"

Seth frowned as he sat down in the other red, overstuffed chair. "Hell, no, my birthday ain't for another two months."

The room was silent for several seconds, and then Wade leaned on the arm of the chair, glanced at the door, and then looked at Seth. "Why'd she buy you the shirt then?"

84

Seth looked embarrassed. "Molly does things like that." Then he leaned forward and lowered his voice. "Don't Sarah do that kind of thing for you?"

Wade grinned, thinking of the new long underwear she bought for him last week. "Yeah, she does."

"Then what's the big deal about my new shirt?"

Wade shrugged with a small smile. "Just asking."

Seth appeared angry as he took another drink of whiskey. "Well, maybe it ain't none of your business."

Wade grinned and took a sip of whiskey. "Just asking Seth."

Having a mind to change the subject, Seth put his glass on the table that occupied the space between their chairs. "You have a chance to nose around Harper?"

Wade took a small drink and sat the glass next to Seth's. "Sure did, and you got yourself a mess here."

Seth frowned. "Hell, I already know that."

"George Hoskins is buying up the town of Harper, just as you said, but were you aware that he was on the board of the bank, and his name is on the window of the land office?"

Seth looked surprised. "The bank don't surprise me none, but the land office..." he let the sentence die.

"The land office," said Wade, "gives him first hand at buying any land the bank forecloses on." Then he sat forward, resting his elbows on his knees, clasping his drink. "I have another bit of news for you, Seth, that you ain't gonna like. Booth Fox is Sheriff Block's new deputy."

Seth sat forward, looking surprised. "His deputy?"

Wade nodded. "You heard, right. He's one of Harry Block's two new deputies."

"Who's the other?"

"Fellah by the name of Lee Jones."

Seth sat back in his chair, considering the name. "Never heard of him." Then he said, "Might be one of Hoskins' men."

Wade took a drink. "I'm sure of it."

Seth looked disappointed. "That doesn't sound like Harry. Why would he be hiring two of Hoskins' men?"

"The town council told him to. Sheriff Block isn't exactly fond of either deputy. He called them both dumb shits."

Seth chuckled. "Sounds like something Harry would say." Then he looked curious. "Why doesn't he just fire 'em both?"

"I don't think he can."

Seth frowned and looked down at the floor. "No, I suppose he can't." Then he turned, looking worried. "With two of Hoskins' men working at the jail, that sort of complicates us arresting Pete Hoskins in Harper."

Just then, Molly appeared in the doorway. "Supper's ready."

"Be right there," said Seth. Then he stood and looked at Wade. "Sounds like we may have to get Pete Hoskins when he ain't in Harper."

Wade stood, looking thoughtful. "That may take some doing. But first off, I want to talk to that farmer friend of yours and that bartender."

"We'll ride out first thing in the morning after breakfast." He pointed toward the door. "Let's go eat before it gets cold."

Nine

Sam Wheeler's Farm

Sam Wheeler was at the pigsty slopping pigs when he heard horses. Turning from what he was doing and seeing two riders, Sam set the bucket down, picked up his rifle he always had with him, and laid the barrel on the top railing of the sty aimed at the two riders.

Seeing the gun, Wade and Seth pulled up a few yards from the strong smell of pigs. "It's Seth Bowlen, Sam!"

"Who's that with ya?" At thirty-five, Sam Wheeler stood an even six feet and had a black, unruly beard, broad shoulders, big arms, and large hands. Dark, black hair flowed from under a floppy brimmed slightly tattered union cavalry hat.

Wade sat back in his saddle. "I'm United States Deputy Marshal Wade Garrison, Mr. Wheeler."

Sam stared at Wade. "Marshal, you say?"

Wade nodded. "That's right, Mr. Wheeler. We want to talk to you if you have a moment."

"Marshal Garrison came all the way from Santa Fe," said Seth. "Mind if we get down?"

Wheeler lowered his rifle, put one foot on the bottom railing, stepped over the top rail of the sty, and leaned the rifle against the sty fence. "Santa Fe?" Then as he walked toward them, he wiped his right hand on his dirty, gray pants and smiled as he offered an outstretched hand. "Pleased to meet you, Marshal."

Wade shook Sam's hand vigorously. "Need to ask you a few questions, Mr. Wheeler."

Sam looked curious. "Sure. Do you want to come up to the house for a glass of water? Ain't got nothing stronger." He looked apologetic. "Guess my missus can fix us some coffee if that'd be to your liken."

Thinking he'd like to get away from the smell of the sty that brought back memories of South Carolina and his childhood, Wade gestured to the corral several yards away. "Let's talk by the corral. No need to bother your missus."

Wheeler glanced back at the sty and grinned. "I forget how bad the smell is. I'm used to it, I guess." Then he walked toward the corral with Wade and Seth following with their horses.

Thankful to get away from the sty, Wade glanced around the place, taking in the small house in need of a new roof and paint nestled among some cottonwoods, the outhouse a safe distance behind it. A new chicken coop sat beside the barn of seasoned gray wood and a new roof. "Nice place you got here."

Sam leaned against the corral fence looking pleased, while Seth tossed his horse's reins over the top railing. "I'm sure the two of you didn't ride out here to tell me I have a nice place. What's on yer mind?"

Having noticed Sam's hat, Wade asked, "You in the Cavalry, Mr. Wheeler?"

Sam looked proud. "Fourth, Michigan."

"You at a place called The Wilderness?" asked Wade.

Wheeler looked curious. "Sure was. Why ya ask'n?"

"My pa died there."

"What outfit was he with?"

"South Carolina, Second Infantry."

Seth looked surprised, having never known that.

Sadness filled Wheeler's face. "A lot of good men died on both sides that day."

Wade nodded. "I guess that's true enough." Then he gestured to Seth. "Sheriff Bowlen tells me you saw three men ride past here the day your neighbor, Tom Lawson, was gunned down."

Wheeler frowned, looking upset. "Yes, sir, I surely did, Marshal." Then he stepped away from the corral fence and pointed to the barn. "I was up in the loft on the other side when I heard the neigh of horses. I walked to the loft window on the far side of the barn and looked out," He pointed toward the tree line and open fields beyond the barn. "Pete Hoskins, and that Booth fellah, who's always with him, and some other fellah I ain't never seen b'fore rode across my field."

"You're sure it was them?" asked Wade.

Wheeler looked offended. "As sure as I see you standing before me."

Wade looked apologetic. "Sorry, Mr. Wheeler, I just want to make sure you know it was them."

Sam frowned. "I'd know them two anywhere's."

Wade glanced at the barn. "Mind taking us up to the loft and show us where they were when they rode by?"

Wheeler shrugged. "Why sure." He led them to the barn, where they climbed up the ladder's wooden steps to the loft. Once in the loft, Wade glanced around at the bales of hay stored in it, then pointed to the window. "That where you saw them?"

"Yep," he gestured around. "I was right here tossing some hay down with my pitchfork to the barn floor for the mules when I heard the horses." Then he turned and walked toward the loft window on the far side. "I walked to this here window and sort of hid behind the wall, like so." He demonstrated this by standing next to the wall with just enough of his face sticking out so he could see. "That's when I saw Pete Hoskins and them other two ride out from them trees yonder." He pointed to the trees as he continued. "Across the open field, they rode, and then disappear behind them birch trees and bushes yonder."

Wade looked from the trees in the distance across the fields to the birch trees. "They see you?"

"Don't know for sure," Wheeler said, looking uncertain. "Don't think so, but when Booth Fox looked this way, I ducked back real quick like so they wouldn't see me, and when I looked out again, they was gone."

Wade stood at the window, estimating the distance from where he stood to where Wheeler saw the three riders and figured it to be close to two hundred yards. "What kind of horses were they riding?"

Wheeler looked toward the field in thought. "Hoskins was on that Appaloosa he's always ride'n, and that Booth fellah, his big gray, and the other fellah rode a roan colored horse."

Wade stared out the window in thought. "Can you describe the third man?"

Wheeler shook his head, looking uncertain. "No, sir, they were too far for that."

Wade turned to Sam. "Then how do you know the other two were Pete Hoskins and Booth Fox?"

Wheeler looked offended. "Cause I know Pete and Booth Fox, and I saw Pete ride by here plenty of times with that Olson girl." His expression turned sad. "God rest her soul."

Wade looked back toward the trees and field, imagining three riders at this distance. He put one hand on the side of the loft window and stared at the clearing between the trees. "They seem in a hurry?"

Wheeler shook his head slowly. "No, sir, they didn't. They's walking their horses. It looked like they were talking about something."

"You got good eyesight, Mr. Wheeler?" asked Wade.

Seth was as surprised at the question as was Sam Wheeler.

Sam looked puzzled. "They're all right, I guess. Why are you asking a thing like that?"

"Nothing personal, Mr. Wheeler," said Wade. "But I need to know how good your eyes are." Then he pointed toward the trees to their right. "I'm going to ride into the woods and then across the clearing. I want you to stand the way you did that day, against the wall, peering out the way you did then."

Sam looked at the clearing and then at Wade. "Mind me asking why?"

"About a year ago," began Wade, "the only witness to a killing in Santa Fe had failing eyes, and the accused was released from jail and quickly disappeared." Wade started for the ladder. "When I get back, Mr. Wheeler, you to tell me what you saw."

Wade rode at a walk from the trees into the clearing, stopping about halfway, looking toward the barn, and was unable to see either Seth or Sam Wheeler. Then he nudged his horse into a walk, rode across the field, disappearing into the cedar trees, circled back to the corral next to the barn. He tied the horse to the corral fence, climbed the ladder to the loft, and stood next to Sam Wheeler. "Tell me what you saw, Mr. Wheeler."

90

Looking puzzled, Sam glanced at Seth, then at Wade. "I saw you riding across the field, stop and look this way, and then ride into the cedars."

"Describe me as best you can, Mr. Wheeler."

Still looking puzzled, Sam looked out the loft window and thought for a moment. "Well, you were riding the sheriff's horse, not yours."

"How do you know that?" asked Wade.

Wheeler scratched the side of his face, looking curious. "The sheriff's horse is gray, and it ain't got white stockings like yours."

Wade smiled. "What else you see?"

"You were carrying that hat of yours in your left hand."

Wade smiled. "You got good eyes, Mr. Wheeler. And to rest your mind, I have good eyes as well, and I couldn't see you from where I rode past."

Wheeler looked relieved.

Wade turned back to the field in the distance and thought about the third man. A minute later, he turned to Wheeler. "Is there anything about that third man you can tell us other than the color of his horse?" Wade was thinking of Deputy Lee Jones, who rode a roan colored horse.

Sam Wheeler thought for a moment, then stared into the clearing as if trying to picture the three men from memory. "Best I can recall is he wore dark clothes and a hat. Sat low in the saddle, like he weren't as tall as the other two, and he looked a mite heavier." Then he turned to Wade. "That's the best I can do."

Wade glanced at Seth with an approving look as he extended his hand to Sam Wheeler. "Thanks for your time, Mr. Wheeler."

Sam smiled, shook Wade's hand, and then Seth's. "Hope I was of some help."

"You were, Mr. Wheeler," replied Wade.

After they climbed down from the loft, Wade and Seth swung up onto their horses and rode away, while Sam Wheeler returned to his pigs.

They had ridden just a short distance when Wade pulled up in the shade of a large oak tree. Seth pulled up beside him and looked at Wade, who was staring at a group of birch trees and red-colored boulders in the distance. The soft sound of buzzing grasshoppers and a slight breeze played with the leaves of the oak tree and moved the tips of prairie grass the way it does with summer wheat.

"I know who the third man was," said Wade softly.

"Who?"

"Deputy Lee Jones, over in Harper."

"If that's true, it's damn good news, but what makes you think so?"

The mare snorted, clearing its nostrils as Wade looked at Seth. "Deputy Lee Jones rides a roan horse."

Bowlen thought on that a moment. "Shit, Wade, there's a dozen or more of them horses in and around Harper and Sisters."

Wade nodded in agreement. "That's true enough, but when I drove your wagon past the Sheriff's Office in Harper on my way back to Sisters, Lee Jones and Booth Fox were standing side by side on the boardwalk." He looked at Seth. "Jones is heavier and shorter." He turned back to the formations of red rocks and birch trees as a hawk screeched as it circled above the trees. "I'm telling you, Seth, the third man in the Lawson killing is Deputy Lee Jones." He looked at Seth. "It all fits."

Seth sighed as he settled in his saddle, looking worried. "You telling me we've two thirds the law enforcement of Harper to arrest?"

"That's exactly what I'm telling you."

Seth thought on that a moment and then grinned. "Wonder how old Harry's gonna handle us arresting his deputies?"

Wade chuckled. "From what I saw, Harry just might be appreciative."

Seth laughed.

Wade spurred his mare. "Let's go talk to that bartender."

Ten

Harper, Colorado

Sarah Garrison drove her father's wagon up the main street of Harper, Colorado, toward Mason's General Store while she and her mother talked about her and Wade's life in Santa Fe. Mrs. Talbert said something that made Sarah laugh while little Emmett quietly took in the unfamiliar sights of the strange town.

Sarah turned the team into the middle of the street and, with the skills of a mule skinner, backed the wagon up, so the side of the wagon was beside the far end of the dock of Mason's Store. Setting the break, she climbed down from the wagon to help her mother and son down.

Sheriff Block, who had watched her with admiration over her handling of a two-horse team, crossed the street. "Mrs. Garrison."

Sarah stopped, turned, and saw who it was. She smiled warmly and waited. Sarah wore a white, big-billed bonnet to protect her face from the sun, apricot, and white striped dress, her hair done up in her usual ponytail. "Good morning, Sheriff."

Sheriff Block took off his gray Stetson hat, held it with both hands in front of him, and nodded politely, noticing she wore a pair of riding boots under her dress, instead of women's shoes. "Nice to see you again, Miss Sarah."

She smiled. "Why thank you, Sheriff, it's nice to see you, also."

Harry accompanied her around to the other side of the wagon, where he looked up at Janice Talbert and smiled. "You look mighty nice, Mrs. Talbert. That a new bonnet?"

She smiled, looking pleased as she touched her big billed white bonnet. "Why, no."

Sheriff Block helped her down from the wagon and turned to help Emmett. As the boy's feet hit the ground, Block patted him on the head. "So, this here's the marshal's boy." Then he turned to Sarah with a smile. "Looks a whole lot like yourself if you don't mind me say'n so, Ma'am."

Sarah smiled proudly. "Why would I mind, Mr. Block? It's his father who may take exception to that compliment."

The sheriff laughed, imagining Wade Garrison's expression at hearing such a thing.

Janice Talbert asked after the sheriff's wife, Dorothy.

"She's doing fine. I'll tell her you asked after her."

Janice turned to Sarah. "We best get out of the sun."

Sarah put her hand on Emmett's shoulder and gently pushed him toward his grandmother. "You go inside with your grandmother. I'll be along in a minute."

Mrs. Talbert took Emmett's hand and walked up the steps leading to the boardwalk and the door to the store.

Sarah turned to the sheriff. "It appears you saw my husband before he left for Sisters."

"Yes, Ma'am," Block said with a quick nod. He gestured to the restaurant down the street with the hat he held in his left hand. "Had breakfast together, as a matter of fact."

"Really," she replied, glad to hear that he had breakfast before starting back to Sisters, and then she wondered how much her husband had told the sheriff. "And what did my husband have to say, Mr. Block?"

The sheriff was a cautious man by habit. "Talked mostly about you and the boy."

She doubted that. "I see." Then she looked across the street, seeing two men wearing badges standing on the boardwalk in front of the sheriff's office. "Town must be getting bigger. I see you've two deputies."

The smile left Harry's face as he turned toward his deputies, but as he turned back to Sarah, the smile returned. "Afraid that's true, Mrs. Garrison."

His expression of contempt didn't go unnoticed. "Well," she said. "If you'll excuse me, I better go inside before mother comes looking for me." She held out her hand. "Nice seeing you again, Sheriff. I'm sure we'll meet again before we return to Santa Fe."

He took her small hand in his big, rough hand, squeezed it gently, saying it had been a pleasure to see her again. Sheriff Block put his hat on, walked across the street to the jailhouse.

Deputy Jones leaned against the post looking at Mason's. "Who's the pretty woman?"

"Which one?" asked Harry, knowing full well that Jones was referring to Sarah Garrison.

Lee looked puzzled. "The younger one."

Feeling contempt for his deputy, Harry stared across the street at Mason's Store. "That young lady is Sarah Talbert, wife of United States Deputy Marshal Wade Garrison. The young lad's their son, and the other lady is Janice Talbert, Sarah's mother."

Booth Fox was staring at the store. "The same marshal you were talking to the other day?"

Block nodded. "Surprised, you caught that one, Booth."

Fox gave Harry a look. "After he rode out of town, I did some asking around and found out that he once worked for the Circle T."

Surprised by that, Block glanced at him. "Since you're so interested, what else did you find out about Wade Garrison?"

Booth looked at Block. "That he trailed the four men that killed his friend clear into Mexico and killed 'em."

"Wade always was a determined man," replied Harry. "A lot of men have found that out."

Having been told the story by Deputy Fox, Lee looked at the sheriff. "What's a United States Deputy Marshal doing in Harper?"

Block lied. "Can't say, and I didn't ask."

Booth, being the smarter of the two, was worried that it had something to do with Sheriff Bowlen and Pete Hoskins.

Not wanting to get into a discussion with his two deputies, Sheriff Block said, "I guess they came to visit her family." Then he turned and walked inside the sheriff's office.

Hearing the door close behind him, Booth glanced at the closed door, believing that Harry knew more than he was letting on, and that frustrated him. He looked at Deputy Lee. "Aren't you a mite curious about a United States marshal coming to Harper?"

95

Lee made a curious face as he turned to look at the jailhouse door. "The Sheriff just said they came to visit."

"I don't believe that!"

"Why not?" asked Lee.

Fox looked at Lee. "Think on it, Lee." Then he looked at the door to the sheriff's office. "We sure won't get anything from that old man."

Lee looked across the street, thinking of Sarah Garrison. "Right, pretty lady."

Booth looked across the street at Mason's. "Wonder what really brought the Marshal to Harper?" He stepped off the boardwalk and while adjusting his hat and gun belt, told Lee to stay where he was.

Jones watched Booth as he walked across the street, wondering what he had in mind. "Where are you going?"

"Have me a little talk with the marshal's pretty, little wife."

Wishing he could tag along, Deputy Lee turned and sat down in one of the chairs on the boardwalk. Getting comfortable, he watched Fox walk across the street, go up the steps to the boardwalk and disappear into the store.

Sheriff Block had poured a cup of coffee and turned to the window just as Booth walked into the store, and quickly thought about rescuing Sarah from the likes of Booth Fox. Then he smiled, remembering that she was one little filly who never needed rescuing. With a wry smile filling his weathered face, he sipped the lukewarm coffee, having just a slight bit of pity for Deputy Booth Fox.

Emmett was at the candy counter, filled with his private dreams of what was behind the glass in the counter. Mrs. Talbert was admiring a set of fine china from a catalog Mrs. Mason was showing her. Sarah was busy looking at a bolt of new material she thought would make a pretty dress and paid no attention to the tiny bell above the door when Deputy Booth Fox walked in.

Closing the door, Deputy Fox paused as his eyes went from the ponytail sticking out from under Sarah's white bonnet to her small waist and curved hips, imagining what it would be like to hold her tiny body against his. Thinking she was as pretty as any woman he had ever seen, he walked toward her, stopping close enough behind her to smell the sweet fragrance of the perfume she wore. He took off his black hat and held it with both hands in front of his stomach. "Excuse me, Ma'am."

Startled, Sarah dropped the bolt of cloth she had been looking at and quickly turned. The badge pinned to the pocket of his brown shirt was the first thing she saw before she looked into the man's dark brown eyes. She recognized him as one of the men she had seen across the street that Sheriff Block seemed to hold little respect for. He was clean-shaven, and his curly, black hair hung over the edges of his ears and coat collar. "I don't appreciate being startled, sir," she said with anger.

He smiled slightly, looking apologetic as he bent down to pick up the bolt of cloth she dropped. Handing it to her, he apologized. "Name's Booth Fox, Ma'am. I'm Sheriff Block's deputy, and I sure didn't mean to scare you none."

Giving him a cold look, she took the bolt of cloth, placed it back on the counter with the others, and turned with a small but friendly smile. "I was startled, Mr. Fox, not frightened. There's a difference."

Standing within inches of her, Booth Fox took in the sweet fragrance of her perfume and looked into her brown eyes. Jealousy over her husband suddenly filled him as he thought about her warm, soft body against his. He smiled. "Yes, Ma'am, I'm sure that's true."

Feeling uneasy, she looked up at him with an expressionless face. "Something I can do for you, Deputy Fox?"

"Yes, Ma'am," he said, noticing Mrs. Talbert walking toward them. "I was just wondering about your husband, the marshal—"

"What about the marshal?" interrupted Janice Talbert.

Booth turned and smiled, thinking Mrs. Talbert reminded him of his Aunt Tess, whom he grew up fearing. "Ma'am," he said politely. "I was…"

"What about my husband?" interrupted Sarah, knowing by interrupting someone, you kept them off balance. Something she learned a long time ago.

Wishing he could finish a sentence, Fox turned from Mrs. Talbert to Sarah, feeling a little uncomfortable and a whole lot outnumbered. "Truth is, I asked around about your husband finding out he once worked for the Circle T."

Mrs. Talbert looked mortified that he would do such a thing.

Sarah quickly asked, "What of it, Mr. Fox, and why is that any of your concern?"

Her abruptness took Booth by surprise, and as he stared into her brown, penetrating eyes, he thought someone should bring her down a peg or two thinking himself as the man best suited for that task. "Didn't mean no disrespect to you or your husband, Mrs. Garrison. I was just curious. It ain't every day that we get a United States Deputy Marshal in Harper."

Sarah felt embarrassed and wondered if she had misjudged the man. Her expression softened as she looked at her mother. "That's all right, Mother, I'll deal with Mr. Fox."

Angrily he considered her words, *I'll deal with Mr. Fox.*

"All right, dear," responded Mrs. Talbert, who gave him a long, disapproving look before returning to the table, and Mrs. Mason with the catalog of fine china.

Sarah waited until her mother was far enough away before she looked at Deputy Fox. "My husband did work for the Circle T, Mr. Fox, and since you asked around, I'm sure you've also heard the story of why he left Harper to become a marshal in Santa Fe."

"Yes, Ma'am, I was told that story, and quite an extraordinary story it is."

Sarah smiled proudly. "My husband is an extraordinary man."

Resentment flowed through Booth, believing he was also an extraordinary man, and he would like to prove it to her. "I'm sure he is."

"Why all the interest?" she asked, looking curious.

"Well, we were wondering if your husband was here on business, and if so, if there was maybe something we could help him with."

Sarah doubted that he spoke the truth as she stared into his dark brown eyes. "We, Mister Booth?"

"That's right, Ma'am, me, and Sheriff Block."

Sarah glanced out the store window of white lettering toward the sheriff's office across the street, considering that for a moment. "That's a mite strange," she said, looking at him. "Sheriff Block didn't mention having any such interest over my husband's visit to Harper when we spoke outside earlier."

Booth lied. "Oh, he's interested, Mrs. Garrison."

98

Sarah hated a liar, and she knew Booth Fox was a big one. "I'm sure that if my husband needed help, he would have asked for it when he talked to the sheriff earlier this week when they had breakfast."

Booth knew he was caught in a lie, and that angered him. "Well, Ma'am," he began with a sly smile. "Sometimes, the sheriff tends to forget things, and, well, I was just trying to be neighborly."

Sarah sensed his anger. "I appreciate that, Deputy." Then, figuring Wade would not want anyone to guess why he was here, she pointed to her son. "It has been a few years since I have been home, and I wanted to visit my mother and father, as well as bring our son to visit his grandparents."

He looked at the young boy and smiled. "He's a fine-looking boy."

She wanted to end the conversation, so she smiled. "Thank you, I think so. Now, if you will excuse me for saying so, Deputy, I don't believe a store is any place to discuss one's personal issues." She glanced at her mother across the room, turned, and smiled, looking friendly. "Have a nice day, Deputy Fox." Then she turned and walked toward her mother.

Booth watched them for a moment taking in her brown ponytail, small waist, and slender hips. Then he looked at the boy and walked the short distance to where Emmett was eyeing the candy counter and knelt. "Lots of good things behind that glass."

Emmett turned from the glass case and smiled. "Sure is."

"What's your favorite?" asked Fox.

"Ain't got one, I reckon. They all look good."

When Sarah turned and saw Booth Fox talking to her son, fear gripped her, and she immediately called out. "Emmett, we'll be leaving soon. Come over here by us."

Booth stood, exchanged glances with Sarah, smiled, then he turned and walked toward the door.

Sarah put her arm around her son as she watched Booth walk outside, close the door, and walk across the boardwalk.

Deputy Lee Jones was still sitting in his chair in front of the sheriff's office, with his feet resting on the post when Booth Fox returned from Mason's General Store. Booth stepped onto the boardwalk, turned, and leaned against the same post, staring across the street at Mason's Store.

Lee grinned, childlike. "She as pretty up close as she is from here?"

"Yeah, but she ain't all that friendly."

Deputy Lee frowned. "She say why her husband came to Harper?"

Booth glanced at Lee, pushed his hat back, and looked across the street. "She said they came here to visit her family."

Jones thought on that a second. "You believe that?"

"Not sure." Booth turned toward the sheriff's office window seeing Block sitting at his desk, reading the newspaper, and thought of what happened in Sisters. "What I do believe is the sheriff and that lady both know more than they're saying."

Jones stood and glanced at the sheriff through the window seeing the reflections of Sarah, Emmett, and Janice Talbert walk out of Mason's carrying packages. He turned in time to see them climb into their wagon and watched as they drove out of town.

Lee looked at Fox. "What're we gonna do about the Marshal?"

"Nothing right now," replied Booth as he stepped into the street, heading for the Blue Sky Saloon. "Be back in a little while."

Eleven

Sisters, Colorado

Wade and Seth rode directly to Pritchard's Saloon, tied their horses at the hitching rail, and went inside looking for Paul Leonard, the bartender. It was early, the place wasn't very crowded, and Jack Pritchard was working behind the bar. "Morning, Sheriff, what'll you have?"

"Paul around, Jack?" asked Seth.

Pritchard glanced at Wade and the badge in his shirt and shook his head. "Has the day off."

Looking disappointed, Seth turned to Wade. "He has a room across the street at Mrs. Harrison's boarding house."

Pritchard wiped the bar down with a wet towel as he looked at Seth. "What's he done?"

"Nothing," replied Seth as they turned, hurried outside, and walked across the street to Harrison's Boarding House. Finding Mrs. Harrison behind the counter, she looked up from what she was doing as the two walked in. She eyed Wade and his badge rather quickly and then smiled at the sheriff. "Good morning Seth," then she joked. "Come to arrest me?"

Seth smiled. "Not today Barbara. Is Paul Leonard in his room?"

"He left about twenty minutes ago. I believe he's down at Molly's having lunch."

Molly's Restaurant was busy but not crowded when Seth and Wade walked in. Molly looked up from what she was doing and smiled at Seth, who gave her a look that was neither anger nor affection. It was a look that she was familiar with, so she went about her business. Paul Leonard was sitting alone at a table in the corner, dressed in a black suit and white shirt, looking as if he was going to church finishing the last of his lunch. As they approached his table, he looked up and stopped eating.

Seth put his hand on a spare chair. "Mind if we sit a spell, Paul?"

He glanced up at Seth, looked at Wade, noticing the badge on his shirt, and then at Seth. "Sure." He gestured to the chairs across the table, giving Wade a long, curious look as the two sat down. Then he turned to Bowlen, who was sitting across from him. "What's on your mind, Seth?"

Bowlen pointed at Wade. "This here's Deputy U.S. Marshal Wade Garrison, Paul, in case you were wondering."

Wade leaned toward him and lowered his voice. "We need to talk about the killing of Jacob Olson."

Paul stared at Wade for a long moment, looked at Seth, then glanced around the room at the other customers while visions of Tom Lawson getting shot ran through his mind. Suddenly, he felt awful warm thinking of what Pete Hoskins and Booth Fox would do if they found out he talked about what happened that Saturday morning. Beads of sweat formed on his forehead as he looked from Seth to Wade.

Wade lowered his voice. "You know damn well that Pete Hoskins killed Jacob Olson in cold blood."

Paul Leonard's face lost its color as his expression turned to fear. He stared into Wade's cold, blue eyes, then he turned and looked at Sheriff Bowlen. "I done told you what happened, Seth."

A waitress approached, said hello to Seth, and asked if they wanted lunch.

Molly hurried over to the table. "That's all right, Mary," she said. "I'll take care of my husband and his friends. Coffee, gentlemen?"

Bowlen smiled, being thankful. "Be fine, Molly, thanks."

She gestured toward the kitchen with a nod, "I'll go make a fresh pot. It may take a few minutes."

After she walked away, Seth leaned on the table with his forearms and lowered his voice. "It's time you owned up and told the truth, Paul. There are too many people dead, including a nice girl and her unborn child."

Paul looked remorseful as his eyes went from Seth to his nearly empty plate. Then he looked at the sheriff and leaned toward him as he whispered, "And I don't plan to put my name on that list." Then he looked at Wade. "I'm sorry, but that's the way it is."

Neither could blame Paul, but they needed to get the truth out of him. "We can protect you, Paul," said Seth above a whisper.

Leonard's eyes went from Seth to Wade and then back to Seth. He wanted to get up and leave, but Wade was sitting in the chair next to him, and he couldn't.

Seth looked at him with an angry expression. "The Marshal and I are leaving on tomorrow's train for Colorado Springs to see a judge." He glanced around the room, looked at Leonard, and lowered his voice. "I'm telling the judge that you saw Pete, kill Olson in cold blood, and then take Olson's gun out his of its holster, and toss it on the floor next to the old man so's it'd look like self-defense."

Paul's eyes bulged with a mixture of fear and surprise. "That ain't fair Seth, I said no such thing, and you know it."

Wade leaned forward, placed one arm on the back of the bartender's chair, and lowered his voice. "It ain't fair that a young girl hung herself neither Mr. Leonard. You may as well own up because once we tell the judge that you saw Pete kill Mr. Olson in cold blood, it won't be long before Hoskins and the others find out."

Leonard stared at him, looking afraid, and raised his voice. "You can't do that!"

People in the restaurant turned to look at them.

Paul glanced around the room, looked at Seth, and lowered his voice. "That ain't right, Sheriff."

Tired of talking, Wade stood, picked up Paul's hat, and handed it to him. "Maybe we should finish this outside." He stood, took Paul by the arm, and helped him up. Seth pushed his chair back, stood, took some money out of his pocket, and tossed it on the table. "City's buying your lunch today, Paul."

With Wade leading Leonard by the arm, they walked outside, where Seth took Leonard by the other arm. Together he and Wade led him around the corner of the building into an alley.

Paul looked from one to the other as they walked toward the back of Molly's. "Where we going?"

"Someplace where we can be alone," said Seth, and when they reached the back of the building, they let go of Paul Leonard's arms. Seth stood in the bright sun and looked up at the blue sky that had but a scattering of clouds. "Looks like a right nice day."

Leonard looked up and then back at Seth, wondering if he had lost his mind talking about the weather.

Seth looked at Paul. "Time's come for you to own up, Paul. What did you see?"

Leonard was fearful, but not of Seth or Wade. He turned away, looked back at the street beyond the building, and thought about Jacob Olson, his daughter, and Tom Lawson. Finally, he took off his hat, turned, looking apologetic, and shrugged as he looked down at the hat he held in his hands. "I was watching Jacob and Pete arguing. Jacob stood, knocking over his chair, and that's when I saw Pete pull his gun and shoot Jacob." He looked at Seth. "That's when I ducked behind the bar."

"Did Jacob pull his gun?"

Leonard shook his head, looking ashamed. "No. He raised his fist to Pete."

Wade stepped closer. "You'll swear to this in open court?"

With fear on his face, he looked from one to the other. "You gotta protect me."

Seth put one hand on Paul's shoulder. "We'll put you someplace until after the trial."

"All right," said Leonard in a trembling, soft voice. "I'll tell you what I saw in court." Then he looked at Seth. "What about my job? I won't be making any money."

Seth thought a moment. "I'll talk to Pritchard after we arrest Pete Hoskins and his friends. What happened next?"

Leonard's face was white, his forehead wet with sweat. "I gotta sit down." They walked to the steps of the back door to Molly's, where he sat on the top step, leaned forward, his elbows on his knees, hands holding his hat. "I could hear old man Olson moaning and gasping for breath. When I stood from behind the bar, I saw Tom Lawson at the back door for a moment, and then he disappeared. Pete was standing over poor old Jacob when he turned and stared at me for the longest time. That's when I looked down and saw Olson's gun lying on the floor next to him."

"You sure he never drew on, Pete?" asked Seth.

Leonard looked up. "Jacob stood, ready to kick the shit out of Pete, not try and outdraw him. Jacob may have been on in years, but he could have beat Pete in a fair fistfight."

"Where was Booth?" asked Seth.

"Standing at the other end of the bar staring at me. Same place he was when you came in." Then Paul looked remorseful. "I heard Jacob take his last breath. That's about the time Deputy Carl came running in, took a quick look, and then hurried out to get you." Paul stood, looking worried. "They find out I talked to you two; I'm as dead as Tom Lawson."

Wade looked at Paul. "Fear makes a careful man as well as a dangerous man, Mr. Leonard."

Paul considered that as he looked at Seth. "Where are you gonna hide me?"

"We'll think on that," said Seth. "But for now, go about your business. No one else knows about this little talk, and no one will, other than Judge Moore. We'll get you to a safe place when we return from seeing the judge."

Paul nodded, looking a little sickly.

Wade was thinking that he may try and leave town. "Don't leave town, Paul," he warned. "If you do, I'll come looking."

Leonard looked at him. "I've no place to go, Marshal." Then he turned and started to leave, but turned and looked at them. "I gave you my word. You know where to find me." Then he walked up the ally, disappearing around the corner.

Deputy McIver was sitting in Seth's chair reading the three day old Sisters newspaper when Bowlen and Wade walked in. Carl looked up with concern and stood as a child would when caught doing something he shouldn't. "I was worried when you never showed up this morning. I went looking for you and ran into Molly on her way to the restaurant." Unhappy about being left out, he looked at Wade. "She said you and the Marshal went for a ride."

"Had some business to take care of," replied Seth, sounding a little irritated.

Looking nervous, Carl stepped away from the desk and watched Seth as he sat down in his squeaky chair.

Seth let out a soft sigh and looked at Carl. "Wade and me are taking the train up to the Springs first thing in the morning to see Judge Moore. I know tomorrow's your day off, but I need you here."

"Sure, Seth," replied Carl, looking curious as he glanced from Wade to Seth. "Whatever you need, but why are you going to the Springs?"

Leaning against the window's sill, Wade was fearful that Seth was about to tell Carl about Sam Wheeler and the bartender.

Seth gestured at Wade. "The Marshal, there's got a personal issue that he needs some legal advice on."

Relieved, Wade looked at Carl. "I'd prefer that no one knew about this."

Carl looked at Wade. "I won't say, nothing Marshal."

Bowlen shrugged. "So, since we ain't got a judge or lawyer in Sisters, I'm taking him to see Judge Moore."

Carl's expression showed his disappointment. "I was hoping it had something to do with Pete Hoskins."

"Why would you think that?" asked Seth, fearful that he saw him and Wade talking to the bartender.

Carl shrugged, "Just hoping we'd get Hoskins for killing old man Olson." He looked at Seth. "Me and you both know he killed Tom Lawson."

Feeling relieved, Seth smiled. "I'm still working on that one." Then he nodded to the coffee pot. "Any coffee?"

"Think so," replied Carl as he looked at Wade. "Cup of coffee, Marshal?"

Wade stepped away from the window and sat down in one of the three chairs in front of Seth's desk. "Don't mind if I do, Carl. Thanks."

While Seth listened to the sounds of tin cups and coffee, he turned to the street outside the window, thinking of Jacob Olson, his wife and daughter, and Tom Lawson and his family. His thoughts of their deaths were interrupted by Carl handing him a cup of coffee. He looked at it, thinking it looked awful strong, and after taking a sip, he wasn't disappointed. "Fire up the stove, Carl. Coffee's getting cold."

While Carl stoked the fire in the potbellied stove, Seth looked out the window, and for some reason, thought of Frank Wells. Taking the makings of a cigarette from the pocket of his white shirt, he rolled his cigarette then offered the makings to Wade.

Wade shook his head no and took another drink of the warm, bitter coffee while thinking of Sarah and Emmett.

Seth put the paper and packet of tobacco back into his shirt pocket, reached into his tan pants pocket, taking out a tin of matches. Striking one across the side of his desk, he lit his cigarette and blew a puff of white smoke, putting out the match. He turned, staring out the window in thought. "Better make your rounds, Carl."

Carl got the sense that something was going on between the Sheriff and the Marshal, thinking they both had troubled looks. While he was curious about what it was, he picked up his hat from Seth's desk and headed for the door.

"Carl."

He stopped and turned.

Seth turned from the window. "There's too much going on right now, but once Wade and I get back from the Springs, the three of us will sit down and have us a long talk."

Carl nodded, looking satisfied, glanced at Wade, grinned at Seth, and walked out the door.

Bowlen turned to Wade, sitting in the chair in front of his desk. "You know, we may get ourselves, Paul Leonard, and Sam Wheeler killed."

Wade stood, walked around the desk, opened the top right drawer of Bowlen's desk, and pulled out an unopened bottle of whiskey. He studied the bottle of cheap whiskey for a moment, looked at Seth, and smiled. "Quite possible."

Seth reached up, took the bottle, and popped the cork while Wade looked for someplace to dump his bitter, cold coffee.

"Not on the floor," warned Seth.

Not wanting to mix the two, Wade gulped his coffee, made a face, and held out his cup.

Bowlen chuckled at Wade's expression as he poured some whiskey into Wade's tin cup, added some to his, put the cork back into the bottle, and held his cup up.

Wade touched his cup to Seth's and looked into his bad eye. "Here's to you, Seth."

Seth chuckled. "Here's hoping we don't get our asses shot off."

"Amen to that."

They took a drink, then Wade returned to his chair and looked at Seth with a big grin. "Wonder how Harry will take us arresting his two deputies?"

Seth chuckled. "Can't say, but I sure don't like the odds." The smile left his face. "Think I'll ask Gil Robinson to lend us a hand."

"That'd help if you think he would," replied Wade.

Seth scowled, looking uncertain. "I doubt he'd turn us down if we asked, but I hate to ask. He almost got killed the last time he gave us a hand."

A small smile filled Wade's face as he remembered the day Gil took a bullet in the shoulder, knocking him from his horse that almost collided with Wade's mare. "Gil's a tough one."

"That's true, but Gil's got a lot more to lose these days."

"He ain't the only one," said Wade, thinking of Molly, little Emmett, and Sarah now with child.

Seth's chair creaked as he leaned forward. "We're gonna have to tell Carl when we get back tomorrow."

Wade thought on that. "Anyone else in town you can count on besides Carl when the time comes?"

Seth thought on that. "Lyle Dickson has helped now and again."

Wade sat his empty cup on the top of Seth's desk, stood, and walked toward the door. "I need to think. I'm going for a walk."

Seth picked up the whiskey bottle, poured another drink, and thought about their trip to Colorado Springs.

Twelve

Sisters, Colorado

Only two passengers occupied the train's first rail passenger car as it approached the depot of Sisters, Colorado. Wade was sitting next to the window, looking out at the landscape of prairie grass, rolling hills, and plateaus of cliffs painted with the same soft, reddish-orange color as the setting sun.

Seth was asleep in a seat across the aisle, and as the train slowed, the jerking motion woke him. Looking confused and half asleep, he glanced around the empty passenger car and then at the buildings of Sisters as they slowly passed by the window. When the train came to a stop, he stood, then he and Wade walked down the narrow aisle toward the rear exit in silence. Stepping off of the train, they walked through the steam that hung over the platform like an early morning fog.

Stepping off the platform into the dirt street, they walked in silence, having said all they needed to say to one another on the ride back from Colorado Springs. Each filled with the resolve that held them tightly in its grasp, and words were of little importance right now. Tucked away in the inside pocket of his coat, Wade carried the four warrants that Seth was so determined to serve. As they walked up the steps to the jailhouse, the sun dipped below the mountains taking with it the evening colors.

Deputy McIver was busy sweeping out one of the cells, whistling a tune, when the jail's front door opened. He stopped whistling, turned, and walked to the door leading to the office, letting the last of the tune die. Seth and Wade walked toward Seth's desk as if they hadn't seen him, and neither spoke. Carl closed the door to the room where the cells were and quietly followed with broom in hand. Bowlen sat down in his creaky chair, looking tired, while Wade, looking just as tired, flopped into one of the three chairs in front of the desk.

"Howdy Seth, Wade," greeted Carl McIver, looking apprehensive as he walked by on his way to the storeroom next to the back door. After putting the broom away and closing the door to the storeroom, he lit several lanterns and then sat down, leaving an empty chair between his and Wade's.

Seth was staring out the window at the lighted windows across the dark street, looking worried. He turned from the window and eyed the coffee pot sitting on the potbellied stove. "Any coffee?"

"I'll make a fresh pot," offered Carl as he started to get up.

Seth quickly raised his right hand. "Never mind, Carl." Then, as McIver returned to his chair, Seth opened the top right drawer, pulled out a whiskey bottle, held it up, and looked at Wade. "Whiskey?"

Wade looked at the bottle as if considering a drink. "Why not?" Then he took off his hat and tossed it onto the empty chair between him and Carl.

Seth looked at his deputy. "Get three cups, will ya, Carl?"

McIver did as asked, placing three coffee cups on the desk, and then sat down looking from Seth to Wade.

Seth emptied the bottle into the three tin cups, shoved the cork back into the empty bottle, and gently tossed it at the trash can sitting next to the potbellied stove, missing his target. As the empty bottle bounced off the side of the trash can, landing on the floor without breaking, Seth glared at the bottle for several moments as if he could will it into the trash can. Turning from the bottle, he picked up two cups, leaned across his desk, handing one to Carl, the other to Wade, and then picked up his cup. His chair creaked and moaned in the stillness of the office as he leaned back and took a quick drink. Wiping his mustache, he put his feet up on his desk, holding the cup on his lap between his hands. He turned to look out the window at the lights in the windows across the street.

To Carl, the clock's pendulum in the corner seemed suddenly loud as it joined the muffled noises of the dark street outside the window and the occasional creak of Seth's chair.

Wade took a drink of whiskey, then stared into it.

110

Seth turned from the window and looked at Deputy McIver. "Carl," he said in a soft voice. "There are some things you need to know."

Deputy McIver sat up in his chair and anxiously waited.

Seth took off his gray Stetson hat and set it on the edge of his desk, resting his forearms on the top of the desk looking serious. "I think it's time you knew what the hell's going on around here."

Carl stared at Seth and waited in silent anticipation.

Bowlen gestured to Wade with the forefinger of his left hand. "Marshal Garrison has four warrants in his coat pocket."

Carl glanced at Wade's coat. "Who they for?"

Seth stood, pushed his hat to one side, and sat on the edge of his desk in front of Carl. "Pete Hoskins, Booth Fox, and a deputy by the name of Lee Jones over in Harper."

Carl's excitement gave away to confusion. "That's only three names."

"Two are for Pete," said Seth. "I'll get to that in a minute, but right now, I need you to be honest with yourself and me, Carl."

McIver was puzzled. "About what, Seth?"

Seth looked worried. "Once we serve them warrants and bring these three back to Sisters, all hell's likely to break loose."

Carl had a look of indifference. "So what?"

Seth glanced at Wade and then smiled wryly at McIver. "You're a good deputy, Carl, but you ain't a gunman."

Carl sat forward in his chair, looking offended. "What're you saying, Sheriff."

Seth was uneasy. "I'm trying to give you a way out of this mess, Carl, before we get you killed."

McIver stood, looking angry. "I ain't no gunman or Pistolero as the Mex's say, but I sure as hell ain't no coward, neither, and I'll kick anyone's ass that says I am."

Seth raised his hand, "Now hold on…"

"Hold on yourself," interrupted Carl in an angry tone as he looked at Wade. "That goes for you, too, Marshal."

Wade grinned and held up his hands, gesturing surrender.

Carl looked at Seth. "I'm no damn coward. Why I was at Shiloh and the Battle of the Wilderness, and Gettysburg, damn it. And not once did I run, or hide, nor shirk my duties."

Seth stood with arms raised. "No one said you were a coward, Carl." Then looking confused, Seth said, "I never knew you were in the war."

"Well, I was," said Carl proudly. "And for three long years, I fought against the union blue, and I never ran or deserted my post."

Seth looked confused. "I thought you were from Pennsylvania."

"I am," responded Carl.

Seth glanced at Wade and then looked at Carl with a confused expression. "Then what were you doing fight'n with the rebs?"

Carl looked stubborn as he adjusted his gun belt. "Because I didn't like Lincoln."

Seth stared at him for a moment and then burst out laughing as he sat back down in his creaky chair.

Wade chuckled, finding humor in the moment.

Carl grinned and then began laughing, not quite sure why he was laughing.

Bowlen sighed and wiped the tears of laughter from his eyes, and looked at McIver. "I'm sorry about all this, Carl. It's just that you seem to sweat a lot when things get a little hairy."

Carl looked embarrassed. "Well, I guess I do that all right, always have, but I ain't no coward. I done my share of killing during the war, and that don't mean I'm proud of taking another's life."

Seth looked at McIver. "All right, Carl, but if you get killed, you only got yourself to blame."

Carl nodded, looking stubborn. "Fair enough."

"Have a seat," said Seth.

After Carl sat back down, he listened as Seth told him about the warrants, Sam Wheeler's testimony about seeing these same three the day Tom Lawson was shot, and about Paul Leonard telling the truth about what happened in the saloon.

Carl looked from Seth to Wade and then Seth. "When we arresting them?"

"Wade and I will be leaving for Harper sometime tomorrow."

Carl looked disappointed. "I ain't going?"

Seth shook his head. "I need you here, Carl. Someone has to keep a lid on this place, and I'm counting on you for that."

Carl nodded with a determined look. "Want me to stay here tonight?"

Seth thought on that for a moment. "See if Lyle will, but don't tell him anything."

"I won't." Then McIver stood, looking concerned. "I'll head over to Lyle's and then go on home to supper."

After Carl left, Wade looked at Seth. "I'd just as soon get to Harper close to sundown."

Seth turned from the window. "Probably a good idea. When Lyle gets here, we'll head to my place for supper."

Thirteen

Harper, Colorado

When Wade and Seth reached the top of the hill overlooking Harper, Colorado, the sun had already set, and the valley below was quickly disappearing as twilight turned into darkness. Images of windows filled with kerosene lamps sprang up like stars on the prairie floor, which seemed to beckon the weary travelers.

Wade wrapped the reins around the saddle horn, took out his long glass from his saddlebag, and looked at the town. "Can't see much from here." He lowered the long glass and pushed it together.

Seth dismounted, and while holding the reins to his horse with one hand, he reached into the pocket of his brown shirt with the other, taking out the tobacco pouch and paper for a cigarette.

Wade climbed down from the mare and took the reins to Seth's horse while he worked on his cigarette. It was quiet except for the horses snorting to clear their nostrils, followed by the mare shaking her head, rattling the bit in her mouth. The cry of a distant coyote leaped at them from the darkness, causing both horses to raise their heads, ears perked with eyes wide.

The cigarette made, Seth put it between his lips, struck a match on his belt buckle, lit the cigarette, blew the match out, and tossed it into the darkness.

Wade looked at the lights in the distance in memory. "Brings to mind Paso Del Rio."

Seth's response was a low grunt as he handed the pouch and paper to Wade and then took the reins of both horses. "There were five of us that night." He looked at Wade's face that was barely visible in the dim light of dusk. "Tonight, there's only the two of us."

Wade rolled a cigarette, gave the makings back, reached over and took Seth's cigarette out of his mouth, and held it against his, then gave it back to Seth. Wade took a deep drag, blowing the smoke into the night air, and thought of Frank Wells, dead in the saloon, and the Indian dying on the boardwalk outside. "Let's give the darkness a few more minutes and then we'll make a wide berth east and come up behind the livery."

"Why the livery?"

Wade stared at the lights of Harper, thinking of Charlie Johnson in Paso Del Rio, and the night he scouted the saloon before the gunfight. "Let's see how old Levi feels about doing a little scouting for the law."

Seth grinned. "This Levi fellah ain't married, is he?"

Wade looked puzzled at the question. "No. Why?"

"Just curious," Then Seth took a quick drag from his cigarette, tossed it on the ground, and stepped on it. "You ready?"

Wade tossed his cigarette on the ground, stepped on it, swung up onto his mare, and settled in the saddle. "We'll circle to the east and come in from the other side of town. That'll put us right at Levi's place."

The moon wasn't up yet, and although the sky held a thousand stars, it was dark as hell as Wade and Seth let the horses find their way toward the yellow light from the windows of Levi Wagner's Livery. As they got closer, the side of the livery filled with tiny lines of light escaping between the weathered boards of the livery. Light from the single rear window left a perfect replica of the window on the dark ground. Stopping several yards away, they dismounted and led their horses toward the lighted livery window.

Hearing the sound of spurs in the quiet night and the neigh of a horse, Levi Wagner walked around the side of the livery to the rear holding a twelve-gauge shotgun. "Mind telling me what you boys are doing sneaking around my place this time of night?"

Startled, Wade looked toward the voice, barely seeing the ghostly figure of Levi covered in the tiny lines of light coming through the wall of the livery. "Hold on, Levi, it's Wade Garrison."

The old man strained his tired eyes, looking at the two figures in the darkness. "Take a few steps this way into the light, and let's see if you're who you say you are. And do it slowly. I got both barrels cocked."

"All right," replied Wade. "Just don't get nervous."

Levi Wagner chuckled and then spit tobacco juice on the ground. "I was born nervous." As the two stepped into the light from the window, Levi recognized Wade, but then he pointed the shotgun at Seth. "Who's that ya got with ya?"

"Sheriff Seth Bowlen from Sisters," responded Wade. "He's a friend."

Lyle turned his head while keeping his eyes on them, spit tobacco juice, pointed the shotgun at the ground, and then lowered both hammers. "I'd think a couple of smart lawmen would know better'n sneaking around someone's place in the dark."

"Sorry," apologized Wade while wondering what he would have done if he and Seth were strangers. "We didn't want to draw any attention to ourselves as we rode in."

Levi spit again and then chuckled. "Not exactly like Indians, are ya? You boys hiding from someone, or just bashful?"

"Long story," replied Wade, finding little humor in the comment.

"Uh-huh," muttered Wagner thoughtfully as he stepped toward Seth with an extended hand. "Name's Levi Wagner. Any friend of Mr. Garrison's is a friend of mine."

Seth shook Levi's hand. "Seth Bowlen."

Levi pointed to the livery. "Let's go inside." Then he turned and walked toward the thin cracks of light coming through the back door while talking over his shoulder. "You can lead your stock around front." Then he disappeared inside.

As they walked their horses around the front, Seth wondered why they didn't go to the front to begin with.

Levi lifted the board holding both doors closed and pushed one open. "Come on inside. I'd offer you, boys, some coffee if I had any," he said as they led their horses past and inside the livery. "A drink, too, if I had any whiskey, but all I got is some water that you're more than welcome to."

Wade looked around the livery. "We're fine, but thanks just the same. Where do you want the horses?"

Wagner paused in thought and pointed to two stalls. "These two will do." Then he stood back and watched as they led their horses into the stalls before he turned and walked toward the back room. "Putting my gun away. Be right back."

Seth noticed the roan in the stall on the other side of the livery as he loosened the cinch to his saddle. "That Deputy Lee's horse?"

Wade looked up from loosening the cinch of his saddle. "Yep." Then he lifted the saddle from off his mare, placing it over the railing of the stall.

Levi returned from putting his shotgun away, hearing what Seth had asked. "It's too bad horses don't know stupid, or he'd buck Deputy Jones right off."

Wade and Seth grinned at one another, finding humor in Levi.

The old man stopped at a post, put a match to another lantern, spit on the floor, and walked toward Wade. "Probably ain't none of my business, but I'm a nosey old man, so I ain't afraid to ask. What the hell are two lawmen doing sneaking into town?"

Seth went about the task of rubbing down his horse with a cloth he found hanging from a nail.

Wade patted his mare on the rump and stepped from the stall. Noticing the old man was wearing the same dark brown shirt and black pants he wore the last time he saw him, he asked, "How's Sheriff Block?"

Figuring the two weren't about to confide in him, he shrugged. "All right, I guess, ain't seen him since he up and quit three days ago."

"Quit?" replied Wade looking surprised.

"Why'd Harry quit?" asked Seth.

Levi looked a little baffled as he scratched his unshaven face. "Never told me. All I know is he up and quit three days ago."

"Who's the sheriff?" asked Wade.

"That Booth fellah."

Not surprised, Wade asked, "Block still around?"

Levi nodded thoughtfully. "Owns a place not far from here. He ain't come to town that I saw since he quit. He's staying home out of the way, is my guess."

"Where is his place?" asked Wade.

"Has a few acres about a mile or so east of here." He paused in thought, then added, "B'lieve he has a few cows, and a few horses, too."

Seth paused at rubbing down his horse and looked at Wade. "Might be a good idea if we talked to Harry."

Figuring their horses were tired, Wade turned to Wagner. "Can we borrow a couple of mounts? Ours could use a rest."

Levi nodded thoughtfully. "S'pose, that'd be all right. I'll pick out a couple while you get your saddles and such." He started walking toward a horse in another stall while talking over his shoulder. "Looks like we got us a big full moon, and that should give you boys enough light to follow the road east. You can't miss the sheriff's place. It's the only place within five miles, and you'll see his lights from the road. Just head due east."

It was easy following the road with the help of the full moon, and when they saw lights in the distance, they turned the horses off of the road and headed for the lights. When they got to the house, they pulled up, and Wade yelled, "Harry Block! It's Wade Garrison!"

The front door opened, casting light and Block's shadow across the porch as he stepped out, pointing a rifle at them. "Climb down and take a few steps closer so I can see you."

They climbed down, and when Wade took a few steps closer to the light, Harry grinned. "Who's that with you?"

"Seth Bowlen, Sheriff of Sisters," answered Wade.

Harry stepped off the porch. "It's just Harry now, Mr. Garrison. I ain't sheriff no more."

Wade thought of their last conversation about what to call him.

Block put the rifle on his shoulder and walked toward them with a hand extended, shook Wade's hand, and then Seth's. "Hello, Seth."

Bowlen smiled. "Been a while, Harry."

"Sure has," said Block, then he looked from one to the other. "What the hell you doing way out here?"

"Need to have a talk with you, Harry," answered Wade.

Looking curious, he motioned toward the door. "Come on in. I'll have the missus fix some coffee."

"No need to bother the missus," said Seth.

"Nonsense," argued Harry as they stepped onto the porch. "Ain't no trouble at all." After they stepped inside, Harry closed the door, took their coats and hats, and set them on a small table next to the door. "Come in by the fire."

An elderly lady walked into the room with short gray hair and soft brown eyes dressed in a black house dress and dirty, white apron. Her face was kindly looking, and her mouth held a soft smile as Harry introduced them to his wife, Dorothy.

Wade and Seth nodded awkwardly, smiled, and said hello.

She smiled, returning their hellos, and then looked at her husband. "Make your friends comfortable, Harry, and I'll put on some coffee."

"No need to bother, Ma'am," protested Wade.

"That's right, Ma'am," smiled Seth. "No need to bother. We're both fine."

She smiled and gestured with a small wave of the hand, discarding their protests. "Ain't no bother, now you sit and visit with Harry while I go fix the coffee. It won't take but a minute."

Wade thought coffee would taste good as he watched her disappear into another room, and then he took a quick survey of the small but cozy and comfortable room with a fireplace that took up most of the north wall.

As the sounds of water, coffee pot, and other noises made their way from the kitchen, Harry motioned to the two chairs separated by a small table. "Have a seat." While they sat down, he hurried into another room, returning with a straight back chair from their dining room, placing it near the fireplace's edge, and sat down. Seth and Wade watched all this while feeling guilty about taking the nicer chairs, but as was the custom, company was always given the better chairs, plates, and cups. That's just the way it was.

"Now," began Block. "What brings you, boys, out here after dark?"

Seth leaned forward, resting his elbows on his knees. "Levi told us you resigned as sheriff a few days back."

Block grinned. "You two come all the way out here, cuz of that?"

"Not exactly," began Wade, "but it is a might curious. You've been sheriff of Harper an awfully long time."

Harry turned to the fire in thought for a moment, and when he looked at them, they could see he was downhearted. "Let's just say things were getting complicated, and I'm getting too old."

119

Dorothy Block walked into the room from the kitchen carrying a big pot of coffee and three china cups. After handing one to each, she poured their coffee, saying she had baked a peach pie that very afternoon and asked if they'd each like a piece.

Having not eaten since Sisters, Wade grinned. "That sounds real good, Mrs. Block."

"It sure does," agreed Seth.

She smiled and turned to walk away but paused and looked at her husband. "You already had a piece. Got to watch your weight now that you ain't working."

Harry looked disappointed, as well as embarrassed, and as she disappeared into the kitchen, bitterness filled his face. "Town's not the same. Neither are the folks running it."

Wade leaned forward. "You referring to George Hoskins?"

Block frowned. "Him and that gutless town council."

"How about the others in town?" asked Seth.

Before Harry could answer, Dorothy walked in, carrying another tray with three pieces of pie and three forks. As Wade and Seth took their plates of pie and fork from the tray, she smiled affectionately at her husband. "Wouldn't be polite for you to stare at the others while they ate."

He grinned, looking happy, took the plate and fork, and then thanked her. She turned to Wade and Seth, said it was a pleasure meeting them and that she had some sewing to do in the other room. They politely stood, careful not to spill their pie, thanked her for the coffee and pie, said goodnight, and returned to their chairs.

Harry shoved a fork full of pie into his mouth, tasting the sweet, syrupy peaches, chewed and swallowed. "The other store owners are too afraid, and most of the small ranchers and farmers owe the bank money that Hoskins sits on the board of, so they keep quiet."

Seth swallowed. "How in the hell did things get so bad?"

Block shook his head thoughtfully as he started to cut the crust with his fork, looked up, and shrugged thoughtfully. "Just happened. No one saw it coming." He stabbed a piece of peach with his fork and shoved it into his mouth. "Anyways," he said softly. "Them's the reasons I resigned as sheriff." He shoved the last of the pie into his mouth and set his empty plate on the floor next to his chair. Then he sat back, wiping his mouth, and stared into the fire, looking sad. "Saw no future in being the law in Harper any longer." Then he turned from the flames and looked at Seth. "I've been an honest lawman too many years, Seth." He paused. "I won't disrespect myself."

Bowlen nodded his understanding as he set his empty plate next to Wade's empty plate on the small table between them, thinking Wade ate awful fast. "And that brings Marshal Garrison and me to our problem."

Harry's interest in their visit suddenly grew. "Problem?"

Wade gestured to his coat on the table next to the door. "I've four warrants in my coat pocket."

Harry Block glanced at the coat and sat back, looking interested.

"One warrant is for Pete Hoskins for the murder of Jacob Olson, and one each for Booth Fox and Lee Jones for the murder of Tom Lawson, and another for Pete Hoskins for Tom Lawson's murder."

Block looked down at the floor, considering all that. "I heard about the killings." Then he looked at them. "Booth Fox is the sheriff of Harper now."

"We know," replied Wade. "Levi told us earlier."

Harry Block chuckled without humor. "You boys have a mess on your hands. I can't recall the last time I knew of a sheriff and his deputy getting arrested for murder."

Wade took a drink of coffee. "Well, the town of Harper's about to see history being made."

Block grinned wryly. "Looks like me retiring was good timing."

Seth picked up his cup to take a drink of coffee. "Can't argue with that."

Wade drank the last of his coffee, set the cup down, and stood. "We best get back to town with Levi's horses before he has a conniption."

Harry stood, shook Seth's hand, and then Wade's. "Saw your missus and son in town a while back."

Wade looked surprised. "You did?"

Block nodded yes. "Sarah's grown into a mite pretty lady, and you've a fine-looking son. You should be proud of both."

Wade grinned proudly while he and Seth walked toward the door.

Harry watched as they put on their coats. "I believe that Sarah of yours gave Booth Fox what for. At least, that's what I heard from Mrs. Mason."

Wade looked worried.

Harry immediately calmed his fears. "Oh, it wasn't anything serious. Seems that after she and I had a short visit in front of Mason's store, Booth Fox decided to ask her a few questions."

"Like what?" asked Wade.

"Oh, trying to find out what a United States deputy marshal would be doing in Harper." Harry paused in thought, looking troubled. "At the time, I just thought he was getting nosey, but after you having these warrants, my guess is he was trying to pump your missus for information." Block smiled as he patted Wade on the shoulder. "Your Sarah straightened him out, and when I saw him coming from the store," chuckled Harry. "He looked a little unhappy."

Wade grinned, knowing that Sarah would never tell anyone any of his business. And he also knew that Sarah could be downright rude when the situation presented itself, and he almost felt sorry for Booth Fox.

Harry opened the door and shook their hands, wishing he were a younger man. "I believe I'd find real pleasure in helping arrest Booth Fox and that little shit, Lee Jones if I was a little younger."

Wade and Seth chuckled, said goodnight, and as Harry closed the door, they stepped off the porch, swung up onto their horses, and rode into the darkness under a full moon toward Harper and Levi's.

Fourteen

Levi's Livery

It was almost ten o'clock when Wade and Seth rode up to the livery, finding it dark inside, the doors closed, and no sign of Levi. They dismounted and knocked on the livery door, waited, and knocked again. With still no response, Wade called out Levi's name in a soft voice. Minutes passed, and Wade started to knock again when a dim light shone through the tiny cracks between the boards of the wall.

"Keep your pants on, I'm coming," hollered Levi. "Who's there?"

"It's us," replied Wade.

"Who's us, damn it?"

Wade became irritated. "Wade Garrison and Seth Bowlen. We were here earlier and borrowed two horses to ride…"

"I remember, damn it," interrupted Wagner. "I ain't stupid, just old. Hang on a second while I put this lantern down and open the door." The sound of the board removed from across the big doors broke the silence, followed by one of the door hinges creaking as it slowly opened.

Levi stuck the lantern and his head out between the small opening of the doors, looking like a man that just got out of bed. "Plum forgot about you, boys." Then he laughed as he stepped back, opening the door so they could bring the horses inside. Wearing only his faded red underwear and black boots, he pointed at two empty stalls. "You boys can do the unsaddling." Then he hung the lantern on the peg of a stall post. "I watered and fed both your horses."

Wade loosened the cinch to his saddle and glanced at his mare, appreciating the care Levi gave her. "We need to talk, Levi."

Levi was tired and wanted to get back to his bed. "We can talk in the morning. I'm locking up soon as you boys leave." Then with a puzzled look, he asked, "Say, where are you two stay'n the night?"

Wade lifted the saddle from the horse, placing it on the top board of the stall, ignoring Levi's question. "Can't wait 'til morning."

Wagner looked irritated. "What the hell's so damn important that it can't wait 'til morning? I'm a tired old man."

Wade finished with the harness, patted the horse on its shoulder, and walked out of the stall. Seth finished with his horse and stood next to his stall, looking at Levi and waiting for Wade to explain.

Wagner looked from one to the other. "Talk about what?"

Wade placed the bit and reins on a hook and looked at the old man, hoping he would do what they asked. "We're in Harper to make a couple of arrests, Levi."

The old man's failing bloodshot eyes lit up with curiosity. "Mind telling me who?"

"Pete Hoskins, Booth Fox, and Lee Jones," replied Wade in a cold, soft voice.

Wagner stared at him for a moment, and then a big grin filled his face. "You're here to arrest the sheriff and his deputy?"

"And Pete Hoskins," reminded Seth.

Levi grinned again as he slapped his leg. "You boys are loco."

Seth chuckled. "I'm sure a lot of people are gonna agree with that come morning."

Levi's face filled with a puzzled look. "Just when is it you plan on doing this?"

"We hope tonight," said Wade. "But first, we need a favor."

The old man raised his brow, looking uncertain as he stared at Wade. He disliked both Booth and Lee Jones and figured the town would be better off without them. "Lee and Booth aren't in town tonight."

Wade glanced at the empty stall where Deputy Lee kept his roan horse. Disappointed, he looked at Seth and then Levi. "Where the hell are they, and who's watching over things?"

Levi glanced from one to the other. "Another no good Hoskins deputy by the name of Chris something or other. Booth and Lee rode out earlier this evening after you two left, and since Lee's horse ain't here, I guess they ain't back yet."

Wade took off his hat and slapped the side of his leg in anger. "Shit!" He looked at the old man. "Are all of Hoskins' men deputies?"

"Sure seems like it," answered Levi.

Wade turned away and stared at the closed livery doors, thinking about their bad luck and loss of surprise.

Seth looked down and kicked at the dirt floor in disappointment. "Damn it to hell."

The old man glanced from one to the other. "Pete Hoskins is in the Blue Sky Saloon. Or at least, he was earlier."

Wade turned, looking hopeful. "Why in the hell didn't you say so?"

Seth wondered the same thing.

Levi looked at Wade with a rueful face. "Didn't have a chance. You were angry over Fox and Lee not being around."

Wade looked regretful. "How long ago was it you saw Pete Hoskins?"

"A couple of hours ago, I reckon," said Levi. "When I stopped in as I do every night for my nightly beer. He was sitting at a table with a whore who goes by the name Julie."

Seth looked hopeful. "If Pete Hoskins is in the saloon, we can grab him and head back to Sisters tonight."

Wade thought on that for a moment in disappointment. "That still leaves Booth and Deputy Jones."

"No matter," said Seth. "I aim to get Pete Hoskins, and our chances aren't likely to get any better."

Wade disagreed, thinking they should wait, but he couldn't blame Seth. He'd been after Pete for a long time. "Booth and Jones will be ready for us when we come back."

"I say we chance that." He looked at Wade. "They don't know about the warrants we have for them."

"You're right." Wade turned to Levi. "Can you run down to the saloon and see if Pete's still in there while we saddle our horses?"

Wagner nodded. "Sure can, right after I get some clothes on. Won't be but a minute." Then he turned and hurried to his room at the other end of the livery.

Wade turned to Seth. "Guess we play the hand we been dealt."

"Guess we do," agreed Seth.

Levi returned, dressed, and looking excited.

Wade stepped from the saddle he had just put on his horse, hoping the old man could do this without giving them away. "Try and see if you can see Pete without going in."

Not clearly understanding why, Wagner nodded and hurried out of the livery, then slowly trotted down the dark street toward the saloon.

Wade and Seth were leading their saddled horses out of the livery when Levi returned, looking excited and sounding out of breath. "Lee just rode in." Then he pointed back down the street toward the saloon. "He's in the saloon with Pete Hoskins."

Wade looked at Seth and then at the lighted windows of the saloon, asking Levi, "Did he see you?"

"Don't believe so. I saw Lee riding up the street and ducked back into the shadows. I was afraid he was coming to the livery, and he'd discover you two but stopped at the saloon instead. After he went inside, I snuck up and peeked in the window, and saw him and Pete sitting at a table with that whore, Julie."

Wade took out his watch and turned toward the dim light from the lamp inside the barn seeing it was twenty minutes to eleven. He put his watch away, glanced down the street at the door and windows of the Blue Sky Saloon, and without turning said, "Better turn them lanterns out, Levi."

Wagner hurried inside, turned them out, and stood next to Wade in the dark while everyone stared down the street at the lighted windows of the saloon.

Seth was standing next to Wade, thinking of Mrs. Lawson and Jacob's wife, daughter, and unborn child.

The street was a mixture of moonlight and reflections of light from the windows and doors of the Blue Sky Saloon and the Sundowner Saloon up the dirt street. The rest of the town was dark. Soft music from the piano spilled into the street from the doorway of the Blue Sky Saloon.

Wade turned to Levi. "How many in the saloon?"

"Four, five others maybe, and a couple more whores."

"Slow night," grinned Seth sarcastically.

Levi shrugged. "It's Thursday night and close to the end of the month. Payday's not 'til Saturday."

Wade looked at the lighted windows and doorway of the Sundowner. "Wonder how many are in the Sundowner?"

Levi stepped closer. "I counted four horses tied up at the rail."

"They could belong to Hoskins' hands," offered Seth.

"Want me to check it out?" asked an eager Levi.

Wade shook his head. "No time for that." Then he looked at the sheriff's office. "Lights are out in the sheriff's office. That's good luck."

Levi stared down the street, "My guess is he's fast asleep. He ain't exactly a go-getter."

Wade turned to Seth. "We've got to move fast if we want to get these two out of town without all hell breaking loose."

Seth was anxious to arrest Pete Hoskins. "Let's get at it."

Wade turned to Levi with an extended hand. "Don't know when we'll see you again, Levi, but thanks for helping us out. We owe you one."

Levi shook the Marshal's hand, grinned, and gave a quick nod of the head. "Anytime, Marshal." Then he shook Seth's hand and watched as they walked their horses along the dark street toward the Blue Sky Saloon. "Good luck to ya," he softly called out, then he hurried inside, closed the big doors, and made his way in the dark to the front window to watch.

The sheriff's office was dark and lifeless as Wade and Seth led their horses along the dark, empty street. Seth took another quick look at the windows and closed door of the jailhouse. "I hope that deputy's a sound sleeper."

Wade glanced toward the sheriff's office but said nothing being more concerned about what awaited them in the saloon. Suddenly, the memory of Emmett Spears lying dead on the same floor came into his already crowded mind.

Stopping at the edge of the saloon building where the boardwalk ends, they stepped into the dark shadows of the alleyway. Seth looked across the deserted street, eyeing the empty boardwalk and dark jailhouse. Wade poked his head out from the corner of the building enough to see the boardwalk filled with light from the saloon's windows and doorway. Soft music from the piano, along with mumbled voices and laughter from inside, made their way through the saloon's swinging doors. Because it was a Thursday night, the usual loud, boastful talk and laughter of drunken cowboys filled with false bravery from too many beers or whiskey was

127

missing. Both felt easier about that because it lessened the danger of a drunken cowboy trying to prove himself to a whore.

Wade took his .45 Colt pistol from its holster, making sure it had six unspent cartridges, while Seth checked his pistol.

Bowlen whispered, "I count six horses."

They tied their horses to the post of the roof of the boardwalk, then Wade glanced at the sheriff's office, seeing it was still dark. He turned to Seth, motioning to the doorway with his pistol as they stepped up onto the boardwalk and walked toward the large window between them and the swinging doors. The piano music suddenly stopped, making the creaking and moaning of the floorboards under their boots seem loud. Stopping at the window, they peered inside as Wade pointed out two men talking to the bartender and whispered, "Two men, from the Double J. They know me, so they won't be any trouble."

"How about the bartender?" asked Seth, thinking of the bartender in Paso Del Rio who pulled his shotgun from under the bar just seconds before Frank Wells put a bullet in his chest.

Wade whispered, "Sam ain't likely to give a shit," remembering he didn't do anything the day Emmett Spears was killed.

Seth looked from them to the three older men sitting at a table near the far wall, playing cards, while two sleepy-looking whores watched. "The three at the table across the room, they look familiar to you?"

Wade stared at them for a moment. "No, but they don't look like they'd be any threat." He looked from them to the empty piano stool, wondering where the player was and curious if he had a gun. Then he saw him at the far end of the bar sipping a beer and talking to Sam. Wade's eyes went from the player at the bar to the table where Deputy Jones was sitting. "There's the deputy," he said softly. "Is the other Pete Hoskins?"

"That's Pete, all right," replied Seth sounding bitter.

Next to Pete was a girl with dark hair dressed in a bright green dress with white lace around the neck and sleeves. She poured Pete another drink from the bottle of whiskey, whispered something into his ear, and then laughed as she stood ruffling his hair with one hand. Hoskins looked up at her with a smile and said something, and she put her head back and laughed.

Wade reached into his coat pocket, pulled out the warrants, and cocked the hammer of his Colt. "When we get inside, you keep an eye on

Sam and them others." Then, remembering his and the deputies' first meeting, he said, "I'll take care of Pete and the deputy." They walked toward the swinging doors and stepped inside, and before the swinging doors closed, Wade held up the warrants. "I'm Deputy United States, Marshal Wade Garrison." Then he pulled his coat to one side, exposing the Marshal's badge. The room fell silent as all eyes turned toward them and then at one another, wondering who he was after. Wade held the warrants into the air for all to see. "These warrants were issued by Judge Moore over in Colorado Springs."

It took bartender Sam Carney a moment to recognize Wade and remembered how angry he was over his friend's death. Sam was skinny, standing six feet, with balding light, brown hair, and a clean-shaven face. Raising his hand's chest high, he dropped the wet towel he was wiping the bar with and backed to the counter behind the bar. With the small of his back against it, he waited to see who the marshal was after. The two men Sam had been talking to also recognized Wade, and like Sam, raised their hands.

Pete looked at Seth and sat back in his chair, knowing one of the warrants had his name on it.

Lee Jones raised his hands, smiled, trying to look unthreatening and friendly as he stood. "I'm Deputy Sheriff Lee Jones, Marshal…"

"Shut up," said Seth in an angry tone.

Lee looked at him, and the .44 Colt aimed at his stomach slowly sat back down and looked at Wade. "Look, Marshal, maybe I can help you with them warrants."

"You already have," smiled Wade. "Your name's on one, and your friend's name on the other."

Surprise filled the deputy's face. "For what?"

Wade ignored the question and looked at Pete Hoskins. "Stand up."

Pete grinned defiantly at Seth as he slowly stood with his hands up, and then he turned to Wade. "You killed my brother six years ago in Sisters."

"That's right," said Wade recalling that night. "He tried shooting me in the back."

Lee started to stand but thought better of it. "What are the warrants for?"

"You'll find out," replied Bowlen as muffled words filled the room.

Seth glanced around the saloon, not wanting a repeat of Paso Del Rio as his eyes settled on the piano layer standing in the corner next to his piano. He was a little man, standing about five-feet-three, with black, greasy hair. He quickly waved his hands in front of him, indicating he was no threat.

Seth looked around the saloon. "Everybody just stay calm; we're taking these two back to Sisters."

Pete smirked at Seth. "I believe I was cleared of old man Olson's death by a judge up in Denver."

"You wasn't cleared," corrected Seth. "The judge dismissed the charges for lack of evidence."

Pete Hoskins looked at Seth. "What's the difference?"

Wade looked at Pete. "It means now that we have proof, we can still charge you with that murder." Then he stepped toward Pete. "Now, turn around and keep them hands up. I wouldn't want you to meet your brother tonight." He took Pete's gun, shoved it under his belt, and then looked at Deputy Lee. "You, too."

"This is stupid," said Lee as he turned with raised hands, as Wade took his gun.

Wade cocked it and shoved it into Lee's stomach. "It'd be wise if you kept your damn mouth shut." Then he looked at the girl in the green dress sitting at the table. "Sorry to spoil your night, miss, but you best get up and move to another table."

She glanced from Wade to Pete with wide eyes as she stood and walked to the table where two other of Sam's girls were sitting.

Wade turned to Pete and Lee, motioning to the door with Lee's gun. "Nice and slow," he said softly. "The four of us are going for a ride."

"We ain't never gonna get there," threatened Pete Hoskins.

"Time will tell," said Seth. He was sure the other men wouldn't interfere, but he was taking no chances and backed toward the doorway, following Wade and their prisoners. "Be a bad idea if any of you were to come outside before we're gone."

Wade led Pete and Lee to their horses, and Seth hurried along the boardwalk to where they left their horses, untied them, and brought them up. Then he held his gun on the two while Wade tied their hands with a small piece of thin rope and helped them onto their horses.

Seth took the reins to Pete's horse, climbed up onto his, and waited until Wade climbed onto his mare, holding the reins to Lee's horse.

Wade glanced around at the empty street while Seth nudged his horse into a walk, tugging at the reins of Pete's horse. Wade nudged his mare and jerked the reins of Lee Jones' horse on purpose, causing it to jump a little. Startled, Lee gave Wade a dirty look thinking he'd done that on purpose.

They rode at a walk along the dark street past the Sundowner Saloon, keeping to the shadows and out of the light from the windows. As they rode past, soft voices and a girl's laughter spilled into the street through the swinging doors as they slowly rode past the saloon toward the edge of town.

Fifteen

Sisters, Colorado

It was just before dawn when the four riders reached the top of a small hill overlooking Sisters and pulled up. Seth stood in his saddle and turned, staring into the first dim light of dawn at the trail behind them. He couldn't see the road in the distance they had traveled from Harper but knew it was there and wondered if Sheriff Booth Fox followed with a posse. His eyes went from the darkness of the road to the light blue sky at the horizon. "Sun will be up soon."

A tired Wade turned to look at the coming sunrise, and sensing Seth's concerns, he glanced back into the dim light they had ridden out of, straining his eyes and ears for Booth Fox. Seeing and hearing nothing that was threatening, he turned to his tired prisoner and checked the deputy's hands, making sure they were still securely tied to the saddle horn.

Pete Hoskins was also standing in his stirrups, looking back toward Harper with the hopes that Booth Fox and a posse would ride out of the darkness. Lee's complaining that his hands hurt went unnoticed. Pete Hoskins relaxed back in his saddle, filled with bitter disappointment.

Bowlen nudged his tired horse down the hill toward Sisters, and Wade turned, took a last look into the darkness and the line of blue sky above the hills and cliffs of the plateaus to the east. Feeling tired, he turned and spurred his mare into a trot, jerking the reins of Lee's roan horse while the deputy fantasized about putting a bullet in the back of Wade's head.

The town of Sisters was quiet and peaceful as the four rode their horses at a walk along the empty street between the canyons of dark buildings toward their destination and safety. Feeling tired, Wade looked up into the sky of stars, then at the sky above the eastern horizon turning a light blue. A dog's barking somewhere mixed with the soft sound of the horse's hooves on the hard, dirt street and the creaking of leather saddles.

Dawn was quickly approaching, bringing light to the street and buildings they rode past as lights began to appear in windows here and there. Seth's tired mind and eyes longed for sleep as he raised his head, seeing Molly's Restaurant and thought of his wife and her soft, warm body curled up next to him in their bed.

Wade drifted in and out of sleep, trying hard to stay awake the last few yards of their journey, and the tired mare bobbed her head and gave out a soft snort in protest of the long night's journey. He looked at the back of her neck and head, knowing it had been a long day for her, reached out, and patted her on the neck. "Soon, girl."

Minutes later, they were at the hitching rail in front of the jailhouse, each glad their journey was over. Wade and Seth dismounted, helped their prisoners off their horses, up the steps, and across the moaning, creaking boardwalk to the Sheriff's Office door. Seth knocked on it lightly and quietly called out to Deputy McIver. "Carl, it's Seth. Open up." Moments later, they heard movement from within, and then light from a lantern appeared in the window and between the cracks of the door while footsteps made their long journey across the floor. The lock turned, and the door slowly opened, revealing a sleepy Deputy Carl McIver holding the lantern while wearing his black pants, suspenders dangling down the sides of his legs. Without speaking, he stepped aside while pulling the left suspender up over the shoulder of his white long johns. He watched as Seth stepped inside, followed by Pete, Lee, and Wade. Carl's black hair was a mess. He looked at each one while pulling the right suspender over his shoulder and said the obvious. "Got 'em, huh, Seth?"

Without answering Carl's needless question, Seth walked to the door leading to the room where the cells were, took the key ring off the peg, opened the door, and turned to Pete and Lee. "In here."

Pete gave Seth a dirty look as he walked into the cell area. "I won't be here long."

Bowlen ignored the comment and gestured to one of the cells. "Take the cell on the right, Pete." Then he looked at Lee. "Take that one," he said, pointing to the cell on the far left, leaving an empty cell between them.

Seth shut and locked the cell doors while Wade untied their hands, and as Lee stepped into the cell, he took off his hat and tossed it across the cell, hitting the brick wall coming to rest on the cot.

Seth chuckled, "Feel better, Deputy?"

Jones gave Bowlen an ugly look as he sat down on the cot and leaned back against the corner of the brick wall. Picking up his hat and tossing it to the bottom of the cot, he lay down, resting his head on the bare pillow. Closing his eyes, he somehow managed to drift right off to sleep.

Pete, on the other hand, gripped the bars of the cell door with both hands turning his knuckles white, and looked at Seth. "You're gonna regret this, Sheriff."

Seth looked Pete in the eye. "I regret a lot of things, Pete, but this ain't one of 'em." Then he and Wade walked out of the cell area, closed the door, locked it, and then hung the keys on the peg next to the door. Bowlen took off his hat, tossed it on the top of his desk, and sat down in his creaky chair, thinking he needed to oil it again. Wade sat down in one of the three chairs in front of Seth's old desk, took off his hat, and tossed it on an empty chair next to him, leaned forward, and rubbed his face, thinking of a good night's sleep.

Seth looked at Carl. "Go home, Carl, get some sleep, and be back here around nine. We'll talk over a mid-morning meal at Molly's."

That brought life to Carl's tired eyes and a grin to his lips. He put the lantern down on the edge of the desk, hurried to the cot he had been sleeping on, and finished dressing. With his shirttail hanging out, he headed for the door. "See you about nine."

Neither Seth nor Wade responded as the door closed.

As Carl hurried across the boardwalk, the thought suddenly occurred to him that his wife may mistake him for a thief and shoot him before Seth could tell him what happened.

Wade looked from the closed door to Seth. "Go home, Seth. I'm sure Molly's concerned."

He could see that Wade was tired the same as he, maybe even more so, but he doubted it. He nodded in agreement and stood. "Think I'll do just that if you're sure you don't mind."

Wade gestured at the cot. "That looks a lot more comfortable than my saddle."

Seth grinned, knowing that was true as he picked up his hat. "I'll take the stock to my place and get them put away." Then he walked toward the door leading to the cells and looked through its small window at their prisoners, seeing that Lee and Pete were both asleep. Wishing Booth Fox occupied the middle cell, he continued his journey to the front door, where he stopped and turned to Wade. "I'll be back after a few hours. Better lock this." Then he opened the door and stepped outside into the early morning.

Wade locked the door, blew out all the lanterns leaving the room in the early morning light, and walked to the cot sitting in the corner against the rear wall, behind Seth's desk. As he approached the cot, he passed a short hall leading to the storeroom and back door with a small, narrow window high on the door. After making sure the back door was locked, Wade stood on his toes and looked through the small window into the early morning, seeing an outhouse next to a large oak tree. Deciding to visit it, he took the board from the door, opened it, and stepped outside.

Feeling dog tired when he returned, he sat down on the cot, took off his boots, socks, and shirt, then laid down in his clothes, pulled the one cover over him, closed his eyes, and fell fast asleep.

Sixteen

The Hoskins Ranch

George Hoskins turned the knob of the door, slowly opened it, and stepped into a dimly lit room containing a pine casket, resting on a table in the center of the room. Glancing around the otherwise empty room, he stared at the casket as he closed the door behind him. As that door closed, another opened behind the casket and a figure dressed in a black robe and hood concealing his face. The figure stepped into the dim room, closed the door, and stood next to the coffin. Then the figure gestured to the casket inviting Hoskins to step closer. George hesitantly took a step backward. "Who are you?" he asked in a fearful voice.

The figure moved closer to the casket, and as he placed his left hand upon it, the lid of the coffin began to bulge, and a voice cried out from within.

George Hoskins opened his eyes and quickly sat up in the darkness of his bedroom. Sweat covered his face, his eyes wide and fearful as he looked around the dark, quiet room at the opened window. The lace curtains moved gently from the soft breeze that invaded the dark, stuffy room, along with the sounds of crickets and frogs. Suddenly, the pounding returned.

"Mr. Hoskins!" yelled a voice outside the window.

Tossing the covers back, he hurried across the room, parted the lace curtains, and stuck his head out, seeing a riderless horse in the yard next to the roofed porch.

136

"Mr. Hoskins," the voice called out again, sounding urgent, followed by more pounding on the door.

Recognizing the voice of Booth Fox, he leaned on the sill with both hands and called out, "That you, Booth?"

Fox stepped from under the roof of the porch next to his horse and looked up. "Yes, sir."

"Stop your damn pounding," responded Hoskins angrily. "You'll wake the rest of the house."

"Sorry, Mr. Hoskins," said Booth in a quieter voice. "But Pete and Deputy Jones have both been arrested."

Hoskins leaned farther out the window. "What the hell do you mean arrested? Arrested for what?" Feeling perturbed, he quickly said, "Never mind, I'll be right down." He turned from the window, talking to himself about stupidity, and lit a nearby lamp. He put on a pair of pants, slippers, and robe then hurried out of the bedroom carrying the lantern. As he walked along the landing to the top of the stairs, another door opened. He paused to look at the elderly housekeeper dressed in a dark robe.

"Go on back to bed. This ain't none of your concern."

The curious housekeeper closed the door partway, watched him descend the stairs, then shut her door, and went back to bed.

Hoskins glanced at the clock at the foot of the stairs as he hurried past it to the front door. Seeing it was only a quarter to four in the morning, he wondered who could have arrested his son, with Booth Fox being the sheriff of Harper. Filled with that puzzle, he held the lantern in his left hand, unlocked the front door, and looked into the nervous face of his sheriff. "What the hell's all this about Pete being arrested, and by whom?" His voice was angry. "You're the damn sheriff, so go let them out! Why bother me with all this nonsense."

Booth took off his hat and held it in front of his stomach, looking nervous. "Yes, sir," he said with a nod of his head. "I would do just that, Mr. Hoskins, but Pete and Lee Jones were both arrested by Sheriff Bowlen from over in Sisters with the help of a marshal by the name of Wade Garrison."

Hoskins considered that a moment looking confused. "Why in the hell didn't you stop 'em?"

"I wasn't in town, Mr. Hoskins, or I would have."

George looked confused and angry. "Well, who the hell was?" He paused. "I pay you to control things, Booth, not to be off poking some whore."

Fox looked apologetic. "Chris Boyd was at the jailhouse."

The old man scoffed with displeasure. "Chris Boyd," he said softly, sounding disappointed. George Hoskins wasn't a very tall man, standing only five-feet-six-inches tall. His messy, balding, gray, and brown hair hung just over the collar of his dark red robe. Bushy eyebrows hooded dark brown, baggy, bloodshot eyes, and his tanned face was full of wrinkles, the gifts of time and weather. Stepping back from the door, he gestured Booth inside. "I need a drink." He turned and walked away, talking over his shoulder. "Close the damn door and come into the library."

Booth closed the door, followed him into the library, and stood at the doorway while Hoskins walked to the liquor cabinet, sitting against the far wall.

"Light another lamp."

Fox did as told while George set the lamp on the dark brown cabinet next to a fancy, clear glass bottle filled with brandy, surrounded by several small glasses. The second lantern Fox lit filled the room with its soft orange light. Looking up from the lantern, he let his eyes wander the room. The walls were decorated with paintings of flower gardens and scantily clad women. Another large painting was of men and women dressed in formal attire, walking along unfamiliar, damp streets. A bigger than life oil painting of a beautiful, young Mrs. Hoskins decorated the wall above the fireplace. It was the only reminder George Hoskins had of his late wife, who had died eight years ago from cancer. Expensive, floral designed, silk woven furniture filled the room of cherry wood tables, area rugs, and a corner curio closet. Unknown to Booth, the room had been Mrs. Hoskins' labor of love. His journey was interrupted by the tinkling of glass.

George finished pouring the two drinks, picked them up, and turned to Booth with a puzzled, thoughtful expression as he held out one of the glasses. "Did you say, Marshal Wade Garrison?"

Fox took the glass and nodded. "Yes, sir. Marshal Wade Garrison from Santa Fe."

George Hoskins stared at him. "What the hell is that man doing in Harper?"

Surprised that the old man knew who Wade Garrison was, Fox explained that Garrison's wife, Sarah, was Jasper Talbert's daughter.

"I know all that," Hoskins said, looking irritated. Then he gestured with his empty hand as if dismissing what Fox had said. "I remember the day that Talbert girl left town chasing him like some dog in heat, clear down to Santa Fe."

Fox sipped his drink, thinking of how good Sarah Garrison had smelled in the store that day, wishing she would chase after him.

Then Hoskins looked at him with cold, narrow eyes. "You knew this marshal was in Harper and failed to tell me about it."

Booth shrugged, looking nervous. "I saw no reason to, Mr. Hoskins. He had just dropped his wife off at the Double J and was headed back out of town. I figured he was heading back to Santa Fe."

"Idiot!" said Hoskins loudly and angrily.

That angered Booth. "You got no call to talk to me that way..."

"As long as I'm paying your wages," interrupted Hoskins. "I'll talk to you any way I damn well please."

Booth's stature slumped in defeat. "Yes, sir."

Hoskins took a healthy drink and looked at him, feeling regret for what he had said, and sighed with a kindly face. "Sorry about that, Booth. I'm just upset and mad as hell right now, and you're the only one close by."

"Guess I'd feel much the same, sir."

Hoskins grunted as he turned and walked to the window where he stared into the darkness, knowing that sunrise was not far off. He sipped the last of his drink and said the name Wade Garrison under his breath. A moment later, Hoskins turned and walked to the fancy bottle of brandy, poured another drink, and when Hoskins finished, he told Booth to sit down. He watched Booth sit down, and then he sat down on the sofa across from him. "Tell me what the hell happened."

Fox sipped his drink. "When I got back to town, it was close to midnight. Chris met me at the door to the sheriff's office, telling me about Pete and Lee getting arrested at the Blue Sky Saloon. I hurried over there and talked to Sam Carney as he was closing up the place, and he told me it was Wade Garrison and Sheriff Seth Bowlen from Sisters."

Hoskins raised his voice. "What the hell's going on around here? And where the hell was Boyd while my boy was being arrested?"

"Sleeping."

"You fire that bastard." Then he glared at Fox. "Thinking on it, I ought to fire you as well."

"Chris is a good man, Mr. Hoskins," said Booth, hoping he would understand. "Shit, there ain't much going on in the middle of the week anyway. For some reason, Chris woke up and looked outside, seeing four men riding down the street toward the south end of town. He didn't think anything of it until he decided that one looked like Lee and decided to walk over to the Blue Sky Saloon. When he walked in, Sam Carney told him about Pete and Lee."

"Why in the hell didn't Chris go after 'em?" Hoskins asked angrily.

Fox shrugged. "He's only one man, and he ain't a gunman. He's just a cowhand you told me to make a deputy 'cause you liked him." He paused. "He's a good man."

Hoskins sighed and gestured with the hand holding the drink. "All right, Chris stays." The room got silent as he took a sip of his drink, thinking about his dream. Moments passed before he looked at Booth. "I should've known that damn Seth Bowlen wasn't going to let this mess be. Pete should never have gotten mixed up with that Olson whore."

"No, sir."

George looked at Booth for a long moment, set his glass on the table, and settled back into the corner of the sofa. He closed his eyes and rubbed his forehead with one hand looking tired. "Do you know who this Wade Garrison is?"

Fox looked puzzled. "Yes, sir."

Hoskins lowered his hand, opened his eyes, and leaned forward, looking at him with a mean and angry face. "I don't think you do, boy."

Booth had never seen George Hoskins in a mood such as this, and it unnerved him as they stared at one another.

The old man moved to the edge of the sofa. "Wade Garrison's the man who killed my eldest son, Daniel, six years ago, over in Sisters."

Having never met Hoskins's eldest son, Daniel, this came as quite a shock to Booth, and he wondered why no one ever talked about it. "Why would a United States Deputy Marshal kill your son?"

George slowly got up from the sofa, looking tired and defeated. "He wasn't a deputy marshal back then." He gestured to the glass Booth held. "Care for another?"

"Yes, sir, I would," replied Fox, who stood with glass in hand and followed him to the table and the fancy glass bottle.

Hoskins had a troubled look on his face as he took Booth's glass, poured him a drink, and handed it back.

Fox took a quick sip, watched the old man pour himself another drink, and returned to his chair.

Hoskins walked to the window and peered through the lace curtains into the darkness. Feeling the weight of the sorrow of six years ago returning, he sipped his drink as he stared into the night. Thinking of the dream he had, he wondered if Wade Garrison was the figure dressed in black, and if that was so, his son Pete was in the pine coffin.

Fox stared at the old man for a long time before he leaned forward in his chair, looking concerned. "Are you all right, Mr. Hoskins?"

As if he hadn't heard, George pushed the lace curtains to the side with his left hand and looked at the light blue sky above the plains and rolling hills in the east. His mind forgot Wade Garrison and Booth Fox for a moment as he stared at the soft light above the eastern horizon while sipping his drink. His thoughts found fonder memories of his wife, their two sons, and baby daughter living in Pennsylvania during happier times. The days then were filled with the laughter of children, and his wife was young and full of life, but the laughter of those days has long since gone silent. He had watched cancer drain his wife of her strength and then of her life, and as he stared at the coming dawn, he found himself wishing they had all stayed back east. He sipped his drink and softly said, "There ain't much separating life from death."

Fox stared at him, confused by that.

Wade Garrison flooded the old man's mind as he returned to the sofa where he sat on its edge, staring into his glass. "I'll not let Wade Garrison take another of my family. I forgave him once, but I won't a second."

Booth stared at him in silence, wondering why the Marshal had killed Daniel Hoskins.

Mr. Hoskins looked at Booth. "I'll kill the son of a bitch and his family before I lose my only son." He took a drink and looked at him, his face hard and questioning. "Talk to me, Booth. I understand the warrant for Pete, but why Deputy Lee Jones? What the hell's he got to do with this?"

Booth stared at him, trying to figure out a way to tell him about Tom Lawson.

The anger in Hoskins rose. "You better talk to me, boy. Why is my son sitting in a two-bit jail in Sisters?"

Fox sat the glass on the table next to his chair and leaned forward, resting his elbows on his knees. He looked down at his clasped hands, fearing what he had to tell him.

"I'm waiting."

Fox looked at Mr. Hoskins and cleared his throat. "Pete killed old man Olson in cold blood."

Hoskins stared at him for a long, silent moment digesting what he just said, thinking of what Seth Bowlen told him about Daniel trying to bushwhack Wade Garrison in Sisters. At first, his mind denied the truth, but then he wondered if it was true. "You and Pete both told me that Olson drew his gun, and Pete shot in self-defense."

Fox looked remorseful. "I was just trying to protect Pete."

George turned toward the window across the room, seeing the hills in the distance were getting lighter as the sun neared the horizon. He spoke softly, sounding disappointed. "All that shit I did up in Denver to protect Pete was based on a damn lie?"

"Yes, sir."

George Hoskins looked angry. "You should have stopped it, Booth. I counted on you."

"I couldn't do anything about it, Mr. Hoskins," he said, looking sorry. "It all happened too fast."

Hoskins stared at him for a long moment. "Anyone else know the truth about Olson?"

"I ain't sure, but the bartender may have. I doubt he'd say anything. He's too afraid."

Hoskins turned in anger. "Damn it, boy," he said in a low, harsh voice. "If this bartender saw what happened, he'll send my boy to the hangman."

"He's too afraid to say anything."

Silence filled the room as George Hoskins stared at Booth with an angry face. "Men like that have a conscience that brings out foolish bravery. You need to take care of this bartender." He turned and looked out the window, fearful of the new day.

Fox looked worried. "Won't that be a little obvious?"

Hoskins scoffed. "One of the things I learned a long time ago is, in a court of law, obvious has to be proven." Then looking determined, he said, "I want this bartender dead. I lost one son to his own stupidity for trying to shoot this Wade Garrison in the back." He looked at Booth. "I ain't about to lose another to the hangman by the same man."

Booth sighed softly. "May take some time," he said thoughtfully. "I can't just ride over there and start shooting."

"I know that. This thing won't go to trial right away. I'll see to that." Then he stood. "I'm tired."

Deciding to tell the old man everything, Booth stood. "There's something else you need to know, Mr. Hoskins."

Half afraid to know what it was, George stared at him. "And what might that be?"

"Better set back down, sir."

George Hoskins sat down and waited with a curious expression. "I'm waiting, Booth."

"When you were up in Cheyenne a few weeks back, you got a letter from your judge friend up in Denver."

"You referring to Ethan Parker?"

"Yes, sir."

Hoskins moved to the edge of his seat, staring at Booth. "How is it you'd know I got a personal letter from Ethan?"

Booth looked apologetic. "Pete opened it."

The old man looked disappointed. "What was in the letter?"

"It said that Sheriff Bowlen had come to Denver with a warrant for Pete saying that he had a witness to the shooting by the name of Tom Lawson. Apparently, this Lawson was willing to testify in court about the killing of old man Olson."

Hoskins stood enraged. "Now, we've two witnesses!"

"Tom Lawson's already taken care of Mr. Hoskins."

George, looking curious as he slowly sat back down, staring at Booth Fox. "What do you mean taken care of?"

143

"Pete was afraid he'd go to jail if Tom Lawson were to tell the truth about what happened."

Hoskins scoffed without humor. "I can understand his fear and rightly so, but how was this Lawson fellah taken care of."

"Pete wanted me and Lee to ride over with him and take care of this Lawson fellah, so we did."

George stared down at his hands, looking like he carried the weight of the world on his shoulders. He wanted to know who killed Lawson, but he was afraid to ask. "Who killed this Tom Lawson?"

Booth hesitated and then lied. "I put the first bullet in him; Lee, the second."

Looking relieved, Hoskins looked up. "Pete, never fired a shot?"

Fox shook his head and lied, remembering Pete putting three bullets in Lawson. "No, sir. It was like I said, I fired the first shot and Lee the second."

Hoskins let out a heavy sigh stood, and walked to the window, thinking about his dream and the man in the black hood. The sun rose above the hills to the east filling the room with sunshine that felt warm and friendly on his face. He thought of his dead wife, the daughter he lost to fever, and his oldest son killed by Wade Garrison. Pete was all he had left from those happier times, the only proof left of his existence. As he watched the sun make its slow climb above the mesa and cliffs in the distance, he knew he couldn't stand by and let Wade Garrison and Seth Bowlen take his only son, no matter what the boy was guilty of doing. He turned from the window and looked at Booth. "Anyone see you and Lee shoot this Lawson fellah?"

Fox thought a moment. "No."

"If they got warrants, they got a witness."

Booth thought about Sam Wheeler but kept quiet.

George looked at the clock in the corner of the room, seeing it was almost five o'clock. "Go wake up, Reese. Tell 'em about Pete and Lee Jones getting arrested and nothing else. Then tell him he's coming with me to Sisters."

Booth followed him out of the room, wondering what he wanted with Reese.

George stopped at the stairs. "You stay on the place and away from town until I see what the hell's going on."

"Yes, sir."

"Tell Reese to get four or five men that can keep their mouth shut to go with us."

Curiosity filled Fox. "Yes, sir."

Hoskins turned and started up the stairs, talking over his shoulder. "I'll be down as soon as I get dressed."

"Yes, sir," replied Fox as he turned toward the front door.

"Booth!" called George from the top of the stairs.

Fox turned and looked up.

"I know you did the best you could watching over Pete, and I'm forever beholding to you for that. But I have to say that you sure messed this thing up."

Booth nodded ruefully, knowing it was Pete that messed everything up. "Yes, sir." Then he turned and walked out the front door to wake up Reese.

Seventeen

Sisters, Colorado

Wade opened his eyes from a short but sound sleep, raised his head, and glanced around the sheriff's office then out the window at the bright sunlight. He thought about last night as he laid his head back onto his pillow, closing his eyes, and rubbed his forehead. His thoughts turned to him and Sarah sitting in bed in the mornings with their coffee, waiting for the day to find them. As the clock on the far wall chimed seven, he looked at it through sleepy eyes, tossed the one blanket aside, and sat up, putting his feet on the cold floor. Dressed in the clothes he had slept in, he rested his head in his hands, thinking of sleep, then put his socks and boots on. Standing, he stretched as he looked out the front window at the buildings across the street and a cloudless blue sky behind them.

Yawning, he walked to the desk, pulled his pistol from its holster, walked down the short hallway to the heavy back door with its small window, looked outside at the oak tree and outhouse he needed to visit. Deciding there was no one around to break Pete and the deputy out of jail, he lifted the board from across the door, opened it, poked his head out then stepped into the crisp morning air.

Wade stood at the jail's big window, thinking of the night before in Harper and the long ride back. Looking out at the town as it started to come alive, he heard the water in the big, dented coffee pot begin to gurgle as it boiled. Turning from the window, Wade moved the pot to the edge of the stove, letting the grounds settle before Wade filled his cup. Thinking of

146

the prisoners, he walked to the jail's outer door and looked through the small window finding them both asleep. Grateful for that, Wade walked back to Seth's creaky chair, sat down, and wondered if Seth ever oiled it. Putting his feet on the desk, he looked out the window and took a drink of coffee to the sound of his empty stomach. Looking at the clock in the far corner by the door, he wondered what was keeping Seth.

Pete Hoskins opened his eyes, got up from the cot, stood with his hands on the steel bars, and called out. "I have to go!"

"Use the bucket!" Wade yelled back with a grin, then sipped his coffee.

"I ain't gonna go in no bucket!"

"Well," Wade yelled. "I guess you can go in your pants!"

"I'll go on the floor instead!"

"You do," replied Wade angrily. "I'll mop it up with your damn shirt and you in it!"

The door opened, and Seth walked in, having heard the last of the conversation. "Trouble?"

Wade grinned. "Pete's refusing to go in the bucket."

Seth chuckled. "He can go in his pants."

Wade shrugged. "Done told him that very thing. Coffee's ready." Then he stood and poured Bowlen a cup and set it on his desk.

Lee Jones, who had been lying on his cot listening, got up and walked to the cell bars, grasping them with his hands. "We gonna get something to eat?"

"It's on the way," replied Seth, sounding irritated.

"I gotta go!" yelled Jones.

Seth chuckled, looked at Wade, and yelled over his shoulder toward the closed door leading to the cells. "Use the bucket!"

Silence followed, and then the sound of the two men filling their buckets echoed from the other room.

Finished, Lee Jones set his buck down. "Just who was it we were supposed to have killed?"

Seth yelled over his shoulder. "Tom Lawson!"

"I don't even know any Tom Lawson," replied Jones sarcastically.

Figuring Jones was lying, Seth, said, "Well, you'll have your chance to tell all that to a judge and jury!"

"Ain't never gonna get that far," said Pete sarcastically.

Looking irritated, Seth told them both to shut up. He took off his hat, placed it on the corner of his desk, picked up the cup of coffee, and sat down in his creaky chair. He took a sip and made a face, thinking it tasted bitter.

The door opened, and Deputy McIver walked in, followed by Seth's part-time deputy, Lyle Dickson. Lyle was close to fifty, thin, about five-feet-seven, with thinning, brown hair, and a clean-shaven face, and had the look of a farmer. He and his wife Barbara owned a few acres just north of Sisters. Lyle closed the door, took off his faded dark brown hat, and followed Carl to Seth's desk.

Deputy Carl was clean-shaven and looked like he'd had a good night's rest wearing a clean, ironed shirt and dark blue pants. "Morn'n, Seth."

Lyle looked at Wade and Seth as he spoke with a heavy southern drawl. "Got here as soon as I could."

Bowlen was leaning back in his chair with his feet on the desk, looking comfortable while sipping his coffee, wishing Wade knew how to make a good cup of coffee. "Wade, this here's Lyle Dickson." Then he grinned. "Lyle's my part-time deputy when his Barbara allows it."

Dickson grinned, looking embarrassed while he and Wade shook hands.

Seth looked at Lyle. "You have breakfast yet?"

Lyle nodded. "Yes, sir."

Seth picked up his hat and gestured to the front door. "Me, Carl, and Wade are going across the street for some breakfast. Be gone for about an hour." Then all three started for the front door.

"Anything I should know?" asked Dickson.

Seth paused at the door and turned. "Food will be here soon." Then he gestured to the stove. "There's a fresh pot of coffee on the stove." Then he grinned. "If you feel kindly, them two in the back can each have a cup. No sense being cruel this early in the morning."

Lyle glanced at the door leading to the cells. "Okay, Seth."

Bowlen put on his hat noticing Lyle's old Confederate pistol and holster. "Leave your gun on the desk until we get back. I don't want one of them reaching for it while you slide their breakfast and coffee through the bars."

148

"Ok, Seth." Lyle already decided that he wouldn't give either a cup of coffee for killing his friend, Tom Lawson.

Bowlen looked at the clock, seeing it was almost nine-thirty. "Lock the door behind us." Then he pointed to the gun rack on the wall above the cot. "Shotgun's loaded."

Seth walked out and started to close the door when he paused and looked back at Lyle. "Don't let no one in here but Sophie from Molly's. I don't give a damn who they are."

"All right, Seth," replied Dickson, and then he grinned as he joked. "Does that go for y'all as well?"

Seth grinned at the humor. "No, Lyle, I believe we're the exception." He shut the door, waited to hear Lyle lock it, then joined Carl and Wade at the edge of the boardwalk. As they stepped off the boardwalk onto the dusty, dirt street toward Molly's Restaurant, he wondered if Booth Fox and rider's from the Hoskins place were on their way.

Wade looked at Seth as they crossed the dirt street, thinking he looked a little worried, and then glanced back at the jailhouse. "Lyle gonna be okay?"

"He's a good man," answered Seth as they walked. "He fought for the South, same as Carl here, but for different reasons." Seth glanced back over his shoulder and chuckled. "Lyle don't think too much of us northerners, so I doubt he'd hesitate much before killing either Jones or Pete. He was one of the last holdouts after the war. The way I heard it, it took damn near the whole Union army to convince him and the rest of his outfit to put down their weapons and surrender." Then Seth chuckled again. "To this day, I doubt that Lyle's fully surrendered."

Wade grinned, thinking people aren't always what they seem.

It was a busy morning in Molly's, and she had just prepared Seth's favorite table by the front window with cups and silverware when the three of them stepped inside. Wearing a white and blue polka dot dress with a white apron that told of a busy morning, she smiled at Seth, telling them to have a seat, and she'd bring their coffee.

Seth smiled, thanked her, and as she walked toward the kitchen, the three men took off their hats and sat down. Seth sat in one of the chairs that faced the window, giving him an unobstructed view of the sheriff's office across the street. Wade sat next to the wall, with the window on his left, while Carl sat next to Seth.

Molly returned with a pot of coffee, wearing a smile meant just for Seth. He looked up and grinned, looking like a young boy as she poured his coffee.

She looked at Carl, "Coffee?"

Carl nodded. "Yes, Ma'am."

Molly looked at Wade. "Coffee?"

"Please."

She poured the coffee, gave Seth a quick look, and then walked away to put the pot on the stove in the kitchen.

Molly returned to their table a few minutes later. "What can I get you boys this morning?"

Carl glanced at Wade, and Molly then looked at Seth. "I already ate breakfast."

Seth looked at Carl, recalling his telling him the night before that they would eat breakfast together. He started to scold his deputy but decided against it. "I think I'll have some eggs, potatoes, and bread."

"I'll have the same as Seth," said Wade.

Carl looked at Molly. "Do you have any pie?"

"We've some apple pie."

Carl grinned. "I'll have a piece with my coffee."

While they drank their coffee and waited for their food, Seth leaned forward, resting on his left forearm, took a sip of coffee, and looked out the window. "I wonder where Booth Fox is right about now."

Wade took a drink of coffee, smiled, and looked at Seth. "I imagine he's at the Hoskins' place, explaining to old man Hoskins about Pete and Deputy Jones."

Carl nodded in agreement, took a sip of coffee, and looked at Seth, waiting to hear what he had to say.

Bowlen took another drink of coffee, and then looking disappointed, stared into his cup. "Sure would've liked to have brought that bastard back with us."

Carl picked up his cup, took a quick sip, set it down, and nodded in agreement several times.

Wade had been watching Carl, wondering if he ever did any talking, then he turned to Seth. "Booth's gonna have to wait." He sat back, looking thoughtful as he stared across the street at the jailhouse. "I don't think we can pull off a second surprise."

Carl grinned, chuckled, and nodded several times as he picked up his cup, took a drink of coffee, put the cup down, and looked at Seth.

Wade wished Carl would stop being so damn agreeable and turned to Seth. "The first thing we got to do is get these two arraigned for murder."

Seth nodded. "I'll get a wire off to Judge Moore as soon as we're finished."

Molly approached the table with their food, and as she put the plates on the table, she told Carl that she would be right back with his pie. After she walked away from their table, Seth and Wade started eating and talking about things they needed to do. Wade said that he would get his gear and the bartender, Paul Leonard, after they finished eating, and head out to Wheeler's place.

Molly brought Carl's pie setting down in front of him on the table.

Carl thanked her, then cut a piece with his fork.

Seth took a sip of coffee and watched as Carl eagerly started on the apple pie. Sitting his cup down, he told Carl that he and Lyle would have to split their time so's one of them was always at the jailhouse with the door locked and shotgun handy.

"All right by me, Seth," replied Carl with his mouth full of pie. "But, you'll need to explain all that to Lyle."

Seth figured that was obvious. "I'll do that after we eat."

Wade paused his chewing in thought and looked at Seth. "I know the windows in the cells are high, but it might be a good idea to board 'em up so's no one can toss a gun through the glass."

Seth nodded, looking appreciative. "Good idea, we'll take care of that today."

Harper, Colorado

Jasper Talbert helped his daughter Sarah up onto the wagon's seat, lifted Emmett so he could sit between them, and then climbed up, sat down in the seat, and picked up the reins to the horses. He smiled at Emmett and then Sarah, thinking how glad he was that they had come to visit. He released the wagon's brake and gently slapped the two horses on their backs with the reins causing the wagon to lurch forward. Startled, Emmett grabbed ahold of his ma, and they laughed.

The wagon moved away from the boardwalk in front of Mason's Store, and then Jasper guided the horses along the dusty street toward the end of town. A drunken Booth Fox who was supposed to stay on the Hoskins spread rode up and stopped in front of them, blocking their way. Jasper pulled up and set the brake. "You crazy?" he asked, looking angry.

Fox ignored Jasper, took off his hat, and smiled at Sarah. "Howdy, Miss Sarah."

"It's Mrs. Garrison," she replied with an annoyed look.

Jasper stood from the wagon seat. "Move your damn horse, young fellah, and let us pass."

Hearing the commotion, Ed Mason, owner of Mason's Store, and two other men walked out of the store and watched from the boardwalk.

Ignoring Jasper, Booth walked his horse to Sarah's side of the wagon, leaned out of his saddle with his face next to hers, closed his eyes, and smelled her hair.

She was afraid and could smell the foul odor of his whiskey breath as she turned her head, wishing he would back away.

Booth Fox smiled. "You sure smell sweet and ripe, Miss Sarah."

Sarah turned and slapped Booth across the face.

Jasper Talbert dropped the reins, stepped past Emmett, in front of Sarah, lept out of the wagon onto Fox, pulling him off the horse. As the two landed on the ground, Booth's horse screamed as it reared up then trotted several yards down the street. Jasper and Booth wrestled near the horses' legs that reared up, pulling at the wagon that had its brake set. Fearful they would get trampled, Sarah grabbed the reins and made sure the brake stayed set to hold the wagon in place. Jasper managed to get up, pull Booth up by the collar of his coat, then hit him in the face, knocking him back into the team of horses Sarah was trying to control.

Sarah yelled at her pa to stop while a frightened Emmett watched as his grandfather got hit in the face by Booth. Jasper hit Fox in the face with his right hand, followed by an uppercut with the left, knocking Booth into the hitching rail. Emmett looked up at his ma as she yelled for Jasper and Booth to stop seeing tears running down her face. The boy quickly slid off the seat, got under it, covered his ears, and began to cry.

Tears ran down Sarah's face as she watched her pa pull Fox away from the hitching rail by his shirt and then hit him in the face knocking him back over the edge of the boardwalk in front of Mason's Store, falling flat on his back.

Afraid someone would get hurt, Ed Mason and another man grabbed Jasper, while the two others stepped between him and Booth Fox.

Booth sat up on the boardwalk and pushed the hand away of the man that tried to help him up. Staring at Jasper, he slowly got up, brushing the dirt from his pants and shirt, and wiped the blood from his face. He smiled at Sarah and then looked at Jasper. "You're one tough son of a bitch old man."

Jasper's face filled with hate and anger. "You ever speak to my daughter that way again, I'll kill you."

Booth looked at Jasper and chuckled. "I doubt that."

"Get back in the wagon, Pa," pleaded Sarah as she stared at Booth.

Deputy Chris Boyd came out of the sheriff's office, rushed across the street, and hurried around the wagon, asking what was going on. When he saw Booth's bloody face, he looked at Jasper and then put one hand on Booth's shoulder, looking worried. "You all right?"

Fox pushed Boyd's hand away. "I'm fine," Then he stared at Jasper while wiping the blood from his nose and mouth. "As I said, you're a tough old bastard."

Sarah wiped the tears from her face. "Get in the wagon, Pa."

Ed Mason put one hand on Jasper's shoulder. "Better do as she says, Jasper."

Jasper looked at Ed, then at a Booth Fox. "Don't ever talk to my daughter in that manner again."

Booth bent down, picked up his hat, dusted it off, put it on, and looked up at Sarah and smiled.

Ed Mason put his hand on Jasper's shoulder. "You best be getting Sarah and your grandson home, Jasper."

Talbert looked at Mason and nodded, then climbed up in the wagon, took the reins from his daughter, released the brake, slapped the horses, and drove the team away from Mason's.

Eighteen

Sisters, Colorado

Seth looked out the window as he lifted his cup to drink the last of his coffee, then he lowered his cup. "Shit."

Wade and Carl turned to see what Seth was looking at and saw two men tying their horses to the hitching rail in front of the jailhouse.

Wade turned to Seth. "Know 'em?"

Bowlen nodded. "George Hoskins is the older man." Then he stood pushing his chair back with his legs. "The other is Jethro Reese, his foreman."

Chairs shuffled across the floor as the three stood, got their hats, and headed for the café door. Molly turned from what she was doing in time to see her husband and the others walk out the door without eating their breakfast.

Bowlen yelled from the middle of the street. "Mr. Hoskins,"

George Hoskins and his foreman stopped, turned, and while he waited, George Hoskins slapped the trail dust from his dark wool suit. Jethro Reese, George Hoskins's foreman, stood five feet ten, with broad shoulders, narrow of waist, dressed in black pants, a black shirt, and a red bandana tied loosely around his neck. His dark brown hair bulged from under a black, dusty hat, and he needed a shave.

Hoskins frowned and was the first to speak with anger. "You got my boy locked up inside, Sheriff?"

Seeing neither was wearing a gun, Seth stopped short of the boardwalk and placed his left hand on the post, his foot on the first step. While he didn't much care for Hoskins' tone, he understood it. "Yes, sir, I do."

George glanced at Carl and then at Wade, seeing the marshal's badge pinned to his shirt. He had never seen Wade but knew he was the man that killed his eldest son. He turned to Seth with a frown. "Mind telling me why?"

Seth gestured to the door. "Might be best, Mr. Hoskins, if we went inside."

"Maybe so," he replied, glancing around at the street and boardwalk, seeing that people were watching.

Seth stepped onto the boardwalk, walked to the door, and called out as he looked at George Hoskins. "Lyle, it's Seth. Put the shotgun down and open the door."

Moments later, they could hear the sound of the board being removed from the door, the key turning of the lock, and then the door slowly opened. Lyle looked at Seth, stepped back and, opened the door.

As they stepped inside, Hoskins asked where his son was.

Bowlen gestured toward the door leading to the cells. "Your son is sitting in a cell through that door, Mr. Hoskins."

George Hoskins started for the door leading to the cells when Seth reached out, putting his hand in front of the man to stop him. "Sorry, Mr. Hoskins. You appear to be unarmed, but just the same, hope you don't mind me checking a little closer before you walk through that door to visit my prisoner."

He smiled at Seth without humor. "I'm not a foolish man, Sheriff."

"Never thought you were, sir," Seth replied as he began searching him for a hidden gun. "But neither am I." When he finished, Seth stepped back and looked at Reese. "Jethro," he said with a nod. "Been a while."

Jethro smiled softly. "That it has, Sheriff."

Seth turned to the others, gesturing to each. "This here's Deputy Marshal Wade Garrison from Santa Fe, my deputies, Carl McIver, and Lyle Dickson."

Each looked at the other while Hoskins stared at Wade, ignoring the others. Wade met his stare while Seth took the keys from the peg next

155

to the door, unlocked the door, opened it, and gestured to Hoskins. "Let's go inside so's you can see your son."

Hoskins looked away from Wade to Jethro. "Have a seat, Reese." Then he walked through the door and smiled at his son, Pete, who was standing at the cell door gripping the bars so hard his hands were white.

Seth left the outer door open, walked over to Carl, and quietly told him to keep an eye on them, noticing Lyle had taken a position next to the front door, looking like a bank guard. Seth walked toward his desk and motioned to the three chairs in front of his desk. "Have a seat, boys. I got the feeling we'll be a while."

Wade followed Jethro Reese across the room, and while Jethro sat down, Wade walked to the window and leaned against the wall next to it, arms folded, eyeing Reese.

Seth sat down in his creaky chair and watched as Reese laid his hat on the corner of his desk, took off his gloves, and placed them next to his hat as the muffled voices of Hoskins and his son escaped through the open doorway where Carl stood. Seth looked at Jethro. "Coffee?"

Jethro shook his head. "No, thanks."

Beyond the door and inside the jail, George Hoskins talked in a low voice with his son so that Carl couldn't hear. Deputy Lee Jones was standing at the bars, trying to listen when Hoskins stopped talking and looked at him. "Mind if I talk to my son in private?"

Embarrassed, Lee Jones stepped away. "Sorry, Mr. Hoskins."

Carl watched Lee walk back to his cot, looking defeated, while George Hoskins continued talking in a voice too low for him to hear.

After several minutes, George Hoskins smiled at his son, reached through the bars, and patted him on the shoulder. Turning, he walked out of the cell area, past Carl to Seth's desk, looking unhappy.

McIver closed the door to the cells and locked it.

Seth gestured to one of the chairs. "Have a seat, Mr. Hoskins. Can I interest you in a cup of coffee?"

Hoskins took off his hat, placed it on the edge of Seth's desk next to Jethro's hat and gloves, and sat down. "Have anything to go with it?"

Seth grinned wryly and opened the bottom drawer of his desk, retrieving an unopened bottle of cheap whiskey. "Probably not what you're accustomed to, but it'll tone down Carl's coffee a bit."

"It'll do just fine," George replied with a small smile but still looking troubled.

Seth set the bottle down, got up to pour the coffee, and looked at Jethro. "Change your mind?"

Reese shook his head no.

"Wade?" asked Seth.

He nodded yes and then stepped away from the window.

Seth turned to the potbellied stove and the coffee pot, poured three tin cups of coffee, handing one to George Hoskins, the other to Wade. Seth picked up his cup, turned, set it down on his desk, and picked up the bottle of whiskey. He poured a little whiskey into each of the three cups, corked the bottle, and sat down. Wade returned to the window, glancing out it to see if anyone looked suspicious, and then turned to watch the others as he sipped the whiskey coffee.

Hoskins took a small sip and then made a face.

Seth grinned with a small chuckle. "Tried to warn you, Mr. Hoskins."

"I've had worse over the years," smiled Hoskins. Then he took another sip, swallowed, and looked at Bowlen. "Just what are you charging my son with, Sheriff Bowlen?"

Seth took a drink of his coffee and swallowed. "Pete's gonna be tried for the murder of Jacob Olson."

"I believe a judge up in Denver settled this thing weeks ago," Hoskins said. "You're holding my son without just cause, Sheriff."

Seth thought things had been going too smoothly as he took a sip of coffee, considering what Hoskins had said. "Well, now, that ain't exactly correct, Mr. Hoskins, because you see that judge up in Denver dismissed charges that were never formally filed. He smiled. "That Judge of yours jumped the gun a bit as they say."

Hoskins drank from his tin cup and stared at Seth over its edge, knowing he was right and was mad at the Judge in Denver for being careless. Then as he swallowed the whiskey coffee, he leaned forward and set the cup down on the desk. Without looking at Wade, the old man gestured to him while looking at Seth. "I'm curious why a Deputy United States Marshal from Santa Fe is helping a sheriff in Sisters, Colorado, arrest my son?"

157

Seth drank the last of his coffee and set the cup down on his desk. "If you recall, me and my deputy came to your place right off, wanting to clear this thing up, and you just sent us packing with our tails between our legs."

Still not looking at Wade, Hoskins raised his voice in anger. "That doesn't explain you asking the man that killed my oldest son to help you destroy my other son."

Not sure what would happen next, Wade stepped away from the window.

Seth leaned forward and spoke in a calm voice. "For some reason or another," he said as he pointed toward the north and Denver. "When I asked for help from that little piss ant marshal up in Denver, I was told to forget it." Seth stood, looking angry. "Just sweep a murder under the rug like it never happened."

Hoskins stood in anger, glaring at him as he yelled, "My son says it was self-defense!"

"I have witnesses that say different," said Seth in a calm voice.

Afraid things were about to get out of hand, Jethro Reese got up and stood next to his boss. "Mr. Hoskins."

Wade set his cup on the sill and watched Reese.

"My boy's innocent, damn you!" yelled Hoskins.

Seth sat back in his chair and softly said, "That's for a jury to decide."

The room fell silent as the two men stared at one another. Jethro had never seen his boss this angry, and being half afraid the old man was going to hit the sheriff, he stepped toward him and spoke in a soft, calm voice. "Mr. Hoskins, this won't do Pete any good."

George turned, giving him a mean look, but Jethro just stood there, staring back like a son would at his angry father. Hoskins sighed, put one hand on Jethro's shoulder, and patted it gently. "You're right, boy. This won't do my son or me any good." Then he reached for his hat. "You'll be hearing from my lawyer, Sheriff."

"Always glad to see a man of the law, Mr. Hoskins," replied Seth.

Hoskins looked at Wade. "You're the man who killed my son, Daniel."

Wade looked into the old man's tired eyes, feeling sorry for him. "I sincerely regret that, sir, but your son didn't give me much of a choice."

They looked at one another for several moments, and Hoskins nodded. "I'm aware of what happened six years ago, Mr. Garrison, and I've never blamed you for that. Dan was headstrong." In the silence that followed, he thought about the dream and knew the man in the hood was Wade that came to kill his son Pete. He turned to Seth. "My attorney will be by in a few days to get my boy released."

Seth stiffened as he looked across the desk at Hoskins. "The last time I let you and your boy walk out that door, I never saw him in my town again. I don't rightly think I'm gonna make that mistake twice."

Hoskins' face flushed as he started to argue the point, but decided against it, put on his hat, and turned toward the door. "Let's go, Jethro."

Reese followed him to the door where Hoskins opened it and then turned. "We'll see about this, Sheriff." Then he and Jethro stepped outside.

Lyle Dickson shut the front door and locked it while Wade turned to the window and watched as they untied their horses and climbed into their saddles.

Seth was standing next to Wade now and watched as they rode past the window. "I believe the old man was a little upset."

Wade drew in a breath, let out a sigh of relief, picked up his cup, and looked at Seth. "Thought you two were gonna go at it for a minute."

"He sure was mad," said Seth in a calm voice.

Wade took a drink of his whiskey coffee that was now cold, thinking it tasted terrible, even with the whiskey. He turned and looked out the window as they rode up the street. "I'm sure they're considering that bartender about now."

"More'n likely," agreed Seth. "I'm sure Sam Wheeler's in their plans now as well."

Wade looked at Seth. "I better get the bartender and head out to the Wheeler place."

"Take Lyle with ya," said Seth in a low voice. "He's a good man."

Wade set the cup on the desk and looked at Lyle standing by the front door. "You want to step over here for a moment?"

Lyle walked across the room, wondering what it was the marshal wanted. Carl and Seth listened while Wade told Lyle about the bartender, Paul Leonard, Sam Wheeler, and their plan to take Paul out to Wheeler's for safekeeping until the judge from Colorado Springs arrives, and the trial begins.

Lyle frowned in thought as he looked at Wade. "Mind me asking how long we're gonna be gone?"

"A few days."

"A few days?" he repeated softly while looking worried.

"Maybe longer," said Wade, looking uncertain. "Can't rightly say for sure just yet, Lyle, but if you can't be gone from your place, I understand."

Lyle looked at Seth and Carl and then at Wade. "It ain't that I can't go. I just wasn't prepared for this." He took off his hat and scratched the top of his head. "You caught me off guard, Marshal." He thought a moment, then looked first at Seth, then Wade. "I'll go, but I've got to make some arrangements and make sure those boys of mine take care of the place while I'm gone."

"Fair enough," said Wade, glancing at the clock. "You go make what arrangements you need and meet me at the livery in two hours."

Lyle gave a quick nod and headed for the door and home.

Seth looked at Carl. "You and me will take turns standing guard and sleeping here at night."

Carl glanced at the familiar cot in the corner. "Anything you say, Seth."

Wade started for the door. "I'm gonna head over to your place, get my horse and rifle, and then pick up our friend."

After Wade walked out the door, Seth took off his gun and holster, laid them on the desk, and looked at Carl. "Go down to the mill and get a few one by six pieces of wood while I get a hammer and some nails from the storeroom. We need to close the windows in the cells and nail them shut. When we're finished with that, I'll go send that wire to Judge Moore."

With the boards securely nailed over the cells' windows, Carl put the hammer and nails away in the storeroom and then stood next to Seth's desk.

Bowlen strapped on his gun belt, picked up his hat, and looked at Carl. "I'm gonna send that telegram to Judge Moore."

"All right, Seth."

160

"Lock up behind me."

After Carl locked the door, he walked to the coffee pot, filled his cup with the last of the coffee, and sat down in Seth's creaking chair, leaned back, putting his feet on top of the desk, and got comfortable. Taking a quick sip and finding it bitter and barely warm, he decided to make a fresh pot when he heard a soft thump come from the back door. Carl put the coffee pot down, turned with his hand on the butt of his .38 Colt pistol, and stared down the short hall at the high, narrow window of the back door. Glancing at the front door wishing Seth would hurry, he heard another noise outside the back door. Little beads of sweat formed on his forehead as Carl drew his pistol and carefully walked into the hall, where Carl stopped a few feet from the door and stared at the narrow window. After listening for a moment, he quietly walked to the door.

The wooden brace was still over the big, heavy door, holding it securely in place, but he checked it anyway. Then he stood on his tiptoes, trying to see out the window, but he was too short. Turning from the window, he wiped the sweat from his face and then wiped his hand on his pants leg. Thinking it was nothing, he started to walk back into the office when he heard what sounded like someone moaning in pain and turned around to the window on his tiptoes. Still unable to see anything, he lifted the board from the door, opened it just a crack, and saw a man crawling along the ground from behind the building next door. Wondering who the man was and if he were hurt, the figure suddenly stopped crawling and collapsed. With gun in hand, Carl carefully stepped outside into the warm sun.

Nineteen

Having sent the telegram to Judge Albert Moore in Colorado Springs, Seth Bowlen walked along the boardwalk of Sisters, thinking about the past few days. He was so preoccupied with his thoughts of the prisoners and the upcoming trial he hardly gave notice to the people he passed on the busy boardwalk.

A woman's voice suddenly called out, "Sheriff Bowlen."

Turning toward the voice, he saw Tom Lawson's widow, Gertie, hurrying across the busy street of wagons, buggies, and riders. As she walked from the sunshine into the shade of the roof covering the boardwalk, he saw a worried, troubled look on her face. Gertie Lawson was a thin, frail-looking woman of thirty, standing just over five feet. Her face was long and slender, as was her nose. She held her light brown faded dress above her ankles with one hand as she stepped from the dirt street onto the boardwalk. An old, white bonnet covered her brown and slightly gray hair. Still wearing the sorrow of Tom Lawson's death on her face, she managed a smile. "Good morning, Sheriff."

He thought she looked tired. "Gooday, Mrs. Lawson, what can I do for you?"

"Is it true, Sheriff?" she asked, looking hopeful.

Looking puzzled, Seth asked, "Is what true, Mrs. Lawson?"

"You've arrested Pete Hoskins for killing Jacob Olson and my Tom."

He felt sorry for Gertie Lawson. What man wouldn't? It's a harsh land for a woman left alone with two children, and as he greeted her with a small, warm smile, he took the package she carried under one arm. "Here, Mrs. Lawson, let me help you with that."

She thanked him and, in the same breath, looking hopeful, asked, "Is it true, Mr. Bowlen?"

"Yes, Ma'am." He tucked the package under his arm. "But we still ain't got proof that he's the one that killed your Tom." Afraid she'd get her hopes up, he quickly added. "No one saw him, you understand. All we know is that Pete shot and killed Jacob Olson, and the rest has to be proven in a court of law."

Desperation joined the sadness on her tired face as she turned and looked up the street at the Sheriff's Office. "I understand, Sheriff." Then she looked at him with gratitude. "Just know'n you ain't forgotten about my Tom eases my pain."

Bowlen felt awkward as he smiled softly. "I ain't forgotten your husband, Mrs. Lawson, and I aim to see justice done."

Looking relieved, she smiled and let out a soft sigh. "God bless you for that, Seth Bowlen."

Feeling embarrassed by that, he cleared his throat. "How are things out at your place?"

Gertie's smile faded as she looked across the street at her two children waiting in the wagon in front of the general store. "Ain't gonna lie to you, Sheriff, things ain't easy for a woman alone with two small children."

"I'm sure it ain't."

A small, sudden breeze blew a thin strand of her hair across her face that she pushed aside with the fingers of one hand as she glanced at her children across the street. "I wrote to my younger brother back in Boston, asking him to come out. I got a letter from him yesterday saying he would come."

Seth felt relieved at hearing that. "I'm sure he'll be a comfort to you, Mrs. Lawson."

She forced a small smile. "Jake and I were always close." The smile faded. "Jake lost his wife and child during childbirth a few months back. I think it's a good thing for him to get away, and I can sure use the help of a man around the place."

"Sorry to hear about your brother's misfortune, Gertie, but as you say, it's probably a good thing for both of you that he's coming out here."

Wanting to get back to the jailhouse and see how Carl was getting along, he placed one hand on her frail arm. "Can I help you to your wagon?"

Looking grateful, she smiled. "No, Sheriff, I'm sure you're busy. I'll take my package and be on my way."

Bowlen handed her the package, smiled, and tipped his hat. "Have a nice day, Mrs. Lawson, and if there's anything I can do, don't hesitate to ask."

"Thank you, Sheriff, but we'll be just fine, and Jake will be here in a couple of weeks." Then with another small, grateful smile, she turned, stepped into the street, and walked toward her children waiting in the wagon outside Baker's General Store.

Seth felt sorry for Gertie Lawson as he watched her give the package to her son of twelve, gather her dress in her left hand, and climb up onto the wagon seat. Taking the reins to the team of horses, she backed the wagon into the street, and as she drove past, she glanced down at him with a small, appreciative smile.

Being filled with the hope that the courts would give her the justice and peace of mind she so desperately wanted, Seth tipped his hat and smiled as she drove by. He watched her until she disappeared around the corner, knowing that nothing would give her peace of mind for the murder of her husband. Feeling sorry for her and the children, he turned and walked toward the jailhouse.

Seth Bowlen was still thinking about Mrs. Lawson when he stepped onto the boardwalk in front of the empty building next to the jail, thinking it had been vacant for a long time. Reaching the door of the jailhouse, he knocked. "Open up, Carl, it's Seth." While waiting, he glanced around at the wagons and riders going up and down the street, eyeing each one, suspicious of anyone he didn't know or recognize.

Wondering what was keeping Carl, he knocked a little harder and then turned the doorknob, finding it locked. "Carl," he said in a louder voice. "Open up!" The moments passed, and getting worried, he walked to the big window, cupped his face with his hands against it, and looked inside. Seeing the door leading to the cells was partly open, he wondered if Carl was inside talking to the prisoners and tapped on the window. When Carl did not show, he started getting one of those funny feelings a person gets when things aren't exactly as they should be. He stepped away from the window, placed his right hand on the butt of his pistol, and hurried toward the small opening between the jail and the vacant building next door.

Thinking he'd try the back door, he hurried through the narrow opening to the rear of the jailhouse. Stopping, he peered around the corner of the building seeing Carl lying on his stomach, his pistol and hat on the ground nearby. Seth drew his Colt pistol wishing Wade was here. He cocked it and peered around the corner of the building at his deputy. Carl was lying on his stomach, facing away from him, but Seth could see blood on his collar and the back of his shirt and hoped Carl wasn't dead. He glanced around the yard, poked his head out far enough to see the back door to the jailhouse was ajar. Fearing the worst, he cautiously made his way to where Carl was lying, knelt, and felt Carl's neck.

Feeling a pulse, he picked up Carl's gun with his left hand, cocked it, and stood against the wall next to the open door. He took a quick look through the open doorway, down the short hall seeing the front window beyond his desk. Straining his ears for some sound inside and hearing nothing, he gave Carl another quick look, then quietly and cautiously, stepped inside. Rushing down the hall to the office, he stopped to peer around the wall into the main room. The door leading to the cells was open as he had seen from the front window earlier, and the big, round keyring of keys was missing from the peg. Knowing what he would find, he rushed to the door and looked inside at the empty cells with doors open. Cursing his bad luck, he kicked at the open cell door where Pete Hoskins should be locked up. He bent down and picked up the keyring, walked out of the cellblock, hung the keys on the wall, and hurried back to the hall and outside to Carl.

Bowlen knelt to one knee, helping Carl sit up against the side of the jailhouse. "You okay, Carl?" Seth asked, looking worried.

Carl was holding his head with both hands. "I think so." Then realizing what he had done, he looked at him ruefully. "Sure, sorry, Seth."

Both mad and worried about his deputy, Seth asked, "What the hell happened?"

Deputy McIver blinked several times with a dazed look as he touched the back of his head and then looked at his bloody hand. "We gotta get after 'em," he said as he tried to get up.

Seth gently pushed him back down. "You ain't going nowhere."

165

Still dazed, he looked at the sheriff. "I'm sure sorry, Seth."

Bowlen looked past the oak tree, north toward Harper, imagining both prisoners riding to freedom with George Hoskins and Jethro Reese. He couldn't help being angry with his deputy, but not knowing how badly he was injured, he didn't say anything. "It could've happened to anyone."

Carl knew better as he slowly stood with the help of Bowlen.

Seth reached over and picked up Carl's hat and help him inside to the cot. "I'll go get the doc."

While Doc Richards tended to Carl, Seth listened to his deputy tell him what had happened. As he listened, his anger returned, and he wondered how Carl could make such a foolish move with two prisoners inside and everyone else gone. Seth paced the floor too angry to sit, thinking Frank Wells would never have fallen for such a trick, nor would Wade. He thought of Gertie Lawson, and Jacob's wife, who also lost a daughter and grandchild because of Pete Hoskins. How was he going to face those poor women and tell them the man who killed their husband's had escaped?

A frustrated Bowlen sat down at his desk watching Doc Richards, who was in his early fifties, work on Carl. He turned to Seth. "I'd say Carl's got a mild concussion." Then he turned to Carl. "Be best if you came over to my place so I can stitch up that cut."

"Don't want no damn stitches," said Carl, looking irritated.

"That cut on your head will heal a lot faster," said Doc Richards, "and there's less chance of infection."

Carl looked at the Doc. "Don't care about that, I don't want to get stitched." He looked at Seth. "We gotta get after 'em, Seth."

Seth was clearly irritated. "Don't be a stubborn ass, Carl. Go with the doc and get that head taken care of."

Carl looked defeated. "All right, Seth." Then he slowly got up with the doc's help. "What about our prisoners?"

"Don't worry about that right now. Soon as you and Doc leave, I'm going to ride out to Sam Wheeler's place and get Wade."

Carl was leaning on the doctor. "He's gonna be madder than hell at me, ain't he, Seth."

Seth looked out the window at the building across the dirt street. "Probably so, Carl, but no more than me." He turned and looked at Carl feeling sorry for him. "But it will pass, as all things do. You go on and get over to the Doc's and let him take care of that head of yours."

Carl looked at Seth. "You and Wade gonna trail after Pete and Lee first to see which way they went?"

Seth frowned. "I already know where they're headed, Carl."

Figuring they headed straight for the Hoskins Ranch with twenty or so men, Carl looked like he was about to pass out, so he sat back down on his cot. "I don't feel so good."

"Of course not," replied Doc Richards. "You got hit pretty hard. Rest a minute, and then I'll help you up slowly, and we'll go to my office. After I've stitched you up, you can rest awhile, and then I'll see you get home."

Carl slowly stood. "I'm okay now."

Seth picked up his hat, followed them out the door, and after locking up, told both men to keep quiet about what had happened, and then he hurried to his place to get his horse.

Smoke lazily rose from the chimney into a calm, clear sky as Seth rode up to the Wheeler place. Seeing Wade and Sam Wheeler walk out of the barn, he pulled up at the corral and climbed down, looking mad.

Recognizing the face Seth wore, Wade asked, "What happened?"

Seth tied his horse to the corral. "Someone broke Lee Jones and Pete Hoskins out of jail while I was sending my telegram."

Sam Wheeler looked worried. "They escaped?"

"Shit," said Wade angrily. "Guess we all know who did it. How's Carl?"

"Bad bump on the head," said Seth. "But he'll be okay."

Wade looked puzzled. "How in the hell did anyone get close enough to hit Carl on the head?"

Deputy Lyle stepped from the house, holding a rifle across his belly and yelling, "Everything is all right, Sheriff?"

"Stay inside with Paul," yelled Seth. "I'll be there in a minute or two!" He watched Lyle go into the house, and then he told Wade and Sam about Carl's carelessness at seeing someone lying behind the jail. "When he went outside, he got hit over the head." Then he told of the boot prints and horse tracks he found in back of the jail. "Looked like six or seven men."

167

Wade took off his black, wide-brimmed hat and slapped it against his right leg in anger. "Son of a bitch!" Then thinking of the deputy, he looked at Seth. "Carl gonna be okay?"

"Doc says he has a concussion, but he's gonna be fine."

Wheeler looked worried. "Think they'll be coming here?"

Bowlen quickly shook his head. "I doubt that, Mr. Wheeler. They're halfway to Harper or the Hoskins' Ranch by now." Then he looked at the house. "How's Leonard holding up?"

Wade glanced at the house. "He ain't much of a farmhand." Then he looked at Seth. "Get'n Pete and the deputy back ain't gonna be easy."

Bowlen looked distraught. "You ain't telling me nothing I don't already know."

Wade turned and walked toward the barn, talking over his shoulder. "I'll get my horse." As he walked, he lowered his voice so no one could hear. "And I hope we don't get ourselves killed in the process."

Seth turned to Sam Wheeler. "I'll leave Deputy Lyle here. He's a good man."

Wheeler looked relieved. "We'll be alright, Sheriff. Just bring the bastards back."

Seth started toward the house, imagining what Paul Leonard would have to say about all this. "Guess I best go tell Lyle what happened."

Carl was sitting on one of the chairs on the boardwalk outside the sheriff's office with his head bandaged when Wade and Seth rode up. He stood, looking sheepish, and waited until they dismounted and tied their horses to the railing before asking, "We going after 'em, Seth?"

"We'll talk on that," Seth said as he and Wade walked up the steps. Seth unlocked the door and stepped inside, followed by Wade and then Carl. Bowlen headed for the gun rack behind his desk, talking over his shoulder. "Me and Wade are heading up to Harper, Carl. You're staying here." Seth pulled a Winchester from the rack, opened the cabinet next to the gun rack, took out a box of shells, and began loading the Winchester. Without looking up, he asked Wade, "You have that Sharps with you?"

"It's on my horse."

With the Winchester loaded, Seth cradled it in his left arm and looked at his sorrowful deputy. "Don't know how long this is gonna take."

Carl nodded his understanding in silence, looking sorry about what happened. "Where's Lyle?"

"At the Wheeler's," answered Seth as he glanced out the window at Molly's. "I'm going over to tell Molly that Wade and I are leaving town, and I'm going to have to tell her why." He looked at his sorrowful deputy. "News is gonna get out real soon about this, and folks will be coming around asking questions." Seth grinned wryly at Carl. "Your punishment is having to tell them."

Carl wasn't too happy about that but knew he deserved the punishment.

Bowlen and Wade started toward the door, but Seth stopped and turned to Carl. "If Gertie Lawson comes by, tell her I aim to keep my word. She'll know what that means." He paused, looking at Carl. "Tomorrow, I want you to head out to the Wheeler place for a couple of days and let Lyle stay close to home. You two can switch off until me and Wade return."

Twenty

Harper, Colorado

It was early evening when Wade and Seth pulled their horses up at the top of the hill overlooking Harper, Colorado. In the stillness of the plains, Wade's saddle creaked as he turned and glanced to the west, wishing the sun that hung above the peaks of the Rocky Mountains would hurry.

Seth's saddle creaked as he turned and glanced back toward Sisters along the narrow stage trail disappearing into the twilight. Turning back to look at Harper in the distance in front of them, Seth saw a rider galloping toward them. "Someone's coming."

The lone rider rode as if trying to outrun the sunset-colored dust thrown up by his horse.

Seth's hand went to the butt of his pistol on instinct.

Wade took the long glass out of his saddlebag, pulled it apart, and stood in the stirrups, and put it to his eye. "Looks like Harry Block," he said curiously.

"What the hell could be chasing Harry out of Harper?"

Wade took the glass away from his eye, pushed it together, and settled back in his saddle. "Good question. I wonder where he's heading in such a hurry?"

Seth held out his left hand for the long glass. "Let me take a look." Taking the glass, he put it to his good eye and looked through it for several moments in silence. Handing the long glass to Wade, Seth, "I don't know. But something's wrong."

Wade put the glass back into his saddlebag and watched the rider. "Guess we'll find out shortly. Let's go meet Harry." They nudged their horses into a gallop toward Harry Block as he raced toward them, leaving a cloud of dust behind him.

Harry waved frantically, yelling something that neither Wade nor Seth could plainly understand. They pulled up to wait for Harry, and as he tried to stop, he couldn't control the animal he was riding. It suddenly turned and bucked a couple of times, looking as if Harry might get thrown. He gripped the reins with both hands, fighting to control his horse while yelling, "Jasper Talbert's dead!"

Wade looked surprised as he watched Harry and his horse go past. "Jasper's dead?"

The horse settled down, and Harry turned him toward Wade. "That's right." Then with a sad look, he told Wade about the wagon rolling over while they were heading home from Harper that morning and that Sarah and his son were badly hurt.

Wade spurred his mare into a run and rode toward the Double J Ranch.

Harry's horse jerked once more and neighed, but he kept the animal under control and yelled after him. "Doc Granger's with them."

Seth looked at Harry. "You got control of that damn horse yet?"

Harry shook his head, looking irritated at the animal. "I just may shoot the bastard and ride back with you."

"Not today, Harry." Then Seth spurred his horse and rode after Wade leaving Harry to his mischievous horse.

Double J Ranch

Sarah slowly opened her eyes to a blurry image sitting in a chair next to her bed. As her eyes cleared, they welled with tears. "Wade?" she said softly as she began to cry.

Wade slid out of the chair, knelt beside the bed, took her hand, and gently kissed it. "Rest easy, Sarah."

Trying to get up, she whispered, "Emmett?"

"Emmett's gonna be fine," said Wade as he gently pushed her back onto the pillow. "His leg's broken, and he has a good bump on the head, but Doc Granger says he'll mend just fine. He gave him something to make him sleep. Your Ma's with him." He smiled tenderly as his fingers gently moved a strand of her hair away from the bandage on her forehead. "You've seven stitches in your forehead, and you dislocated your left shoulder, but you'll heal in no time."

Tears flowed down her cheeks. "Pa's dead, Wade."

"I know," Looking sorry, he leaned closer. "Can you tell me what happened?"

"My head and shoulder hurt something awful."

"Try not to move around. Doc says you need to rest."

She licked her lips, looking tired. "I'm thirsty."

Wade poured a glass of water from the pitcher on the nightstand and helped her take a small sip. As she swallowed, he set the glass on the table, sat back down in the chair next to the bed, and took her hand.

She looked frightened. "Don't leave."

"I'm not going anywhere. I'll sit here and watch you sleep."

"No," she said, squeezing his hand. "Lay with me, Wade. I'm afraid."

"No need to be afraid, Sarah." He stood from the chair carefully, sat on the edge of the bed, and smiled reassuringly. "You're gonna be all right, and so's Emmett."

She managed a small smile. "I'm so glad you're here. Promise me you won't go."

"I promise. Now rest, please."

"Lay down beside me," she said as she pulled at his arm, and as he lay down next to her, she closed her eyes, only to open them a few moments later to see if he was still with her.

Wade smiled and gently stroked the side of her head. "I'm right here, Sarah."

She closed her eyes and calmly drifted off into a restless sleep.

He looked at her bruised face and bandaged shoulder that held her arm securely against her body. Thinking that he came close to losing both her and their son and suspecting she may be pregnant, he worried about the unborn child. The minutes passed, and as the day settled in on him, he carefully got up, turned down the kerosene lamp, and watched her sleep for several more minutes. Looking at the closed door, he thought of their son across the hall, his leg broken, and the bandage on his head covering four stitches. Knowing that Mrs. Talbert was at Emmett's side gave him comfort, but he knew she was also grieving for her husband.

Sarah let out a small whimper, and her breathing became fast and shallow, so he sat back down in the chair and gently stroked the side of her head, wondering if he should get Doc Granger. He wanted to know what happened, but the only two people that could tell him were Sarah and Emmett, and neither would be able to tell him for some time. Feeling the weight of the day, his eyes grew heavy, and not wanting to sleep, he quietly got up.

He stood beside the bed for several moments, watching her sleep and thinking she looked peaceful. He quietly left the room and walked across the hall to Emmett's room. Slowly and quietly, he opened the door and stuck his head in, just enough to see Mrs. Janice Talbert sitting in an overstuffed chair next to Emmett's bed. Wade thought she was asleep and started to close the door when she turned and motioned with her hand to wait. Mrs. Talbert quietly got up, and as she stepped away from Emmett's bed, she motioned Wade inside. Stepping into the room, he closed the door, thinking she looked tired, knowing Jasper's death weighed heavily on her. Her black and gray hair, which she usually wore in a braid around her head or a bun, hung loosely down her back, past her waist, which surprised Wade. Wiping the tears from her dark, sunken eyes with a hanky, she managed a small smile as she put her arms around him. Neither spoke as they embraced.

Wade wanted to say something about how sorry he was about Jasper, but he knew words were empty, so he just held her and tried to comfort her.

She stepped back and looked across the room at her grandson and whispered, "Emmett's resting."

Wade looked past her to his son. "Has he been awake any?"

"Off and on," she whispered as she took his hand and led him back to Emmett's bed, where she bent down and gently touched the boy's head with her hand. "Still no fever," she whispered, sounding relieved. Then she turned, letting go of his hand. "Doc Granger says that's a good sign."

"He's young," Wade whispered. "Doc says he'll mend quickly."

She sat down in the overstuffed chair and looked down at the crumpled wet hanky she held.

Even in the dim light, he could see the sorrow in her eyes.

She looked up. "I'm so glad you happened to come back." Then she looked down at the wet, crumpled hanky she held. "I don't know what we'd have done without you here." Then she looked up with a worried face. "Do you think Sarah will be all right?"

He smiled reassuringly. "She'll be fine, Mrs. Talbert." Then he looked at his son. "Same as Emmett." He paused then quickly added, "Providing no complications come about." Wade gently put one hand on her shoulder. "Does anyone know what happened?"

She looked up, appearing helpless, and then looked at the hanky she unfolded and refolded. "All we know is the wagon tipped over." She put the hanky to her face, quickly turned away, and sobbed for a moment, and then she looked down at her hands and the hanky she held. "They said it looked like Jasper was driving awful fast."

Wade thought on that for a moment, wondering why Jasper would be driving so fast that he'd lose control of the team and wagon.

Mrs. Talbert looked up questioningly. "Do you think a snake could have spooked the team?"

"Maybe," he said thoughtfully. "We won't know until Sarah can talk."

She put one hand on his that was resting on her shoulder, patted it, and then stood to adjust the covers Emmett had kicked off. As she sat down and watched her grandson sleep, she said, "He's so innocent." The room filled with a heavy silence as she watched her grandson sleeping. Her face bore the sorrow she felt for her husband. "Jasper's dead, Wade. What am I going to do?"

Wade could find no words of comfort for her as he gently patted her shoulder, wishing that he could say something that would ease her sorrow.

She wiped the tears from her face and eyes with the already wet hanky and looked up. "Doc Granger's going to spend the night so that he can check on Sarah and Emmett during the night."

"That's good."

She smiled. "You go on now downstairs with the other men. I'll stay with my grandson."

He bent down, kissed the top of her head, and whispered, "I'm going to go talk with Doc Granger."

She patted him on the hand. "Please give the others my apologies for being a poor hostess."

He smiled warmly. "I'm sure they understand, Mrs. Talbert. You look like you could use some rest."

"I'll sleep in this chair for the night. Emmett may need me."

He smiled at her. "I'll check in on you later."

As he started to turn, she grabbed his hand. "I need to ask a favor."

He looked into her grieving eyes. "Sure thing, Mrs. Talbert."

"My Jasper needs to be taken to the mortician in Harper first thing in the morning. I'd be ever beholding if you would take care of that for me."

"I'd be honored."

"He always liked you." She said. "I don't want him buried in that cemetery in town." Then she looked at the open window into the black of night. "There's a nice spot under that big oak tree, at the bottom of the hill, away from the house that overlooks the ranch. He always liked sitting under it with Willie in the evenings." She smiled in memory. "Jasper would sit against the tree, smoking his pipe, with his hand on Willie lying next to him." Suddenly, she stopped talking, looked down at her hands, and then back at the window, as she spoke in a choked voice. "The tree will give shade in the summer, and its leaves, warmth in the fall and winter." Then she looked at Wade and smiled. "Jasper will be happy there."

"I'll see to it, Mrs. Talbert."

Looking tired, she turned in the chair, rested her head against its back, and watched her grandson as Wade quietly left the room.

Wade paused at Sarah's room, quietly opened the door, and looked inside. Seeing that she was sleeping peacefully, he closed the door and walked toward the staircase, greeted by mumbled voices from the living room below. Pausing, he looked down at Tolliver Grimes, saying something Wade could not hear from this distance. Doc Granger, Seth, and Harry Block were sitting in separate chairs, listening.

Grimes looked up as Wade started down the stairs, stood, and walked to the bottom of the staircase. As Wade stepped from the last stair, Tolliver asked, "How's Sarah and the boy?"

Wade's face filled held concern. "As good as can be expected." Then he looked at Doc Granger. "Mrs. Talbert says you're spending the night."

Doctor Samuel Granger was a man in his late fifties, short and heavyset, with gray hair, bushy eyebrows, and blue eyes. He smiled a soft, comforting smile as he looked at Wade. "Under the circumstances, I believe it best that I stay close for at least twenty-four hours. After that, they both should be out of any danger."

"Danger from what?" asked Wade, looking worried.

"Head injuries are always a danger," said the Doc. "And should be checked on every couple of hours."

"I just left her," said Wade, "she's resting comfortably."

Granger nodded. "I gave her a little laudanum for the pain, so she'll sleep for a spell. Same with Emmett."

"Mrs. Talbert," began Wade, "says Emmett wakes up once in a while, and he ain't got any fever."

"No fever's a good sign," offered Granger. "As far as waking up, he'll drift in and out for a while yet. That boy took a damn hard knock on the head, and so did your Sarah."

Seeing the worry on Wade's face, Doc Granger stood, walked the short distance to his side, and put one hand on his shoulder. "They'll both be fine, son. They're strong and healthy, and you'll not lose them over this."

Wade smiled, looking relieved, and thought about the baby but didn't want to ask in front of the others.

"Sorry about Jasper," said Harry Block.

Wade glanced at Harry and nodded, looking appreciative.

Seth and Wade exchanged quick looks. Seth knew the moment was beyond any words he had to offer, and he was certain Wade already knew how he felt.

Feeling awkward, Wade let out a soft sigh. "I could use a drink." Then he walked across the room toward the liquor cabinet in Jasper's study. Pulling the cork out of a bottle of Jasper's fine brandy, he poured some in a shot glass and gulped it down. He looked back at the others.

"I'm sure we could all use a drink. Why don't you boys come in here and pour yourself a drink?"

While the others poured their drinks, Wade walked back into the living room to the open front door and leaned against its frame, staring out into the warm night. As the sounds of tinkling glass made their way from the study, he stared into the darkness, thinking of Sarah, their unborn child, and little Emmett. Night noises of crickets and owls filled the silence left by the absence of tinkling glass as his thoughts went upstairs to Sarah and their son. Then he thought of Jasper Talbert lying upstairs in one of the spare rooms, covered by a sheet, waiting to be taken to the mortician.

Taking a sip of brandy, he recalled the words of Mrs. Talbert when she asked, "What am I going to do?" Feeling pity for her, he took another drink, looked into the black night, and listened to the mumbled voices of the men in the room behind him reclaiming their seats.

Tolliver Grimes stood next to Wade, put one hand on his shoulder, and smiled softly. "Your wife and boy are gonna be okay, son."

Wade looked at him with hope, took a small drink of brandy, and turned to stare into the night, imagining the accident. "I sure would like to know what the hell happened out there. It ain't like Jasper to ride a team so hard he'd lose control of a wagon with his daughter and grandson riding with him."

"That's a mystery, alright," said Grimes thoughtfully. Then he turned toward the living room and gently tugged at his shoulder. "Come back in and sit down. We won't know anything until Sarah's well enough to tell us what happened."

Wade downed his drink, turned from the night, and followed Tolliver into the living room, but kept walking into the study. He poured another drink, then returned to the living room with the bottle setting it on the coffee table in front of the sofa. He took a seat next to Seth and looked at Doc Granger, sitting across from him. "Mrs. Talbert asked me to take Jasper into Harper in the morning and make the arrangements."

Granger grimaced and gestured with his empty hand. "I'll come along. After we drop Jasper off at Perkins Mortuary, we'll go see preacher Jonas Drake about burying Jasper in the Harper Cemetery, behind the church."

Wade shook his head in disagreement. "That ain't gonna happen, Doc. Mrs. Talbert wants her husband buried here on the ranch."

The doctor gave a quick, thoughtful nod. "Probably just as well. The cemetery's a long way from the ranch, and I'm certain Janice and Sarah will find some comfort with Jasper resting nearby."

The men talked until Doc Granger admitted to being tired, said his goodnights, and went upstairs to check on Sarah and Emmett before retiring to one of the guest rooms. After a few minutes, Harry Block stood, saying he had better head for home, as did Tolliver Grimes.

Wade looked at Block. "I'm curious about something, Harry. In all the excitement, I forgot to ask. How did you know we were on the road from Sisters?"

Harry glanced at Seth and shrugged. "I told Seth earlier that as soon as I helped Doc hitch up his buggy so he could come out here, I sent a telegraph to you in Sisters saying I'd wait for a reply. Deputy C. McIver answered a little while later, saying the two of you were on your way to Harper. So, I decided I'd ride out and give you the bad news in person."

"And now the whole town, including old man Hoskins, knows we're in Harper," added Seth, looking disappointed.

Wade looked at Bowlen. "Don't matter none at this point, Seth. I'm sure they knew we'd be coming anyways." He looked at Harry Block. "You did the right thing, Harry, and I'm obliged."

Harry smiled then looked at Tolliver. "You ready?"

Seth stood, shook both their hands, said goodnight, and sat back down in his chair while Wade walked Tolliver and Harry to the front door. After shaking their hands and saying goodnight, Wade watched them climb onto their horses, and as they rode away, he contemplated the accident. As the sound of their horses faded, he closed and locked the door, then walked back into the living room, telling Seth he'd show him to his room.

Wade turned all the lamps out, but one he carried upstairs to a spare bedroom for Seth. They said goodnight, and then Wade quietly slipped into Emmett's room, finding Mrs. Talbert asleep and resting peacefully. He quietly closed the door and looked at the door where the body of Mr. Talbert lay under a sheet.

A door opened, and Doc Samuel Granger poked his head out of his room and whispered, "Got a minute Wade?"

Fearful and curious about what the doctor wanted, Wade entered his room, seeing the bed hadn't been turned down, and the doctor was still dressed. Granger looked worried as he walked to the bed and sat down, offering him the only chair. "There's a couple of things I have to tell you that I haven't told anyone else."

Becoming curious, Wade sat down and looked at Doc Granger, anticipating bad news.

Doc Granger's face filled with a frown as he stared down at the floor before he looked up. "Jasper Talbert was shot in the back."

Wade sat forward, looking surprised. "Who would shoot Jasper in the back?"

Granger reached into his vest pocket and handed Wade a mangled bullet. "I dug that out of Jasper."

Wade examined it. "Looks like a Winchester."

Doc had a worried face, looking like he carried an awful secret. "It looked like the wagon wheels had run over him. Several ribs were broken, his left shoulder and left forearm both broken with each having pieces of bone sticking out of his dirty and bloody skin." Doc Granger shook his head. "Jasper was a mess." The doctor paused for a moment. "I was a battlefield surgeon during the war between the states and saw plenty of mutilated and mangled bodies, so I have a trained eye for seeing things most other people would miss."

Wade sat back in his chair, looking puzzled. "Why didn't you say something?"

Doc Granger looked regretful as he gestured with both hands. "Scared to, I guess."

"Why?" asked Wade.

"The day of the accident, Sheriff Booth Fox and Jasper got into one heck of an argument in front of Mason's Store that came to blows."

Surprised that Jasper would be in a fistfight, Wade leaned forward in his chair. "An argument over what?"

Granger shrugged. "Don't know exactly. The only one that does for sure is lying in bed with a pretty good bump on her head. But whatever it was about, I heard that Jasper jumped clean off the wagon and pulled the sheriff off his horse."

Wade frowned, looking curious. "What would make Jasper Talbert so angry that he'd attack the sheriff?"

"Don't know," said Doc Granger, "but it took Ed Mason and a farmer by the name of Jed Brown to pull Jasper off Booth Fox."

He considered all that Doc Granger had said as he looked at the bullet he held and then at the closed door thinking of Sarah. "Guess I'll have to ask Sarah when she's up to it."

"I've seen a lot of head injuries," said the doctor with an uncertain face. "And that wife of yours has a bad one. The mind's a funny thing and does things the way it wants. I've seen people with complete memory loss lasting days, weeks, even months."

Wade looked at the doctor. "You telling me we may never know what happened?"

The doctor nodded. "I'm just telling you that she may not wake up tomorrow and start telling you what happened. It may take a few days. Just be patient with her."

Wade nodded thoughtfully. "I will, Doc. What about her shoulder?"

"Shoulder's fine, but it'll be sore for a few more days." Doc Granger had an uncomfortable look as he got up and stood by Wade's chair. "There's something else you need to know, son."

Wade looked up, fearing what the Doc was about to tell him.

"Your wife lost the child she was carrying."

Wade slumped a bit in the chair and looked at the floor. "Does Sarah know?"

"I believe so. I told her, but she was in a lot of pain at the time. Lucky for her, she wasn't that far along." He paused, adding, "Be best if she spent a few days in bed."

"I know Sarah, and she won't miss Jasper's funeral."

Doc Granger chuckled. "Probably not, just keep an eye on her. If she starts bleeding, get her into bed and fetch me if I ain't here for the funeral."

Wade looked puzzled. "Bleeding from what?"

Granger looked at him. "She just lost a child."

Wade looked thoughtful. "Alright, Doc, I will." Wade paused a long moment, then looked at Doc. "What was it?"

"It was too early to tell."

"Does Mrs. Talbert know?"

Doc Granger shook his head. "Not under the circumstances. I thought it best not to tell Mrs. Talbert with the loss of Jasper and all."

Wade had been thinking about the fight between Jasper and the sheriff when he looked up. "Do you think Sheriff Booth Fox is the kind of man that would shoot Jasper in the back, causing the accident?"

The doctor shrugged and returned to the edge of the bed. "Don't know, and I ain't about to speculate." He looked at Wade. "You asked why I never said anything. Well, with all things considered, who the hell was I going to report this to?"

Wade considered that. "I see your point, Doc."

"When you showed up and being a Deputy US Marshal, I figured I'd tell you when the time was right and let you handle it the way you see fit."

Wade looked thoughtful. "It might be best if we continue to let this be our little secret for a few days, Doc. No sense adding any more to Sarah and her mother's grieving right now."

Granger's face turned sad. "Well, I couldn't bring myself to tell Mrs. Talbert."

Wade stood and extended his hand. "You did the right thing, Doc. I'll tell both Mrs. Talbert and Sarah when the time's right."

Doc Granger raised his brow, looking unsure as they shook hands. "I sure hope I did." He followed Wade to the door, and before he opened it, he asked, "Can I ask what you plan on doing about this?"

Wade quickly considered the question as he looked down at the bullet. "Not rightly sure at this point, Doc. I need to get the family past the funeral and the next few days before I consider what to do." His mind went to the warrant he was still carrying for Booth Fox and saw no sense in burdening the doctor with that information.

Doc Granger sighed. "Maybe I'll sleep a little easier tonight."

Wade looked troubled. "Well, Doc, I'm sure you'll sleep better than I will." He said goodnight, slipped the bullet into his pocket and stepped out of the room. He walked down the hall to where Sarah was sleeping, considering all that Doc Granger had told him. Pausing at her door, he glanced at the door to Emmett's room, hoping his son would be alright as Doc had promised. Wade opened the door to his and Sarah's room and stepped into the dim room filled with soft shadows from the single lantern on the small table next to the bed. Pausing a moment while looking at his wife, he quietly walked to her bedside and looked down at her. Wondering what Booth Fox had done that would have infuriated her pa, Wade took the extra pillow from the bed, picked up the lamp, and walked to a small sofa near the window. After tossing the pillow on the sofa, he set the lamp down on a small table, lay down, and watched Sarah sleeping until he fell asleep.

The smell of fresh coffee and bacon frying filled the air as Wade walked down the stairs into the dining room, finding the table set and ready for breakfast. Walking past the table into the kitchen, he was surprised at finding Mrs. Talbert busy over the stove frying bacon. She looked up from the stove, smiled warmly, and told him to sit down at the small kitchen table where Jasper always had his first cup of coffee. He did as told, and she quickly poured him a cup of coffee and returned to the bacon.

He thanked her and took a small drink of hot coffee, thinking it tasted good. As he watched her, she no longer looked tired but peaceful as if she had come to terms with life. "I checked in on Emmett before I came downstairs," he said. "Looks like he had a good night."

"He did," she said. "Only woke up a few times but always went right back to sleep. Doc Granger even came in a couple of times. He said you were sleeping on the sofa and that Sarah was resting peacefully."

Wade thought about the doctor coming into the bedroom and wondered why he never woke up. Doc Granger was either awful quiet or himself very tired.

She put the fried bacon into a metal pan and bent down, putting the pan into the oven to keep it warm. Standing upright, she turned to him, "Take that coffee pot into the dining room for me, Wade, please, and set it on the table. And then go upstairs and fetch that friend of yours and Doc Granger."

After breakfast, Wade hitched up the wagon, drove it to the front door. Then he, Seth, and Doc Granger carried Jasper's covered body downstairs and outside to the waiting wagon under the watchful, teary eyes of Mrs. Talbert. Seth asked Wade if he wanted him to tag along, but Wade shook his head no, telling him that he'd appreciate his staying close to the house. Seth said he would and walked up the steps to the porch where he stood next to Mrs. Talbert. Wade looked at Bowlen with a worried face. "Stay close, Seth."

Bowlen watched Wade and the buggy head for Harper and the Undertaker. He put his arm around Janice, feeling sorry for her loss. Wishing he could say something that would bring her peace, she wiped her eyes with her apron, then turned and walked into the house.

After the door closed, Seth thought about how Wade looked at him when he told him to stay close. He turned and walked to the door, paused and took a good glance around, then stepped into the house and up the stairs to get his gun before he checked on his horse in the barn.

Twenty-One

The Funeral of Jasper Talbert

Four days after the accident, a gathering of friends and neighbors stood under the oak tree next to Jasper's pine coffin, resting on two boards spanning the grave's width. An elderly preacher by the name of Jonas Drake dressed in a black suit and tieless, white shirt buttoned to the collar stood at the head of the grave. He had a long, thin, somber, clean-shaven face, and his thinning, gray hair fluttered in the slight breeze. His soft but powerful voice read the words printed on the flimsy paper of the Bible he held. The gentle breeze played in the leaves of the oak tree above the grave, accompanied by chirping birds that seemed happy on a day of sadness.

Wade stood behind Sarah with his hands gently on her shoulders as she sat on a wooden, high-back chair next to her mother. Sarah and her mother held one another's hand, their free hand holding white hankies on their laps, already damp from tears. As the words of the Bible flowed from the preacher's mouth, Wade stared into the distance at the Rocky Mountains as his thoughts found his son lying in bed, his leg broken, and his head bandaged. He looked down at his wife, Mrs. Talbert, at Seth, and finally, the pine coffin holding Jasper's broken body, wondering if Booth Fox was responsible.

"Amen," said the preacher

Wade looked from the Rocky Mountains to the pine casket hearing the silence that seemed everywhere as he, Tolliver Grimes, Harry Block,

184

and Seth Bowlen walked to the edge of the grave and the pine coffin. Wade and Tolliver bent down, picked up two ropes, and handed the other ends to Seth and Harry Block. Then, as if rehearsed, they slid the ropes under the ends of the coffin and lifted it so the two wooden planks could be pulled from under it.

Everyone was standing with heads bowed, looking solemn as wives held onto their husband's arms while small sobs mixed with the sound of the lowering of Jasper Talbert's casket. Janice stood at the edge of the grave and looked down at the coffin that held her dear, dead husband. Sarah put one arm around her mother and gently moved her back as shovels of dirt were tossed into the open grave, sending back lonely, thunderous echoes that seemed so final to Janice Talbert.

Food to Ease the Sorrow

As is the custom, neighbors, friends, and ranch hands gathered on the front porch, in the yard, and inside the main house to talk of Jasper's life. While the women went about the business of food, several ranch hands gathered chairs and placed them around the yard so people would have a place to sit and eat.

Janice Talbert made it a point to visit and thank each person for coming to Jasper's funeral, making sure they partook in the food. Wanting to keep busy, Sarah fixed a plate of food for Emmett, who was now awake and complaining about everything. While she took the plate upstairs to her son, Wade fixed himself a plate and went outside to look for a lonely spot away from all the noise and talking. After a few minutes of searching, he found a flat rock to sit on beneath a tall cottonwood, a reasonable distance from the house and the others where the air carried the sweet smell of Lilacs.

It wasn't long before Seth found him. "Wondered where you were."

Wade looked up and pointed to a nearby stump. "Have a seat."

Seth sat down, careful not to spill his food or coffee. After setting his cup on the ground next to him, he shoved a fork filled with fried potatoes into his mouth. "Sarah looks a mite tired."

Wade looked concerned. "I tried to get her to go up and rest." He played in his potatoes with his fork the way a child does when not hungry. "But she'd have none of it." He watched the fork move through the potatoes and chuckled with a little humor. "She sure is stubborn."

"Most of 'em are," grinned Seth, and then he took a bite of food.

Wade smiled and nodded in agreement as he shoved a fork of food into his mouth. He glanced at Seth, thinking he should tell him of his and Doc Granger's talk the night before. Deciding to let it be, for now, thinking he was hungrier than he realized.

The late afternoon sun hung low above the mountains as the women who had helped with the preparing and serving the food finished washing the dishes. Friends and neighbors gave their condolences to the family, and as they left, Wade stood by the front door, thanking each one for their kindness.

After the last of them had gone, Wade walked into the study to the liquor cabinet, poured a glass of Jasper's favorite Tennessee Bourbon, raised the glass in a toast toward the oak tree where Willie the dog lay on fresh dirt and took a drink. He took another swallow and looked around the room of empty chairs and sofa, then walked into the living room, finding another room of empty chairs. The piano sat smugly in one corner, and the paintings of faraway cities and landscapes that were unfamiliar to him hung on the walls. Stillness held the room as his eyes went to the stairs and then the second floor's railing. And as he took a drink of bourbon, he wondered where Seth might be. Imagining Janice Talbert upstairs with Emmett, he was glad that Sarah had decided to retire early. He took another drink and headed for the front porch, where he could watch the last of the day quietly go.

Walking out the front door into a warm, peaceful evening, he paused at the porch railing by the steps, leaned against the porch post, and took a drink of bourbon. Looking to the west, he watched the sun fight to give up the day as it slowly slid behind the mountains. As far as he could see, the landscape of rolling hills and prairie grass carried the soft, reddish-orange colors of sunset. A coyote somewhere in the distance broke the quiet stillness as it hunted for its dinner, and a hawk high above him screeched as it headed home to its chicks.

"Always seems deathly quiet the evening after a burial," said Seth from a chair in the far corner of the porch.

Startled, Wade turned, seeing Seth sitting in one of the white, wooden chairs with his feet resting on the porch railing. "Seems like," replied Wade as he turned back to the scene of tall, dark mountain peaks. A scattering of clouds hanging above the peaks took on the sunset colors of red, pink, and orange. Night and its darkness were not far away, he thought as he sipped his drink. Without turning away from the scene, he asked, "You have anything planned for tomorrow?"

Thinking it was a strange thing to ask, Seth took his boots from the railing, got up, walked across the porch of moaning boards, and stood next to Wade. He leaned against the other side of the same post and stared at the mountains, getting dim now that the sun was gone. "If you don't mind, I'd like to get back to why we came here."

Wade took a drink of bourbon, deciding that it was the time for him and Seth to have their talk. "Doc Granger called me into his room the night before we took Jasper to the mortician."

Seth turned to Wade, filled with curiosity.

Wade glanced back at the open front door and then at the porch ceiling, remembering that all the windows upstairs were open, and pointed toward the yard. "Let's take a walk."

Bowlen followed, and after they had walked a good distance, Wade stopped, drank the last of his bourbon, and told Seth everything that Doc Granger had told him, including the part about the baby.

"Sorry about the baby," said Seth as he stared at the tiny line of what remained of the day above the jagged peaks. Having heard about the fight between Jasper and Booth, he looked at Wade. "You thinking Booth Fox killed Jasper?"

"I do. Can't prove it, but I sure as hell do."

A moment passed before he recalled Wade's earlier question. "You have something in mind for tomorrow?"

Wade nodded. "I do."

"Mind telling me what it is?"

Wade looked into Seth's good eye. "We're paying Sheriff Booth Fox a visit."

Seth thought on that as he looked at Wade, hoping he wasn't thinking of revenge. "We arresting him?"

Wade nodded, patted him on the back, and smiled. "We are. I'm going upstairs. Mind locking up before you turn in?"

Seth said he would and watched Wade walk across the yard, up the porch's stairs, and into the house. After the door closed, Seth turned to the mountains now hidden in the darkness of the night sky filled with stars and worried about Wade as he pondered what might go wrong tomorrow.

Dressed in a yellow nightgown covered by a white robe, Sarah was sitting on the small sofa in the dark when Wade stepped into their bedroom. "I'm here," she said softly.

He paused to look at her sitting on the sofa in the dim light of dusk and shut the door. "How are you feeling?"

"Better," she said with a smile. When Wade got to the sofa and sat down next to her, she took his hand. "My shoulder is still sore, but I'm thankful to have that awful wrap and sling over with."

He glanced around. "Why are you sitting in the dark?"

She looked down at their hands, put her other hand over them, and turned to the window. "I have to tell you something."

Anticipating what she was going to say, he told her that Doc Granger already told him about the baby. "I'm so sorry, Sarah. I know you wanted this baby."

She nodded several times and wiped her eyes as she began to sob. "Yes, I did."

Wade sat quietly on the sofa next to her, feeling useless as he wondered what a man could say to a woman that just lost her child.

"Have you checked on Emmett?" she asked, wanting to think about something other than the baby.

"Your mother is with him, and he's sleeping." He glanced around the dim room and started to get up. "I'll light a lamp."

She pulled him back onto the sofa. "Don't."

"Are you sure you're all right?"

She nodded as he smiled at her. "I'm fine."

As the room fell silent, Wade settled back on the sofa. "Doc Granger said he'd stop by in a day or two and check on you and Emmett."

She smiled, looking thankful, but her eyes began to well with tears once again, so she turned away.

"Emmett's gonna be all right, Sarah," he reassured her.

188

"It ain't Emmett I cry for, Wade. It's our baby, and my pa I cry for."

He put one hand on her shoulder. "Do you remember anything about the accident?"

"A little," she said, wiping the tears from her eyes and face with a damp, crumpled up hanky.

"Tell me what you do remember."

She looked down at the hanky, barely visible in the darkness. "I've had so many bad dreams. It's hard to tell what's real and what isn't."

Thinking of his own dreams that haunted him when he returned from Mexico and remembering Doc Granger's advice, he sat quietly and let her think about it.

She stared down at her hands in the dim light of the room. "I remember the wagon was swaying this way and that, and I feared for Emmett." She looked at Wade's face in the darkness. "I remember yelling at pa to be careful." She paused to wipe her eyes once more, looking regretful. "I can't remember anything else."

He smiled and squeezed her hand gently. "Take your time, Sarah. Doc says you may not remember for a spell yet."

She became flustered. "I'm trying to remember, but I can't."

"I know you are." Then he thought that if he told her about Jasper, she might remember. Holding her hands tighter in his, he looked into her eyes, hoping he was doing the right thing. "I have something that I need to tell you about the accident."

She looked into his eyes. "What is it?"

"Doc Granger says that Jasper was shot in the back."

She pulled her hands away from his, looking terrified. "That can't be," she said. "Doc Granger must be wrong."

"He's not wrong, Sarah."

She turned to the window and the darkness outside, trying to remember that day. Flashes of this or that spilled through her mind, but they were all jumbled up and out of order. She turned to him. "Who would hate my father enough to shoot him in the back while he was with his grandson and me?"

"That's what I'm trying to find out. That is why I need to know what happened that day."

189

Looking flustered, she shrugged and gestured with her hands. "I can't remember, Wade. And now you say that papa was shot, and I don't remember why, or by who." Her eyes welled, and her forehead furrowed. "How can that be?"

Wondering if he had done the right thing, he put his arm around her. "I'm sorry, Sarah. I didn't mean to upset you. I just thought that if you knew the truth about your pa, you might remember more."

"I know," she said in an understanding voice while wiping her tears with the crumpled hanky. "But I just can't remember."

He knew she must be exhausted. "Maybe what you need is a good night's sleep."

"Maybe," she said, admitting she was tired.

Wade helped her up and into bed, covered her, and started to return to the sofa, thinking she would rest better if left alone.

She reached out and grabbed his hand. "Lay with me."

He took off his boots, got undressed, climbed into bed, and held her. She settled in against him, her head resting in the crevice between his chest and shoulder. Within minutes, her soft breathing told him that she had fallen asleep. He listened to her shallow, soft breathing as he stared out the window listening to the crickets talking, and thought about Jasper being shot. Knowing he would add to Mrs. Talbert's sorrow by telling her about Jasper, he decided it was best she never knew and suggested Sarah not to tell her mother in the morning.

The room was still dark when Sarah opened her eyes from a bad dream about the accident. Relieved at finding herself still in Wade's arms, she let her body settle against his and stared out the window into the dark, starry sky. A hoot owl's soft cry invaded the quiet room through the open window, and as she lay next to Wade, she thought about the baby she would never hold.

Wade opened his eyes, and knowing she was awake, looked at her. "You all right? You seem restless."

"No," she said softly as that terrible day in town flooded her mind, and she remembered what Booth Fox had said to her and the fight that followed. She moved away from him, sat up against the headboard, and considered the consequences of telling him. "I remember now."

He sat up next to her, leaned against the headboard, and waited.

Sarah pulled her legs up to her chest, wrapping her arms around them, and began by telling Wade of how Booth Fox smelled of whiskey, what he did, and what he said to her and of her slapping his face. She went on to tell how her pa jumped past her, dragging Fox off his horse, and the terrible fight that followed.

Wade wished he had been there but was glad that Jasper took Sheriff Fox down a peg and knew that he and Booth Fox would have a little talk.

She continued. "We rode out of town toward home, and soon, Emmett stopped crying and had settled down in the seat between pa and me." She looked at Wade with a frightened look. "I could see a look on pa's face. I ain't ever seen before."

"What kind of look?"

"He looked worried, even scared," she said thoughtfully. "I've never seen pa scared before. I've seen him angry as hell lots of times, especially when he went after Booth Fox, but never scared." She paused in memory. "Pa began looking at the road behind us, saying he wished he'd brought a gun with him. I was glad he hadn't, thinking he would have shot Sheriff Fox." She looked at him. "Now, I know pa wished he'd had his gun to protect Emmett and me." She turned to the window and continued. "We were only a mile or so from home when pa looked behind us once more and told Emmett and me to hang on, and that's when he slapped the team with the reins, and we raced toward home. The wagon was bouncing all over the road, and Emmett started crying, and I held onto him real tight. Then I turned, seeing a rider coming after us riding hard. I couldn't see clearly," she said thoughtfully. "The wagon was kicking up a lot of dust." She paused, looking sure of what she was about to say. "But I know it was Sheriff Booth Fox."

Wade thought she was probably right, thinking that Jasper was a man well-liked, and it would take a man filled with hate to kill him.

Sarah pulled her legs tighter into her chest with her arms. "Pa yelled at us to get on the floor of the wagon, so I helped Emmett get down under the seat. Soon after that, pa lost the reins, leaned forward to get them, and fell from the wagon. That's when the wagon began tipping over." She paused and looked at Wade. "That must be when he shot pa."

Rage filled Wade thinking that's when Jasper was run over by the wagon, causing it to turn over.

She looked away. "I remember screaming as the wagon rolled over, thinking Emmett was going to get killed. The next thing I remember was looking at Billy Murray, one of pa's ranch hands. I must've blacked out again, because when I woke up, I was up here in my old room, hurting something awful with Doc Granger over me." She turned, looking worried. "Does ma know about pa?"

Wade shook his head. "No, I haven't told her yet, nor have I told her about the baby."

"I don't want her to know about either, Wade. It'd kill her to know that someone hated pa enough to shoot him in the back."

Wade considered that. "I was thinking the same thing."

She turned from the window and looked at him. "What are we going to do?"

"Get some sleep," he said. "I'm tired, and I think you are on the verge of collapsing. You've been through a lot these past few days, and I'm surprised you have any tears left." He snuggled down under the covers, turned onto his side, and closed his eyes but couldn't close off his mind. She slid under the covers, turned on her side, facing his back, put one arm around him, and held him tight as she closed her eyes.

The sky was bright blue and cloudless as Wade walked the yard thinking about Booth Fox and what he and Sarah had talked about in the darkness of their bedroom. As they sat watching the morning from their bed, he had told her about arresting Pete Hoskins and Deputy Lee Jones for murder, only to have someone break them out of jail, after the visit by George Hoskins and his foreman, Jethro Reese.

Now, Sarah sat in the window seat of her bedroom dressed in her yellow nightgown and white robe, watching her husband walk the grounds wrestling with what she had told him. She wanted justice for her father's death, the death of their unborn child, and for what they did to their son. Sarah wanted her revenge and wanted Booth Fox dead. She wanted what Wade got when he avenged Emmett Spears. With tears in her eyes, she got up, hurried downstairs, and rushed out the front door to her husband.

Seth had just stepped to the window after shaving when he saw Wade walking in the yard, and then Sarah, in her robe, running from under the porch roof and across the yard into Wade's arms. Hoping nothing was wrong, he thought of Molly and missed waking up next to her in the mornings, and hoped this would be over soon. Seth wanted to return to Sisters and his wife. Watching Wade and Sarah a moment longer, he turned from the window and finished getting dressed.

"Is something wrong with Emmett?" asked Wade as he held her.

"No," she said, then she stepped back, taking his hand. "Walk with me." As they walked toward the archway, the morning sun felt warm and peaceful. "We never talked about the men you hunted after the death of Emmett Spears."

Wade looked at the mountains looming in the distance as they walked and wondered why she brought that up now.

"I was so happy to see you when you returned, and I couldn't understand why you rode away a second time when I begged you not to go."

He recalled that day, the look on her face and the tears in her pleading eyes.

"Tell me about it, Wade. Please."

His memory rushed to the body of the little boy lying on the floor of a cabin, the tiny little dog licking the blood from the boy's face, the boy's murdered parents that he buried after placing the boy in his mother's arms. "Why do you want to know such things?" As they reached the fence next to the archway and road leading up the hill, he turned, looking back at the house and barn beyond, not remembering their walk from there to here.

"It's important to me."

He looked at her, wondering why, and then he turned to the mountains, remembering the others they had found murdered. They saved the two little girls from the four murderers, the family in Mexico, and the slow, agonizing death he left for Paul Bradley. "Some things are better left alone, Sarah."

She turned away angry, looking disappointed. "Damn it! Tell me how you felt the day you brought Dog with you to tell me you weren't staying."

"What I felt?" he asked, looking puzzled. "I don't rightly understand."

She turned, looking angry.

He saw something in her face he had never seen before.

"God forgive me," she said as she turned, looking off into the distance. "But last night, I think I finally understood why you went after those four men." She put both hands on the fence railing, gripping it tightly with her frail hands. "If I were a man, I'd go after the man responsible for my pa and our child, Wade. Just as you did six years ago, and I'd kill him just as you did."

That surprised Wade. It was unlike Sarah to be filled with so much hate, and it unnerved him.

She paused, looking at the expanse before them. "Sometimes I fantasize about taking my pa's pistol, and when I ride into town to do some shopping, I walk into the sheriff's office with it hidden in the folds of my dress, and I kill Booth Fox."

Wade stared at her for a long moment in the silence, thinking that maybe she did need to know. "When I finished in Mexico, I fulfilled a promise to an Indian on my way back. That's why Seth got back to Sisters long before I did."

She was curious about the promise but never asked. Instead, she continued to stare into the distance, hoping for more of an answer.

"It was after that promise, while I was on my way to Gil Robinson's place over in Roscoe's Creek, that I knew I had changed inside, and I wasn't the same as I had been before I left. I felt different. Inside I felt different." He paused to look at the house, thinking of Seth. "Seth tried to warn me the first day we met."

"Warn you?" she asked, looking curious. "About what?"

He looked down at the weeds at his feet. "Finding something I may not be prepared for." He paused and turned to lean on the top railing of the fence, looking out at the expanse of prairie, blue sky, and mountains. "I was filled with hatred when I got to Gil's place. When I saw Dog and those two little girls we saved, playing and looking happy, I knew I had to ride away. Gil asked me to get down, come in, visit with his family, and have some dinner. He wanted me to see how well the two little girls were getting along with his wife and daughter. But I couldn't. All I could think about was that my revenge was responsible for getting Frank Wells, Dark Cloud, and Todd Jewett killed, along with an old sheriff in some town, and Gil badly wounded to satisfy my revenge. I had to leave."

"Why?"

"I'm not sure I can explain it. Right now, I think it was because they were reminders."

"Reminders of what?

194

"All the hatred, revenge, and violence that had become a part of me."

She turned and looked at him. "But I wasn't part of that, Wade. Why did you leave me?"

"Yes, you were Sarah, so was the Circle T, and all of Harper." He filled his lungs and let out a long, soft sigh in thought. "I spent so many days and nights filled with hate, revenge, and killing, I guess I lost myself. I didn't know who I was any longer." He paused. "Hate and revenge may give you something for the moment, Sarah, but it takes something worthwhile away." He looked back at the house. "Men like Seth and Billy French understand that, and I think that's why Billy offered me the job in Santa Fe. He knew I would never be able to do anything else." Then he turned and looked into her eyes. "That's why I was so upset with you when you followed me to Santa Fe."

She smiled. "You were upset, alright. Are you glad I did?"

A small grin found his mouth. "Yes, I'm glad."

She turned away and stared at the mountains, looking troubled. "How do I get past the hate, Wade? I know Booth Fox is responsible for all of this, and I want him dead."

He shrugged. "I don't know what to tell you, Sarah. Hate and revenge are mighty powerful. They're both powerful enough to destroy the very person that feeds on them."

"Do you still hate the four men you hunted?"

He looked down at the ground in thought. "I don't know anymore." As he looked up at the mountains, his mind found Paul Bradley's screams while the vultures began to feed on him. He looked at her. "Sarah, let me worry about justice for all this. I still have that warrant for Booth Fox, and I aim to serve it. By this afternoon, Booth Fox will be in jail, so let me use the law and the courts to give you justice for your pa, our unborn child, Emmett, and you. Don't go taking on something you have no idea of what it will do to you. You'll get lost in it. One of us getting lost is enough. Emmett needs his mother."

She stepped into his arms, filled with love and the need to believe him.

He gently kissed her and then held her, feeling her warm body against his. "It's gonna be all right, Sarah. I promise."

She stepped back, took his hand, and smiled as they started walking toward the house. "I better get dressed and help ma with breakfast."

Twenty-Two

A Question of Justice

Wade told Sarah he would check on Emmett while she got dressed, and when he walked into Emmett's room, he found a frowning, unhappy, and complaining Emmett Garrison.

"My leg hurts," whined the boy.

Wade sat down on the edge of the bed and noticed the blanket Mrs. Talbert had been using was missing from the stuffed chair next to the bed. "Did your grandmother sleep in here last night?"

Emmett shook his head no. "I'm hungry, and my leg hurts Pa."

He reached out and touched the leg gently. "I know." Then he smiled. "There's nothing I can do about your leg, Son. It has to heal, and it will hurt from time to time. You're just going to have to man up and deal with it." Then he looked at the crutches sitting in the corner that Doc Granger had brought out. "You need to learn to use them crutches, boy."

"I don't want no crutches. My leg hurts."

"You can't just stay in bed asking for things," Wade replied harshly.

"Where's Ma?" whined the boy, figuring his pa wasn't about to be sympathetic.

Having the fill of his son's complaining, Wade stood and started for the door. "She's getting dressed." He opened the door and turned. "I want you on them crutches by the time I get back from town." Closing the door, he walked across the hall, deciding the boy needed a firmer hand, opened the bedroom door, and stuck his head inside.

Sarah was sitting at her dresser in front of the mirror, fussing with the bangs of her hair, trying to cover the stitches on her forehead. "Be glad when these are out, and my hair grows back." She looked up at his reflection. "How's Emmett?"

"Whining like a pup wanting his mother."

Disappointed at the way she looked, she gently tossed her brush on the dresser as her shoulders slumped. "Tell him I'll be there in a minute."

"I ain't going back in there. Time the boy stopped whining and started using them crutches Doc brought out."

Irritated by what he said, she frowned at his reflection. "He's just a child, and he's been hurt and through a terrible thing."

"I know that," said Wade in an irritated voice. "But he can't just lie around in bed until his leg heals. Doc says Emmet's got to get up and use it."

She turned from the mirror, looking like she was in the mood for an argument, and gave him a look.

Not wanting an argument, he stepped into the hall, closed the door, and walked downstairs, figuring she could baby the boy if she wanted.

Walking into the dining room, he found evidence that Mrs. Talbert was up and about. Three candles sat in the center of the table, ready to be lit, and her best china and silverware decorated the table as if she were expecting guests.

Mrs. Talbert backed into the room through the swinging door carrying a steaming platter of scrambled eggs. She smiled at him as she placed them on the table, wiped her hands on her apron, and glanced at the table with pride. "Mr. Bowlen is on the front porch with a cup of coffee. Would you please tell him that breakfast is ready and then tell Sarah?" With that, she turned and disappeared through the swinging door.

Bowlen was sitting in one of the white wooden chairs, his feet propped against the porch railing, a cup of coffee resting on his lap between his hands. He turned and grinned. "Morning." Then he lifted the cup and took a drink of coffee.

"Breakfast is ready."

Seth stood wearing the same gray shirt and tan pants he had arrived in a few days ago, but thanks to Mrs. Talbert, they had been washed and ironed. Walking toward the front door, he looked at the Rocky Mountains looming in the distance. "They have a magnificence about them."

198

Wade looked at the mountains, thinking they did, then he turned and followed Seth inside just as Sarah was walking down the stairs without Emmett. Disappointed, he waited for her at the bottom, and together they walked into the dining room, joining Mrs. Talbert and Seth for breakfast, neither mentioning Emmett.

After breakfast, Sarah filled a plate of food and took it upstairs to Emmett while Wade argued that the boy needs to come downstairs. Sarah ignored him while Mrs. Talbert sided with her daughter.

Knowing his friend was in a losing argument, Seth wiped his mouth with the linen napkin and placed it on his empty plate. He stood, thanking Mrs. Talbert for a fine breakfast, and told Wade he was going upstairs to get his gear and head for the stable and their horses.

Wade placed his napkin on the table, stood, and thanked her for breakfast, excused himself, and went upstairs. Gathering his Sharps rifle, bandolier of cartridges, brown duster, and a black wide-brimmed hat, he walked into the hallway. After shutting the door, he set everything on the floor next to the stairs and opened the door to Emmett's room. Sarah was reading a story aloud, while the half-eaten plate of food was sitting on the floor. She paused, looked up, and then closed the book on her finger to mark her place.

"We're leaving," he told her while standing in the doorway. Then he looked at Emmett. "How's the leg?"

"Still hurts some," the boy replied. Then as if trying to please, his father added, "But not as much."

Wade smiled warmly. "It'll mend soon enough, Son."

Emmett looked doubtful. "When you coming back, Pa?"

"Later today." Then he looked at Sarah. "We'll try and be back b'fore dinner."

"Pa," said Emmett sadly, "I wish Dog were here."

Wade thought on that a moment. "Well, there's Jasper's dog, Willie."

"Willie's still sitting on Grandpa's grave."

Wade walked to the window and looked down at Jasper's grave, seeing Willie lying on top of it in the shade of the oak tree. The old man and his dog were never too far apart, and if Jasper were busy at something, the dog would lie near him and wait. Willie was a ten-year-old border collie that once belonged to a sheepherder, and how Jasper ever ended up with a sheepdog on a cattle ranch is still a mystery, even to Janice. He turned from the window, feeling sorry for Willie. "Dog ain't here right now, and it looks like Willie wants to be near your Grandpa, so I guess you'll have to make do with your ma and that book." Hearing horses, he looked out the window, seeing Seth with two saddled horses.

Emmett looked disappointed. "Yes, sir."

Wade looked at Sarah. "Seth's waiting. I best go."

She set the open book upside down on the small table next to the chair and stood. "I'll walk you out."

As he walked past the bed from the window, Wade reached down and gently touched the toes of his son's unhurt leg. "Start using them crutches."

Emmett frowned. "Yes, sir."

Sarah closed the door behind them and followed him to the railing at the top of the stairs.

Wade stopped and turned. "Don't let that boy run you ragged, Sarah. He's well enough to get up on them crutches and walk around a bit."

She smiled. "I know." She put her arms around him and held him tight, her head against his chest, thinking about what he told her at the fence. "Be careful."

Wade could smell the familiar aroma of perfume and soap and suddenly imagined Booth Fox putting his face next to hers, sniffing her as a dog would another dog. He put his hands on her waist, gently pushed her away, and smiled. "I promise."

She fussed with the faded, red neckerchief he wore and then nervously smoothed out the front of his yellow shirt. "How long will you be gone?"

Wade studied her face, forehead, and stitches for a moment, then looked into her brown eyes," Be home sometime tonight. He smiled and gave her a quick, reassuring wink, then he reached down, picked up his gear, and started down the stairs.

She stood against the railing, watching as he walked down the stairs, putting on his black, wide-brimmed hat, and walked out the front door. Sarah hurried into Emmett's room, where she stood at the window.

200

Wade rolled his duster up and tied it to the back of his saddle, and knowing she would be watching, he took the reins from Seth, swung up onto his big sorrel mare, and looked up at the window. Smiling, he tipped his hat, turned the mare away from the porch, and trotted toward the road to Harper.

Seth looked up at her knowing she was full of worry, turned his gray, and rode after Wade.

She watched as the two rode under the archway, up the hill, and out of sight, wishing she had never said anything to Wade.

Seth caught up with Wade, and as he looked at him, he could tell something was eating at him and wondered if everything was alright between him and Sarah. "Saw you and Sarah this morning before breakfast out walking. Don't mean to pry, but is everything alright?"

Wade thought about all that Sarah had told him and decided to tell Seth some of it. "You know about the fight between the Sheriff and Jasper?"

"Yeah, but not the why?"

"Sarah told me last night that the Sheriff was drunk when he rode up next to the wagon in front of Mason Store that day. She said he leaned over and told her she smelled ripe. Sarah slapped his face, and then Jasper stepped past her and jumped the Sheriff."

Seth stared at the road ahead of them. "Can't blame Jasper for that. I'd done the same." He looked at Wade. "Maybe you're right about Booth Fox shooting Jasper. It fits."

Harper

It was a little afternoon when Wade and Seth pulled up at the rear of Levi's livery.

Wade looked at Seth. "Let's see if Levi's seen or heard anything about Pete Hoskins."

"Good idea," agreed Seth. "Liveries are as good as a saloon when you want to find out something."

They dismounted, tied their horses to an old buggy rusting away, and walked in the rear door.

201

Levi Wagner was busy cleaning out a stall when he looked up, seeing the two as they walked in. He leaned the shovel against the wall and stepped out of the stall pulling a dirty rag from his hip pocket. As he wiped his hands with it, he grinned. "I was wondering how long it'd be b'fore the two of you showed up." Then he gestured toward Sisters with the hand holding the rag. "Heard about the jailbreak."

Seth looked past the open doors toward town. "Haven't seen anything of Pete Hoskins and Deputy Lee, have you, Levi?"

Wagner looked at Seth's bad eye and then at the good one. "No, I ain't, Sheriff, and don't want to neither." Then with a sad expression, he looked at Wade. "Sorry to hear about Jasper Talbert. He was a fine man."

"Yes, he was," agreed Wade.

Levi quickly asked about Mrs. Talbert, his wife, and son.

Wade smiled appreciatively, saying they were all doing fine, but he couldn't stop thinking about Booth Fox with his face against Sarah's.

Wagner shrugged, looking guilty. "I'm sure sorry for not making it to Mr. Talbert's bury'n."

"Don't worry yourself about that, Levi." Wade turned toward the open doors of the livery, looking at the streets of Harper. "Have you seen Sheriff Fox today?"

"Saw him and his deputy walk in the Blue Sky Saloon a while back."

Wade and Seth glanced at one another.

Wagner grinned. "That was some fight he and Mr. Talbert had a few days back."

Wade looked at him. "You saw the fight?"

Levi shook his head. "No." Then he smiled mischievously. "But I hear'd old Jasper did a fair job of kicking the shit out of our sheriff." Seeing that neither was laughing, he looked out the big, open doorway. "Least that's what I heard."

Wade walked across the livery dirt floor of strewn straw and tiny lines of sunlight coming through the cracks in the walls. Reaching the doorway, he stopped and leaned against it, staring along the busy street deep in thought. Several horses were tied to the railings in front of the Blue Sky and Sundowner Saloons, patiently awaiting their riders. A few more here and there at hitching rails along the street. Wagons made their way up and down the street among a few riders coming and going. Here and there, pedestrians crossed the street or walked along the boardwalk, some with packages. The town was busy.

As Seth watched Wade, he worried that he might be harboring deep anger over what Fox had said to Sarah and his shooting of Jasper.

Wade stepped away from the door and walked past them toward the rear door where their horses waited outside. "Let's go see Booth Fox."

Seth followed, not seeing that Wade had taken off his Marshal's badge and put it in his shirt pocket as he walked. Climbing onto their horses, they rode at a walk past the livery toward town.

Levi walked outside, stepping into the sunlight just as they rode past and watched them ride at a walk along the hot, dusty street past Mason's Store and several other shops toward their destination, the Blue Sky Saloon.

Seth nudged his horse, and as he caught up to Wade, he glanced at the side of his face, "You ain't aiming to kill Sheriff Booth Fox, are you, Wade?"

Wade never looked away from the street and doorway of the saloon. "I plan on serving him this warrant I've been carrying all folded up in my shirt pocket. What the sheriff does after that's up to him." Then he turned to Seth with a stern look. "That meet with your approval?"

Seth looked at Wade, thinking he was in a foul mood, and that worried him. "It does."

"Good," barked Wade., then he nudged the mare into a trot toward the hitching rail.

Stopping at the hitching rail in front of the Blue Sky Saloon, the two climbed down, then wrapped the reins of their horses around the railing. As they walked up the steps to the boardwalk, they slipped the thin leather straps over the hammers of their Colts that held them securely in their holsters. Pausing to look over the swinging doors thinking it was a busy afternoon, Wade pushed them open, then he and Seth stepped inside the dim saloon. Greeted by piano music and cigarette smoke, their eyes adjusted to the dim light as they walked toward the busy bar finding an empty spot at the corner where the bar turns to meet the wall.

Wade bellied up to the bar, where he could see images in the big mirror on the wall behind the bar. Seth took up a position beside Wade, where the bar turns toward the wall so he could see the bartender and the faces of those standing at the bar.

Wade nodded to Sam Carney and held up two fingers indicating two beers, then looked in the big mirror on the wall behind the bar taking in the crowded tables of drunks and whores.

Seth leaned toward Wade. "Table with the blonde whore dressed in yellow." Seth lowered his voice. "The man with his back to us is Booth Fox."

"I see 'em," said Wade as he looked in the big mirror. "The other with the badge facing us must be Deputy Chris Boyd." Wade leaned on the bar with his elbows, glanced over his shoulder at the table, and then turned to Seth. "Looks a mite young."

Seth looked past Wade's shoulder. "Sure does."

Sam Carney approached with the two beers remembering the last time the two were in his saloon. As he set the two beers down, his eyes immediately went to the table where Sheriff Fox and Deputy Chris Boyd were sitting. He looked at Wade. "Hello, Marshal. Sorry to hear about Jasper Talbert. He was a good man."

Wade looked from the image of Sheriff Fox in the mirror to the bartender. "Thanks, Sam. Appreciate the sentiment."

Wade glanced at the piano player in the corner that never looked up from the soft tune he was playing and the whore standing next to the piano, listening in memory of some happier time. The soft music mixed with the inaudible words and laughter filled the room of cowboys and whores as Wade looked at Sam. "Busy for a weekday."

Carney nodded as he looked around the saloon. "It's Friday and payday for a few ranches. It looks like some are getting an early start. We'll have a bigger crowd Saturday night." He looked at Seth's bad eye before looking into his good one. "Afternoon, Sheriff."

"Sam," nodded Seth as his eyes moved to the table where Booth Fox sat, then glanced around the crowded room.

Carney asked Wade how his wife and child were.

Wade took a drink of warm beer, wiped his mouth, and told him they were both doing fine, and tossed some money on the bar for the beers.

Thinking Wade was in a foul mood, Sam bent down behind the bar, bringing out a bottle of whiskey. "This here's the good stuff," he said as he reached behind him and got three whiskey glasses from the counter behind the bar. Pulling the cork out of the bottle, he poured three drinks.

Wade stared into the mirror behind Sam at Booth's image watching as he laughed while talking to the whore at the table.

Finished, Sam gave one glass to Seth, the other to Wade, and then lifted the third glass in a toast. "Here's to Jasper Talbert."

Seth raised his glass, "To Jasper Talbert," then drank it down.

Carney gulped his drink, corked the bottle, put it back under the bar, and then pushed Wade's money toward him. "All on the house tonight Marshal."

Wade thanked Sam, picked up his whiskey, drank it while eyeing Booth in the mirror, then set the empty glass down, picked up the money, and looked at Carney. "Ain't seen Pete Hoskins have you, Sam?"

Carney took the towel off his shoulder and began wiping the bar down, looking worried. "I heard about Pete and Lee Jones breaking out of jail over in Sisters." Sam glanced past Wade at Sheriff Fox and lowered his voice. "I ain't seen either Marshal, and I'd appreciate it if there weren't any trouble in my place today."

Wade looked in the mirror, seeing Deputy Chris Boyd was staring at him. "Well, Sam, we never figured Pete and Lee would be dumb enough to come into town anyways. As far as trouble, that's not up to us. It's up to Sheriff Booth and his deputy."

Chris Boyd leaned forward and said something to Sheriff Fox, who turned in his chair and looked at Wade and Seth.

Wade picked up his mug of beer and took a small drink while his eyes met Booth Fox's in the mirror.

Seth watched Fox and his deputy as he leaned against the bar, resting on his left elbow. His right hand found the butt of his Colt pistol as he picked up his beer with his left hand and took a small drink.

Sheriff Fox slid his chair back, stood, and walked toward the bar, adjusting his holster. Pushing his way to the crowded bar next to Wade, he leaned on the bar with both elbows and asked Sam for a beer.

Sam looked worried. "Don't want no trouble in here, Sheriff."

Booth gave Sam a look. "Just get me a beer, Sam."

Wade looked at Booth's reflection in the mirror and thought about his face next to Sarah's. Then he looked at Deputy Boyd's reflection, thinking he looked even younger up close as he walked past, taking a spot at the bar between him and Seth.

Deputy Boyd glanced at the back of Wade's hat, then turned and looked at Seth, noticing his scar and right eye. He had never seen anyone with a bad eye before and had a hard time looking away from it. Feeling nervous, he turned away and looked at Booth in the mirror. Chris Boyd was lean, his young face absent of scars and wrinkles. He stood about five-feet-seven, with sandy hair and blue eyes.

Sheriff Booth Fox took a drink of beer, wiped the foam from his mouth, and grinned at his deputy in the mirror, and then at Wade's reflection. "You come to Harper looking for them two prisoners that escaped from your friend's jail in Sisters?"

Wade took a drink of beer and set the mug down. "No, we aren't. Something else brought us to Harper."

Seth figured the deputy wasn't more than twenty, if that old, and hoped he didn't do anything foolish.

The piano player in the corner stopped playing and glanced around to see what everyone was staring at. Sam Carney stood several feet away, wiping the bar with a towel, hoping there wouldn't be any trouble, but something in Wade's eyes told him differently.

Booth Fox took a drink of beer, wiped the foam from his mouth, and lowered his voice. "How's that little wife of yours doing."

Seth couldn't hear what Booth said but knew the sheriff was filled with false bravery from drinking and figured Wade was going to tell Booth Fox about the warrant.

Wade thought about him killing Jasper and smelling Sarah as if she were a dog in heat. His right hand dropped to his holster, and he softly said, "I think you're a bully and a drunk Booth. We'll see how brave you are at your hanging for killing Tom Lawson."

Booth's hand with the glass of beer paused in midair and then continued the slow journey to his lips. He stared into Wade's cold blue eyes over the rim of his beer mug as he took a long drink, knowing Wade was here to arrest him. Booth wiped the foam from his mouth with the sleeve of his brown shirt, set the mug on the bar, and noticed Wade was not wearing his badge.

Seth watched the two wishing he knew what Wade had said, and then he turned his attention to the deputy, hoping he didn't have to kill the young man.

Wade's heart was beating fast against his chest, and he wasn't sure he could beat Fox to the draw, but he remembered the night Billy French went up against a faster gun in Santa Fe. Billy was a firm believer in the badge winning, and being fair was foolish, as well as deadly. "In a few minutes, I'll put that badge back on and serve you with this warrant I have in my pocket. Until then, I'm just a man in a saloon having a beer."

Booth stared into Wade's eyes, knowing why he came to town and knew it wasn't to serve any warrant. He had already made up his mind that he wasn't going to jail or a hanging. Fox had killed a few men in bar fights and figured he could outdraw the marshal. Booth glanced at Chris facing Seth and was sure Seth would kill the boy, but then he could take care of the Sheriff after he took care of Wade Garrison. He smiled, thinking he was going to make a widow out of Sarah Garrison.

Seth's eyes went from Chris Boyd to Wade, to Booth Fox, and then back to the deputy.

The sound of chairs sliding away from tables as Sam Carney stared on in fear at the two who were no longer talking. The men at the bar standing behind Booth Fox backed up and got out of the way.

Adrenaline flowed through Booth then, having made up his mind, he went for his gun.

Wade pulled his gun with his right hand and, at the same moment, reached down with his left, pushing Booth's right hand that held his gun toward the bar.

Looking surprised and fearful, Fox pulled the trigger. His gun exploded, sending the bullet past Wade's leg through the side of the bar, breaking bottles of whiskey, ending up on the floor behind the bar.

Wade pulled the trigger of his Colt, feeling the gun kick as the bullet ripped through Booth's heart, clipping the side of his spine as it exited, putting a hole in the side of the bar. Wade stared into Booth's wide, surprised eyes and thought of Jasper and Sarah as he watched Fox fall backward, still holding his gun. Wade knew he was dead before he hit the floor.

Deputy Chris Boyd was looking at Seth and his bad eye when he heard the gunshot. Turning, he saw the sheriff falling back along the bar, knocking over a spittoon that rolled along the brass foot railing, coming to rest against an old man's foot. Boyd turned to Seth with surprise and an unsure look.

"Don't," said Seth, but he was too late. Chris Boyd clumsily went for his gun, but Bowlen was too quick and shot him in the stomach, knocking him backward onto an empty table. The deputy's pistol had barely cleared its holster as he fell back, but he managed to squeeze the trigger, putting a hole in the corner wall behind Seth.

The saloon filled with a silence that matched the explosions of their guns, as customers and whores watched in disbelief at their sheriff and deputy lying dead on the saloon floor. Some stood knocking over their chairs, ready to run, while others sat in their chairs, held by the moment. Sheriff Booth Fox lay on the floor, eyes open, his lifeless face still holding the mixture of fear and surprise. Deputy Boyd was lying face up on a table close to the bar, his gun still in his hand.

Seth moved to the edge of the bar and looked at the young boy he just killed, filled with regret.

Wade turned to the crowd and pulled the warrant from his shirt pocket. "I'm United States Deputy Marshal Wade Garrison, and we came in here to serve a warrant on Sheriff Booth Fox for murder." He looked down at Booth's body and the hole in the center of his bloodstained shirt. "The sheriff thought it best to fight than go with us and stand trial." When he turned to look at Boyd, Seth noticed the absence of his marshal's badge.

Wade pointed to Boyd's body. "The deputy wasn't wanted for anything." He paused a moment looking sad. "His only crime was being foolish, and that cost him his life."

The room was deathly silent as people glanced at one another, stared at the two bodies or Wade and Seth. Some began sitting down while others still stood, yet others picked up the chairs they had knocked over, unsure if they should stay or run, but all were watching Wade and Seth.

Wade turned to Sam Carney. "Better send for the undertaker, Sam." Then he holstered his gun and started for the door.

Bowlen starred at the body of deputy Boyd, holstered his gun, and followed Wade through the swinging doors into the warm sun and through the small crowd that was gathering along the boardwalk.

Reaching their horses, an angry Seth grabbed Wade's arm and turned him. "What was that all about between you and Booth, and where the hell's your badge?"

Wade pulled away, looking angry, grabbed the reins to his mare, climbed up, settling into his saddle. As he backed her away from the hitching rail, he looked down at Seth. "Coming?" Then he turned his mare north and trotted up the street.

Seth looked back at the saloon door imagining Booth and the Deputy lying dead, climbed onto his horse, and rode after Wade wondering what he had said to Booth Fox to make him draw and why he had taken off his badge.

Twenty-Three

Seth rode a few yards behind Wade, playing the scene in the saloon over in his mind, wondering what it was that he had said to Booth Fox to make him draw. As they rode toward the ranch, Bowlen wondered if Wade made the trip into Harper to kill Booth over what he had said to Sarah. Angry at being played the fool, he spurred his horse and yelled, "Pull up, damn it!"

Wade pulled up, turned his mare, and waited for Seth.

Seth pulled up and looked at Wade. "What the hell was that back there?" He glanced at Wade's shirt that now held his marshal's badge, turned in the saddle, and pointed back toward Harper. "Where in the hell was your badge back there?"

Wade looked at him. "You know where in the hell it was, Seth."

Bowlen was mad as hell. "You can't serve a warrant without wearing your damn badge."

Wade thought on that. "Wearing the badge doesn't make me a deputy marshal, Seth. Taking the oath does."

That angered Seth even more. "Don't play me like a damn fool, Wade, not here, not now." Then he looked at him with narrow, accusing eyes. "You wanted Booth to draw on you so you could kill him for what he said to Sarah, didn't you?"

Wade thought of Sarah as they stood by the fence that morning, saying she wanted Booth Fox dead for her pa and unborn child. He looked at Seth. "It goes deeper than that."

"Well, just how deep does it go, Marshal?" Seth asked sarcastically.

Wade stared at the long dirt and red, sandy road disappearing into the distance. It was warm, the blue sky above held a scattering of white puffy clouds, and the sound of grasshoppers filled the breezeless air. He looked at Seth. "What Booth Fox said to Sarah was in a drunken stupor, and had I been there, I'd have kicked the shit out of him myself."

"Then, why?"

"You and I both know that Booth Fox killed Jasper and Sarah's unborn, not to mention almost killing both her and Emmett."

"No, I don't for sure, and neither do you," replied Seth in a loud, angry tone.

"C'mon, Seth," he said angrily. "Do you honestly believe after what happened in town between Jasper and him that someone else just happened to shoot Jasper in the back?"

Seth looked doubtful. "No, I don't, Wade, damn it. But we can't go around killing someone because we believe they did something." He pointed an angry finger at the badge on Wade's shirt and raised his voice. "We arrest men for doing that, damn it. Then we let the courts and juries decide." He paused. "You so much as killed Booth Fox in cold blood."

Wade gave him an angry look and yelled. "Then arrest me!"

Silence filled the prairie as Seth let out a soft sigh, took off his hat, and wiped the sweat from his forehead with his forearm. He looked out across the expanse, then as he put his hat on, he spoke in a soft, weary voice. "You know I won't do that."

Wade spurred his mare into a trot and yelled over his shoulder. "Then leave me alone, damn it!"

Still angry, Seth spurred his horse and caught up with Wade, reached out and pulled at his arm, telling him to pull up, and when he did, Seth looked at him. "You crossed the line, damn it, Wade, you crossed the line."

Wade stared at Seth with a weary look. "There is no line, Seth. All I see is a country full of bad men that rape, kill children, rob banks, and make life miserable for others."

Seth heaved a disappointed sigh. "We had a warrant for Booth Fox for killing Tom Lawson," he said, looking despondent. "He'd have gone to prison, maybe even hung."

Wade thought about that as he looked off into the distant snowcapped peaks of the Rocky Mountains. He took off his hat and wiped the sweat from his forehead, then put his hat back on and softly said, "I didn't know Tom Lawson."

"Well, I knew Tom Lawson," said Seth bitterly. "And I know his widow. What about her, Wade? What about his widow and the justice she deserves?"

Wade stared down at his hands, resting on the saddle horn holding the reins to his horse, and thought about Lawson's widow. Moments passed, and then he looked up. "Let me ask you something, Seth. Do you think Mrs. Lawson cares if the men who killed her husband got hung by the county or shot, as long as they're dead?"

Seth looked uncertain. "I can't answer that." Then he scowled. "But maybe I should've asked her before we left, so you'd know."

"Maybe so," said Wade in anger.

They stared at one another as a heavy silence fell, each having nothing more to say.

Seth settled back in his saddle and sighed, looking worried. "Are you gonna take Pete and Lee back for trial, or are you gonna kill 'em?"

"We'll take 'em both alive if that suits you."

Seth lifted his head, looking angry. "It does."

"Good," responded Wade with a mean look. "But I'll tell you this much, Seth: If either draws down on me, I'll kill 'em, just as sure as I killed Booth Fox for drawing on me. And I won't even think about Widow Lawson or the Widow Olson." He spurred his mare and trotted away, anxious to get home.

Seth watched him for a few moments, wondering what happened to the young man who walked into his office all those years ago, half wishing that French had come instead of Wade. Filled with disappointment and apprehension about Pete Hoskins, and having nothing more to say, he spurred his horse and followed at a distance.

It was midafternoon when Sarah happened to look out Emmett's window just as Wade crested the hill and rode down the road toward the archway, with Seth several yards behind him. Thinking it strange they weren't riding beside one another, she rushed out of Emmett's room, hurried down the stairs, and out the front door. Her hair wasn't in its usual ponytail but hung loose and soft over her shoulders. Knowing that her husband was safe, she lifted the bottom of the white gingham dress with puffy sleeves so she would not trip and paused at the edge of the porch to watch him. Filled with relief and excitement that he was home, she hurried down the steps into the yard where she waited by her mother's rose garden next to the hitching rail.

Wade rode toward the house, while Seth rode toward the barn. Sarah raised one hand to wave at Seth, but he looked straight ahead, and she sensed something was wrong between the two. As Wade pulled up next to the hitching rail, she asked, "Seth looks upset. Is everything all right?"

Wade climbed down, tied his horse to the railing as he watched Seth ride past the corner of the house. Not wanting to discuss it, he said, "I think he's just tired."

She stepped toward him, put her arms around his waist, her head against his chest, and closed her eyes, thankful he was back in her arms. "I was worried. Did you arrest Booth Fox?"

He put his arms around her and looked toward the Rocky Mountains thinking of the surprised look on Booth's face as he fell backward to the saloon floor.

"Wade?" She paused. "Wade, has Sheriff Booth Fox been arrested?"

"Sheriff Booth Fox is dead, Sarah," he said, still staring at the mountains.

She stepped back with a surprised look fearing the answer to the question she had to ask. "Did you kill Booth Fox?"

He looked at her. "I had no choice," he said, knowing he had goaded Booth into drawing. "He drew on me in the saloon when I tried to serve the warrant and arrest him for the murder of Tom Lawson."

She looked away with mixed feelings. "I won't lie to you," she said softly. "I'm glad he's dead, but I was looking forward to seeing him in court, and him seeing me, and Ma. I wanted to see his face with him knowing he was going to hang for killing pa and our unborn child."

Wade thought of the widow's Lawson, and Olson wondering if Seth hadn't been right. "Was that so important?"

She nodded, looking disappointed. "Yes, it was."

Wanting to get the mistake of Booth Fox out of his mind, he asked, "How's Emmett?"

"He's fine," she said with a smile, and then with a tender hand, touched the side of his face, looking worried. "You look tired."

Wade sighed, raised his brow, and nodded. "I am, and a bit hungry, too."

She gently tugged at his arm. "Come inside. I'll fix you and Seth something to eat, and then you can put your horse away."

Thinking of how mad Seth was, he was sure it would be a quiet meal and gestured at the mare. "I'll put her away first." Thinking he and Seth needed to talk, he added, "Then we'll be in."

She smiled. "All right."

Bowlen was rubbing down his horse, having already unsaddled it when Wade walked the mare into the stall next to them. Wade took a quick look around to see if anyone else was in the barn, then turned, looking over the stall railing at Seth. "I know you disagree with what happened back in Harper…"

"I do," interrupted Seth as he continued brushing his horse.

Wade watched him for a moment, reconsidering his need to talk to the man but knew he couldn't leave it. "Tell me the truth, Seth. If it wasn't for both Mrs. Lawson and Mrs. Olson, would you have given a shit?"

Bowlen stopped brushing the horse and stared at its gray coat, sighed softly, and lowered the hand that held the brush, the other holding the long, gray mane. He looked at Wade over the back of his horse and the wall of the stalls between them. "I don't know the answer to that because that ain't the way it is. But I remember asking if you were going to kill Booth Fox as we rode down the street today." Seth frowned. "Do you recall that?"

Wade nodded, looking regretful. "Yeah, Seth, I do."

Bowlen's expression changed to one of sadness. "I had to kill a boy today no older than nineteen or twenty, and that young man had nothing to do with this mess." He sighed and looked out the barn door at the sunlight and shadows. "I've killed a lot of men over the years, and most deserving, but damn it, it'll be a long time before I forget the look on that young fellah's face as he died." He looked at Wade. "It's shit such as that what gets a man pissed." Then he turned and began brushing his horse.

214

Wade stared at him for a time, knowing he had put something between them that he may never put aside. Seth was right. The death of Deputy Boyd was an unnecessary thing. Feeling regretful about the deputy, he turned away and began unsaddling his horse and thought about Emmett Spears' killing in that same saloon. Thinking about what Sarah had said, he loosened the saddle cinch and then turned his head toward Seth. "I was wrong, Seth. If I could change it, I would. I killed Boyd, not you."

Seth paused his brushing the horse. "It was my bullet," he said softly as he returned to the task at hand.

Silence filled the barn while Wade lifted the saddle from the mare and put it over the stall railing, followed by the blanket folded neatly over the saddle. The harness and bit off the mare and hanging on a peg, he turned to Seth. "I wanted Booth to draw on me, Seth. But I never thought he would. Not until the moment, he drew his gun." He put his forearms on the top railing of the stall, looking regretful. "I admit that I wanted him to, but I thought he would let us arrest him and fight us in court using George Hoskins' money. But in truth, I wasn't disappointed."

Seth continued brushing his horse while thinking about Jasper Talbert, Sarah, Emmett, and the unborn child and knew that if someone were to kill Molly, he'd not rest until they were dead. He stopped brushing his horse, put the brush on a shelf in the stall, and turned. "What was it you said to Fox that made him draw on you?"

Wade stared out the barn door at the hills in the distance. "I told him he was a bully and a drunk, and we'd see how brave he was at his hanging for killing Tom Lawson." He looked at Seth. "Booth got a funny look on his face and just stared at me for a moment. Then he did just what I wanted him to do. he drew his gun."

Seth thought about that. "You goaded him into drawing. Like I said before, Wade, there's a fine line we have to adhere to." He sighed. "No sense in going over it. What's done is done. I just wish that damn kid hadn't gone for his gun."

Wade looked at Bowlen. "I never figured that one, Seth. The boy got caught up in something he shouldn't have, and that's on me." He gestured toward the house. "Sarah's fixing something to eat."

Seth stepped out of the stall and waited while Wade pushed the mare to one side and stepped out of her stall. "You ever pull that crap on me again, and I'll slap you shitless."

Wade smiled but knew he meant exactly what he said.

The evening was calm and warm as Wade and Seth sat on the porch after dinner, watching the last of the day when Sarah and Emmett walked out the front door.

Wade turned in his chair, pleased at seeing his son using the crutches. Sarah held a small basket in one hand and a small plate of what looked like meat scraps in the other. "Where you two off to?"

Sarah smiled. "Pick some flowers for Pa's grave." She waited, looking worried while Emmett managed the three steps on his crutches. "Emmett wants to try and get Willie off the mound with this bowl of meat."

Wade silently wished the boy luck, while Seth turned away and looked at the Rocky Mountains set against a dim, blue sky and thought of Deputy Chris Boyd.

Sarah went about cutting flowers to put in the basket she would place on Jasper's grave while Emmett waited patiently, and when she finished, they walked to her pa's grave where Willie lay. Sarah put the plate of food on the ground, then bent down and placed the flowers she had cut neatly on her father's grave at the headstone.

The dog lifted his head, looked at them, whined softly, and then lay his head back down on his front paws, looking sad.

Emmett called to him. "Here, Willie."

Willie raised his eyes without raising his head, looked at Emmett, and then looked off into the distance in memory.

Emmett laid his crutches on the ground, managed to slowly sit down at the side of the grave, put one hand on Willie's back, and petted him. "He looks sad, Ma."

She stood and looked at Willie with pity. "He is sad. He misses pa as much as I do, I reckon. See if you can get him to eat something."

Emmett reached behind him, picked up the plate of meat scraps, and set it down in front of Willie, but the dog turned its head away. Emmett picked up a small piece of meat, scooted a little closer, and held it in front of Willie's nose. "Here, boy."

Willie smelled it briefly and then gently took it.

Emmett looked up at his ma with a big smile, picked up another, and then another until Willie had eaten it all.

Wade stood from the white wooden chair, went inside, poured two small whiskeys, then returned to the porch giving one to Seth. He sat down and took a quick sip. "I'm sure Hoskins knows about his sheriff and the deputy."

Seth took a small drink. "I'm sure he has. Bad news always travels fast."

Wade wondered how loyal the Talbert ranch hands were if he needed them but then decided this wasn't their fight. "What do you think his first move will be?"

Seth thought as he stared at the mountains growing fainter in the dim light of dusk with each passing moment. "I'm more concerned about our next move." He looked at Wade. "We still have two men to arrest, and that won't be easy after what happened in Harper."

Sarah and Emmett walked around the corner of the house returning from Jasper's grave. Wade stood and went to help Emmett up the steps, but Emmett told him he could do it. Wade stood back with pride and watched as his son struggled up the steps. Then he noticed Willie standing a few feet from the porch. "Looks like someone's following you, Son."

Emmett turned and grinned happily.

"Call to him, Son," said Wade.

"Here, boy. Come, Willie."

Willie hesitantly walked to the porch steps where he stopped and looked up with dark, searching eyes, at Emmett then turned his head, looked at the corner of the house toward Jasper's grave, and whined. Unsure what to do, the dog looked at the open doorway Emmett was standing in. Willie was never allowed in the house and always slept on an old blanket in a room off the back porch.

Janice Talbert appeared at the front door, looking curious. "What's going on?"

Emmett turned with a big grin. "Willie followed me." Then he looked back at the dog. "I think he wants to sleep in my room."

Mrs. Talbert's eyes grew wide, her expression unyielding. "Willie has always slept in his bed."

Emmett turned, looking disappointed and sad. "But he's lonely and misses grandpa."

Taking pity on the dog or feeling love for her grandson, she smiled warmly. "Well, I guess it won't hurt no one."

"Call him again, Son," Wade told him. "See if you can get him to go upstairs with you."

Emmett slapped his leg and called Willie once more.

Willie whined as he looked back toward Jasper's grave then at Emmett as if deciding. He took a hesitant step while eyeing Janice and stopped at the door.

She looked at the dog, stepped aside, and motioned him inside with one hand. "Well, come on. I ain't gonna carry you."

Willie hurried past her into the house with head and tail down, turned, and waited for Emmett.

"I'll be damned," said Wade with a smile.

Willie followed Emmett and Sarah upstairs to his room, where he jumped up onto the foot of the bed near the window overlooking Jasper's grave.

Sarah stepped from the house onto the porch and stood by the porch railing, looking up into the black starry sky. She turned to Seth. "I bet Molly's worried."

Seth knew she would be. "I meant to send her a wire while we were in town." He glanced at Wade then looked at Sarah. "But things happened a little differently than I expected." He smiled. "I'll send her a message tomorrow."

Wade looked at him. "Think going into town tomorrow would be a smart move?"

Bowlen thought on that a moment. "Maybe not, but I gotta get word to Molly somehow."

Sarah stepped next to Wade's chair, putting her hand on his shoulder, and looked at Seth. "Perhaps we can send one of the hands into town to send one for you."

Seth liked the idea. "Could do that, I suppose."

Sarah played with the hair on the back of Wade's head. "You could write it down, and one of the hands can take it in first thing." Then she bent down and kissed Wade on the cheek. "I'm going upstairs."

Wade smiled up at her. "Goodnight." Wade's eyes followed her across the porch to the front door until she disappeared into the house, thinking of her warm body next to his.

Seth broke the stillness bringing Wade back from his desires. "My guess is Hoskins will yell at the town council first, demanding our arrest, and then he'll head up to Denver to see that judge of his."

Wade turned from the empty doorway. "I don't see a judge getting involved in this thing now. Pete Hoskins was arrested with a legal warrant then broke out of jail by his pa."

Seth nodded in agreement. "Let's not forget that it was George Hoskins' own paid sheriff that drew down on you while you were trying to serve a warrant for his arrest."

Wade looked at Seth, wondering if he had forgiven him or was making a joke. "Any judge worth his salt would think the risk too high right now. My guess is he'll advise Hoskins to avoid bloodshed, turn his son in, and fight this in a court of law."

Seth thought on that a moment. "Sure would make this a hell of a lot easier." Then he thought of his deputies and Paul Leonard staying at Lawson's place and chuckled. "I wonder how Ted Lawson is getting along with Paul and my deputies?"

Wade softly laughed, then thought of Sarah sitting upstairs at her dresser wearing one of her soft nightgowns getting ready for bed. He drank the last of his whiskey, stood, stretched, and said he was turning in. "See you in the morning, Seth."

Seth said goodnight, saying he'd lock up and stayed in the chair a while longer, looking into the darkness that had swallowed up the plains and the mountains. His mind filled with Molly, knowing she would be getting ready for bed about now the same as Sarah. Feeling lonely, he stood and went for a short walk in the yard under the black sky of a thousand stars before turning in.

The next morning, Wade and Seth sat on the front porch after breakfast with their feet on the railing, listening to the sounds of the ranch, letting their breakfast settle. They were discussing ways they might arrest Pete Hoskins and Lee Jones without creating a small war. Wade sipped his hot coffee thoughtfully, looking at the empty road and hill beyond the archway. "There has to be a way to get Pete and Lee Jones away from the Hoskins' place."

Seth scratched the side of his face searching for an answer. "Whatever it is, it's going to have to be soon. We can't stay up here forever, and Paul Leonard can't stay at the Wheeler place much longer." He grinned at Wade. "I've got to get back to Sisters before Carl does something I might regret, and Molly runs off with pot salesman."

Wade smiled at Seth's sense of humor, and as he turned and looked at the road, a solitary rider crested the hill and rode toward the archway. "Rider," he said softly.

Seth looked toward the rider and watched as he rode under the archway toward the ranch house. "Looks like Harry Block."

Wade set his empty cup on the floor next to his chair, stood, and walked to the edge of the porch. "Bet you a dollar its Harry's visit has something to do with last night."

Seth stood and followed Wade, stopping next to him at the edge of the porch. "I'm sure your right. Things may get a little interesting around Harper in the next few days."

"Hope so," replied Wade thoughtfully as they watched Harry ride up to the porch and stop short of the rose bushes and hitching rail. "Hello, Harry," greeted Wade with a grin. "What brings you out here this time of day?"

Seth stepped from the porch, taking the reins to Block's gray horse so he could get down, noticing he had a troubled look.

Wade stepped into the yard as Harry dismounted, taking notice of the sheriff's star pinned to his dark blue shirt.

Block pulled a hanky from his inside coat pocket, took off his gray Stetson hat, and wiped his forehead and inside of his hat as he talked. "You boys stirred up a hornet's nest in town yesterday morning." Then with a serious face, he put his hat back on and looked at one and then the other. "We haven't had a killing in Harper in years."

"Not since Emmett Spears," responded Wade dryly.

Ignoring the comment, Harry motioned to the chairs on the front porch. "Mind if I sit?"

Wade gestured to one of the chairs. "Help yourself." As they followed him up the stairs to the porch, Wade said, "I see you have your badge back."

Harry sat down in one of the white, wooden chairs, took a deep breath, and stared at the scenery. "Sure is a pretty view of the country from here."

Wade and Seth sat on the porch railing and looked at Block. "Drink, Harry?" asked Wade.

Block folded his hands in his lap and shook his head. "No, thanks." He frowned as he looked down at his folded hands and then looked at Wade. "You two have got the whole damn Hoskins' place riled up. They're all mad as hell. If you weren't a United States Marshal, there'd be a lynch mob riding over that hill."

Wade looked doubtful. "Booth Fox wasn't the sort that had that many friends, Harry."

Block looked across the yard, considering that. "You're probably right, but some of them boys are looking for a reason to raise some hell." He looked first at Seth and then Wade. "George Hoskins came into town late yesterday and met with the town council saying he was afraid you two were gunning for his son Pete and Lee Jones."

"No one's gunning for Pete and that Lee fellah," replied Wade. "All Seth here wants to do is take them both back to Sisters to stand trial. That's what we attempted to do with Sheriff Fox, but he had different ideas."

Block took off his gray hat, scratched his head, and then looking uneasy, he put it back on and looked up at Wade. "Soon after Hoskins left, the town council came out to my place and asked me to take my old job back. They wanted me to look into what happened." Harry coughed, leaned forward, and spit over the railing, then sat back in his chair. "I talked to Sam Carney, and he said the sheriff drew first." He looked at Seth. "Says the same about Deputy Boyd." Then he looked at Wade. "I'd like to see that warrant."

Wade stepped away from the porch railing. "I'll go get it."

Seth asked Harry if he'd like a cold glass of water. He said he would, so Seth went inside and, in a few minutes, returned with the water and handed it to Block.

Wade stepped outside and waited until Harry drank his water and then handed the warrant to him.

Harry unfolded the piece of paper and started reading. When he finished, he folded it and handed it to Wade. "You better keep this," he said thoughtfully. "I'll tell the council that I saw the warrant with Booth Fox's name on it, signed by Judge Moore in Colorado Springs." He looked at both and then shrugged. "Looks like a clear case of Booth Fox resisting arrest is what got him killed." Then he nodded, thinking of the deputy. "Too bad Chris Boyd didn't keep his gun holstered."

Seth glanced at Wade, then softly said, "He'd be alive today."

Wade knew what Seth was thinking and then thought Harry didn't seem to be broken up by Booth's death. "How's old man Hoskins gonna take the news that we were in the right?"

Sheriff Block raised his brow, looking worried. "I haven't talked to old man Hoskins, and I ain't about to ride out there and deliver the news. I'll leave that up to the town council or one of his men." He paused and looked from one to the other. "It might be best if you two headed back to Sisters and let this mess blow over."

"Ain't leaving," said Seth, looking determined.

Wade nodded in agreement. "Not without Pete and Lee."

Disappointment filled the sheriff's face. "No, I suppose not. I suspected as much, but I had to try."

"You sure about that drink, Harry?" asked Wade. "You look like you could use one."

"I'm sure I could use one, but no, thank you." He stood, looked off into the distance in thought for a moment, and then turned. "George Hoskins can be a vengeful man." He looked at Wade. "You killed his oldest son, and he ain't about to risk his other son to the same man." He looked from one to the other. "Be careful." Then he turned and walked down the steps to the hitching rail, untied his horse, climbed up in the saddle, and looked down at them. "Anything you boys would like me to tell the town council b'fore I resign?"

Surprise filled Wade's face. "Resign?"

"I'm getting a little old for what might be heading my way. I only took it so's I could talk to you two and find out what happened."

Seth understood Harry's feelings. "Do me a favor, Harry, and send a telegraph to my wife, Molly Bowlen, telling her I'm fine, and I'll be home in a few days."

Block smiled and nodded once. "Consider it done."

"Do me a favor, too?" asked Wade. "Since you're already sending a wire for Seth, send one to Marshal Billy French in Santa Fe, informing him I may be here longer than expected."

"I'll send it. You, boys, be careful." Harry turned his horse and rode toward the archway and up the hill.

Seth looked worried as he took a deep breath and let it out slowly. "Sure would like to know what Hoskins has in mind."

Wade looked worried as well, mulling over all that Sheriff Block had said, especially about Hoskins being a vindictive man.

Sarah opened the front door and stepped onto the porch, wearing a light pink dress, her hair in a ponytail. She walked to the edge of the porch, watching a rider disappear over the hill.

Seeing where she was looking, Wade said, "Harry Block stopped by."

She turned to Wade. "I couldn't help but hear through the open window." Embarrassed at her eavesdropping, she looked at Seth.

He smiled an understanding smile and started for the steps of the porch. "Think I'll go check on my horse."

She waited until he was around the corner of the house, then she turned to her husband. "There's going to be trouble, isn't there?"

Wade's expression couldn't deny there would be. "More'n likely."

"This isn't your fight, Wade," she argued.

"It is my fight, Sarah. This is no different than anything I've done in the past with Billy."

She sighed and turned away, looking discouraged. "Wish we'd never come with you. My pa would be alive if we hadn't."

Wade looked at her worried face. "Maybe you and Emmett should go back to Santa Fe."

"I ain't leaving Ma," she said stubbornly.

"Take your ma back with you. This place ran without them before when they came to Santa Fe, I'm sure it can run without her for a while."

She shook her head. "I'll not leave without you."

He looked past her head to the mountains in the distance, wishing she would take her mother, Emmitt, and head back to Santa Fe. "Then we've said all there is to say."

She turned. "I'm scared, Wade."

"I know," he said softly. "It'll all be over soon."

"I hope so. I best check Emmett." Then she walked into the house.

He stared at the closed door for a moment considering her stubbornness, turned, and stepped from the porch to find Seth while thinking of Harry Block's warning.

Twenty-Four

Unable to sleep, Wade walked the front yard in thought about the past few days. Reaching the fence by the archway, he put his hands on the top rail and looked up at the few remaining stars in the morning sky, hearing a coyote cry out somewhere. Turning, Wade put his back against the railing and looked at the house barely visible in the early morning light wishing he had a cup of Mrs. Talbert's coffee. He thought of his unborn child, Jasper Talbert, Booth Fox, and young Deputy Chris Boyd. Then his mind found Dan Hoskins, whom he killed six years ago in Sisters, knowing had that never happened, everything would be different today.

The tip of the sun, bright and warm, broke over the eastern horizon, catching the tops of trees, while the land beneath waited in the dim light of dawn. He watched the sun as it continued its slow climb into the blue sky, knowing that Jasper and his child would be alive if he hadn't brought Sarah with him. Sarah just wanted to visit her parents and let them get to know their grandchild. Such an innocent thing, he thought. Turning away from the sun in the east, Wade leaned on the top rail with his forearms and watched as the sun touched the tips of the snowcapped mountain peaks in the distant west. Wishing things were different, he looked up into the early morning sky and wondered what God thought of all this.

A rooster crowed its hello to the early morning, breaking the silence, and as he turned from the mountains to the house, he saw smoke from the chimney of the kitchen stove and knew that Mrs. Talbert was up. As if someone had awoken the world, the silence filled with horses, cows, sheep, and chickens waking to a new day. Stepping away from the fence, he thought of a cup of coffee and started walking toward the house.

Barefoot, Sarah stepped out of the house and walked to the edge of the porch dressed in her white robe, wearing a smile as she wrapped herself in her arms. "Couldn't sleep?"

He walked up the steps, put his arms around her, and gave her a quick kiss. "Morning."

She felt warm and safe in his arms. "Are you worried about what Sheriff Block said yesterday?"

He couldn't lie to her. "That and a few other things."

She looked up at him. "Such as?"

He let go of her and looked at the mountains drenched in sunshine. "I thought that if I had never brought you and Emmett up here, your pa would be alive, and so would our child."

She looked up at his unshaven face and into his sad, blue eyes. "You couldn't have stopped me from coming along, Wade. You're not to blame for any of this." She paused. "We both know who's to blame."

He knew he would never have been able to stop her once she knew he was coming to Harper. Sarah was one stubborn woman.

She put her arms around his waist and pulled herself into him. "Let's go inside, and I'll help ma while you go up and shave."

Stepping into the house, she asked, "You and Seth heading out after breakfast?"

Wade had decided while watching the sun come up that they needed to scout around both the Hoskins' place and the town of Harper. He closed the front door. "Might be gone most of the day."

She took his hand as they walked across the floor. "I washed and ironed that blue shirt you like."

He smiled and thanked her, telling her he needed a cup of coffee, and she better put her slippers on.

Reaching the staircase leading upstairs and the doorway to the dining room, she watched him walk toward the kitchen for his coffee, then she hurried up the stairs for her slippers and to check on Emmett.

Wearing his freshly ironed blue shirt, Wade and Seth rode under the arch toward the top of the hill just as Doc Granger's buggy crested the top of the hill. They pulled up and waited until he stopped his horse and buggy. "Hi, Doc," greeted Wade.

Seth merely nodded hello, looking friendly.

Doc Granger set the brake and rested his foot on the front railing of the buggy. "I saw what was left of Fox and Boyd after you two left town." Being a man of healing, he couldn't say he approved but kept quiet.

Wade had no desire to talk about what happened. "You gonna take Sarah's stitches out?"

Granger looked up with a small smile, thankful that Wade changed the subject. "More'n likely. They have been in long enough. Could have taken them out a couple of days ago, but knowing Sarah, she'd shoot me if they left a scar."

Wade chuckled. "That she might, Doc." Then he pulled the reins to his horse, turning her toward the top of the hill. "Emmett's been using the crutches you brought out. Getting pretty good with them, too."

Doc Granger smiled. "Glad to hear it. I'll check on him while I'm here." Then he released the brake but held the reins tight. "How's Mrs. Talbert holding up?"

"She's doing good, Doc," replied Wade. "She's keeping busy."

"Glad to hear that. Well, I guess I better be getting down to the house." Then he slapped the horse on the back with the reins, bid them both a good day, and guided the buggy under the archway.

Wade and Seth turned their horses and rode up the hill where they parted company. Seth headed to a hill of boulders behind Harper, where he would use his long glass, checking all riders in and out of Harper. Wade headed west to a cliff overlooking the Hoskins' place that he and his friend, Emmett Spears, found years ago.

Neither Wade nor Seth had seen any sign of Pete Hoskins or Lee Jones. Wade had spent most of the afternoon of the third day hidden in the rocks under one of the few trees atop the cliff overlooking the Hoskins' Ranch. Pushing the long glass together, he set it down on the rock next to him, and deciding to check on the mare, he got up from the trunk of the tree he was leaning against. Taking a drink from the canteen, Wade poured some water into his hat and watched the mare drink. "Maybe we should head back," he said as if she understood. When the mare finished drinking, he put his hat on and wrapped the canteen's straps around the saddle horn.

Deciding to stay a while longer, he patted the mare on the rump and returned to his place by the tree and rocks where his long glass waited. Getting comfortable, he picked up the long glass, pulled it apart, and looked first at the barn, then the bunkhouse, and finally the main house. Two men hurried from the main house and ran toward the barn waving their arms at two other men standing outside the bunkhouse. The two men from the bunkhouse followed the others into the barn, and minutes later, all four rode out of the far side of the barn and headed north, disappearing behind the trees and rolling hills west of the ranch.

Taking the glass away from his eye, he looked up at the late afternoon sun and realized he had been careless in letting the afternoon sunshine reflect off the lens of his long glass. "They know someone's up here," he said aloud as he stood and put the glass back to his eye. Searching the rolling hills to the north, he soon saw them ride out of a ravine and turn east, disappearing into a stand of trees. Knowing they were on to him, he picked up his Sharps rifle and bandolier and ran to the mare. He shoved the rifle into its scabbard, put the bandolier around the saddle horn, and tightened the saddle cinch then untied the mare. Swinging up onto the saddle, he turned her east and rode at a fast trot, figuring they would be on him soon.

As he rode away from the cliff at a fast trot, he glanced over his shoulder several times before seeing the riders break out of the trees and ride after him. Not wanting to turn the mare loose just yet, and knowing their horses would soon tire, he continued at a fast trot, wanting to save the mare's speed for when he needed it. Reaching the edge of a wide gully, he paused to look back, and now he could hear the soft thunder of their horses' hooves on the hard soil as they closed in on him. Nudging the big mare into the gully, he rode through it to the other side and pulled up. He looked back at the four riders coming at a fast gallop and quickly estimated their distance. Knowing he had but a minute to let the mare rest, he watched as they raced toward him ahead of the dust cloud they created. One man stood in the saddle, and Wade saw the puff of smoke as he fired his Winchester, but the bulled landed several yards short. The mare grew anxious, sensing the danger, and eager to run. She turned in a tight circle head up, tail out several times. Feeling it was time to run, he nudged the mare, leaned forward against her neck, and let her have her head. Several minutes passed, the mare's breathing was getting labored, and he knew she could not last much longer at this speed. He turned and looked back just as the four riders came out of the draw and slowed, giving up the chase.

Wade sat up and slowed her to a trot and looked back at the riders, who had turned heading back to the Hoskins ranch. He slowed the mare to a walk, pulled her up and looked behind him to make sure the others had not changed their mind, and patted the mare on her shoulder. Deciding to let her walk a spell, Wade climbed down, giving her a much-deserved rest, and as they walked, he wondered how Seth was making out in the rocks behind Harper. The thought occurred to him that maybe he and Seth should head back to Sisters for a few days.

An hour later, he rode under the archway to the ranch seeing two men and a woman sitting on the front porch. The woman he figured was Sarah, one of the men looked like Seth, but he wasn't sure about the other man. Seeing Wade, all three stood and walked to the edge of the porch, and it was then that he recognized Billy French. Curious why French was in Harper, Wade rode across the yard to the hitching rail in front of the porch, stopped, and climbed down.

Billy French stood at the edge of the porch looking like he was dressed for a wedding in tan pants neatly tucked into a pair of Mexican boots, and under the long, tan coat, he wore a white shirt buttoned to the collar. On his head of dark, brown hair sat a wide-brimmed, tan Texas flat hat, and the bulge of his coat boasted of the Colt pistol he wore. Stepping off the porch, Billy grinned. "What sort of mess did you let this old dog get you mixed up in, Deputy?"

Wade shook Billy's hand and grinned. "It is a hell of a mess at that, Billy."

Sarah looked at Wade. "I'll go in and help ma with supper. It'll be ready soon, so you boys best go out back and wash up. I'll get some clean towels." She gave Wade a quick smile before she turned and went inside.

Puzzled at why Billy was in Harper, Wade asked, "What brings you to Harper?"

French grinned. "That little bastard dog of yours is eating me out of house and home, not to mention the little guy shits all over the yard, so I brought him along."

Wade looked surprised. "You brought Dog?"

"Never saw a dog shit so much," said Billy, then he shrugged. "I figured since I was coming this way anyway, Emmett could use some perking up." He paused. "After seeing the boy, I'm glad I did."

Wade looked curious. "How'd you know about that?"

Billy nodded to Seth. "His deputy sent me a wire a while back."

Seth had heard all this before, so he just listened.

Wade remembered the wire Sheriff Block sent to him in Sisters while he and Seth were on their way to Harper. He also thought Deputy Carl had been a little bit of a busybody.

French looked serious. "Truth is, I got a message from Sheriff Block saying you were having some difficulties. Putting that message with the first one, I figured there was a hell of a lot more going on up here than I knew about." He shrugged. "And, since I'm nosey by nature and there wasn't much going on in Santa Fe, I loaded my horse on the train and headed to Sisters with that damn little dog in a wooden box I made. I visited the jail and talked to Seth's deputy, and he told me about the jailbreak, so I rode into Harper…"

Seth interrupted. "I saw him riding up the street through my long glass." He chuckled with a big grin. "Scared the shit out of him when he rode past where I was hiding in the rocks." Seth chuckled again, looking proud. "Thought he'd done shit his pants."

Marshal French didn't see the humor. "You're damn lucky I didn't shoot your ass."

Sarah appeared at the door. "Supper's ready. You boys need to wash up. I don't want it getting cold."

Wade motioned to the side of the house. "You boys come around back and wash up while I put my horse away. Wade asked one of the hands to put the mare away, and after they washed up, they went inside to dinner.

Conversation during dinner was casual and covered anything, except why the men were here the accident and Jasper's death. For a while, it was as if none of it had ever happened. Sarah asked about Mrs. French, their

230

children, and what news, if any, in Santa Fe. Billy smiled, saying his family was doing good, filled her in on what little gossip he knew, and anticipating her next question, said her house was being looked after.

Dinner over, Wade, Seth, and Billy French sat in Jasper's study of books, desk, and expensive furniture, sharing a bottle of his brandy. While Seth had earlier told Billy most of what had been going on, Wade filled in the gaps.

Billy looked worried. "You boys have a mess on your hands."

"Can't argue that, Billy," agreed Wade. Then he said they've been trying to find a way to get Pete Hoskins and Lee Jones off the Hoskins' Ranch so they could arrest them, without getting into a gun battle with the Hoskins men. "We considered riding out there, but there ain't no one in town willing to join a posse."

French looked thoughtful. "I can understand their reluctance. Maybe what we need to do is light a small fire under this George Hoskins."

Wade sat forward, looking curious. "How we gonna do that?"

Billy took a thoughtful sip of brandy. "You boys know this George Hoskins better than I do, and from what you've told me, maybe we should go at this from another angle."

Seth and Wade looked interested.

"Go on," said Wade.

"Well," began French. "What if I were to send a wire to the US Marshal's Office up in Denver asking for help and a few of his deputies?"

Seth scoffed. "That piss ant isn't going to help us. I already went down that road with the little bastard. He and Hoskins are friends."

Billy grinned. "It ain't important if he helps. What we want this George Hoskins to know is that a United States Marshal has come to help his deputy and is asking for assistance from another United States Marshal. This marshal should be smart enough to know that asking for help from the military is my next move."

Wade looked at the marshal. "Might work, Billy.' He grinned. "It just might work."

French looked at Wade. "I'm sure this old man doesn't want a posse or a company of soldiers with a United States Marshals riding onto his place."

Seth looked hopeful. "Maybe he'll send his son and Lee Jones into Harper to surrender themselves."

French didn't look so sure about that. "Maybe, maybe not," He took a sip of whiskey and stared into his glass. "My guess is the first thing he'll do is head up to Denver and see if he can stop this."

Sarah suddenly appeared in the doorway, and all three stood and smiled. She excused herself for interrupting and then looked at Wade. "Emmett's ready for bed."

Seth drank the last of his drink, set the glass down, and looked at the others. "I believe I'll turn in."

"I'm tired, as well." Billy French smiled at Sarah. "Thank your ma for a right, nice dinner, Sarah." Then he drank his drink, set his glass on the table, and looked at Wade. "I think I'll go on upstairs myself. It's been a long day." He smiled at Sarah. "Goodnight, Sarah."

She smiled. "Sleep well, gentlemen." She stared after them as they left the room, and then she turned to Wade. "I'm glad Billy's here."

Wade wasn't at first, but now that they had a new plan that may end this thing and let him and Sarah returned to Santa Fe, he was. After turning out all of the lamps but one, he picked it up, locked the front door, and then he and Sarah went upstairs, stopping to check on Emmett. Finding Dog and Willie cuddled up on the foot of the bed together and the boy already fast asleep, they closed the door and went to their room. Wade got undressed and lay in bed, while Sarah put on a pale green nightgown. He watched as she sat at the dresser, brushing out her hair as she had done every night since they got married.

She looked at his reflection in the mirror and smiled, put the brush down, blew out the lantern, got into bed, and curled up next to him. Staring across the darkroom and out the window, she listened to the crickets and other night sounds, thinking of her father lying in his grave.

"You okay?" asked Wade.

"Thinking about pa lying out there under that tree instead of in bed next to Ma."

"I'm sorry about Jasper," he said sadly.

"I know you are." Then she put her arm across his naked stomach, kissed his ear, and whispered, "I've missed you."

Wade opened his eyes the next morning to the mountains out the window covered in sunshine. Realizing he had overslept, he sat up to the sounds of horses, cows, chickens, a hammer on an anvil, and other ranch sounds that floated through the open window. Resting back on his elbows, Wade looked at the empty bed next to him and wondered where she was. Tossing the covers aside, he sat on the edge of the bed, yawned, and looked at the clock sitting on the nightstand, seeing it was already seven-fifteen.

The door opened, and Sarah stepped into the room wearing her white robe and carrying two cups of coffee. She smiled. "Good morning."

He smiled. "Why'd you let me sleep so long?"

She sat both cups on the table next to the bed and then fluffed the pillows. "Because you needed your rest."

Only a woman thinks that way, he told himself, and then asked, "Coffee in bed?"

She smiled, telling him it was a special treat. "Now, move over." As he did, she handed him a cup of strong-smelling coffee and sat down beside him. She leaned back against the pillow, resting against the headboard, and sipped her hot coffee while looking out the window at the distant mountains.

Wade got comfortable and took a sip of the hot, strong coffee, and thought about last night and how soft and warm her skin felt against him. They sat in the silence and safety of their room as if they were hiding from everything and everyone. Outside in the hall, a door opened, dogs barked, and Emmett laughed.

Sarah sighed, shaking her head, looking disappointed. "That didn't last long." She set her cup down on the table, got up, and opened the door to the hall, finding Emmett standing at the top of the stairs leaning on his crutches. Hearing the dogs downstairs clawing at the front door, she asked what he was doing.

"Sorry, Ma, I thought I could let 'em out."

She smiled, turned to Wade, telling him she'd be back in a minute, closed the door to the bedroom, and patted her son on the head as she walked by. "Go back to your room." She hurried downstairs, opened the front door, and both dogs bolted across the porch into the front yard, where they started playing. She watched them a moment, glad that Billy brought Dog for Emmett, then closed the door and went back upstairs. Finding Wade half-dressed, she had hoped they could have a little more time together and felt disappointed. "Why are you getting dressed? We haven't finished our coffee."

Buttoning his green shirt, he turned. "I am finished."

233

"Well, I wasn't," she said.

Recognizing her disappointment, Wade smiled as he grabbed her hand and pulled her onto the bed.

Laughing, she told him to stop.

Fearful he would hurt her, he stopped and smiled warmly. "Drink your coffee. I'll finish dressing later."

She sat up looking happy, picked up her lukewarm coffee, and took a sip. "I miss our little house."

"You do?" he said, looking surprised.

She nodded several times, looking happy. "I love it."

He gestured to her mother's house. "Better than this?"

"Hmm hmm," she said while nodding. "It was our first. The house where Emmett was born and our second child..." she let the sentence die.

He leaned over and kissed her shoulder. "We'll have another."

She smiled at him as she set her cup down. "I best get dressed and help, ma."

Wade walked downstairs, finding Seth on the porch sitting in one of the three white chairs nursing a cup of coffee. He turned to Wade. "Mrs. Talbert has coffee ready."

"Had a cup upstairs with Sarah."

Seth thought on that a moment, remembering coffee with Molly. "Billy rode into town about an hour ago to send that telegram. Said he'd wake the telegraph operator if necessary."

"Billy's not one to tarry," grinned Wade as he thought on the conversation in the study the night before. He walked to the edge of the porch and watched Dog running circles around Willie as the two played, thinking Dog was good for Willie. "Sarah asked me to see how things are going around the ranch. She and her ma are afraid things aren't getting done."

"I'll tag along if you want."

Wade looked appreciative. "Thanks, I'd appreciate the company."

Seth grinned. "As long as I don't have to shovel horse shit and cow manure."

Wade thought of his chores as a child back in South Carolina, and then of his mother, who passed away a few years ago.

234

The door opened, and Mrs. Talbert, donning a gray dress and white apron, poked her head out. "Breakfast is ready. Get washed up."

"Yes, Ma'am," both replied, and then they stepped off the porch and walked around to the back of the house, where they could smell Mrs. Talbert's cooking as they washed up.

Marshal Billy French returned too late for breakfast, finding Wade and Seth in the barn saddling their horses. They listened as he told of waking the telegraph operator to send the wire to the marshal in Denver. "I told him I'd wait for an answer at the sheriff's office." He grinned. "Sherriff Block was kind enough to buy my breakfast, and after we finished, we walked back to his office and waited for my reply. Well, the reply from Marshal Lewis was not what I expected. He said he'd look into the matter."

Seth scoffed without humor. "Sounds like the little banty rooster dipshit."

French chuckled as he continued. "I asked the operator if he had a message for George Hoskins, and he said he did. It took some prying, but Sheriff Block managed to get him to tell us that Lewis suggested Hoskins come to Denver and explain what was going on. Sheriff Block got a big grin on his face and told the telegraph operator that he'd deliver the telegram in person." French grinned mischievously. "The sheriff said George Hoskins would have the news before I got back here."

"Now, all we do is wait," said a grinning Seth Bowlen.

"Right," agreed French. "Let's give the old man a day to get to Denver and back."

Wade nodded. "That'll give Seth and me some time to see how things are around here. We're heading out now. You're welcome to tag along if you have a mind to."

The marshal considered but a moment. "I'm a bit hungry after the ride back." Then he looked at Wade with a hopeful face. "Wonder if Mrs. Talbert or your wife would fix me something to eat?"

Wade shrugged, wondering how many meals a day Billy needed. "Don't know. You'll have to ask them."

"I think I'll do that," he said as he patted his horse on the rump and walked toward the back door of the house, talking over his shoulder. "I'll catch up."

Wade and Seth rode out and spent the rest of the day with Ted Bennett, foreman of the Double J Ranch. He was a man in his late forties, with a thick head of black, curly hair, bushy eyebrows, dark eyes, and a beard. By all accords, he was a good looking man and saved his money to buy a small piece of land a few miles east of the Double J.

They accompanied Ted as he checked on the other hands, helped him rescue a calf from a mud sinkhole, and herd cattle from one section of the ranch to another to prevent overgrazing. Billy never did catch up.

It was dark when they returned to a late dinner, and after they ate, both turned in, leaving Billy alone on the front porch with a glass of whiskey. Wade checked on Emmett, seeing the dogs were settled in, and then went to his room, finding Sarah sitting on the small sofa reading a book. Wade quietly got undressed and climbed into bed. He was dog tired as he looked at her. "Coming?"

She closed the book, made the short walk across the room, and climbed into bed.

Wade was on his side facing the wall, with his back to her.

As she lay against him with one arm around his stomach and closed her eyes, she felt content and happy.

In the silence, just before sleep took him, Wade thought about Booth Fox falling backward in the saloon with that surprised look on his face.

Seth woke early the next morning, dressed, and went downstairs, greeted by the aroma of fresh coffee and bacon at the foot of the stairs. When he walked into the kitchen, Mrs. Talbert was busy over the stove.

She turned with a questioning look while wiping her hands on her white apron. "The others up?"

Seth wondered why she didn't have a cook since she could certainly afford one. "I think so. Least, I heard movement behind the doors on my way down."

"Good," she said and went back to her cooking. "There's a big cup Jasper used to have his coffee in." She pointed to the cupboard with the fork she was using on the potatoes she was cooking. "Second shelf in that cupboard over there. Pour yourself a cup, go outside and have a seat. It'll be a few minutes before everything's ready."

Feeling funny about using Jasper's favorite cup, Seth did as told, poured himself a cup of coffee, and started to head for the front porch when she called to him. He turned, looking curious. "Yes, ma'am?"

"Mind me asking you a question, Mr. Bowlen?"

He smiled politely, already knowing what the question was. "Why, no, ma'am, I don't mind at all."

She stared at his cloudy eye for a moment and then looked into his good, blue one. "Can you see out of that bad eye?"

He grinned and nodded. "Yes, Ma'am. Not as good as the other, but I can see."

"Strange," she said softly as she stared at it for another moment. "Hmm," she said, then turned back to the stove.

He smiled as he turned and walked out of the kitchen to the front porch, greeted by the warm Colorado morning air. Closing the door behind him, he walked to one of the white, wooden chairs and sat down, careful not to spill his hot coffee. Taking a small drink, he looked west across the ranch and plains at the Rocky Mountains and took another small sip enjoying the stillness of the porch, the scenery, and thought of Molly. A faint breeze rustled the leaves of the tree next to the house mixing with the early morning sounds and smells familiar to a ranch that was waking up.

Feeling hungry, he wondered how long it would be before Mrs. Talbert had breakfast ready. Taking a sip of hot coffee, he wished he was back in Sisters with Molly in her restaurant. Seth missed her coffee and the way she would fix his breakfast and then sit down and watch him eat. He missed the smell of her in the morning while she slept and the way she laughed when he said something that wasn't particularly funny. Smiling from memory, he drank his coffee and thought about being with her.

The front door opened, and Wade stepped from the house, cup in hand, closed the door and walked to the edge of the porch.

"Morning," said Seth.

Wade took a small drink of his coffee without looking at Seth. "Morning." Taking another quick drink, he walked the length of the porch and sat in one of the white, wooden chairs next to Seth, and put his feet on the railing of the porch. "Nice morning."

Seth took a drink of coffee, listening to his stomach, growling softly, and looked at the mountains as a rider crested the hill and headed down the slope toward the archway. "Rider."

Wade nodded. "I see 'em."

Moments later, the rider rode under the arch and turned his horse toward the house.

"Looks a bit like Stu from the Circle T," said Wade. "Wonder what brings him to the Double J?" He set his cup on the small table, stood, and walked to the edge of the porch, wondering what he was doing here this time of the day.

Seth stood with his cup in hand, followed Wade, and stood next to him, watching the rider as he drank his coffee.

Stu Parks' face held a mixture of excitement and worry as he stopped his horse by the hitching rail. He was breathing hard from the ride, as was his mount, and as he looked at Wade, he pointed toward the mountains. "Pete Hoskins rode out just b'fore sunup, heading to Oregon."

Wade and Seth glanced at one another. Then Wade asked, "How do you know that?"

"A friend of mine by the name of Josh Martin, who works out at the Hoskins Ranch, told me not more than thirty minutes ago."

Wade and Seth glanced at one another, suspicious of this Josh Martin. "Stu, this is Seth Bowlen from Sisters."

"Yes, sir, I know who Sheriff Bowlen is."

"Why would this Josh ride over and tell you about Pete?" asked Seth.

Stu looked at Seth and paused, noticing his eye. "Cuz he's a good friend of mine."

Wade looked up at Stu, sitting his horse. "Makes no sense Stu, why would he do that?"

Stu made a curious face and shrugged. "Cuz we're friends, I guess." Then he looked upset. "Josh says he's heading back up to Wyoming to his pa's place."

"He quit the Hoskins?" asked Wade.

Parks nodded several times. "Josh thinks old man Hoskins has gone and lost his mind. Says he's get'n meaner every day, so he's heading home." Then Stu looked worried. "Said he ain't about to get caught up in something that could get him killed when the shooting starts."

238

Seth looked to the west and let out a soft sigh of disappointment, thinking of the Widows Lawson and Olson. "He'll be hard to catch."

Wade contemplated that for a moment and then quietly said, "Maybe."

Seth looked at Stu. "With Pete gone, there won't be any shooting."

Parks nodded, looking encouraged while trying not to look at Seth's eye. "Hope you're right about that, Mr. Bowlen."

Wade looked at Stu. "Thanks for coming over, Stu. You best get back before Tolliver misses you."

"He knows I'm here, but just the same, I got work to do." He turned his horse, saying, "Good luck." Then he rode away at a slow trot.

Wade turned to Seth, looking anxious. "You best wake up, Billy, while I talk to Sarah."

Seth followed Wade inside, up the stairs, and while Wade went to his and Sarah's room, Seth walked down the hall to Billy's room and knocked on the door.

Billy French softly called out in a drowsy voice, "Who is it?"

"Seth."

"Just minute."

Hearing movement from inside the room, Seth stepped back and waited.

Billy opened the door enough to look at Seth. "What?" He asked, looking tired and confused.

Seth looked into the sleepy face of Billy French. His gray and brown hair was a mess, and his handlebar mustache didn't look much better. "Need to talk," replied Seth. "Can I come in?"

Billy stared at him for a moment, wondering what could be so important, then stepped back and opened the door. After Seth was inside, Billy closed the door and walked to his bed, wearing only the bottom of his white long johns. Feeling the cold floor on his bare feet, he sat down on the bed and looked up. "What time is it?"

Seth shrugged. "About six-thirty."

French glanced out the window and then looked at him with a puzzled look. "What the hell's so important?"

Seth apologized for waking him and then told him about Stu and his story of Pete Hoskins leaving for Oregon.

Billy scratched his already messed up hair and quietly said, "Damn it." Then he looked at Seth. "Looks like old man Hoskins made that trip to Denver all right, but instead of turning his son in, he helped him leave the country." Then he looked down at his bare feet, sighed in disappointment, and looked at Seth. "Should have guessed as much. I must be getting old. All right," he said softly as he scratched the top of his head. "I'll be down soon as I clean up and get dressed." Then he stood and gestured to the door. "Show yourself out."

Seth walked out, closed the door, and when he reached Wade and Sarah's room, he paused at the door to knock, hearing voices from within. Their tones told him that Wade and Sarah were having words. Reluctantly, he knocked lightly on the door and softly called out to Wade. The voices went silent, and moments later, the sound of heavy footsteps he knew was Wade's approached, and the door opened. Seth noticed the deputy marshal's badge pinned to the pocket of his shirt and his wide-brimmed hat on the bed. Sarah was dressed in her robe, standing next to the window with arms folded.

Wade looked troubled. "I'll just be a minute."

Seth nodded his understanding and then gestured toward Billy's room. "French says he'll be down as soon as he gets dressed."

"All right," Wade said softly. "I'll be down in a minute." Then he closed the door.

Seth turned from the muffled voices inside and walked down the stairs, figuring Sarah was arguing with Wade about leaving, and couldn't hold any blame for her fears after all that has happened.

Mrs. Talbert was holding the big pot of hot coffee when Seth walked into the dining room. "Breakfast is ready. Everyone up?"

"Wade and Billy will be down soon."

She put the coffee pot down and pointed to a chair at the table. "Have a seat." Then she turned and disappeared through the swinging door into the kitchen.

Seth sat down, filled his cup with coffee, and waited for the others. As he sipped the hot, strong coffee, he pictured the scene upstairs between Wade and Sarah. He was glad he was down here in the stillness of the dining room and wished the others would hurry so he could eat.

The Chase

Wade, Seth, and Billy French rode northwest past the Hoskins' Ranch looking for signs of Pete Hoskins. Wade was sure they'd head for Whisper Creek, but Billy wanted to find their tracks to be sure, and after twenty minutes of searching, Billy let out a yell. He climbed down from his horse while Wade and Seth galloped to where French was kneeling.

Billy stood as they rode up. "I make it three riders and two packhorses." He pointed at the tracks. "These shorter strides are a little deeper, indicating heavy loads. Them others carry riders."

Wade considered that. "Makes sense they'd have two packhorses if they're heading up to Oregon."

"You still think they're headed to Whisper Creek?" asked Seth.

Wade rested his hands on the saddle horn and looked at the tracks. "They're heading in that direction. It's the last town before they cross into Wyoming."

"They could turn and go elsewhere," said Billy as he climbed up onto his horse. "How far to this Whisper Creek?"

"It's a ways," replied Wade. "Almost to Wyoming. It's just a little town that sits at the base of the mountains."

Billy looked in the direction Wade pointed. "Let's keep after their tracks." Then he spurred his horse and followed the tracks while Wade and Seth followed with the two packhorses.

They followed the trail for the better part of the day, and now the bright afternoon sun hung low in the sky just above the rugged snow-capped peaks of the Rocky Mountains. The bright, reddish-orange sun in their eyes obscured the land, the foothills to the west, and the mountains beyond. Behind them to the east, the prairie's grass and hills were covered in the late evening colors of burnt orange.

The horses were tired and needed to rest, so they stopped near a shallow gully of sagebrush and fir trees and dismounted. The prairie was quiet, not a hint of a breeze or a bird broke the stillness, and no one spoke as Billy gave his horse a drink from his hat, as he stared off into the distance in thought. Seth checked the supplies on the packhorse, loosened the cinch to his saddle, and gave both some water. Smelling the water as Wade poured it into his hat, the impatient mare tried to drink before he had water into the hat.

241

The quiet minutes passed, and thinking they had rested long enough and feeling anxious, Billy French climbed up onto his horse and took the reins of Seth's packhorse. "Take point for a while. We'll follow their tracks until it gets too dark."

Seth was in the lead, followed by Billy and his packhorse, then Wade with his packhorse. They rode at a walk in a line following the tracks that would lead them to Whisper Creek. Wade had fallen behind, bringing up the rear thinking about Pete Hoskins and the others riding all the way to Oregon while leaving an easy trail. He had followed easy tracks before, and these were no different, but even so, he was apprehensive, and then he thought of Stu's friend. "Hold up!" he yelled.

French and Seth turned in their saddles to look back as they pulled up and waited

"What is it?" asked French.

Wade stood tall in the stirrups and looked past them into the sun about to set. He raised one hand, blocking the sun from his eyes, and stared into the shadows beneath the mountains.

"What is it?" repeated French.

"Not sure," Wade said. "Just doesn't feel right." He turned, looked behind them at the landscape covered in the colors of the setting sun and back into the dark shadows beneath the mountains and sunset ahead of them. "We're in the open riding out of the light into the dark shadows."

Seth and French looked back in the direction they had come and then into the setting sun just as the stillness was broken by a thud, followed by distant rifle fire. Billy's gray horse reared up, throwing him just as a second bullet hit Seth with a thud knocking him off his black horse, followed by distant rifle fire. Both horses, along with Seth's packhorse, bolted north as another thud hit the supplies on Wade's packhorse. He turned his big sorrel mare and spurred her into a fast gallop east, riding in a zigzag pattern with the packhorse in tow. Bullets kicked up dust ahead and on either side of him as he headed for a small formation of rocks for cover they had recently passed. The packhorse was slowing him down, so he tossed the reins, lowered his head, and galloped toward the formation, hoping Billy and Seth were alive.

Reaching the rock formation that gave good cover, he dismounted and tied the mare to a dead tree. He pulled his Sharps from its scabbard, grabbed the bandolier of cartridges from the saddle horn, and ran into the rocks and trees. Taking a position in the rocks, he loaded his Sharps and looked through the rifle scope for Seth and Billy. The sun was gone, but there was still enough light, and it took a minute, but he found them lying against the wall of the shallow gully. A bullet kicked up dust near Billy, followed by the sound of distant rifle fire. Wade waited for the next shot, and after seeing the flash in the dim light in the foothills, he aimed at the flash and waited. He didn't have to wait long and fired at the next flash. After firing several rounds, Wade stopped and stared at the spot he had been firing at, waiting for another flash. Glancing back to check on the mare, he returned his gaze to the foothills in the distance and waited. After several minutes of silence, Wade thought about the canteen hanging from the saddle horn.

A coyote cried out south of him, making the mare nervous, so he got up and walked back to the mare, rubbed her nose and shoulder, and spoke in a soft voice to calm her. Putting the Sharps away and the bandolier over the saddle horn, he took the canteen of water off the saddle and took a good drink. He poured a small amount in his hand for the mare and hoped Billy and Seth were alright. Looking up at the sky of stars, then toward the east, wondering when the moon would rise so he could see more than just a few feet around him. Putting the canteen away, Wade turned and looked at the stars above the mountains, getting a fix on his directions that would take him back to Seth and Billy. Picking a bright star that hung low in the sky to navigate on, he untied the mare and started walking.

The minutes passed, and when he looked back over his shoulder, a full moon had risen above the eastern horizon. Another coyote cried out, and the mare snorted, raised her head and ears, looking alert and nervous. He drew his Colt pistol, cocked the hammer, and glanced around into the darkness, hoping they didn't run into wolves. Hearing a sound off to his right, he strained to see into the darkness, and seconds later, he saw a large, dark figure. The mare stopped, turned her head, and nickered softly and getting a nicker back, Wade knew it was the packhorse he had lost earlier. Talking to the packhorse in a soft voice, he reached down, took the reins, and tied them around his saddle horn.

Another coyote called out from somewhere behind them, causing the packhorse to tug at its reins while holding its head high with eyes wide, looking nervous as it let out a soft whinny. The mare's ears perked, and her head turned toward the sound. "Easy, girl," he whispered, wishing the coyote would keep his damn mouth shut. He climbed up on the saddle and rode at a walk toward the bright star, hoping he'd stumble onto Seth and Billy. After several minutes, he stopped and called out in a loud whisper. "Billy. Seth." No answer, so he continued for several more minutes and called out again.

"Over here," answered French in a loud whisper.

"About time you showed up," whispered Seth.

Wade stopped and peered into the darkness looking for them, nudged the mare into a walk toward the voices. After a few moments, he saw their figures in the light of the full moon, lying against the side of the shallow gully. He climbed down. "Shit, I feared you were both dead."

Billy was lying on the ground, and Seth was sitting next to him, holding his Colt pistol across his lap.

"Got me in the left thigh," said French. "Wrapped my belt around it to stop the bleeding." Then he quickly added. "I can't believe we were that damn stupid."

Wade looked at Seth. "You hit?"

"Left side," Seth said. "Went clean through. I'll be all right. Shoved it full of dirt to stop the bleeding."

Wade looked at Billy's leg and the belt he was using as a tourniquet. "Been loosening that?"

"Think I don't know any better?" asked Billy in an irritated voice.

Wade chuckled. "Just ask'n."

"Well, ask something smarter next time," said French. "Glad you kept ahold of the packhorse. I think that's the one with the medical kit."

"That's a bit of luck," said Seth with a chuckle. "At least, we won't die hungry while Wade's doctoring us." Then he looked at Wade. "Hope you got one of them, bastards, you were shooting at."

Wade was doubtful as he unsaddled his mare. When he finished, he gave the saddle to Billy to use as a headrest. "I'll see if I can find the horses at first light. They're probably holed up someplace for the night." Concerned over the marshal, Wade hobbled the horses, unpacked the supplies, and rummaged through them until he found the satchel of medical supplies. He knelt next to French and felt his head, finding it warm and wet. "Wish we could have a damn fire so I could see what the hell I was doing." He leaned closer to French, trying to see in the faint moonlight. "I need to clean this, Billy."

French nodded, knowing it was going to hurt. "Do the best you can."

Wade loosened the belt as carefully as he could and slid it from under the leg, feeling around the wound and under the leg as gently as he could. "There's no exit wound, so you still got the bullet in you." Then he sat back, looking concerned. "I can't dig it out; it's in too deep." He paused, looking back toward Harper. "You need a doctor."

"Do what you can," said Billy.

"I'm gonna have to cut your pants away so's I can wash the wound, put some salve on it, and then I'll bandage it." Wade looked hopeful. "That should make it feel better." Then he turned to Seth. "I'll tend to you when I'm done here."

"I can wait," replied Seth, then sat back to watch Wade as he started on Billy's pants with his knife.

Wade cut Billy's pants leg away, washed the leg around the wound with water from his canteen. Then he put salve on the wound and wrapped the leg with a roll of clean bandages. When finished, he sat back, looking tired. "How's the leg feel?"

"Not good." Then Billy nodded at Seth. "Better take a look at Seth."

"It'll keep 'til morning," replied Seth.

"Needs to be cleaned out, Seth," argued Wade.

Bowlen stared at Wade in the dim light. "I've done this b'fore. It'll keep 'til morning when you can see what the hell you're doing."

"Better let him look at it, Seth," argued Billy.

Bowlen shot him a look. "Go to sleep."

Knowing it was a lost argument, Wade helped French get comfortable against his saddle and then covered him with their only blanket. Seth lay back against the gully wall, trying to get comfortable when Wade covered him with his slicker. "Only had the one blanket."

"This'll do." Seth looked at Wade. "What about you?"

"I'll be alright." Wade sat down on the cold ground between them, hoping to get a little heat from each, his rifle and bandolier lying in front of him, his pistol in his right hand resting across his lap. He put the saddle

245

blanket over his legs and wrapped himself in his arms, hoping the light coat he wore would be warm enough while he kept guard over his friends.

Wade had fallen asleep at some point, and now the sun peeked over the top of the horizon, and feeling the warmth of it, he slowly opened his eyes and sat up. He turned to look at Seth and then Billy. Both appeared to be sleeping restfully.

Stiff and sore, he started to get up but thought about the bushwhackers. He looked toward the west and the foothills, wondering if they were still there, waiting for him or the others to show themselves. Staying low, he got up without disturbing the others, pulled the long glass out of his saddlebag, leaned against the wall of the gully, and began searching the distant foothills sitting at the base of the Rocky Mountains. His glass found a small line of cottonwoods he thought might be along the South Fork River. Worried about Seth and Billy, he decided to take the chance and gather up something to build a fire. Mindful of the bushwhackers, he walked in a crouch picking up a few pieces of wood that would be enough to make a small fire for breakfast. Within minutes, the sound of the fire and the smell of strong hot coffee filled the chilly morning air of the gully.

Seth raised his head and looked at the small, beat-up coffee pot. "You got a steak to go with that?"

"Afraid not," smiled Wade, then he picked up a tin cup, poured coffee into it, and handed it to him.

Billy was awake now, looking like he'd had a rough night.

Wade knelt next to him, felt his forehead, and was relieved at finding no sign of a fever. He helped him sit up against the saddle and then handed him a cup of coffee. "Need to take a look at that leg."

French took a couple of sips and watched as Wade took off the bloody bandage.

Wade examined the wound. "Don't look too bad. I'll clean it, put some more salve, and a clean bandage." Then he looked troubled. "Wish I could take that bullet out." He leaned forward and carefully touched the edges of the wound with his fingertips. "That hurt?"

Billy winced. "Shit, yes."

"Big baby," said Seth as he lay against the gully wall.

Wade chuckled.

246

Billy ignored the remark and took a drink of hot coffee.

Wade sat back. "Think you can make it back to the ranch so's they could send for Doc Granger?"

French nodded. "I can manage. Been hurt a hell of a lot worse than this." Then he motioned to Seth. "Better take a look at Seth."

Wade picked up his medical satchel and knelt next to Seth, who had tossed the slicker aside and began unbuttoning his shirt. Wade helped him off with his shirt, then the top half of his bloody long johns, and looked at the wound that was close to the scars of being shot in Paso Del Rio. "Need to clean this," he said, reaching for the water bag he had taken off of the packhorse.

Seth watched in anticipation as Wade poured cold water over the wound.

"Baby," said Billy with a grin.

Seth grinned. "Up yours, Billy."

Wade smiled at the two as he cleaned the wound, put salve on it, wrapped a bandage around Seth's midsection, and then helped him back on with his clothes. He turned to Billy and apologized for needing the saddle he was resting against. "I'm gonna see if I can find your horses."

Billy pointed north. "The last I saw of my gray, he was headed in that direction."

After saddling the mare, Wade put his foot in the stirrup, climbed up, nudged her into a walk, and smiled. "Don't wander off."

"Funny," responded Seth.

Bowlen was cooking breakfast when Wade rode up, leading his black and Billy's gray along with the other packhorse. He looked up from the small frying pan. "Where'd you find 'em?"

"In a little draw not far from here." Wade looked at Billy. "Your gray was a little skittish. It took him a minute to trust me, or I'd have been back sooner."

"Always was a good judge of people," said French.

Wade failed to see the humor.

"Sit down," said Seth. "Grab a plate, and let's eat."

"What is it?" asked Wade.

Billy looked at Wade. "You don't want to know."

It was decided while they ate that Seth would return to the ranch with Billy and the packhorses, and Wade would go it alone. Seth helped Wade pack up after they ate and saddled the horses, then he turned to him with a concerned look. "I don't much like you going it alone."

Wade paused to look in the direction he would travel. "I'd feel better if you and Billy were coming, that's for sure." Then he turned and pushed dirt over the fire with his foot. "Seems this is the hand we were dealt Seth, and I ain't about to toss it in." He felt he could travel faster without a packhorse in tow, giving him a better chance of catching up with them at Whisper Creek. He opened the cloth bag Mrs. Talbert had packed and took half of the bread, part of the cooked meat, and some jerky out of another. After he packed them in his saddlebag, he tied one packhorse to the other and offered to help Seth onto his black.

Seth motioned him away. "Help the baby," he said, referring to Billy.

After Billy was on his gray, Wade handed the reins of the lead packhorse to Seth, who tied them around his saddle horn. He looked down at Wade and held out his hand. "You be damn careful."

"I intend on doing just that, Seth." Wade shook his hand firmly. "I'll try my best to bring them back to stand trial, Seth."

"I know you will. Just be careful and bring yourself back."

Wade turned to Billy and shook his hand. "Take care, Billy."

"You be careful," Billy told him. "Lots of places for an ambush, and they won't miss you again."

Wade considered that. "I know." Then he stepped back. "You, boys, be careful. Tell Sarah not to worry."

"We'll do both," said Seth, then he nudged his black into a walk across the empty plains back toward the Double J Ranch. Billy looked at Wade full of worry, nodded once as he nudged his gray into a walk following Seth.

Wade looked after them for several minutes, hoping Billy would be all right. He was sure that Seth would be, but he worried about Billy because he felt a little warm when he touched his forehead.

The morning air was calm, the sun warm, and friendly. A single magpie broke the stillness of the prairie as it landed on a rock several yards away to watch the solitary stranger. Wade glanced skyward, seeing it was going to be a nice day, and then checked his pocket watch. Giving one last look at the two figures riding away from him at a slow walk, he swung up in the saddle, took one last look at the two men, turned his mare, and headed in the direction where the gunfire had come from.

French turned in the saddle and looked back, seeing Wade riding toward the foothills, hoping he would be all right, then remember other times Wade tracked wanted men alone. He turned and looked at the back of Seth's head. "You should have gone on with him."

Seth felt the same, but he knew that Billy was too badly hurt, and he had to see that he made it back to the ranch before an infection could take his leg.

Twenty-Five

Finding several sets of tracks heading north out of a wooded area, Wade climbed down from the mare, knelt to one knee, and examined them carefully. Although they were heading away from the wooded area, he wanted to see where they came from and climbed back up on the mare. Wade followed the tracks back to the edge of a wooded area where he pulled up, drew his Colt, and cocked it. He nudged the mare into a walk and followed the tracks with caution, glancing from this tree to that, half expecting to see the bushwhackers. Hearing the excited cawing of crows, he nudged the mare deeper into the woods. Coming upon several big crows feeding on uneaten food strewn around an empty camp as most flew off, but one stubborn crow returned to reclaim its prize. A curious red squirrel darted up an aspen tree and stopped on the first branch. The squirrel chattered with tail twitching as it watched the horse and rider stop next to the dead campfire. The occasional caw of the determined big, black crow that bounded around the food joined the sounds of the noisy squirrel.

Ignoring both the crow and squirrel, Wade studied the campsite for several moments before holstering his Colt and climbing down. He knelt to one knee, studying the different boot prints that had trampled the dirt around the fire pit of stones. Taking the glove off his right hand, Wade held his hand over the ashes, finding them cold. Sticking one finger deep into the ashes finding they were cold to the ground, he considered Stu's friend thinking that maybe Billy was right. It was Pete's plan all along to get them out here in the open, so he could kill all three and bury their secrets with them. One thing was certain. They knew he, Billy, and Seth would be coming after them.

Bored with the intruders, the squirrel ran down the tree and disappeared into the thick underbrush. Wade stood, put his glove on, and tied the mare to a tree. He was looking at the many boot prints that led into the trees toward the east. Following them, Wade came to an opening of rocks, bushes, and boulders atop a fifteen-foot cliff that fell away to trees and rocks below. He had a clear view of the prairie and the place where they were ambushed and spent the night without a fire. In his mind's eye, Wade pictured Seth, him, and Billy riding into the sights of Pete and his friends hiding behind these very rocks. He looked back toward the camp, knowing he would not have been able to see their fire from where he, Billy, and Seth had spent the night due to the trees and thick underbrush. They picked their spot well, he thought.

Seeing several spent cartridges on the ground, he bent down, picked one up, and examined it carefully. It was a .45 caliber cartridge and probably belonged to a Sharps or a Hawkins rifle. Picking up two more, he looked out into the plains and tried to picture him and the others riding into their sights. Tossing the empty cartridges over the cliff, he turned and walked back to his horse, untied her, and swung up. Taking a last look around, he turned the mare and followed the tracks out of camp, leaving the crows to finish their meal. Certain their destination would be the town of Whisper Creek, and fearing another ambush, he left their trail that would have passed through the forest of aspen, along the South Fork River, and kept close to the low lying hills instead.

By late afternoon, he came across a dry riverbed that he remembered passed close to the town of Whisper Creek. He paused to look around, remembering the day that he, Mr. Grimes, and Emmett Spears tracked a grizzly Emmett had wounded along this same riverbed. They found the dying bear, killed it, and after skinning it, they rode to Whisper Creek and the saloon, where they got drunk and spent the night.

Nudging the mare into the sandy bottom of the dry part of the riverbed, he turned north and rode at a slow trot next to a small trickle of water nearly two feet wide and maybe six inches deep, making its way south along the west bank. A rabbit scurried along that same bank,

251

disappearing into a thicket hiding from a screeching hawk that flew past at treetop level, having missed its meal. Watching the hawk land on a branch in one of the tall pines, Wade hoped the rabbit stayed in the thicket. He guided the mare out of the riverbed and nudged her into a faster pace, anxious to catch up with Pete Hoskins and company.

Whisper Creek

Beyond the foothills, the sun sat motionless above the mountains, painting the soft landscape tones of oranges and reds as he slowly rode in the sandy creek bed called Whisper Creek. It had been several weeks since the creek saw any real water and wouldn't again until the next heavy rain or snowfall. The creek's high banks were covered with rock, dry weeds, small cactus, and an occasional blue Columbine flower. As he rode along the sandy creek bed, his thoughts were of Sarah and young Emmett. He would be glad when all this was over, and he and his family could return to Santa Fe and their little house Sarah said she loved.

Rounding a bend, the rooftops of Whisper Creek rose over the thick bushes lining the side of the creek bed, all dwarfed by the tall mountains that loomed behind them. Stopping next to a dead tree lying in the sandy bottom of the creek bed, he pulled up, stood tall in the saddle, and looked over the bank of the creek at the tops of the buildings, and then dismounted. The town sat at Harlow Peak's base, taking the name from the same creek he now waited in that flowed out of the mountains between Harlow Peak and Cougar Mountain. For a few short weeks each spring, the creek overflowed into a raging river, giving life to the prairie before drying up to what the town's people called a whisper of water, often going dry in the heat of summer.

The town of Whisper Creek consisted of several buildings whose gray, weathered wood had been aged by the elements and time. Unlike most towns, all of the buildings lined the west side of the dirt street, facing east to take advantage of the warm sun during the winter months. The site was often used as a meeting place for mountain men, when each spring, they brought their winter's catch and Indian Squaws for trade. During a week or more of getting drunk, they played games only they understood the rules of, and after they were broke and the whiskey was gone, they headed back into the high mountains. No one knows for sure how the town came to be.

He looked up in time to see the last of the sun disappear behind snow-capped Harlow Peak and the other mountains that, because of their size, looked a lot closer than they were. With the sun gone, the late afternoon breeze carried the coolness of the snow and glaciers from high up in the mountains. Feeling a sudden chill, he adjusted his duster lapel and collar around his neck, opened his saddlebag, and took out his long glass. While the mare drank from the small stream that quietly wound its way along the bank, Wade climbed over the dead tree and hurried up the bank. Pulling the long glass apart, he studied the street, buildings, doorways, and windows until he came to the saloon he remembered from years before. Several saddled horses and two packhorses were tied to the railing next to the boardwalk. Believing the horses belonged to Pete Hoskins and his friends, he shoved the glass together and stared at the saloon in thought.

As before, when he had found the men he hunted, adrenalin heightened all of his senses, filling him with an excitement unparalleled by anything else he ever felt. His mouth went dry, so he left the bank, took a drink from his canteen, and returned the long glass to his saddlebag. Standing in the dry creekbed, he looked over the bank at the rooftops of the town in anticipation of finding Pete and the others. He swung up onto his mare and guided her up the bank between two bushes and rode at a slow walk toward the buildings of Whisper Creek. With the sun gone, darkness rushed toward the town, turning everything dark and shapeless shades of grays and blacks. Warm, soft lights from kerosene lamps filled the windows of the dark, weathered buildings and the scattering of shacks that dotted the higher landscape behind the town.

Riding toward the lights of the saloon, he thought of Billy French and Seth Bowlen, hoping they made it back to the Double J.

In the dim light of evening, only a few people walked along the street and boardwalk, none of whom appeared interested in another solitary rider. Paying them little attention, he focused on the last building bearing a weathered white sign above the door: "SALOON" in red faded letters. He rode at a walk down the street next to the boardwalk as muffled laughter and piano music softly made their way past the single closed door and dirty windows. Eyeing the horses tied at the railings in front of the boardwalk as he rode to the end of the hitching post, he pulled up, dismounted, and tied his mare to it.

Taking off his duster, he placed it over his saddlebags and tied it securely across the back of his saddle while glancing at the windows, door, and empty boardwalk. Reaching into his saddlebags, he took out an extra Colt pistol and shoved it in his belt next to his stomach. Then he took out three sets of handcuffs, walked around his mare. Glancing around, he stepped between two of the horses tied to the hitching rail, not surprised at finding all were carrying the Hoskins brand.

Walking up the steps to the boardwalk with the handcuffs in his left hand, he pushed the leather strap over the hammer to his Colt. Standing by the wall next to the window, he adjusted the second gun in his belt and peered inside, seeing Pete Hoskins and two men sitting at a table with two whores. Pete Hoskins stood, as did one of the girls taking Pete's hand, while the other hand reached for the bottle of whiskey. Glancing at the other two men, Pete smiled, said something, and then he and the girl walked up the stairs to the second floor, disappearing into the third room.

Wade returned his attention to the two men at the table. One, a big man sat with his back to the door; his black, tattered hat pushed back. The other, a young man of maybe eighteen facing the door, smiling at the pretty whore as she talked. After taking a quick inventory of the customers at the bar and tables, he opened the door, stepped inside, greeted by warm, smoky air, piano music, and laughter, and closed the door.

The girl sitting at the table had long, black hair that looked soft and shiny as it lay across her left shoulder, partially covering one breast of her bright green dress. She turned and smiled at Wade as he approached, but upon noticing his badge, the smile left her pretty face as she leaned close to the young man and whispered into his ear.

The young man looked at Wade and then his badge as fear filled his face. He looked at the other man that had his back to Wade and said something causing the other man to turn and look over his shoulder. He looked to be about thirty, unshaven, with brown, unruly hair.

Wade stepped toward them and tossed the handcuffs on the table. "Put 'em on."

The older man stared at Wade with something all too familiar in his expression that warned Wade of what was coming moments before he stood and went for his gun. Wade drew his Colt and fired, hitting the man in the center of his chest before he cleared his holster. The force of the .45 Colt at this close range knocked the man back onto another table, turning it over, sending beer mugs, cards, and money all over the floor. Women's screams mixed with the sound of chairs sliding from tables as people ducked and scrambled to get out of the way, including the fat piano player.

In the next instant, and before the smoke cleared from Wade's Colt, the younger man stood and clumsily went for his gun. Wade fired, hitting him in the right side of his chest, sending him backward, sprawling against the floor. Neither man got off a shot. Wade quickly glanced around the silent room while drawing his spare Colt from his belt with his left hand. Letting his eyes settle on the heavyset, curly-haired bartender. "Name's Wade Garrison. I'm a United States Deputy Marshal." He gestured at the two men with his pistol. "I've been trailing these two and another since yesterday."

"What are they wanted for?" asked the bartender.

"For bushwhacking federal officers a day's ride from here." Then he motioned to the stairs. "The one upstairs is wanted for four murders in Sisters, Colorado." Seeing the young man lying on the floor trying to get his gun that lay a few feet away, Wade walked over and kicked the gun away. Kneeling, he looked into the young face as blood oozed from the wound and the corners of his mouth. The young boy looked afraid as tears fell from the edges of his eyes.

"What's your name?" asked Wade, already suspecting who he was.

He coughed several times. "Josh Martin." He looked up at Wade. "I don't want to die."

'I know," said Wade in a soft voice. "That was a foolish thing to do, Josh."

Martin looked up into Wade's blue eyes, moved his lips as if he was going to say something, then he slowly closed his eyes and went limp. Wade checked Josh Martin's neck for a pulse, and finding none, he stood. As he stared down the young face in regret, he remembered how Seth felt after he killed Deputy Chris Boyd.

"Look out," someone yelled as Pete Hoskins fired at Wade from the second-floor balcony, narrowly missing his head. Wade turned and fired back, hitting the post of the railing next to Pete's head. Hoskins fired another errant shot as he turned and ran back into the room, slamming the door shut.

Wade hurried up the stairs, stood with his back against the wall, and tapped on the door with his pistol.

Hoskins fired two shots through the door, causing Wade to flinch to one side, and then with his back against the wall, he kicked the door ·open with his right foot. The girl inside screamed as Pete fired two more shots at the empty doorway. Knowing Pete was out of ammunition, Wade dove inside the darkroom, getting off a quick shot at a figure disappearing out the window. Getting up, he hurried to the window in time to see Pete Hoskins galloping up the street through the lighted images of the windows on the dirt street then disappear into the darkness.

Cursing to himself, Wade turned and ran past the good looking redheaded whore sitting against the headboard, holding a sheet over her breasts, looking terrified. He quickly apologized, hurried out the door and down the stairs, past a small crowd that had gathered around the two bodies. Pausing to pick up the handcuffs, he headed out the door.

A short, elderly, heavyset man wearing a brown hat, dressed in black pants and gray shirt, boasting a sheriff's badge, and holding a shotgun met Wade on the boardwalk. "Hold on, there."

At seeing the shotgun and badge, Wade thought he didn't have time for this.

The sheriff noticed the marshal's badge. "Sorry, Marshal, I heard the shooting and came running."

Figuring Pete would ride his horse until he couldn't run anymore, Wade holstered his gun, shoved the other into his belt, thinking the man was a little old to be wearing a badge, but then he thought of Harry Block. "I'm Deputy Marshal Wade Garrison. I've been trailing three men, and the two inside drew on me, and I had to shoot. The other man I'm after just rode out of town."

The fat man looked up the dark street in thought as he held his shotgun. "Mind telling me what them boys were wanted for?"

"Murder."

The fat man with the badge considered that. "You going after him tonight?"

Wade glanced at his horse, waiting at the hitching rail. "Thought about it. Unless you're arresting me."

The sheriff chuckled. "Not likely." Then he pointed to the saloon door. "What do we do with the two inside?"

"Bury `em." Looking irritated, Wade stepped off the boardwalk.

"And their stock and personal belongings?" asked the Sheriff.

Wade stopped and turned, wanting to get after Pete. "Take what you need to pay for their burial, send the rest back to the Hoskins Ranch near Harper." Wade walked to his horse, put the handcuffs in his saddlebag, and as he untied the mare, he looked at the fat man. "Something else on your mind, Sheriff?"

"I just thought it might be best if you waited 'til morning. The trail will still be there."

Wade couldn't disagree. "There a livery close by?"

He gestured toward the other end of town. "There's a livery behind the hotel. It isn't much, but the hay in the stalls is clean, and your horse will have a meal of oats and freshwater. And the price is right."

Wade doubted that. "How about the hotel?"

"It ain't much neither," he replied with a smirk. "The beds are lumpy, and the walls are paper-thin, but my missus changes the sheets every third guest."

"You own the hotel?"

"And the livery." Then the fat man walked down the steps and offered his hand. "Name's Kyle Fisher."

Wade shook his hand. "A night's sleep in a bed, even a lumpy one, sounds good."

Sheriff Fisher gestured up the street toward the livery. "I'll help you with the other fellah's stock."

Recalling a younger sheriff that arrested him, Mr. Grimes, and Emmett Spears for being drunk the last time he was here, Wade asked, "You been in Whisper Creek long, Mr. Fisher?"

"Be six years this November. Me and my missus moved here from New York."

Curious about that, Wade asked, "How did you settle in this place?"

Kyle looked disappointed. "Bought the place unseen. Pig in a poke, you might say."

Wade didn't need any further explanation. A lot of people from the east bought farms, ranches, and businesses in such a manner. Most of the time, they got what they paid for, but others, like Mr. Fisher, ended up disappointed.

They put Wade's horse up for the night and the Hoskins horses, and then they went to the hotel where he was introduced to Mrs. Fisher. Kyle excused himself and returned to the saloon and the two dead men. Mrs. Fisher was a short, plump woman, her face was rough and wrinkled, and her gray hair cropped short like a man's. The brown dress she wore was faded, the white apron soiled and torn in two places, and she had the look about her of a hard life. As they climbed the noisy stairs following the light of the lantern Mrs. Fisher carried, she made small talk by asking questions about where he was from and if he was married. Reaching the second floor, they walked down a narrow, creaky hall to a door she unlocked, opened, and then stepped inside.

While she lit another lamp, he put his saddlebags on a chair, leaned his Sharps against the wall between the bed and the door, and then tossed his tan duster and hat on the bed.

Mrs. Fisher checked the small stove in the corner, saw plenty of firewood in the bin, turned, smiled, and handed him the key. "Hope you sleep well tonight, Mr. Garrison. If you get cold, you can build a fire, but it'd be best if you waited until morning. There ain't enough wood to last the night, and you've plenty of covers to keep you warm."

Wade returned the smile and took the key. "Thank you."

Mrs. Fisher walked to the door she had left open and turned. "Breakfast is at six. Sleep past that, and you go hungry. I don't cook all day." She closed the door, and as the day caught up to him, he listened to her footsteps disappear down the hall. He felt tired as he sat on the edge of the bed that looked lumpy and uncomfortable. He took off his boots and shirt, leaving on his pants and socks, turned down the lamp, and climbed between the covers of the lumpy bed. He pulled several heavy blankets over him then closed his eyes, thinking of Josh Martin's tearful face. Recalling the last words of Tim saying he didn't want to die, the last thing Wade thought of was Martin's mother never knowing what happened to him.

Twenty-Six

The Canyon

Wade sat his horse at the mouth of a narrow canyon, not liking where Pete Hoskins trail had led him. He had been on his trail for two days and came close to catching him twice when they exchanged gunfire, but both times Hoskins managed to escape. Not having eaten for a day, Wade thought of a hot cup of coffee, eggs, and a big slice of ham while glancing around at the trees, shrubs, and steep rocky sides of the canyon. He was tired of chasing Pete and tired of eating jerky. The mare was tired also, and she protested by blowing through her nostrils and then shaking her head, rattling her bridle and bit. He reached out and stroked her neck. "Can't go home just yet, girl."

The canyon's rocky cliff walls were steep, close to one hundred feet in places, and sparsely covered by pinyon and sagebrush growing out of the crevices of the canyon walls. Above the cliffs, a mixture of aspen and pine trees blanketed the sides of the mountain. The taller mountains beyond were still covered in trees that got sparse as they reached timberline where a thin layer of early snow blanketed the rough, rocky terrain to the summits. Wade couldn't see the creek off to his left, but he could hear the water as it made its way over and around rocks and boulders on its way down to the flatlands. The mare raised her head, perked her ears, and flared her nostrils smelling the water.

Wade climbed down, knelt to one knee, and studied the familiar tracks of Pete Hoskins that led up the canyon floor, and he could find no signs of his tracks coming back out. Either there was another way out, or Pete was up there somewhere waiting for him. Suspecting the latter, he stood and studied the narrow trail that snaked its way up the mountain between the canyon walls. Knowing he had no other choice but to follow the tracks left by Pete Hoskins, he drew his pistol, cocked it, and cautiously led the mare on foot into the entrance of the canyon.

It was quiet, except for the sounds of the creek he could not see, a slight breeze in the pine trees, and a few birds. The sun was high and warm, and he began to sweat a little as he walked up the gradual slope keeping a keen eye out for Hoskins. A few minutes into the canyon, he heard a horse bray somewhere up ahead. Stopping, he turned his head slightly to listen for any sound that shouldn't be there. Hearing nothing but the breeze, he continued past a crevice that ran up the length of the canyon, stopping next to a large spruce tree. Thinking of water, he glanced back down the canyon, then at the trail leading up the canyon, and listened to the silence.

A bullet glanced off a large rock formation sticking out from the slope behind the tree, spraying the side of his face with the stinging dust followed almost immediately by the sound of the rifle. Dropping the reins of the mare, he jumped behind the tree as another bullet struck the tree trunk above the mare's head. She turned and galloped back down the canyon, taking Wade's Sharps, the long glass, and water with her. Knowing she wouldn't run far, he took off his hat and peered around the trunk of the tree, looking for some sign of Pete Hoskins. "No sense in running anymore, Pete. Give yourself up!"

"That's easy for you to say, Marshal," yelled Hoskins with humor. "You're not the one that's gonna go to prison."

"Better than getting yourself killed."

"I have no intention of dying, Marshal. But today, you'll meet my brother in hell. He's waiting for you."

Wade considered that while remembering that day in Sisters. "I'm sure he is." Wanting to find out where Pete was hiding, Wade fired a quick shot into the canyon, hoping Hoskins would return fire. As planned, Pete returned fire, hitting the tree Wade was hiding behind, not realizing the smoke from his rife would give away his position. It was clear to Wade that Pete was out of his Colt's range, and he wished he had his Sharps. As Wade took another quick look from behind the tree trunk, Pete fired, hitting the tree. Wade recognized the distinct sound of a Winchester and not a Sharps or Hawkins. While he thought of his promise to Seth about not killing Pete, he glanced around, knowing he couldn't stay where he was for long without water. Wade remembered walking past a deep crevice in the rock wall a few yards back, big enough for him to hide in. If it went all the way to the top, he might be able to climb up out of the canyon. To do this, he needed to draw Pete's fire again so he could make a run for the crevice while he was injecting another cartridge into his Winchester. It was a slim chance, but he knew that Pete was no marksman, or he'd be lying on the canyon floor dead with the first shot. Taking aim at Pete's position, he raised his sights above it to compensate for the distance, fired twice. As Pete fired, Wade turned and ran toward the crevice. A bullet ricocheted off the canyon wall and another just as he made it into the crevice. Pete fired twice more at the back of the crevice so the bullets would ricochet into it, and as both hit above Wade's head, it caused him to doubt his own decision.

He looked up the crevice toward the top of the canyon, thinking it would be a difficult climb, but he was sure that he could make it to the top while hidden by the sides of the crevice. His only concern was if Pete moved from where he was, so he fired another shot and then crouched down as close to the ground as he could while Pete fired several shots into the back wall of the crevice. Bullets ricocheted off the wall covering him in rock dust. Pete stopped firing, and after Wade brushed the dust off his shoulders and hat, he reloaded his Colt, reconsidering his promise to Seth.

"You okay, Marshal?" yelled Pete with humor.

"You came close," hollered Wade while taking off his spurs, boots, socks, and hat, placing them on the ground behind him.

"You've no place to go, Marshal! How's the water holding out?"

"What water?" he yelled as he stuffed his socks into his back pockets and began his climb up the crevice in his bare feet.

Pete laughed. "You can share mine! All you have to do is come and get it!"

"For some reason," yelled Wade, "I don't think I could trust you!"

Pete laughed. "You may have a point there, Marshal!" Pete Paused. "You ever think about how different things might be if Dan and I had left town that night?"

Wade continued his slow climb up the crevice. "Never entered my mind, Pete!" He paused and climbed a few feet. "But I have wondered what Dan would be like if I hadn't killed him!"

"Me too," yelled Pete.

Neither spoke anymore, and by the time Wade reached the top, he was tired, hot, and his bleeding feet hurt. He drew his pistol, crawled out of the crevice, and tiptoed across the rocky surface on sore feet, hoping Hoskins hadn't left his hiding place. Reaching a large rock, he sat down, looked at his feet, thinking of his boots back down in the crevice, then put his socks on to ease the pain. The top of the canyon was a rocky surface covered with pinyon and sagebrush, leading to a thick wall of fir and aspen trees that went up the mountain's slope. If his calculations were correct, Pete should be hiding west of him, and knowing the rocky surface was going to hurt his feet, even with socks on, he stood. Wade crouched down and hurried to the next boulder and then the next until he was behind a rock overlooking the canyon cliff and the creek below.

Wondering where Pete was, he looked up at the sun, wishing he had his hat and some water. It was hot, he was thirsty, and he couldn't help but think of the water in the creek below. Wade looked at his bloody socks wishing he had his boots. He crawled toward the edge of the cliff, hoping he was above Hoskins. Lying on his belly, he carefully peered over the edge, seeing the canyon's dead-end about three hundred yards to the west. A waterfall cascaded down the side of the canyon into a large pool of water that was the beginning of the creek flowing down the canyon to the flatlands. Wade thought the cold water would feel good on his sore feet.

Wade crawled closer, sticking his head farther over the edge, looking for Pete but couldn't see him, and from this vantage point, everything looked different. Now he wasn't sure if Pete was to his left or right, and he could see the tree he had hidden behind and the crevice below, but no Hoskins. Moments passed, and then hearing something off to his left, he turned, seeing Pete standing next to a boulder about the same time Pete saw him. Looking startled, Pete raised his rifle to shoot, but Wade got off the first shot. His aim was off, and his bullet ricocheted off the rock next to Pete's face, splattering him with bits of splintered rock. Pete grabbed his face, and as he turned away, he tripped over a rock then screamed as he disappeared over the steep edge of the cliff.

Wade got up, limped on sore, bloody feet to the edge where Pete fell and looked over the edge. Pete Hoskins was lying on the rocks at the edge of the stream, blood from his head covering the rocks. Wade thought about Pete's father, George Hoskins. Having already taken the life of the man's oldest son six years ago, he had wanted to take Pete alive, not for Pete but for his father. Feeling sorry for Mr. Hoskins, he turned away, limped back to the crevice, and climbed down.

Harper

The late afternoon sun cast long shadows across the street of Harper as a weary Wade Garrison rode at a walk leading Pete Hoskins black horse up the street. Pete's body was wrapped in his slicker and draped over the saddle. The residents of Harper watched in silence while recognizing the black stallion, and knowing who was draped over the saddle, whispers repeated Pete Hoskins' name. Fearing the wrath of George Hoskins that he may in some way blame the town for his son's death, women hurried their children along the boardwalks.

Wade pulled up outside the office of Doc Granger, climbed down, tied his mare to the hitching rail, and without glancing around, stepped up onto the porch. He walked across the boardwalk, opened the door, and stepped inside to reappear moments later with Doc Granger. Together, they carried Pete's body inside, and after they laid the body on a table, Wade asked about Billy and Seth.

"They're both doing fine." Doc looked at Wade with concern. "But you don't look so good. When was the last time you slept or ate a good meal?"

"Been a while," admitted Wade in a tired voice. He sat down looking tired, then told Doc Granger how he tracked Pete and of him falling off the cliff.

Doc stared down at the lifeless face of Pete, picturing what happened, covered him, and then offered Wade a cup of coffee.

Wade refused, saying he wanted to get home, and then he shook Doc's hand. "Would you have someone take Pete's horse to his father? I don't think he'd take kindly to me bringing it back?"

Knowing Mr. Hoskins would probably kill Wade, he nodded. "I'll see it's taken care of."

Wade glanced back at Pete Hoskins body wrapped in his slicker, turned to Doc, thanked him, said goodbye, and stepped outside. He never noticed the streets were deserted as he climbed into the saddle and rode toward the Double J, hoping to be there before dark.

The ride from Harper to the ranch passed quickly, and it was almost dark when he reached the top of the hill overlooking the peaceful setting of the Talbert ranch house nestled among the cottonwoods. Soft, orange light from kerosene lamps filled the windows, and he thought of Sarah, food, and sleep. Sensing a warm stall, fresh hay, and oats, the big mare needed little prodding as she trotted down the hill and under the archway.

Seth Bowlen stood from the chair he had been sitting in and disappeared inside, reappearing moments later, with Sarah. Pausing at the edge of the porch, she lifted her dress as she ran down the steps and across the yard toward her husband.

Spurring the mare into a gallop, Wade rode across the yard, pulled up, jumped down, and braced himself as she ran into his arms.

They held one another, and then she looked up with tears in her eyes. "I've been worrying myself sick, Wade Garrison." Then she stepped back and looked at him with a worried look. "Are you alright? You're not hurt, are you?"

Wade smiled, feeling happy to be home. "I'm fine, Sarah."

Seth Bowlen smiled, turned, and walked inside, giving them the few moments they needed.

Smiling with tears on her cheeks, she said, "You look tired. Are you hungry?"

He put his arm around her and walked toward the porch while the mare tagged along. "I am tired as hell, and I'm hungry."

"When was the last time you ate?"

He thought about that for a moment. "Not sure. A couple of days ago, I imagine. Some little town west of here."

"And you wonder why I worry."

He smiled. "You always worry." Then he asked about Emmett.

She wiped her tears of happiness away and smiled. "He's doing fine and walking with only one crutch. I think he's asked me when you were coming home just about every hour. You should go up and see him."

"I will in a minute." Then he shifted his attention to the front door. "How's Seth and Billy?"

She laughed softly. "You'd think they were married to one another." Then she looked worried. "What about Pete Hoskins?"

Wade looked sad. "He's dead."

Worry over what Mr. Hoskins would do filled her.

"I didn't kill him, Sarah. He tripped and fell off a cliff. The fall killed him."

She looked relieved as she put her arm around his and pulled herself closer, and then they started toward the porch. "Dinner's almost ready. I'll have one of the hands put your horse away and bring your things up to the house."

"I can do it."

"No," she insisted. "You go up and see your son, and I'll lead the mare into the barn and have someone care for her."

He chuckled softly. "All right, but make sure she gets plenty to eat and a good rubdown."

She smiled. "I'll take care of it. Now go."

Walking into the house, Wade found Seth sitting in the living room with a small glass of whiskey.

Seth grinned as he got up to greet him with an open hand. "Glad you're back."

"How's the side?"

"Good as new almost."

"And Billy?"

Seth glanced around to see if anyone was listening. "He's a big baby."

Wade chuckled.

"What about Pete Hoskins? "asked Seth. "Did you get him?"

Wade frowned, looking regretful, and shook his head. "I'm sorry, Seth. I tried, but Pete's dead. So are the others."

Seth's face filled with disappointment. "What happened?"

Wade put his hand on Seth's shoulder. "I didn't kill him if that's what worries you. We'll talk after dinner. I want Billy to hear the full story."

"All right," said Seth, feeling relieved yet disappointed about having to wait. Then he gestured toward the stairs. "You best get up to that boy of yours. Seeing you again is all he's talked about."

Emmett was putting on a clean shirt for dinner while Willie and Dog watched from the bed, their heads slightly tilted, and as the door opened, all heads turned. Dog was the first to jump off the bed, barking and tail wagging, with Willie close behind whining and wagging his tail. Wade knelt to greet the pair, getting his face licked while petting both dogs. He looked prideful at his son. "Your ma tells me you're getting around pretty good."

He smiled proudly. "Yes, sir."

Willie and Dog made it back to the bed, where they watched from the comfort of thick, soft covers while Wade walked to the bed. He sat down beside Dog, reached down and petted its head, and then petted Willie's neck and back. He looked at Emmett. "We'll be heading home in a few days."

"Good," he said, looking happy.

"Miss your friends?"

Emmett nodded. "Mostly." Then he asked his pa bout his trip and if he had caught the bad men. Wade frowned, looked down at Dog's black eyes, and said that he had. Silence filled the room until Emmett said he could do some tricks with his crutches. Wanting to think of something other than Pete Hoskins and the others, Wade looked up and smiled. "Well, let's have it."

Emmett showed him some tricks he could do with one crutch, which weren't actually tricks at all, but cute just the same.

Sarah opened the door and stuck her head in. "Dinner's ready." She smiled at her husband for a long moment, drinking up the image of him sitting on his son's bed with Dog and Willie. "Better get washed up." Then she closed the door.

Wade stood and waited while Emmett got his crutch, and as Wade opened the door, Willie and Dog darted out and ran down the stairs, past Sarah to the front door. While they waited patiently, tails wagging for her

266

to let them out, Emmett proudly refused any help from his pa down the stairs on his one crutch. Having let the dogs out, Sarah waited for her husband and son at the bottom of the stairs, and together, they walked into the dining room.

Looking happy, Janice Talbert greeted Wade with a big hug, telling him she was glad to have him safely back, then told him to sit at the head of the table in Jasper's place. Wade said hello to Marshal French, who was sitting at the other end of the table, the material of his left pants leg cut away at the thigh above his bandage, and his foot resting on an empty chair. After everyone was seated, Wade asked him how he was doing.

French said it was healing, thanks to Doc Granger.

Mrs. Talbert said a quick, thankful grace and then smiled at Wade as she handed him the mashed potatoes. "You had us all worried, Wade, and now my Sarah can sleep once again."

Sarah gave her mother a disapproving look that her mother ignored.

After dinner, Seth helped Billy up from the table, handed him his crutches, and followed Wade into Jasper's library. Seth helped Billy get settled into a chair and sat next to him as Wade poured their drinks. He handed each a drink, dropped easily into another chair, and took a quick sip while thinking of where to start his story. Having decided, he set his glass down on the table next to his chair and began with the empty campsite, then of Whisper Creek and killing Josh Martin and the other man in the saloon.

"I figured that little bastard was in on it," said French.

Seth nodded in agreement, then took a small drink of whiskey.

Wade went on to tell of how he trailed Pete Hoskins for two days, cornering him in a small canyon, of the ambush, Hoskins' fall to his death, of bringing him back and leaving him at Doc Granger's place.

Seth's face held disappointment in it as he thought of Gertie Lawson and Mrs. Olson.

Wade looked at Seth and thought about their argument over Booth Fox. "I tried to bring him in alive, Seth, but Pete said he wasn't going to prison."

Seth looked up with raised brow and a small smile. "I'm sure you did. But the only thing George Hoskins will understand is that you are responsible for the death of both of his sons."

Wade looked down into his glass in sadness. "I can't do anything about that. Both of his sons tried to kill me."

"Just be careful," offered Billy. "And mindful of what goes on around you until you get back to Santa Fe."

Wade considered that briefly as he looked at him. "When can you head back?"

Billy glanced down at his leg, looking unsure. "Soon as I can ride."

Wade sat back in the chair, looking curious. "I wonder if Lee Jones is still in the territory. I half expected to find him with Pete."

Billy looked unsure. "Good question."

Seth stared at the floor and then looked at Wade. "I have a feeling he ain't gone far. Deputy Lee impressed me as the sort that stays where the money is, no matter what." He thought of Paul Leonard, Sam Wheeler, and Kyle. "I better send a wire to Carl and tell him to tell everyone to go home."

Wade suddenly felt exhausted, drank the last of his drink, and stood. "Sorry, boys, but I'm tuckered out."

"I'm tired myself," said Billy.

Seth stood and helped French up while Wade turned out all the lanterns but the one he carried upstairs. After seeing Billy and Seth to their rooms, he checked on Emmett and the dogs before going to his room.

Sarah looked up from the book she was reading as the door opened. She smiled, closed the book, set it on the nightstand, and watched while he sat down and began taking off his boots. "Are you going to tell me what happened?"

"I already told you about Pete. There's not much to tell." He placed the boots next to the chair, stood, and began undressing. As he did so, he told her about the ambush and spending the night without a fire. He told her of patching both Seth and Billy up and following the others to Whisper Creek. He got in bed, rested against the headboard, and watched the slight breeze come through the open window to play with the lace curtains. He stared at the darkness out the open window and finished the story by telling her how Pete Hoskins died, and then about his older brother Dan Hoskins six years ago in Sisters.

"You never told me that," she said, looking surprised.

He shrugged. "Never saw the need."

She looked sad. "Poor Mr. Hoskins." Then she looked worried. "Do you think there will be trouble?"

"Not sure," he said thoughtfully while looking out the window. "I killed both of his sons." Then he turned to the kerosene lamp on the table next to the bed, turned it off, and lay back on his pillow, staring up at the black ceiling. "We've been gone too long from home. Maybe it's time you thought about taking Emmett and heading back to Santa Fe."

"I'll not leave without you. We all leave, or we all stay."

He was in no mood for an argument. "Let's talk about this later. I'm tired." He scooted down under the covers, turned onto his side facing the door, and closed his eyes, thinking of the face of Josh Martin as he died, and the surprised look on Pete's face as he fell to his death screaming.

She put one arm around him and held him tight. "I've missed you."

Wanting to rid his mind of Pete Hoskins and Josh Martin, he turned over, took her in his arms, and kissed her.

The ground was soggy from an August rain that pelted the plains of Eastern Colorado as Wade and Ted Bennett sat their horses hunched under their slickers staring through the blurry, gray curtain of rain. As the rain poured from their wide-brimmed hats, they watched the ghost-like figures of cattle standing like statues in the heavy rain. Wade thought of hot coffee and dry clothes as quiet thunder without lightning rolled out of the gray, metallic sky, making the mare and Ted's horse nervous.

The rain soon let up to a drizzle and then stopped as the sky to the west suddenly opened, allowing the late afternoon sun to spread its light and warmth across the prairie with a gift of a large colorful rainbow. The cows that had been huddled in small groups now walked leisurely with tails swishing, nibbling on the wet, prairie grass.

"It'll be dark in a couple of hours," offered Wade. "We should head back."

"You go on ahead, Mr. Garrison," replied Ted. "I want to check a couple of things first."

"All right," said Wade, then he turned the mare and rode north toward the barn and ranch house, thinking of a hot cup of coffee.

Wade rode into the yard, and toward the barn, the gray clouds that had rained on him were far to the north. The sky above and south was blue, filled with a spattering of white, puffy cumulus clouds looking like cotton. He rode into the barn, unsaddled her then took off his wet slicker. He slipped a bag of oats over the mare's head, and while she worked on the oats, he dried her off, gave her a rubdown, then covered her with a blanket. When he finished, he went into the house, where Sarah greeted him with a hot cup of coffee, telling him supper was almost ready.

Sarah helped her mother clean up the dinner dishes while Emmett sat on the front porch's steps, throwing a stick for the dogs to fetch, but Dog chased Willie instead. Wade, Seth, and Billy sat on the porch, enjoying the last of the day watching the boy's frustration with the dogs. It was quiet and peaceful when Sarah appeared at the door and called to Emmett. "Time to come inside."

Emmett stood with the help of his crutches, turned, and called to the dogs. Being quicker than the boy, they ran past him and his ma, disappearing inside the house. Emmett laughed at the two while Sarah waited for him at the door, and after he went inside, she smiled at Wade and told Seth and Billy goodnight.

Wade stared at the closed door, thinking about going home to Santa Fe and leaving all of this Hoskins stuff in Harper. He drew in a deep breath and let out a soft sigh. "We need to end this thing."

Seth shifted in his chair and thought of Molly. "What's on your mind?"

French was sitting in one of the white chairs with his injured leg resting on a short stool. "I ain't gonna be much use with this leg."

Wade stood, combed his brown hair back with the fingers of his right hand, feeling anxious as he sat on the railing of the porch. "We can't just sit around." Then he looked at Seth. "You up for a ride into Harper, to see if anyone knows where Lee Jones is?"

Seth shrugged. "Sure. When?"

270

"Right now," shrugged Wade, then he looked out toward the yard. "If he's left the country, ain't any sense in us hanging around, and I'd like to know right now if he has."

Seth stood, knowing Wade was as anxious as he was to get out of Harper. "I'll go up and get my gear."

"I'll meet you in the barn," Wade said, and then he looked at Billy. "You gonna be all right?"

French nodded. "I'll stay out here a while and then go upstairs. Doc Granger's supposed to come by tomorrow and check on this leg. If he says I can ride, I'm heading back to Santa Fe."

"Maybe me and the family will tag along," said Wade. "You can ride in the back of the wagon. I'd like to get back."

Billy played with his mustache as he looked at the setting sun. "This thing has about played itself out." Then he looked at Wade, "I think Seth can live with the results. I need you back in Santa Fe."

Wade gave a quick nod feeling glad it was over, and headed upstairs to get his gear. Finding Sarah in Emmett's room, he told her that he and Seth were riding over to see Tolliver Grimes and maybe ride into town.

She didn't mind the Circle T but argued against Harper.

He smiled reassuringly. "It'll be all right."

"Just the same," she said, looking worried, "I wish you wouldn't."

He smiled and kissed her cheek. "Be back in a couple of hours. If Lee has left the territory, we're heading home."

Sarah didn't look too sure about that. "Ma still needs me, Wade."

He thought about that a moment. "We'll talk when I get back." Then he turned and went to their room across the hall, strapped on his gun belt, and checked his pistol making sure it was loaded. He picked up his wide-brimmed, black hat, his saddlebags sitting in the corner, the Sharps and cartridges, and walked out of the room. He hurried downstairs to a cabinet in Jasper's study, took out two Colt pistols, and made sure they were loaded. He shoved them into his saddlebag, walked through the house and out the back door to the barn.

Harper, Colorado

271

Lamps filled the windows of Harper with soft, orange light when they reached the one place in town they knew they'd be welcome. Hearing horses, Levi picked up a lantern and stepped outside, holding the lantern above his head, peering into the darkness.

"Hello, Levi," said Wade.

Levi grinned. "I'd offer you, boys, a drink to celebrate, but all I got is water."

Wade and Seth glanced at one another, and then Wade asked, "Celebrate what?"

Levi looked at them in astonishment. "Ain't you heard? We're a state now. Came in over them darn telegraph wires late this afternoon."

"I'll be damned," uttered Seth with a soft chuckle looking pleased.

Wade wondered how long before New Mexico would become a state, then asked Levi, "We're here looking for Lee Jones. He been around?"

Levi thought for a minute. "I ain't seen him. Don't want to neither, but I did hear he was staying out at the Hoskins' place." He paused, looking thoughtful. "Keeping low, I guess." Then he turned toward town. "Figured there'd be more celebrating, but the town's gotten awfully quiet since you came back with Pete Hoskins draped over his saddle."

Wade pondered that for a moment and then nudged his mare into a walk. "Take care, Levi."

"Levi," said Seth as he nudged his horse and followed Wade.

The old man watched them for a moment, wondering what trouble they brought with them this time. He stepped back inside the safety of his livery, closed the big front doors, and put the big board across them to secure them in place, and waited for the shooting to start.

Wade and Seth rode at a walk up the dirt street, passing through images of doorways and windows made from the light of kerosene lamps. Passing the restaurant, they could see customers enjoying their meals and conversation. The boardwalks had but a few people leisurely walking toward some destination. There were but a few horses at the hitching rail in front of the Sundowner up the street and the Blue Sky Saloon.

They turned their horses toward a hitching rail that wasn't crowded with horses in front of a store, climbed down, loosely tied their horses to it, and glanced up and down the boardwalk as they dusted off their clothing. A man walked out of the swinging doors of the Blue Sky Saloon then staggered along the boardwalk, disappearing into the darkness. Piano music drifted through the swinging doors, followed by soft laughter and inaudible words as Wade turned to his saddlebag, took out one of the Colt pistols, and shoved it under his belt next to his stomach. Taking off his duster, he draped it over his saddle, took out the second pistol and walked around Seth's horse, and waited.

Seth took off his duster and laid it over his saddle, and looked at the pistol Wade was offering.

"It's loaded," said Wade noticing Seth's white shirt had a dark spot of blood that had seeped through the bandage. "You okay?"

Seth took the pistol and just looked at him thinking it was an unnecessary question, and shoved the gun under his belt. They walked up the steps to the boardwalk, paused at the door to slide the thin, leather straps over the hammers of their Colt pistols. They stepped through the swinging doors, greeted by piano music, laughter, cigarette smoke, and the smell of dance floor sawdust. Making their way along the wall, past the big window of painted designs and white letters spelling Saloon, they stepped up to the bar where Wade shot and killed Booth Fox.

Sam Carney, dressed in his usual dark pants, white shirt, gartered sleeves, and a folded apron tied around his waist, was at the far end of the bar, talking to two men. When he looked up, seeing Wade and Seth, worry replaced the smile as he picked up a towel from the bar, tossed it over his left shoulder, and walked toward them. Remembering Booth Fox and Deputy Boyd the last time the two were in his saloon, Sam nodded at Wade. "Marshal," then he looked at Seth. "Glad to see you're up and around, Sheriff."

"Thanks, Sam," responded Seth knowing he wasn't really.

"How you doing, Sam?" asked Wade.

He shrugged. "All right, I guess." Then he looked regretful. "Too bad about Pete Hoskins."

Wade glanced around. "Looks like a good crowd celebrating Statehood."

Sam leaned against the bar with his hands noticing they each had an extra gun tucked under their belts, and lowered his voice. "I don't want any more trouble in my place, Marshal."

Wade smiled at Carney. "Didn't come looking for trouble, Sam, came looking for Lee Jones. Ain't seen him, have you?"

"No, I ain't," Sam said, looking worried. "But some of the Hoskins boys are in here."

Wade's demeanor changed. "I don't care about them."

"Well, maybe you should," warned Sam in a soft voice. "Word is some of them boys are looking for a fight with the two of you."

Seth leaned against the bar. "How many of the Hoskins' hands are in here?"

Carney quickly glanced around, looking nervous as he leaned a little closer. "Three at the table in the back next to the stairs."

Seth looked at Sam. "That's all? You'd think more would be here celebrating."

Sam looked at the three in thought. "That is a little strange, but maybe they're celebrating out at the ranch." He looked at Wade. "Or maybe they feel bad about Pete."

Wade doubted that as he took a quick glance at the three men. "They leave us alone, we leave them alone" He looked at Sam Carney. "Now, how about a couple of beers to celebrate?"

Carney glanced at the table by the stairs where the Hoskins men were sitting as he turned to get their beer, hoping no more Hoskins men came in.

Wade looked in the mirror behind the bar, searching the room until he found them talking to three of Sam's girls. Seth took a quick look, and then he glanced around the room at the other faces, trying to anticipate who would be trouble. Other than the three Hoskins hands, there were a few older men, a mixture of men living in town, a few farmers playing cards or just talking over a beer, and a few men from other spreads. None of them looked the type to get involved in anything other than what they came in for.

Sam placed the two mugs of beer on the bar. "The first one's on the house to celebrate us becoming a state."

"Thanks, Sam," said Wade.

Carney smiled nervously at the two, then turned and walked along the bar to the two men he had been talking with earlier.

Wade picked up his beer and looked at Seth. "Here's to statehood." He took a quick drink and wiped the foam from his mouth

274

with his sleeve. He set the mug on the bar, turned, and looked at the table near the stairs where the three Hoskins men were sitting. The three Hoskins crew seemed to be enjoying the company of Sam's girls, and he hoped they would stay interested. He had no quarrel with any of the Hoskins' hands.

Seth took a long drink, wiped his handlebar mustache with the forefinger of his right hand, set the mug down, and let out a soft belch as he glanced around. The piano player suddenly stopped playing, reached up, and grabbed the beer Sam had placed on top of his piano. He took a quick drink, set the mug down, and went back to the lively song he was playing while the couple on the dance floor beyond the piano continued dancing.

Wade picked up his beer and took a drink while considering he and Seth leaving, thinking the trip had been a waste of time. He set the mug down, wiped his mouth, and started to turn to Seth to say they should leave when Lee Jones walked through the swinging doors. Wade watched in the mirror as Lee glanced around the place without seeing him and Seth and then headed for the table with the three Hoskins men.

Seth leaned on the bar with his elbows, thinking the same thing as Wade about leaving when he saw Lee Jones in the mirror and nudged Wade.

"I see him," said Wade. "I can't believe the dumb shit just walked in here."

Seth looked at Wade. "We gonna arrest him in here?"

Wade stared at Lee. "You want to forget Lee and head back, or take him with us?"

Seth frowned. "I'd like to leave with one warm body. Carney ain't going to like it, but let's take the dumb shit with us."

Upon seeing Jones, Sam hurried along the bar to Wade. "You promised no trouble."

"Sorry, Sam," said Wade. "We still have a warrant with his name."

Carney looked disappointed and then asked with a pleading look. "Try not to kill anyone this time."

"That's up to Lee," chuckled Seth without humor.

Wade pushed his mug toward Sam, turned, and started walking toward the table where Lee Jones and the others were sitting. Seth walked to the other end of the bar near the piano player and watched as Wade approached the table.

Sam stared after Seth and walked a few feet to where he kept a double-barrel shotgun. Just then, two more men from the Hoskins Ranch walked through the doorway and stepped up to the bar.

Wade was almost to the table when Lee Jones turned, searching for a waiter, and found Seth standing a few feet away by the piano. He started to get up when he saw Marshal Wade Garrison making his way past the chairs and tables to his left.

The other three men at the table turned to see what Lee was looking at and saw Wade, but they never saw Seth because they watched Lee to see what he was going to do.

Lee stood and looked at Wade, knowing he would be arrested, and went for his gun.

Wade pulled his gun and got off the first shot, hitting Jones in the left chest, knocking him back against the wall next to the stairs.

Lee still managed to pull the trigger getting off a wild shot that put a bullet in the wall behind the bar above Sam's head.

Wade got off another shot hitting Lee in the face. Deputy Lee Jones was dead by the time he slid down the wall to the floor.

The other three men sitting in their chairs wisely and quickly raised their hands, not wanting any part of what just happened. They looked from Lee and then to Wade and Seth. "We ain't part of this!" yelled one.

Sam Carney cocked both hammers of the shotgun he had taken from behind the bar and kept his eye on the two men at the bar. As one stepped away from the bar and drew his gun to shoot Wade in the back, Sam's twelve-gauge shotgun exploded like a cannon. The force of the shot knocked the man several feet onto a table filled with beer, cards, and money. The second man turned to Sam with wide eyes, as he took a step back, with his hands in the air, he said, "Want no part of this, Sam."

Sam glared at them. "Don't you move, damn it." Then, looking angry, his eyes went from Wade to Seth and the others as he yelled, "That's enough. No more killing in my place. We're supposed to be celebrating statehood."

Wade looked at the other Hoskins hand standing at the bar. "Take your gun out, drop it on the floor, and kick it away."

Sam looked at the Hoskins ranch hand. "Do as the Marshal says, damn it." Then he looked around at the faces of the crowd. "The next asshole that goes for his gun's gonna eat what's in this here twelve gauge." Then he looked at Wade. "I told you no trouble. Time to leave."

Wade gave him a quick nod and walked over to Lee Jones, knelt, and looked into his open eyes. Closing them, he stood and looked at the three sitting at the table with their hands up. What are your names?

"Tim Howard," said the man closest to him.

"Clay Edwards," said the second.

Wade looked at the third man. "What's your name?"

"Joel Grayson."

Wade told him and the other man to take their guns out, put them on the table, and step back. After they placed their guns on the table, he picked them up, unloaded them, and tossed the guns back at them. "When you load those, think about Lee Jones."

Wade holstered his gun, walked to the bar, picked up his beer, took a drink then lowered his voice. "Thanks, Sam, but Mr. Hoskins ain't gonna take kindly of you shooting one of his men to save my life."

"I'm sure of it," replied Sam, looking a little worried.

Wade looked at the Hoskins man standing at the bar with his hands raised. "What's your name?"

"Ron Nelson," he replied. "Why?"

Wade stared at him a moment. "Let's say I'm curious and leave it at that." He starred into Nelson's eyes for a moment, then turned to Seth, "It's time to leave."

Seth stepped away from the piano, holding his Colt, and walked toward the swinging doors.

Wade gave a quick look around and then followed Seth outside into the small crowd, pushing their way through asking questions. They walked along the boardwalk to their horses, swung up into their saddles, and rode north toward the Circle T Ranch.

Lights from the bunkhouse windows reflected across the ground as they rode past it toward the main house, where they pulled up in front of the porch, dismounted. They tied their horses to the railing, walked up the steps, and knocked on the door. A few moments later, Bertha opened the door holding a lamp in one hand, dressed in her usual dark blue shirt and

277

floor-length red skirt. Looking irritated, she glanced from one to the other. "What you want?"

"Hello, Bertha," greeted Wade. "We'd like to speak to Mr. Grimes if he's up."

Expressionless as usual, she stared at Wade the way she always had and then stepped back. "Come in. I get him."

They took off their hats and stepped inside.

Still staring at Wade, she closed the door and then walked across the room, disappearing into Tolliver's library.

Seth looked at Wade after she disappeared into the other room. "I don't think she likes you very much."

"She's warming up to me," grinned Wade. "She just holds things in."

Seth laughed.

Tolliver Grimes walked out of his office, all smiles.

Bertha walked past Wade staring at him, looking a little on the angry side. "Why you come so late?"

"That'll do, Bertha," scolded Tolliver with a humorless smile as he shook their hands. "Drink"

Wade looked at Mr. Grimes. "No, thanks. We stopped by to see if it'd be alright if we talked to Stu."

He nodded and looked a little puzzled. "Sure, he's more'n likely down in the bunkhouse."

Thinking it would be polite to explain why he and Seth wanted to talk to Stu, Wade asked if they could sit down. Grimes motioned to a couple of chairs, and as they sat down, Tolliver sat on the sofa. He listened while Wade told the story of the ambush, Whisper Creek, where Stu's friend Josh Martin got killed, and the canyon where Pete fell.

Grimes already knew about Pete Hoskins but didn't know the full story, so he quietly listened, and when Wade finished, Tolliver sat back on the sofa looking worried. "George Hoskins buried his son this morning next to his oldest son Daniel."

Wade looked down at the hat he held in his hands, feeling sorry for Mr. Hoskins. "I feel bad about Pete Hoskins, Mr. Grimes. I tried to bring him in."

Tolliver shrugged. "The choice was his, Wade. You didn't make it for him. Pete wasn't liked by many people outside of the ranch." He

278

paused while looking toward the bunkhouse. "Stu's gonna take Josh's death hard. I'm sure he never knew the little bastard was helping set a trap."

"I'm sure he didn't," said Wade.

Tolliver looked at Wade. "I said not many outside the ranch liked Pete, but there were plenty at the ranch that did." He looked at them. "I'd be damn careful."

Wade thought about Lee Jones and the other men in the saloon, none taking part trying to help Lee Jones by gunning down he and Seth.

Mr. Grimes looked curious and listened while Wade told him what happened with Lee Jones in town. Tolliver sighed, looking troubled. "Harper's becoming a graveyard."

"This ends it," said Wade. "I'm gonna leave in a couple of days with Billy, Sarah, and Emmett. We're heading back to Santa Fe to let this thing cool off." He nodded to Seth. "Seth's heading back to Sisters tomorrow."

Grimes looked relieved. "The sooner you're all gone, the better. You being around is a constant reminder to George Hoskins."

Wade stood and held out his hand. "I'll stop by before we leave."

Tolliver shook their hands firmly and then walked them to the door, said goodnight, and watched as they walked off the porch and led their horses toward the bunkhouse.

Seth stayed outside while Wade walked into the bunkhouse, and after he greeted the others and answered a few quick questions, he asked Stu if he could speak to him outside.

Looking puzzled, Stu glanced at the other hands, followed him outside, said hello to Seth, and then listened while Wade told him about Josh Martin.

Stu looked sad, and then his sadness was replaced by worry. "I never thought Josh was going with them, Wade. I swear."

Wade smiled as he put his hand on Stu's shoulder. "We know that, Stu. We're not holding you to blame over this." He nodded to Seth. "We both know you were just trying to help."

Stu looked relieved and yet angry. "I was, Wade. I was only trying to help you and Seth catch and arrest Pete Hoskins."

Wade held out his open hand. Stu looked down at it, smiled, shook it, and then shook Seth's hand.

Twenty-Seven

Act of vengeance

The night was calm, the black sky filled with stars, with the full moon lighting their way as Wade and Seth rode at a slow walk along the road that led to the Double J Ranch. They talked and laughed in memory of Frank Wells, Gil Robinson, and the Indian, Dark Cloud, then of going home now that the Pete Hoskins ordeal was finally over. It hadn't turned out the way Seth wanted it to, but they found justice for Jacob Olson, his daughter and unborn child, and Tom Lawson's wife. In the stillness of the moment, Seth pulled up and pointed to a red glow reflecting off the low clouds along the northern horizon. Wade pulled up, and both stood in their stirrups.

"What the hell's that?" asked Seth.

"Looks like a fire," said Wade.

Seth looked at Wade. "Ain't that about where the Double J is?"

Wade spurred the mare and galloped toward the glow as Seth spurred his big gray and followed.

When Wade and Seth reached the top of the hill overlooking the ranch, flames were leaping from the windows and doors of the ranch house. The bunkhouse was consumed in flames and the rear of the barn on fire. The night sky was thick with white and gray smoke as it rose to meet the stars hiding the moon. Pulling up, they looked at the scene for only a moment, then Wade fearing for his wife and child, spurred his horse down the hill. Seth paused to look a little longer, then followed under the archway toward the house. Wade pulled up as he glanced around, then jumping down from his horse, he yelled, "Sarah, Emmett."

Seth pulled and watched in disbelief while ranch hands fought a losing battle fighting all three fires with buckets of water. Men ran in and out of the barn, rescuing the animals or carrying out saddles and harnesses, or whatever else they could find. Suddenly, the big two-story house roof collapsed into the second story with an explosion that sent sparks and flames into the air, frightening Wade's mare. She reared up, letting out a loud squeal, and pulled at the reins to run away from the fire, but Wade fought for control of the mare. Hearing Sarah call his name and still fighting the horse, he saw her kneeling next to Emmett and the others, huddled together by the oak tree where Jasper was buried. Wade calmed the mare enough to walk her toward Sarah and the others.

Seth climbed down and started to lead his horse toward the tree where everyone had gathered when the house's front wall collapsed, sending sparks and smoke into the already smoky sky. His horse pulled free and bolted toward the archway, chased by Seth's loud cursing.

Wade's mare tried to break free, but he managed to keep control of her, and after she settled down, he tied her to the tree.

Sarah got up and ran into his arms, crying as she watched the fire destroy the house where she grew up.

"Are you all right?" he asked.

"Billy got us out." Then she looked up at him with a frown and tears on her face. "Where have you been?"

Without answering, he took off his duster, put it around her, and then helped her back to where the others were. He helped her sit down next to Emmett, who was crying as he melted into his mother's arms. It was then that Wade saw Billy French sitting on the ground, his white shirt and pants filthy with black soot, his face dirty, and the bandages on his leg dirty and bloody.

Mrs. Talbert stood a few feet away wearing a blue nightgown that showed evidence of the fire. Wrapped in her own arms, she cried as she stared at what was left of her home.

Seth took off his duster and put it over her shoulders.

Worried about Emmett, Wade knelt to his son, put one hand on his head, and asked if he was all right.

The boy looked up with eyes and face wet with tears. "I think so," then looking worried, said, "Willie and Dog ran off."

"They'll show up, Son. They're just a little afraid right now." He thought of Seth's horse running in fear and hoped she would stay close enough to get her at daylight. He looked at his son once again. "You sure you're all right, son?"

"My leg hurts. Mr. French dropped me from the porch roof."

Wade kissed the top of his son's head, thankful he was alive. "I'll take a look at it later." The barn roof collapsed, and as Wade watched the barn burn, he asked Sarah what happened.

Billy answered before Sarah could. "Bastards burned it down, Wade. They just rode in and burned it down."

Wade turned and looked at him, seeing the anger in Billy's dirty face. "Who rode in and burned it down?"

French looked puzzled. "Hooded riders is all I can tell you." Then he looked at Wade. "But, we both know who ordered it."

Wade stood and looked back at the fire thinking of George Hoskins. Concerned over his friend, Wade turned to Billy. "You all right?"

French nodded. "I guess. I ain't dead if that's what you're asking." He looked at the fires. "Some son of a bitch is gonna regret that I ain't."

Wade looked at Seth standing next to Mrs. Talbert and motioned with a nod of the head for him to take a look at Billy. While Seth did that, Wade glanced around at the ranch hands that had lost their fight against the fires. Some still holding buckets, others with their arms folded, all watching the fire as it consumed the house, barn, and bunkhouse. Two horses galloped past them, heading into the dark of night, several goats and sheep ran past, and chickens were everywhere, having been set free from the burning coop.

Sarah was still holding Emmett in her arms as she looked up at Wade and again asked, "Where were you?"

Wade knelt next to her. "What's this about hooded riders?" he asked, avoiding her question.

"I was in with Emmett when I thought I heard you and Seth ride up. Then I heard the sound of glass breaking and ran to the top of the stairs. The living room was on fire, so I yelled for ma and ran back to

283

Emmett's room. That's when I heard gunshots outside and from Billy's room." She paused and looked down at her son. "By the time I got Emmett out of the room, Willie and Dog were with ma at the top of the stairs barking at the fire." Sarah had a scared look on her face. "The stairs were on fire, and there was no way down. Then Billy opened his door and yelled for us to come into his room, where he helped Emmett out the window and onto the roof." Then she started crying, unable to talk.

Wade held her and looked at Billy.

Billy looked from the fire to Wade. "I lay on the porch roof and lowered the boy as far as I could and then dropped him. He landed on his good leg then rolled just like I told him to." He gestured to Sarah and Janice. "Then I used a sheet and lowered Sarah, Mrs. Talbert, and then the dogs."

Wade looked grateful and wondered how he did that with a bad leg. "I'm forever beholden to you, Billy."

"You'd have done the same for me," replied French.

Sarah continued as she wiped her face with her hands. "After me and ma were on the ground, two riders came around the side of the house, and they started shooting at us." She glanced at French. "Billy shot back, and they rode off."

French looked angry. "I think I got one of them bastards. At least, he bent over and rode off like he was hit."

Then Sarah continued. "After they rode off, Billy climbed down, and we hid behind the berry bushes away from the house. After a few minutes, when Billy thought it was safe, we came over here to the tree." Then she looked at Wade. "What took you so long?"

"We stopped by to see Stu on our way back from town."

She hugged her son. "You should have been here."

He put his arm around her. "I wish I had been. I'm sorry."

She wiped her nose and wet face with the sleeve of her robe and softly said, "I know you are."

Wade looked at Seth. "How's Billy's leg?"

"I think it's all right. His upper arm and shoulder are burned. I don't think it's too bad, but just the same, I think Doc needs to take a look." Then Seth looked around. "No telling who else is hurt."

Wade glanced down at Emmett, glanced around, and then looked at Seth. "I'll send someone to fetch Doc Granger on my mare."

"I'll go in a few minutes," volunteered Seth, then he stood and gestured at the burning pile of rubble that was once a house and thought of the women. "Once that goes out, it'll get dark and chilly as hell." Then he saw some men covering a body with a yellow slicker. "Who's that?"

Wade stood. "Don't know." Then he walked over and stood next to the foreman, Ted Bennett. "Who's that?"

"Billy Murray," replied Ted.

"Ain't he the one who found Jasper, Sarah, and Emmett?" asked Wade.

Bennett nodded. "The same; got shot in the back." He looked at Wade. "We never had a chance to fight back, they set the bunkhouse on fire with bottles of kerosene, and we barely got out."

Hearing horses, they turned, seeing a group of riders approaching the archway. Wade drew his Colt pistol as he motioned at the others, telling them to take cover, then he moved closer to Sarah, telling her to get down.

The riders stopped, and a voice called out. "It's Tolliver Grimes."

Relieved, Wade stepped from behind the tree and waved. "Come on in."

Tolliver and the six men with him rode in, stopping near the tree. "One of my men saw the glow on the horizon." Then he glanced at the faces gathered around the tree. "Everyone all right?"

Wade gestured to the others. "The women are scared, so's Emmett, and he may have hurt his leg again. Billy's got some burns that need tending, and it looks like the wound on his leg is bleeding."

Grimes glanced around. "What the hell happened?"

Wade stepped closer. "Billy says some hooded riders rode in and torched the place." He looked angry. "Two of 'em took shots at Sarah and her mother." He pointed to the covered body. "Billy Murray is dead got shot him in the back."

"Who'd do such a thing?" asked Tolliver, looking shocked.

Wade gave him a stern look. "You and I both know the answer to that Tolliver."

Grimes rested his hands on his saddle horn, looking unsure. "Hoskins is a hard man, I'll give him that, but it's hard to believe he'd be behind such a thing."

"I believe it," replied Wade as he shifted his attention from the fire to his family. "No sense arguing about it now." Then he turned and gestured to Sarah and the others. "We need to get them to your place, Tolliver. It'll get cold soon."

Grimes turned to Jessup and Haggerty. "You two head back and get a couple of wagons." Then as they rode away, he looked at Stu. "You head into Harper and get Doc Granger and bring him to my place." Then he looked at Wade. "Your boys can bunk with mine."

Mrs. Talbert stepped closer to Wade. "Who was it you said was dead?"

"Billy Murray, Mrs. Talbert," replied Wade softly.

Her sad face somehow became even sadder as she turned away, wiping at her eyes and wondering who would do this to her and her family.

Sarah held Emmett, remembering it was Billy Murray, who found them right after the accident.

"Anyone else hurt?" asked Grimes.

"Some have minor burns," replied Wade. "I'd say, all in all, we were pretty lucky."

Tolliver climbed down, took off his hat, and put one arm around Mrs. Talbert to console her. "Sure, sorry about this, Janice."

She looked at him with welling eyes. "What am I going to do, Tolliver?"

He looked at her with kindness on his face. "It may not seem like it now, Janice, but everything's gonna be all right, and so are you."

She looked doubtful. "I don't see how." Then she looked down at Jasper's grave. "If only Jasper were here. He'd know what to do."

"I'm sure he would, Janice," replied Tolliver.

Tolliver Grimes was sitting on the ground next to Mrs. Talbert when Haggerty and Jessup returned with the wagons, and as the wagons stopped, he helped Mrs. Talbert up. "We'll get everyone to my place. You can stay with me until you rebuild."

Wade helped Sarah into the wagon while Dobbs picked up Emmett and placed him in the wagon next to his mother. Wade climbed up on the mare, ready to fight if the hooded riders returned. Seth helped Billy into the wagon and sat next to him while the ranch hands climbed into the wagons or rode double with Tolliver's men.

286

Sitting on the floor of the wagon, Janice Talbert looked at the few small fires still feeding off the pile of burnt smoldering rubble. The air was heavy with the smell of disaster, and her voice was soft and broken. "Everything Jasper and I had is nothing but ashes now." She touched her nightgown. "This is all that I have left."

Tolliver moved his Appaloosa closer to the wagon. "Mason's Store and the others in Harper have lots of clothes, Janice, and if they don't have what you need, I'll take you to Denver myself." He reached out and touched her shoulder. "Right now, we need to get you and the rest to my place and out of this chilly night air."

She looked up and smiled while touching his hand. "You're a good man, Tolliver. You've always been the best of friends."

He smiled affectionately. "And I always will be, Janice." Then he looked at the others, making sure everyone was ready. "All right, let's go."

Hearing the sound of a horse, Seth turned and saw his big black standing a few feet away from the tree. Happy to see his black horse, he climbed down and walked toward him, talking softly so he wouldn't spook him.

Twenty-Eight

Circle T Ranch

Doc Granger unrolled his white shirt sleeves as he started down the stairs in silence, looking tired.

Wade got up from his chair, walked to the bottom step, and waited anxiously to hear about his family.

Seth, Tolliver, and Harry Block got up from their seats and waited for the news.

At the bottom step, Doc Granger smiled as he put one hand on Wade's shoulder. "They'll be fine. I gave Mrs. Talbert, your wife, and son something so they'll sleep through the night. But they'll be just fine."

Looking relieved, Wade asked about Billy French.

Granger looked at the coffee pot and cups sitting on the low table in front of the sofa and gestured to them. "Any coffee left? I sure could use a cup."

Tolliver started toward the coffee pot. "Have a seat Doc. I'll pour you a cup. Black if I recall correctly."

"Black is fine, Tolliver." Then Doc looked at Wade with a kindly smile. "He'll be fine." Doc sat down, picked up the cup of coffee, and took a quick drink. "The wound in his leg opened up and needed cleaning, and I'm not concerned about infection." He took a thoughtful sip. "He wants to head back to Santa Fe, but I told him he could go in a day or two if he goes slow and doesn't ride hard."

Wade thought on that and then looked at Mr. Grimes. "It might be best, Mr. Grimes, if you had one of your men take him to Sisters in the wagon with his horse tied behind so he could catch the train to Santa Fe."

Tolliver looked at Wade. "I can do that, but aren't you and your family leaving as well?"

Wade eased into the sofa next to the doctor. "I haven't decided on that just yet." Then he looked at Doc Granger and leaned forward in his chair. "You treat anyone for a gunshot before you came out here?"

The question caught Doc Granger with his cup at his mouth. He paused as he looked at Wade, then Doc took a small sip, swallowed, and glanced at the others as he lowered the cup to his lap. "Well, as a matter of fact, I pulled a slug out of Joel Grayson's left shoulder about an hour before Tolliver's man Stu, came for me." He paused. "The bone in his shoulder was broken."

Wade looked across the room, thinking he should have shot the bastard when he had the chance in the saloon. Then he looked at Seth. "Billy thinks he wounded one of the riders that shot at Sarah and her mother." He paused while staring at Seth. "Do you recall that little shit at the table in the saloon? The one that was doing all the talking."

"Vaguely," said Seth. "I was a little busy."

Wade got an angry look that Seth had never seen before. "His name was Joel Grayson."

Doc Granger looked surprised. "You think Grayson was one of them?"

Block leaned forward with his forearms on his knees and looked at the doctor. "This man Grayson say how it happened?"

Doc Granger shrugged. "Said it was an accident."

Tolliver had a puzzled face as he looked at Wade. "What does Joel Grayson have to do with this?"

Wade told Grimes about the men at the Blue Sky Saloon and his conversation with Grayson. "Joel Grayson knew what was going to happen." Then Wade looked at Seth. "That's why there weren't many of the Hoskins drovers in town. They were getting ready to raid the Double J."

Tolliver Grimes looked puzzled. "But why attack the place if the man you're after ain't' there? His men would surely have told him where you were."

Seth turned. "That's the whole point, Mr. Grimes. I don't think Hoskins is after Wade just yet. If he kills Wade, it's over, but if he kills his son…" He let the sentence die.

"What do you mean?" asked Doc Granger with questioning eyes.

Seth's eyes hardened. "He wants Wade to feel what he's felt with the loss of his two sons."

The doctor looked shocked. "I can't believe Hoskins would be that cruel." Then he glanced around at the others and then at Wade. "Your son's just a child, and Sarah's never hurt anyone that I'm aware of."

Wade stared across the room and out the window into the darkness, deep in thought, and never answered.

"Revenge is a cruel business, and the crueler, the better," offered Tolliver while he looked at Wade as he continued to stare out the lace curtains.

Not liking what was being said here and fearing more deaths, Doc Granger looked at his watch, drank the last of his coffee, and stood. "It's late. I best be heading home." He looked at the others. "I find it hard to believe that any man would be so cruel as to harm a child and an innocent woman."

Wade turned from the window. "I've seen the things a man can do to a woman and a child Doc that would make you sick and curl your hair." He paused. "And I hope you never do."

Granger looked at Wade. "Maybe so, but I hope you're wrong."

"How else do you explain this, Doc. These weren't riders from hell set free by the devil."

Doc Granger just looked at Wade, seeing the hate in his eyes.

Harry Block stood and motioned toward the door. "I'll ride for a ways with you, Doc. Time I get home."

Wade stood and held out his hand to Granger. "Thanks again, Doc." They shook hands, and then he shook Block's firm hand. "Thanks for coming out, Sheriff."

Block nodded thoughtfully as they shook hands, considering some advice for Wade, but quickly decided against it. He knew that advice was not something Wade needed at the moment, nor would he listen to it. It was too late for advice.

While Tolliver saw Doc Granger and Harry Block to the front door, to say goodnight, Wade and Seth returned to their chairs in silence,

290

and when Tolliver returned to the room, the clock tolled midnight. Wade turned and looked at the big clock sitting next to the stairs, realizing he hadn't slept in a while.

A knock came at the door, and when Tolliver opened it, he was looking at Ted Bennett, foreman of the Double J, and two other men. "Could we talk to Mr. Garrison?"

Hearing that, Wade stood and walked to the door. "Everything alright, Ted?"

Bennett stepped back. "Could we talk out here?"

Wade stepped outside, closed the door, and waited.

Ted looked at the other two. "We'd just like you to know that if you need any help getting even, a few of us are willing?"

Wade smiled. "Thanks, that's good to know. Now go on back and get some rest. You boys have had a hard night."

"Yes, sir," each said as they turned away.

Wade watched as the three stepped off the porch, then he went inside, closed the door, and returned to his chair.

Grimes dropped onto the sofa across from them and looked at Wade, seeing he was deep in thought. "Everything alright?"

Wade nodded it was, and then he took a drink of coffee.

"What are you planning, son?" asked Tolliver.

Wade was already making plans for the Hoskins' Ranch as he looked up with a lie in his mouth. "Nothing right now."

Seth looked at Grimes and then Wade. "First thing in the morning, we get Billy and head to Denver for the marshal and his men, and then we pay Hoskins a visit."

Tolliver nodded in agreement. "Good idea." He looked at Wade. "Stay within the law, son. It's the only way."

Wade appeared tired as he looked at Seth. "Billy's in no condition to travel." Then he stood. "I'm tired. We'll talk in the morning over breakfast with clearer heads about what to do."

"Good idea," said Tolliver as he stood.

Seth stood, saying he was tired as well.

Wade said goodnight and then walked upstairs to Sarah and Emmett, leaving the tasks of lamps to Mr. Grimes.

Wade quietly opened the door, walked into the moonlit bedroom, closed the door, and melted into an overstuffed chair next to the bed. He looked at the faces of Sarah and Emmett bathed in moonlight from the window and thought of how much he loved them. Getting comfortable in the chair, Wade sat in silence and listened to their sleeping noises. While watching them sleep, he realized that he had almost lost them to Hoskins and his men for the second time since they had come to Harper. He knew he couldn't prove anything against George Hoskins, and if he brought up Joel Grayson, every man on Hoskins's payroll would claim it was an accident. George Hoskins would remain free for another attempt at destroying his family. Looking from Sarah to the black night out the window, he thought of what Seth had said about not wanting him dead so he could suffer. Fear and anger filled him, knowing the next attempt on his family may prove fruitful. It was clear that George Hoskins wanted blind revenge on the Garrison family for what two Hoskins boys had caused. He remembered Pete's question in the canyon about Dan Hoskins. Wade thought about Dan and wondered how different life would be if he hadn't stopped in Sisters all those years ago and had never met Dan and Pete Hoskins.

The clock at the foot of the stairs chimed and then struck the hour of two, echoing through the still house like a lonely ghost searching the night. Wade opened his eyes from a brief sleep, turned, and looked at the closed door. As the clock sounded another chime, he got up from the chair and looked down at Sarah and Emmett, sleeping peacefully. Glad that Doc had given them something to make them sleep, Wade bent down, gently kissed Sarah on the forehead, did the same to Emmett, then picked up his gun and holster from the bedpost. He strapped them on, tied the holster down, put on his hat and duster, picked up his saddlebags, and tossed them over his shoulder. Tiptoeing to the door where his Sharps rifle and bandolier waited, Wade picked them up, turned, and took one last look at Sarah and Emmett sleeping. He quietly opened the door and stepped into the hall, closing it behind him.

Walking down the hall, Wade stopped at the top of the stairs and glanced back down the hall at the bedroom doors hoping everyone was sleeping. He walked down the stairs into a living room filled with moonlight from the windows, giving the room an eerie contrast of soft moonlight and dark shadows. Wade walked to Tolliver's study, went inside, lit a lamp, and sat down at the desk. He took out a piece of paper and pencil from a drawer and scribbled a quick note. He folded the paper and stuffed it into an envelope, and wrote "Sarah" on the front of it.

Placing the envelope on the center of the desk, he blew out the lantern and made his way in the moonlight of the living room to the kitchen, greeted by the same soft light and shadows. He leaned his Sharps against the wall and laid the bandolier of shells on the table next to a lantern, took out a match from his shirt pocket, and lit the wick. Lowering the glass bub, he turned the lamp down, filling the room with long distorted shadows that followed him and the lantern into the pantry. Quietly rummaging around, he soon found what he was after; glass jars and lids sitting on the bottom shelf. He knelt to one knee, placing the lantern on the floor next to him, and started to take six glass jars from the shelf when he noticed several empty whiskey bottles with corks sitting on the floor in the corner. Deciding they would fit his purpose better, he took six bottles, shoved them into his saddlebags. After he buckled the flaps, he picked up the lantern, stood, and turned, looking into the chubby face of Bertha.

Wearing a long white nightshirt that fit loosely over her large body, she stared at him in silence. Her long, black hair hung over her large, round breasts and past her waist. The dim light of the lantern lit up one side of her expressionless face of dark accusing eyes and firm, thin lips. In her hand, she held a large butcher knife she slowly lowered while staring at him. "I thought you were a thief." Then she made a cutting motion with the knife. "I was ready to cut your throat."

He knew that she would have done just that, and thinking of the bottles, he felt like a thief.

"What do you do with empty whiskey bottles?" she asked as she backed out of the pantry.

He stepped out with his saddlebags, set the lantern on the table, and looked at her, hoping she would be quiet. "I need them for something."

She looked at him with narrowed, accusing eyes. "Strange thing to look for so early in the morning." She paused, making a cutting motion. "Like a thief."

He wished she would put the knife away go back to bed.

She walked to the island countertop and set the butcher knife down, turned, and looked at him with a different look than she usually had for him. "The men who burnt down other ranch will come here looking for you. They will burn this house down and maybe kill Tolliver Grimes."

He shook his head. "They won't hurt Mr. Grimes, Bertha."

"How you be so sure?"

He never answered, and instead, he asked, "I need a favor."

She looked at him with a curious face thinking of why he needed the empty bottles. "What sort of favor you ask so early in the morning?"

"I need you to go back to bed and not tell anyone about this."

She glanced at the saddlebags. "You going to kill the men who burned down Mrs. Talbert's ranch?"

"Go to bed, please."

It was one of the few times he had ever seen her smile. "Bertha thinks you go kill these men. That is why you steal bottles in the middle of the night like a thief, so no one sees." Silence fell as they stared at one another, then she pointed toward the back door. "Kerosene for lanterns on the back porch in big cans. Small funnel on top of can."

He turned and looked at the back door. "What makes you think I need kerosene?"

She looked at him. "What makes you think I'm a dumb Indian?"

He had no answer but found humor in her question.

"It is middle of night," she said, and then she pointed to the Sharps rifle. "Your long gun is there, and you steal empty whiskey bottles like a thief. Bertha thinks you will burn down ranch of man who hates you." She paused. "Bertha, not dumb." Then she turned and walked to the door where she stopped and turned. "Bertha, not tell of whiskey bottles, but you must keep Tolliver Grimes safe." Then she looked at him for a moment. "It is good you do this thing." Then she walked out of the kitchen and disappeared into the darkness of the other room.

He stared after her knowing she would not tell anyone about the bottles and kerosene, picked up his Sharps, bandolier of cartridges, and walked out the back door where he filled the whiskey bottles with kerosene. When he finished, he shoved the corks in tightly and carefully put them in his saddlebags, three on each side. After he blew out the lantern, he walked to the barn, lit another lantern, and began saddling his mare. Wade had just finished with the bit and bridle when the side door of the barn opened, and Bill Dobbs stepped just inside the side door of the barn. At forty-six, Dobbs stood about six-one, had graying, rusty red hair and beard, and blue eyes. He was the old man of the Circle T hands. His Winchester was pointed at Wade, and upon recognizing him, he lowered it looking both apologetic and curious. "Didn't expect to find anyone saddling their horse this early, Mr. Garrison."

Wade had forgotten about the guards Tolliver had posted. "Since when did you start calling me Mr. Garrison?"

Dobbs grinned. "Since you became a Deputy United States Marshal."

Wade chuckled. "Can't sleep." Then he turned and tightened the saddle cinch.

Dobbs watched him for a few moments from the doorway and then walked across the barn. "Need some help?"

Wade shook his head with a friendly smile. "No, I'm done." Then he took the saddlebags from the stall's top railing, placed them on the back of his saddle, and tied them down.

Hearing the clinking of bottles, Dobbs asked, "I didn't mean with your saddle."

Surprised, Wade looked at him for a moment, then took the reins to his mare, backed her out of the stall, and swung up in the saddle. As he settled into it, he looked down at him. "You're better off staying out of this, Bill."

Dobbs looked disappointed as he nodded his understanding and turned toward the big doors. "I'll turn out the lamp and then get the door." After the lamp was out, he lifted the plank holding the barn doors closed, opened one of the big doors, and stepped outside into the moonlight.

Wade nudged the mare into a trot and rode past him, disappearing into the darkness.

Hoskins Ranch

The sky in the east was turning a light blue, and the stars were slowly disappearing when Wade stepped down from the saddle and walked his horse to the edge of the trees some twenty yards from the Hoskins' bunkhouse. In the dim light of predawn, he stood in the shadows and looked at the three windows not yet filled with light from lamps. Figuring there were three more on the other side, Wade considered his plan. Tying the mare to a bush, he moved a little closer to the bunkhouse seeing the back wall was solid; no door or window, and the only way out was at the far end of the building. Hurrying back to the mare and the trees, Wade took the six bottles of kerosene from his saddlebags and knelt to one knee. Hearing a door close, he looked toward the bunkhouse seeing a dark figure round the far corner of the building, walk along the bunkhouse and go into the outhouse.

Knowing that everyone would be getting up soon and they would take turns to visit the outhouse, he set the bottles on the ground and silently crept across the yard. Standing at the side of the outhouse next to the door, he drew his hunting knife, hearing the man inside grunt as he did his business and wished he would hurry. Moments later, the door opened, and as the figure stepped out, Wade stepped behind him and shoved the knife against the man's back. "Don't say a word."

Startled, the man put his hands up and glanced over his shoulder, thinking he had a gun in his back. "You shoot, and you'll wake everyone up."

"And you'll be dead," whispered Wade as he recognized Ron Nelson from the Blue Sky Saloon.

The man quickly considered that. "What do you want?"

"You know who I am?"

He nodded, yes. "Marshal Garrison."

"Then you know why I'm here."

"It was orders," he said, sounding afraid, "we were just following orders."

"Hoskins in the big house?"

Thinking Wade came for his boss, he shook his head no. "He's in Denver. He left late yesterday."

Wade thought about that and silently cursed his bad luck. "Guess he didn't want to be around when the shooting started. Get on your knees."

"Please don't shoot Mr. Garrison. I was only following orders."

"I ain't gonna shoot you," whispered Wade.

The man did as he was told and got down on his trembling knees.

Wade's heart pounded so hard he could hardly fill his lungs with the cool morning air. He looked up at the dark sky and stars, and then the blue sky above the horizon, thinking the sun would be up soon, and the men inside would wake up.

"Please don't shoot me," whimpered the man.

"No, I won't." He looked down at the hatless head and, in one motion, grabbed his hair, pulled his head back, cut his throat then pushed him forward. The man fell onto his stomach, thrashing like a fish out of water while the gurgling sound of air and blood escaped the large, long gash. By the time Wade knelt next to him, the man was dead. Wade cleaned the blood from his knife and hand using the man's shirt, then stood and put his knife in its scabbard. Knowing his time was running out, he hurried to where the mare and bottles of kerosene waited, opened one side of the saddlebags, took out two Colt pistols, and stuck one under his gun belt next to his belly, the other under his belt in the small of his back.

He knelt next to the six bottles, pulled the corks out, and tossed them away. Then he pulled the rag out of his coat pocket he had taken from the pantry and tore it into six strips. He stuffed one in each of the six bottles, picked them up, holding them in his arms as he hurried across the open ground to the rear of the bunkhouse. Kneeling not far from the man he just murdered, he carefully set three bottles down, and then staying low, he hurried past the three dark windows to the front of the bunkhouse. He knelt and put the bottles on the ground, took a match out of his shirt pocket, struck in on his belt buckle, and touched it to the rags of each bottle. As the rags burned, he tossed one against the buck house door, the second and the third he threw against the walls under the first and second windows.

While the flames quickly spread, he ran to the three remaining bottles, lit the rags, tossed one at the wall under the third window. Then he ran around the side of the bunkhouse and threw one at the wall under the next two windows, leaving one window for the men inside to escape. As flames consumed the dry wood on the outside of the bunkhouse, it quickly spread inside. He pulled the two extra guns from under his belt and walked along the side of the bunkhouse, feeling the heat from the hot, quickly spreading fire. As the men woke to the heat of the fire, someone yelled, the place is on fire, and then chaos filled the bunkhouse.

297

Reaching the front of the bunkhouse, he stood by the woodpile so he could see the door and the window he left free of fire and waited. Someone kicked the front door open, and Wade fired into the flames that consumed the door and wall. Moments later, a man fell through the flames to the ground with his clothes on fire while another jumped out and started to run. Wade aimed and fired, hitting him in the back. A man appeared at the window he left for escape and began to crawl through, but Wade fired and hit him in the chest. The man fell on the window ledge half in and half out. Another man pulled the dead man inside and then dove through the window only to be shot as he got up to run. The fire had quickly spread inside, and now bunks, inner walls, and the ceiling were on fire. He could see the men inside fighting desperately to put out the fire with blankets that soon became blankets of fire.

Wade aimed at the window and shot four men that were fighting the fire. The air filled with the smell of kerosene, burning wood, black smoke, screaming, and shouting. He shot two more as they climbed out of the window he left for escape. Panicking, two men dove through the windows that were on fire, catching their clothes on fire. As they got up to run, he shot both. Thinking they were escaping from the other side of the long building, he ran the few yards as three men, one with his clothes on fire, ran toward the barn. He took aim and shot each man, then turned and ran back to the woodpile and shot two more men inside fighting the fire.

A man with his clothes on fire dove through one of the burning windows, got up, and ran across the open ground screaming with flailing arms. Wade took aim and fired, and as the man fell, he shot him a second time. A man appeared at one of the windows, fired his gun blindly into the night, and then dove out the window. As he stood, Wade aimed and shot him in the chest. Turning back to the window, another man, his clothes on fire, was halfway out of the window; when Wade fired and hit him in the chest, knocking him back into the burning bunkhouse. By now, the dry wooden roof and floor inside was a firestorm of intense heat, and each time a man appeared at a window to crawl out, Wade showed no mercy.

Filled with hate, anger, and fear for his family, he reloaded his gun and fired into the walls below the windows, thinking that if anyone was left alive inside, that was where they were hiding. He wanted no one to get out of the inferno alive giving them the same fate they had planned for his family. As he knelt to load his pistol, three men jumped out of the burning bunkhouse door and ran toward the barn before he could get the shot off. With his Colt reloaded, he stood and started to go after them when someone from a second-story window of the big house fired, grazing his right leg. Falling to one knee, he fired back, dove for cover behind the woodpile, and watched as the three men disappeared into the barn. He checked his leg, seeing that it was only a flesh wound and then hearing a crashing sound, looked at the roof collapsing into the bunkhouse, and knew there was no one left alive inside.

Someone from the second story window fired again, hitting a log in the woodpile. Looking over the top of the woodpile at the house, he wondered if the man he had killed earlier had lied to him about George Hoskins being in Denver. Whoever it was, fired again, hitting the woodpile inches from his head. Ducking down, he heard the sound of horses and looking toward the barn. Three men galloped away from the barn heading north. Cursing the person inside that he hoped was George Hoskins, he reloaded his guns and shoved one under his gun belt. Wade looked at the dark windows of the two-story house and the closed-door beyond the front porch. Firing several times at the dark second-story window, Wade made a run for the big house and dove rolling across the porch and stood with his back against the outside wall next to the front door. The flames painted the yard and white house a soft orange, and it was eerily quiet except for the burning bunkhouse.

Kicking the front door open, he dove inside the darkroom and rolled across the floor to the front of a white silk sofa. Carefully lifting his head, he looked over the rear of the sofa at the walls, staircase, and a closed-door by the stairs all lit up by dim, flickering light from the fire outside. Getting to his knees with a gun in each hand, he glanced around the room, at the empty staircase, then stood, and ran across the room. Standing with his back against the wall, he looked up the stairs to the railing along the second floor. Hearing a door close, he knew Hoskins was somewhere upstairs.

He slowly walked up the stairs with a gun in each hand, keeping his back against the wall, eyeing the second-floor railing. Reaching the turn in the staircase, he paused and then slowly walked up the stairs pausing when the second floor was at eye level. Looking up and down the hallway, he continued to the top step eyeing the four closed doors along the hall and wondered which door Hoskins was hiding behind. Hesitating, he listened for some sign of the man he came to kill. The dim light from the fire outside came through the window at the end of the hall. The sound of a creaking door caused him to turn, and at seeing someone move inside the darkroom, then the barrel of a gun, he pulled the triggers of both pistols, hearing the scream of a woman followed by the sound of someone falling to the floor.

Wondering who he just shot, he rushed across the hall and pushed the door open with the barrel of one of his guns. In the flickering light that came through the closed lace curtains of the window, he saw a woman dressed in a dark robe crawling on her stomach toward the bed. She reached up, pulled at the covers, and then collapsed onto the floor. Realizing he had shot a woman, he rushed to her, set his guns on the floor, and turned her over. Seeing she was an elderly woman that held fear in her face and eyes. He looked down at her bloody robe and the two bullet holes an inch apart, then into her soft eyes. "I'm sorry," he said in a sad voice. "I thought you were George Hoskins."

"He's in Denver," she whispered, and then she let out a soft breath, closed her eyes, and went limp in his arms.

Wade picked her up, laid her on the bed, and looked at her kindly face wondering who she was. Remembering the wooden chairs by the flower garden outside, he wrapped her in a blanket, picked up his guns, gently picked her up, carried her downstairs and out the front door. Pausing at the edge of the porch, Wade looked at what remained of the burning bunkhouse. Stepping from the porch onto the hard ground, he carried her across the yard and placed her in one of the two chairs, then fussed with the blanket, making sure she was covered except for her face. He stepped back, looking at someone he had never meant to harm, thinking she looked peaceful as if she were sleeping. "I'm sorry, Ma'am," he said softly. "I meant you no harm." It wasn't until that moment that he realized the sun was above the horizon, and as he looked at it in the quiet death he created, it felt warm and soft on his skin. Looking down at the housekeeper for a long moment regretting that he had mistakenly killed her, he turned and went back into the house to finish what he had come to do.

He went upstairs to her room, where he lit a lantern and tossed it against the wall setting the room on fire, then to another room that looked like George Hoskins' bedroom. He lit a lantern and threw it on the floor that exploded into flames that quickly spread to the bed and furniture. He visited one more room to do the same, and then carrying a lamp from that room, he walked down the stairs stopping at the turn where he tossed the lantern onto the stairs above him, leading to the second floor. As the glass of the lantern shattered, catching the stairs on fire, he hurried down the stairs to the library. He lit a lantern and started to throw it against the stone fireplace but paused to look up at the painting of a beautiful woman that appeared to be staring down at him. Thinking of the woman outside in the chair, he figured the lady in the painting must be George Hoskins's dead wife he had heard about. He raised the lantern in a silent apology then threw it against the stone fireplace. The flames quickly spread to the floor and up the wall, catching the bottom of the painting on fire.

Walking toward the door, he stopped, turned, looked up at the burning painting into the woman's dark eyes, then turned and hurried out of the room. Pausing in the living room while the rest of the house burned with a fire that roared like a train racing along the rails, he took a last look around then walked outside. Standing on the porch, he looked at the pile of burning wood that was once a bunkhouse and thought of the three men that got away. Certain they were heading for Denver to warn Hoskins, he hurried down the steps, ran past the bodies lying on the ground, and the pile of burning wood to the waiting mare. The stench of black smoke, burning wood, clothing, and flesh filled the morning air as he put the two guns back in his saddlebag, untied the mare, and swung up into the saddle. The sun was bright and warm as he rode past what was left of the bunkhouse, past the barn, and headed north, searching for the tracks of the three men.

Circle T Ranch

Sarah sat up, giving out a soft cry from a nightmare, looked at Emmett sleeping, and wondered where Wade was. Feeling tired from the medicine Doc Granger had given her, she figured he must be downstairs, so she put her head on her pillow and closed her eyes.

When Sarah next opened her eyes, the sun was above the eastern horizon filling the bedroom with its soft, warm light. Glancing around the room, wondering where her husband was, she looked into the innocent face of her son as he lay sleeping. She laid her head back on the pillow and looked out the window, thinking of all the bad that had happened since they came to Harper and wished she had never left Santa Fe. A soft breeze carried the peaceful morning sounds of ranch noises through the open window. Emmett moaned softly, bringing a smile to Sarah's face as she watched his sleep of funny expressions. She returned her head to her pillow, put her arm around her son, and held him as she closed her eyes, thinking of the safety of Santa Fe.

Hearing inaudible words from the yard below that made their way through the open window, she wondered if that's where her husband was. There was soft laughter and then the words 'thank you' spoken by Mr. Grimes, followed by the sound of horses hooves and a buggy. Careful not to disturb Emmett, she got up, walked to the open window, and peered into the yard below, seeing Harry Block and his wife in their buggy as it passed the barn toward the gate and road beyond. Curious about the early morning visitors, she noticed a thin trail of smoke in the distance and wondered what it was. She turned from the window, picked up her robe, put it on, stepped into the hall, and went down the stairs.

Tolliver Grimes was sitting at the head of the table in the dining room, looking troubled as he stared into the bottom of his cup. He looked up, smiled, and motioned for her to join him. "Coffee's hot."

She walked into the dining room, sat down at the table set for six guests, and fussed with her dirty robe as if she were embarrassed. "Have you seen Wade?"

Tolliver looked concerned as he filled the cup in front of her with coffee and shook his head. "Why, no. I thought he was upstairs with you."

She had a worried look about her as she picked up the cup of coffee. "He was gone when I woke up." Then she took a small sip of the hot coffee, feeling the steam on her face thinking it tasted good.

Grimes looked at her with a worried, furrowed brow. "Maybe he couldn't sleep and is out walking around the place." He didn't believe that after seeing the expression on Wade's face the night before. Wanting to get Sarah's mind off her husband, he asked. "How's Emmett?"

"Sleeping."

Grimes looked relieved. "Good."

She took a sip of coffee and thought about the mornings when she and Wade would have their morning coffee in bed back in Santa Fe. "Was that Mr. and Mrs. Block that just left?"

Tolliver glanced toward the front door. "Yes, it was." He took a drink of coffee, swallowed, set the cup down, and smiled. "Being the kind and generous soul she is, Dorothy Block brought over a few things for your mother, saying they're about the same size." He paused while picking up his cup. "She also said there might be a thing or two for you if they weren't too matronly."

She smiled warmly, thinking the only thing she had to wear was the robe and nightgown she had on. "That was nice of her."

"Yes, it was."

"Does Mother know?" she asked.

He took a drink of coffee and nodded. "She heard voices, came downstairs, and visited for a spell, then thanked Dorothy with a hug and took the clothes up to her room." He took another drink of coffee then put his cup down on its saucer. "I believe she was a bit overwhelmed by the generosity." He looked at her with a hopeful look. "Sure, you won't have something to eat? Bertha's in the kitchen cooking breakfast as we speak."

She shook her head no, put the cup to her mouth, took a sip of hot coffee, and as her eyes followed the cup back to the table and saucer, she wondered where her husband was.

The room suddenly got quiet as Grimes took a drink of coffee and stared at the doorway with a thoughtful look, wondering where Wade was. As he put his cup down, he thought it was strange that he hadn't come in for something to eat or a cup of coffee, then the sound of knocking at the door took his mind from Wade.

"Mr. Grimes," a voice called out, sounding important.

He excused himself as he stood and walked toward the living room and front door.

Sarah watched him disappear through the dining room doorway as she drank her coffee and wondered who it was.

Opening the door, Tolliver looked into the worried face of Stu Parks. "What is it, Stu?"

Stu pointed to the smoke in the west. "Looks like smoke coming from the Hoskins place."

Hearing that, Sarah thought of the smoke she saw from her window, got up, and walked toward the voices finding Tolliver and Stu Parks on the porch, staring at a trail of smoke far to the west.

Grimes immediately solved the mystery of why Wade wasn't around. He looked at Stu. "Have you seen Wade this morning?"

Sarah was standing at the door and suddenly became worried about her husband.

Stu shook his head, looking curious. "No, sir, I ain't."

Tolliver put one hand on Stu's shoulder. "Go down to the barn and see if Wade's mare and Seth Bowlen's black are there."

Stu gave a quick nod, jumped from the porch, and ran toward the barn.

"What is it?" asked Sarah, looking worried.

Grimes pointed to the faint trail of smoke that was barely noticeable. "Looks like a fire at the Hoskins' Ranch. Or what's left of one."

Sarah became frightened. "What does it mean?"

He stared at the smoke in the distance. "We'll know in a few minutes."

"Know what?"

Watching for Stu, he said, "Where your husband is."

She walked to the edge of the porch, put one hand on the porch post, the other over her heart, and stared at the thin trail of smoke in the distance. Filled with the fear of what her husband may have done, she worried that he might get killed.

Stu ran out of the barn and headed for the porch, and as he approached, he said, "Wade's mare is gone, but Mr. Bowlen's black and Marshal French's gray are both in the barn."

Tolliver nodded. "Figures he'd go it alone."

Sarah looked frightened. "Go where?"

Grimes looked away from the smoke with a worried look. "To the Hoskins' Ranch." Then he looked at Stu. "Saddle my Appaloosa and Mr. Bowlen's black."

"Yes, sir." Stu turned and ran to do what he was told, while Tolliver turned to her. "Sorry, Sarah, but I think Wade's taken the war to George Hoskins." He put his hand gently on her shoulder. "We'll be back

304

as soon as we can." Then he walked inside, hurried upstairs, and knocked on Seth's door.

"Come in."

He opened the door, finding Seth sitting in a chair, putting his boots on. "You up for a ride?"

Hearing the urgency in Tolliver's tone, Seth nodded with a curious face as he pushed his right foot into his boot. "Where we going?"

"I'll explain on the way. Meet me downstairs after you're dressed." Then he turned and hurried out of the room.

Bertha walked to the front door and stood in the doorway, looking at the smoke in the distance, knowing what it meant. She was glad to see the smoke and hoped Wade Garrison was alive.

Sarah turned with tears in her eyes. "Have you seen my husband?"

Bertha thought of earlier that morning when she found him in the pantry, where he asked her to keep quiet. She looked from the smoke to Sarah in silence and turned and walked back inside without answering.

Tolliver hurried down the stairs and paused at the bottom. "Won't have time for breakfast, Bertha." Then he hurried across the room, disappearing into his library just as Seth appeared at the top of the stairs. Bertha looked up as he started down while putting on his gun belt, carrying his coat under his arm, asking if there was any coffee.

"I'll pour you a cup," Bertha told him.

He followed her into the dining room, noticing Sarah on the porch, and wondered where Wade was. While Bertha poured the coffee, he put on his coat, then picked up the cup and thanked her. He took a quick small drink of the hot coffee, swallowed, took another, and swallowed as he heard Tolliver on the porch telling Sarah, "Your husband left this on my desk."

Sarah took the note cautiously and walked to the edge of the porch.

Curious about the note, Seth walked out of the dining room, through the living room, and stood in the open doorway. Drinking his coffee, he watched Sarah and wondered what the note said, and then he noticed the smoke in the distance.

She opened the envelope and took out the folded piece of paper.

Mr. Grimes stood next to Seth in the open doorway and watched as she turned away and read the note, hoping it would tell them where he was.

Sarah,

You and Emmett will be safe with Mr. Grimes.

Wade

She crumpled the note, held it against her heart, and looked toward the faint column of smoke against the mountains and blue sky through welling, red eyes.

Seth moved across the porch, stood beside her, and gently put his hand on her shoulder. "What is it, Sarah?"

She handed him the crumpled note without looking away from the smoke.

He set the cup down on the railing, opened the note, quickly read what the note said, and then handed it to Tolliver.

He quickly read it, folded it, and held it out for Sarah. "I'm sorry, Sarah."

Sarah looked up at Tolliver with red eyes and wet cheeks, fearing for Wade's life, then looked at the folded paper he was holding. Hesitantly, as if she were afraid to hold it, she slowly took it and held it tightly in her fist against her heart.

Stu approached the porch leading Tolliver and Seth's saddled horses.

Grimes looked at Seth, knowing he had figured out what was going on, then Grimes stepped off the porch to meet Stu and the horses. Tolliver took the reins of his horse, climbed up onto his saddle, and waited for Seth.

"Sorry, Sarah," Seth said in a soft voice as he stepped past her and hurried down the steps to his waiting horse. He took the reins from Stu, swung up into the saddle, and followed Mr. Grimes toward the smoke.

Curious at what was going on, Stu looked up at Sarah, took off his hat, and asked, "You all right, Ma'am?"

She nodded in answer, picked up Seth's empty coffee cup, turned, and walked inside. After setting the cup on the table in the dining room, she went upstairs, where she lay on the bed next to Emmett and cried in silence. Gripping the note in her hand, she prayed that Wade was alive.

The bunkhouse was a smoldering pile of wood, and so was the big ranch house as the two men rode up and stopped. Tolliver Grimes and Seth Bowlen sat speechless in their saddles, not believing their eyes as to what remained of George Hoskins's vast empire.

Moments passed before Tolliver uttered, "My God." And while Seth looked around, Grimes slowly stepped down from his Appaloosa. With reins in hand, he walked toward the charred, smoldering body of a man he could not recognize.

Seth's black horse was nervous and acting fidgety at the smell of burned flesh and smoldering lumber. Lifting his left leg over the saddle horn, he slid down from his saddle and held the reins of his horse tight to steady her. He glanced from this body to that one imagining the slaughter. "Bastard's never had a chance," he said softly. "How many men did Hoskins have on the payroll?"

Grimes glanced from the bodies to the pile of burnt wood, seeing one charred arm sticking through the charred wood, a head of another, and a couple of more partial bodies. He took several steps toward the burned building and stopped feeling sick. "Not sure," he said softly. "Fifteen, twenty maybe."

Seth saw two bodies close to the trees several yards from the pile of rubble, picturing them trying to make a run for cover only to be shot in the back. "I ain't never seen anything like this."

"I did once," said Tolliver. "But it took twenty Indians." Tolliver pointed to an unburned body next to the outhouse. "There's another over there."

Seth glanced at it. "My guess is he was Wade's first. Caught him coming out of the shitter most likely." Seth turned to the smoldering pile of wood that was once the big house. "Who the hell is that?" he asked, pointing to the figure wrapped in a blanket sitting in the white, wooden lawn chair.

Tolliver squinted as he stared with his tired eyes. "Why, it looks like someone's sitting in the lawn chair wrapped in a blanket." Then he called out. "Hello, there. Are you all right?"

The figure never moved.

"Think it's George Hoskins?" asked Seth.

Grimes thought for a moment. "Don't know." Drawing his gun, he gripped the reins of his horse and led it toward the figure with Seth right behind him. Reaching the body, Tolliver bent over, moved the blanket so he could see the face, and recognizing Hoskins' housekeeper, felt her neck. "She's cold as death." Then he opened the blanket seeing the bullet holes and bloody robe. "Ah, shit." He said sadly. "Wade killed an innocent woman."

Seth leaned over and looked at her. "I can't believe he would have shot her on purpose." He stepped back. "Look how he wrapped her in a blanket as if she'd get cold." He looked at the pile of charred wood that was once a grand six-bedroom house and the smoke that lazily rose from the charred wood. "He must have carried her outside before he set fire to the place."

Grimes stood. "You might be right." Then he looked around. "Wonder where he is?"

Seth shrugged as he glanced around. "My guess is he still hasn't finished what he came to do, and we won't see him until he has." He paused in thought. "Maybe not even then."

Tolliver gestured at the slaughter and spoke in a soft, sad voice. "Be better for him if we never see him. He'll not escape this."

Seth looked at the house, the bunkhouse, and the bodies. "If it were your family, these men tried to kill and burn your home, what would you have done?"

"Ain't saying I wouldn't have done the same, Seth, but that doesn't make it right either."

"Maybe not," replied Seth in a soft, low voice feeling regretful about Wade and wishing he had never sent that telegram.

Tolliver stared at the body of the housekeeper. "I won't judge him, but I'm afraid the law will."

Seth knew that was true and hoped Wade would keep going when he finished what he had to do, traveling far from this terrible place. He put one hand on Tolliver's shoulder. "I'll go into town and get Harry Block and Doc Granger or the undertaker while you stay here and make sure nothing bothers the dead."

Tolliver shook his head. "No, I'll go. If it were Sisters, I'd let you go."

"All right."

Grimes climbed up on his horse. "I'll stop by the ranch and tell Sarah." He paused, looking sad. "Ain't looking forward to that." Then he turned his Appaloosa toward his ranch.

Seth watched Tolliver ride away and then continued to look around, wondering which way Wade rode off. As his eyes settled on the trees behind the outhouse where Wade's first victim lay, he tugged at the reins of his black horse and led it toward the trees, hoping that he'd find signs of Wade there. He wasn't disappointed. Finding six corks, he knelt and picked one up, knowing what they were for. He looked around at the ground seeing where Wade had waited, finding the boot prints leaving and coming back a couple of times. The piles of manure shit belonging to the mare told him she waited for a time. He walked his horse out of the trees to the body by the outhouse. He paused to look down at the deep gash in the man's throat.

Turning, he paused at the rubble that was once a bunkhouse and looked at the charred wood seeing broken whiskey bottles that belonged to the corks he found in the woods. He tugged at the black horse and followed Wade's tracks that led away from the burned, smoldering pile of wood to the barn. Following the tracks through the barn and out the other door, he lost them among countless other tracks. Being persistent, he looked around, and he found them once again and those of three other fresh tracks heading north. He swung up onto his horse, followed the tracks for a while, then stopped and looked north. Imagining the three men riding like hell, and Wade, determined as always, on their trail, he felt no pity for the bastards. Turning his horse, he rode back to the scene of the slaughter to keep the vultures away, hoping George Hoskins was one of the three men Wade was trailing. He wanted the man to experience the fear he had planned on giving to Wade Garrison.

Twenty-Nine

Wyoming Territory

It was getting too dark to follow the tracks of the three men, so Wade pulled the mare up, climbed down, and started to make camp when he saw a dim light in the distance. Hoping it was their campfire, he took the long glass out of his saddlebags and looked toward the campsite, but it was too far away to see if it was the camp of the three men he had been trailing, Indians or some others. Taking the glass from his eye, Wade stared at the tiny light, pushed the long glass together, and shoved it back into his saddlebags. Taking the reins of the mare, he started walking toward the light. "Sorry, girl," he told the mare, "But we can't rest just yet."

Reaching an arroyo not far from the campfire, he hobbled the mare, took the long glass out of the saddlebags, and leaned against the embankment of the arroyo on one knee, putting the long glass to his eye. Through the long glass, he could see three men sitting about the campfire, but the dim light of the fire and this distance made it impossible to see who they were. Confident it was the three men he had been trailing, he shoved the long glass together and put it away. Unsaddling the mare, he covered her with the one blanket he had rolled up behind his saddle. Wearing his black duster, he lay on the side of the hill in the arroyo with his Sharps rifle close by, watched the light from the campfire, and waited for sunrise.

Opening his eyes, Wade pushed his hat back as he sat up, turned, and peered over the top of the arroyo at the campsite several hundred yards to the north. Thinking they were foolish in underestimating his determination

310

or that he would go to Denver for Hoskins. Feeling the Wyoming morning chill as Wade lay on the embankment of the dry creek bed, he looked at the blue sky above the eastern horizon wishing the sun would hurry. The mare he had hobbled in the arroyo a few yards behind him was awake, clearing her nostrils, shook her head, rattling her bit and reins. Pushing off the duster he had used as a blanket, he slid down the embankment and hurried along the sandy, dry creek bed to quiet her before she warned the horses of the men he followed. At seeing him, the mare perked her ears and softly snorted as if saying hello. He checked her front legs, making sure her tethers were secure, adjusted the blanket he had draped over her for warmth, then patted her neck and whispered, "Be quiet."

Returning to the embankment, he lay down next to the Sharps rifle and rod he had placed in the ground earlier to steady the sharps. He turned and looked over his shoulder at the light, blue sky above the horizon, noticing the stars above him had all but disappeared. Feeling the early morning chill as he lay on the embankment, he shrugged into his duster, wrapped his arms around himself to keep warm, and waited for the sun. Minutes passed, and a solitary coyote in the distance sang its lonely song as the sun peeked over the rocky cliffs to the east, leaving ghostly shadows and darkness beneath the rocky plateau. The sun rose higher, spreading its warmth across the desolate but beautiful Wyoming landscape. Knowing the men he hunted would be up soon, he slid down the embankment, hurried to the mare, and quickly yet quietly saddled her. He rolled the blanket up and tied it to the back of the saddle, left her tethered, and returned to the bank of the arroyo and his Sharps rifle.

Now that the sunlight had fallen on the campsite, he could see it clearly and estimated the distance to be around two hundred yards. He put the Sharps barrel in the u shaped rod and looked through the scope at the camp. He could see three saddled horses standing motionless a few yards to the right and the three bedrolls where the men he hunted slept. One of the men sat up, adjusted his hat, and glanced at the horses, the rising sun. He tossed off his blanket, stood, and stretched. He was too far away to see his face clearly, but the sling holding his right arm told him it was Joel Grayson, the man that shot at Sarah and Emmett while the house burned. While the rod steadied the Sharps, he took careful aim putting the crosshairs of the scope on Joel's good shoulder, going for a wound and not a kill. He figured that he wasn't quite done with Mr. Grayson as he pulled the first trigger, steadied the gun then pulled the second trigger. Feeling the Sharps recoil against his shoulder as the cartridge exploded into the quiet Wyoming morning, he saw Joel Grayson go down with a violent twist of his body.

Startled by the sound of the gun that rolled across the prairie like thunder, the three horses in the draw lurched, raised their heads with ears high, and pulled at their reins. The other two men sat up, tossed their blankets off, and at seeing Grayson lying on the ground, they headed for the horses. Having already reloaded, Wade put the scope to his eye, took aim at the closest man, pulled the first trigger, then the second. Feeling the Sharps recoil as the shell exploded across the quiet prairie.

As he reloaded again, the third man grabbed the reins of a horse, cut the tether on its front legs with his knife, and led the horse into a deep ravine. By the time Wade looked through the scope, the man and horse were gone. "Damn it!" he said in anger as he stood, picked up the bandolier, then pulled the rod out of the ground and ran to the mare waiting in the arroyo. Shoving the rod into the slot on the scabbard, Wade tossed the bandolier over the saddle horn, untied the rope, and swung up onto the saddle holding the Sharps in his left hand. He rode up the bank out of the arroyo toward the campsite seeing the third rider galloping out of the ravine riding north. Wade pulled the mare to a stop, stood tall in the stirrups, and took aim. He pulled the first trigger, then the second just as the rider disappeared around the rocky cliff of a low-lying flat hill. Seeing dirt splatter as he looked through the scope, he knew he missed.

Cursing his luck, he turned the mare and looked at the campsite just a few yards away, seeing that Grayson was trying to crawl away. Not done with the man, he shoved the Sharps into its sheath, climb down, dropping the reins of the mare. Wade drew his Colt and walked toward Grayson, leaving the mare to nibble on some grass. He walked up behind Joel Grayson, seeing his pistol was still holstered, cocked his Colt, and pointed it at the back of Grayson's head. "Move, and I'll blow your damn head off."

Grayson stopped, partially rolled over onto his side, and looked up. "I need a doctor."

Wade stepped closer, wondering if he had a gun hidden under him. "I'm going to turn you over, Grayson, and if I see anything that looks like a gun, you're dead."

Grayson's breathing was labored as he looked up at Wade. "I got no surprises, Marshal."

Wade put the toe of his boot under Joel's side, turned him over, and looked down at the man that tried to kill his wife and son.

Grayson grimaced and moaned as he rolled over onto his back.

Wade looked down at the man and his bloody shirt, seeing the shoulder bone had shattered. He bent down, pulled Grayson's pistol from its holster, and tossed it several feet away. Recalling the hidden knife of Paul Bradley in Mexico and the derringer the man pulled on him in New Mexico, Wade was taking no chances. Seeing that both of Grayson's hands were empty, he knew there would be no surprises.

Joel's face filled with perspiration from pain as he looked up at Wade. "Reese said you'd go after old man Hoskins."

Wade glanced toward the north. "That who just rode out?"

Grayson grimaced and stiffened in pain without answering.

Wade glanced at the other man he shot. Figuring Joel would pass out from the pain soon, he turned to him. "Reese was wrong. You should have kept riding."

Grayson's breath was heavy. "I told him that very thing."

Wade put the barrel of his Colt pistol against Joel's coat and moved it so he could see the bloody shirt. "You've lost a lot of blood."

"I need a doctor."

Wade looked at his bandaged shoulder, knowing it was Billy's bullet that Doc had dug out, then glanced around for something to sit on. Seeing a small rock close by, he sat down, looked into Joel Grayson's dark eyes, and smiled. "Well, you won't find one out here."

Grayson didn't see the humor. "You gotta get me to a doctor."

Wade felt no pity. "I know you were shot by Billy when you tried to kill my wife. Who told you to kill my family?" Wade knew the answer, but he had to hear the name.

Grayson's breathing was labored, and suddenly his body stiffened in pain, his forehead and face covered in sweat. "Reese," he said. "It was Reese. He said it was orders from the old man. Something about giving you the same pain you gave him. Every man who rode got a hundred dollars cash."

Wade considered that. "Why didn't you shoot me in town?"

"Orders. You were not to be harmed. Just your wife and that kid of yours."

Wade thought about Lee Jones and how none of the other five Hoskins hands in the saloon took part and knew Seth had been right about George Hoskins. "That's a lot of money." He paused, then asked, "If that's true, why did Lee draw on me?"

"Lee didn't want to go to prison." Grayson looked up at Wade with pleading eyes. "I need a doctor."

"You'll feel better soon. How many men took the money?"

Grayson couldn't believe all the questions. He looked at his bloody shoulder and then into Wade's cold eyes, hoping he wasn't going to leave him. "We all did," he said, sounding tired and out of breath. "Can I have some water?"

Seeing a canteen a few feet away, Wade stood, and walked over to it while keeping an eye on Grayson, picked it up, gave him a drink then asked, "Where's Reese headed?"

Grayson's face was wet with sweat as he smiled, then clenched his teeth in pain. "Go to hell."

Wade chuckled. "I've always been amazed at how brave some ass holes are when they're dying." He gestured over his shoulder at the sun. "Once that sun gets high and hot, your lips will chap, and your tongue will swell, and you'll do anything for a drink. I can wait." Thinking of Mexico, he smiled. "The big birds will start arriving soon for their breakfast. They can smell death miles away."

Joel looked at the sun sitting just above Wade's left shoulder. "Get me to a doctor, and I'll tell you."

Wade considered that as he stared at the man, then he slid off the rock to one knee and punched Grayson in his bloody, wounded shoulder.

Grayson screamed in pain and gave Wade a dirty look. "Damn you to hell."

"Sooner or later, you'll tell me, Joel. It'd be better for you if it were sooner."

Joel blurted out, "A place called Friendly's." He gestured with a nod of the head. "It's north of here on the Sweetwater River."

"Friendly's?" repeated Wade with a puzzled look.

Grayson closed his eyes in pain then looked at Wade. "His brother owns a damn trading post a few miles north of here named Friendly's. Now, can I have some more water?"

Wade picked up the canteen, gave him another drink, and then fussed with Joel's wounded shoulder as if he was concerned. "Looks bad. Your shoulder bone is shattered. The bone is sticking out of your shirt." Wade looked at him. "Why didn't you head up to Denver to warn Hoskins?"

"Like I said. Reese figured you'd go after the old man instead of trailing after us, and he figured the Marshal and his deputies would take care of you."

Wade had all he wanted from Grayson. "Want some water?"

Joel nodded.

Wade put the canteen to Grayson's lips, and while he drank, Wade reached around to his back and pulled out his eight-inch hunting knife. He looked into Grayson's dark eyes, then suddenly dropped the canteen, put his left forearm across Joel's chest, leaned into him, and felt the knife go deep into Grayson's chest, hitting the backbone and whispered, "Going after a man's family is a big mistake."

Feeling a last gasp of Grayson's breath on his face, Wade stared into his open, lifeless eyes for several moments before he pulled the knife out and cleaned it on Grayson's shirt. He turned and looked in the direction Jethro Reese had ridden, thinking he'd be easy to track. Remembering that he had no money, he reached into Grayson's pants pocket and pulled out two fifty-dollar gold pieces. After finding the same on the other man whose head resembled a mushy melon, he gathered the two horses and cut away their ropes. Putting the knife away, he grabbed their reins, climbed up on his mare, and rode out of the camp leading the two horses following Jethro Reese's trail as if he was in no hurry.

An hour into the chase, Wade came upon a ranch house nestled at the bottom of a small, flat, tabletop plateau of rugged cliffs, about two hundred yards to the north of him. He pulled up, wondering if Jethro had taken shelter here, and was watching him over the sites of a Winchester from inside. With that in mind, he followed Jethro's tracks cautiously, keeping an eye on the house, the few sparse trees, and rocks big enough to for a man to hide behind. The trail he followed suddenly turned away from the house and headed northwest. He followed Jethro's trail for a short time, then pulled up and took his long glass out of his saddlebags. Putting it to his right eye, he found no sign of Reese or any other rider on the open ground before him and the trees in the distance. Returning the long glass to his saddlebags, he considered the two horses he now owned and turned in the saddle, looking back in the direction of the house that he had passed earlier. Taking one last look at Reese's tracks, thinking he would let Reese believe he got away, Wade decided to drop the horses off at the house he passed. He turned the mare, yanked at the reins of the two horses, then rode at a trot back in the direction of the house.

Several minutes later, he pulled up atop a small hill overlooking the house he passed earlier, sitting several hundred yards to the east. He took the long glass and studied the long single-story house with an almost flat roof. A thin trail of smoke drifted lazily out of a metal chimney he figured belonged to the kitchen stove and imagined someone cooking a meal, and suddenly he was hungry. The long glass found the rock chimney on the other end of the house smokeless. A covered porch ran the house's length, sheltering the door and windows from the weather and offering shade on warm afternoons. An empty hitching rail waited in front of the porch, and about fifty yards to the right sat a small, weathered barn and corral containing two horses. Next to the barn was a small chicken coop with several chickens pecking about the yard. In the open land beyond the barn, a dozen or so cows roamed here and there, grazing lazily in the warm sun. It looked peaceful, and the scene reminded him of one of the farms they came upon when he, Seth, and the others hunted those four killers six years ago.

A man stepped out of the house carrying a bucket and walked past an outhouse and windmill that turned lazily in the soft breeze, pumping water into a large, metal tub. He watched as the man stopped at the pigsty, dumped what was in the bucket, and then walked back to the house. After he went inside, Wade pushed the long glass together, put it away, and nudged the mare down the small hill toward the house.

Pulling up several yards away from the front door, Wade wrapped the reins of the two horses around the saddle horn of his saddle. He pushed the leather strap off the hammer of his Colt pistol then rested his hand on the grip calling out. "Hello, inside."

The door slowly opened, and a man in his mid-thirties cautiously stepped out carrying a shotgun. "What's on your mind, mister?"

"I mean you no harm," yelled Wade. Then letting go of the reins to the mare with his left hand, he slowly opened his duster, exposing his marshal's badge. "Name's Wade Garrison, United States Deputy Marshal."

The man on the porch stood five-feet-seven, had sandy-colored hair, light blue eyes, and needed a shave. He was thin and had the look of a man who worked hard. His gray shirt and faded blue pants were a little big, and his shoes looked like military issue. He took another step to the edge of the porch. "I saw you on the hill watching the place. Mind telling me why?"

Wade smiled a friendly smile. "I'm trailing a man wanted for attempted murder, among other things down in Colorado." Wade looked to the west and gestured with his left hand. "His trail broke off a ways back. I think he's headed to a place called Friendly's."

The man nodded. "That'd be Ed Reese's place."

"You know this, Ed Reese?"

He shrugged. "Not well. Been in his place a time or two over the years."

Wade was curious about this Ed Reese. "He a family man?"

"His wife died several years ago," replied the man sadly. "And they never had any kids."

Relieved that the place wouldn't be crawling with family, Wade asked, "What sort of man is this Ed Reese?"

The man shrugged, looking uncertain. "Can't say. Seems nice enough."

Wade pondered that while thinking about the brother, Jethro. "Mind if I step down?"

The man smiled as he lowered the hammers on the shotgun. "Sorry, Marshal." Then holding the shotgun in one hand, he gestured inside with the other. "Can I offer you a cup of coffee?"

Wade nudged the mare toward the house, thinking a cup of coffee sounded good. "I'd be grateful. It's been a couple of days since I've had a good cup of coffee." He pulled up and climbed down.

The man stepped off the porch and extended an open hand. "Name's Charlie Peters, Marshal Garrison." Then Charlie noticed he had no packhorse with supplies, just two saddled horses. "Hard traveling without any supplies, ain't it?"

Wade shook the man's hand. "You might say I left in kind of a hurry. How long have you been living here?"

"Close to twenty years." Then he motioned to the corral. "You're welcome to put your horses in the corral. There's some oats and fresh hay if they're hungry."

Wade looked surprised. "Where do you get the hay?"

He gestured south. "I tote it up from Rawlins."

"Be glad to pay for the hay and anything else the horses eat."

Charlie grinned, being thankful. "That'd be right generous of you, Marshal. I'll help you put them in the corral, and then we'll go inside and have that coffee." As they walked toward the corral, he glanced at the two horses and their saddles. "Never saw a man with two spare horses b'fore and no packhorse."

"I suppose not," replied Wade thinking Mr. Peters was not going to let up about the packhorse and thought of how he'd explain them.

Disappointed in the answer, Peters gave him a troubling look as he slid the corral railings to one side so they could walk the horses inside. He watched Wade as he led the three horses into the corral then as he loosened the cinch to the mare. Feeling useless, Charlie started with the saddle of one of the horses, curious about them but not enough to ask. They worked in silence, and when they finished, they stepped out of the corral, and Wade waited while Charlie slid the rails back in place to close the corral. Then he watched as Charlie set three buckets half full of oats down for the horses they eagerly started on. They walked to the house where Peters opened the door and stepped back so his guest could enter first.

Wade took off his hat as he stepped inside, finding a thin woman of barely five feet wearing a faded red housedress, busy over the stove.

She turned, looking surprised, and smiled as her husband introduced her.

"This here's my wife, Nora," said Charlie.

She did a quick curtsey, looking somewhat embarrassed, and like her husband, her teeth were yellow and uneven. She had green eyes, her face was freckled, and looked to be the same age as her husband, but out here in this harsh land, it was difficult to tell. Women seemed to age early, but he thought she was attractive, just the same. Her long, red hair was

318

done in a braid and hung over her left shoulder, covering her small breast. He saw no signs of children or childlike things about the place.

"I offered the marshal a cup of coffee, Nora."

She looked from her husband to their guest. "I was getting ready to fix Charles some eggs and bread I baked yesterday, Marshal. Have plenty if you're hungry."

Wade was very hungry. "If it wouldn't be any bother," he said with a friendly smile as his mouth began to water at the thought of food, not remembering the last meal he ate.

She grinned shyly. "Taint no bother at all." She turned to the stove while her husband pulled one of eight chairs away from a long dining room table. "Have a seat, Marshal."

Thinking the table was a might big for two people in such a desolate country, Wade looked for a place to set his hat.

"I'll take that," offered Mr. Peters, who took the hat and placed it on a peg next to the door, then sat down opposite Wade and watched as his wife poured their coffee.

Wade thanked her and sipped the hot coffee as he looked around at the meager furnishing of the kitchen to his left and a large single room to the right of the table. A black iron stove, small counter, and steel sink next to the inside water pump filled the kitchen. Seeing an open doorway, he figured the bedrooms were down the hall. A large, stone fireplace took up most of the east wall of the living room, and two chairs covered with old blankets and an old-looking leather sofa sat around a bear rug, minus the head and claws. The board walls were empty of pictures and decorations, and to his surprise, the coffee tasted good. He smiled at her. "Coffee's mighty tasty, Ma'am."

She smiled with a blush, thanked him, and turned back to the stove.

As silence filled the room, Wade asked, "Where do you folks go for your shopping?"

"Rawlins," replied Peters. Then he glanced at his wife. "We drive the wagon in every month for supplies, feed, and a little hay. It's a far piece, so we generally spend the night. Sometimes we go to Casper."

Wade smiled. "Sounds like a nice time." He took a small drink of coffee as his thoughts turned to Jethro Reese. "How far is this place called Friendly's?"

Charlie sipped his hot coffee in thought. "About a two-hour ride northwest along the Sweetwater River. You familiar with Wyoming, Mr. Garrison?"

He shook his head. "No, I ain't, Mr. Peters."

Nora Peters approached the table carrying two plates of fried eggs and bread, sitting one in front of Wade, the other in front of her husband.

Afraid he was taking her breakfast, Wade asked, "Aren't you eating, Mrs. Peters?"

"She doesn't eat breakfast generally," smiled Charlie answering for her. "She eats a noon meal with me and then supper."

She smiled shyly. "I've never liked breakfast much, even as a child."

The smell of food found Wade and his hunger as he asked, "Do you have any children?"

She glanced at her husband. "Had two sons and a daughter," she said sadly. "All three died their first year."

Wade thought of Sarah and the baby she lost. "Sorry to hear that." Then he cut into the eggs, watching the yellow yolk fill the plate.

Charlie glanced up at Nora, seeing the look she gets whenever someone asks about children, and changed the subject gesturing with his fork. "If you ride northwest when you leave here, you'll run into the Sweetwater River. Head south a bit, and you won't have any trouble finding Friendly's."

Wade thanked Mrs. Peters for the coffee and food, took his hat from the peg by the door, and followed Charlie out to the corral. Peters started to saddle one of the other horses when Wade stopped him. "No need for that, Mr. Peters. They ain't coming with me."

His mouth agape, Charlie turned to Wade with a puzzled look.

Wade put the saddle blanket on the mare, turned for the saddle, lifted it off the corral fence, and placed it onto the mare's back. "Consider 'em both gifts, Mr. Peters." Then he looked at him and smiled. "For the generosity and kindness you've shown me and the oats for the horses."

Peters looked at the horses with a skeptical look. "That's a lot for a howdy, a cup of coffee, some eggs, and oats."

Wade chuckled. "I guess it is at that, but the truth is, I can't be taking them with me." He put one hand on the saddle horn and looked at him. "I was trailing three men from Colorado; all wanted for attempted murder. I came across them a few miles back and had to kill two." He glanced at the horses and then at Peters. "These were their horses. I only brought them along, so's the wolves or coyotes wouldn't get them."

"Gee, I don't know," he said, looking uncertain as his right hand went to his chin.

Wade tightened the cinch to his saddle. "No one's going to come looking. You have my word on that."

Charlie looked at the three horses and thought on that for a long moment.

Wade started with the harness, and when he finished, he turned to him. "If it'd make you feel better, I'll give you a note or even a bill of sale."

Peters looked at the horses thinking they were fine stock, both males who could mate with their two mares. "I lost my stud a few months back and could sure use a couple of good studs." He looked at Wade ruefully. "No offense Marshal, but I'd sleep better if I had that paper."

Wade smiled and gestured toward the house. "Let's go back inside, and I'll write that note."

Thirty

Circle T Ranch

Tolliver Grimes stopped by his place and told Sarah that the Hoskins place had burned to the ground, and all of the Hoskins riders were dead.

"What about my husband?" She asked.

"There was no sign of Wade," he said. "Only what he had done." He paused. "I'm sorry to have to bring this bad news to you, Sarah."

She looked past him to where the smoke was earlier. "Is George Hoskins dead?"

"I don't know." He paused to look back in the direction of the Hoskins place, thinking Wade probably went after Hoskins.

Worried about Wade and about to cry, she walked to the corner of the house and stared off across the land, afraid she may never see him again, she lowered her head and softly cried.

Tolliver watched Sarah as she stepped off of the porch and walked to the cottonwood tree near the top of the small hill sit down melting into the tall, brown prairie grass.

Billy stepped out of the house. "Did you and Seth find Wade?"

Tolliver stepped close to Billy and told him what he and Seth had found, and there was no sign of Wade.

Billy thought about that. "If he's gone, he's trailing someone."

"You're probably right," said Tolliver. "If you'll excuse me, Billy, I have to head into town for the sheriff." He stepped off of the porch, climbed up on his horse, and looked toward Sarah as she sat in the tall grass. "See if Mrs. Garrison is alright." Then he turned and rode toward Harper.

Billy stared after Mr. Grimes for a moment, then turned and limped around the corner of the house. "Sarah," he said in a low soft voice.

Startled, she turned away and quickly wiped her eyes and face with her hanky.

"Mind if I sit?" he asked.

She turned, forced a smile, and gestured with the wet, crumpled hanky she held in her hand. "Of course not. Please."

Billy slowly eased himself into the tall grass near the white picket fence that surrounded the graves that Tolliver visited each night. "I wish there were some words of comfort I could give you, Sarah."

Her eyes filled with tears. "This is too much, Billy." Her face held a puzzled look. "Why couldn't he let the law take care of Mr. Hoskins and his men?"

French pulled at a grass stem and tossed it away. "The law would have been of no help to you and Wade, Sarah. We had no proof that George Hoskins or any of his men had anything to do with what happened. Even if we had arrested all of them, a good lawyer would have gotten them all off, and you still wouldn't be safe." He paused and looked toward the Hoskins ranch. "Wade knew that."

She considered that for a moment as she wiped her eyes. "We could have left for Santa Fe."

Billy nodded in agreement. "Yes, you could have. But then, late one night, while Wade was off chasing some bank robber or murderer, someone would visit you and little Emmett."

Fear filled Sarah while she pictured that in her mind's eye, knowing Billy spoke the truth.

"George Hoskins was or is, if he ain't dead yet, a man filled with hate and revenge to the point of being insane. He wants Wade to feel the pain he's felt from the loss of his two sons."

She considered that. "It's hard to believe anyone would be that cruel."

"Cruel has got nothing to do with it. The man's insane. He already proved that at the Double J. It wasn't enough that he burned the place down. His men meant to kill you, your ma, and Emmett. It takes an extremely hateful and dangerous man to plan vengeance on a man's family." Silence fell as he slowly stood with the help of the fence and looked down at her. "Wish there was more I could do. I hate to leave at a time like this, but I've got to get home. I'll be leaving in a day or two, and I half suspect Seth will, too."

"I know," she said sadly as she looked up with a kindly face. "I'm glad you were here."

He gave her a small, comforting smile, turned, and limped back to the house, leaving her to sort out her feelings about her husband.

Friendly's on the Sweetwater River

Friendly's trading post sat on the east bank of the Sweetwater, just before the bend of the river became shallow as it widened and turned west, making it an ideal place to ford the river. Rich grasslands of sagebrush flowed out of rolling hills to the thick groves of green leafy trees lining both sides of the river. The trading post of logs and shingled roof was no small place, having a big front porch and a second story in the back where Ed Reese lived. This was where trappers and mountain men stopped for supplies and took part in rough tasting whiskey. An occasional wagon heading north into Montana or west into Oregon would rest for a few days. Even ranchers used Friendly's as a stopping place while herding cattle up and down the Great Basin.

The late afternoon sun hung low in a blue, cloudless sky when Wade rode into a small grove of pine trees and rocks several hundred yards from the trading post. Pulling up, he dismounted, took the long glass out of the saddlebag, found a comfortable rock, and sat down. Wade pulled the glass apart and studied the trading post and the four horses tied up at the hitching rail. Moving his glass along the building to the rear, he saw a small corral next to a weathered barn with several horses, one of which he recognized as the horse Jethro had ridden. Chickens poked and pecked about the yard in front of a small chicken coop not far from a pigsty reminding him of Wheeler's place. After the glass found the outhouse several yards from the rear of the trading post, he lowered it from his eye and pushed it together. Looking at the sun setting low above the mountains, he knew it would be dark in a couple of hours and decided that was when he would visit Friendly's. Putting the long glass away, he unsaddled the mare and hobbled her near a clump of grass to let her feed. Wade tossed his saddle down next to the rocks, laid down with his head on his saddle, and closed his eyes.

The sound of the mare neighing softly woke Wade from a sound sleep. Pushing his hat back, he raised his head, looked at her, and then west, seeing the sun had set, leaving behind a sky of red, purple, pink, and a few gray clouds above the mountains. As darkness approached, he was anxious to end this war with the Hoskins's hands so he could get after George Hoskins to ensure Sarah and Emmett's safety. Kerosene lamps lit up Friendly's open windows and doorway that reflected off the prairie like tiny islands of light. The hitching rail was empty, and it looked peaceful enough, so he got up, saddled the mare, took off his duster so his badge would show, and swung up on the mare. Turning her toward Friendly's, he nudged her into a walk toward the soft light of the open doorway that shone across the porch, spilling a few feet onto the prairie grass.

Riding past the hitching rail so he could see inside the open doorway and not seeing anyone, he continued to the corner of the porch. Climbing down, he loosely tied the mare to the railing and made sure the leather strap was off the hammer of his Colt pistol. He glanced around as he softly stepped up onto the wooden porch, stepped through the open doorway, greeted by a big man of six feet with broad shoulders and a robust chest. He was dressed in a white shirt, unbuttoned vest, and slumped over the counter, looking at a piece of paper. Wade immediately recognized the resemblance between the two brothers, both having brown hair, brown eyes, and a wide mouth with thin lips.

The sound of crackling wood made its way from the fireplace at the rear of the big room crowded with tables of clothing and other things one might need. Ed Reese smiled warmly, and then seeing the badge on Wade's shirt, fear replaced the smile. Placing both hands on the countertop, his eyes suddenly looked to Wade's left.

Wade turned toward the movement while drawing his gun, but before he cleared the holster, Jethro fired, hitting him in the left side. At about the same moment, Wade fired while falling back against a post hitting Jethro in the chest, killing him instantly, and knocking him back against a counter filled with clothing. As the smoke cleared, Wade heard the click of the hammer of another gun, and as he turned, Ed Reese was pointing a small pistol at him. The gun went off, and a bullet ripped into Wade's left shoulder, but he managed to get off a shot hitting Ed just below the neck in the chest. The bullet from Wade's Colt knocked Ed Reese backward against the wall behind the counter. Ed Reese dropped his gun and grabbed at the bleeding hole below his neck, gasping for air. His surprised eyes met Wade's as he slid down the wall and disappeared behind the counter.

Wade cocked his Colt pistol, glanced around the room, and walked toward Jethro as he lay on the floor, his face covered with a new pair of pants that had fallen from the table. Wade reached down, pulled the pants from over Jethro's face, and looked into his open eyes. Dropping the pair of pants to the floor, he picked up Jethro's gun and tossed it across the floor. Remembering the money old man Hoskins paid each man to kill Sarah and Emmett, Wade searched Jethro's pockets and took the money. Standing, he looked at the wound in his side and left shoulder, then walked to the counter. Looking at the lifeless body of Ed Reese sitting on the floor with his back against the wall, his legs bent and his eyes open, he wondered why he made the move. A small-caliber pistol lay on the floor next to his leg and open hand.

Wade turned from Ed Reese, holstered his Colt, and again looked at the hole in the shoulder, his bloody shirt, and then at the hole just above the belt of his pants and knew he was hurt bad. As the blood oozed from both wounds and the pain set in, he walked to a pile of blankets on a table a few feet away. Taking his knife, Wade cut a piece of blanket, put it under his shirt against the wound in his side, and then did the same for the wound in his shoulder. Cutting a length of rope from a roll, he wrapped it around himself, pulled it tight to slow the bleeding, and tied it in a knot. He tried doing the same for his left shoulder but could not secure the rope with one hand. Feeling weak and sweaty, he cut a second piece of rope, turned, and started for the door. Stopping at the counter, Wade looked down at Ed Reese's open eyes, picked up the lantern, and tossed it against the wall setting the place on fire. As the fire blazed and quickly spread, he stepped outside, climbed up onto the mare, and turned her away from Friendly's.

Circle T Ranch

326

It had been three days since the Hoskins Ranch incident, and now Billy French and Seth Bowlen were getting ready to ride out of the Circle T for Sisters, where Billy would board a train for Santa Fe. There had been no further word from Wade, and the endless worry held Sarah like a storm holds the wind.

Holding his hat in one hand, Seth turned from telling Mrs. Talbert and Tolliver Grimes good-bye, took Sarah's hand, and gently held it in his. "Sorry about leaving, Sarah, but I have to get back to Sisters."

"I understand," she said, looking sad while wishing they would both stay and help look for Wade.

Seth let go of her hand, looked out at the western sky and blue haze of mountains thinking of Wade. He turned with a frown of regret. "I truly am sorry about asking Billy for help. Had I known..."

She placed her fingertips on his arm and smiled affectionately. "Don't go blaming this on yourself. I'm certain that if any of us had any notion, all this would happen, none of us would have left our homes."

He looked down at his hat, while his hands unconsciously played with it and nodded several times, feeling relieved. "Mighty kind of you to say so, Sarah."

The smile left Sarah's face, replaced by hatred. "We all know who is to blame for this, Seth." She rose onto her tiptoes, kissed his cheek, and settled back onto the soles of her feet. "Tell Molly I said hello."

Thinking of Molly, a big smiled filled his face. "I'll do that." Then he put his hat on and walked down the steps of the porch to his saddled, black horse. Swinging up into his saddle, he settled in and looked at Emmett. "You take care of your ma, young man, until your pa returns."

"Yes, sir," replied Emmett.

Billy shook Tolliver's hand and then turned to Mrs. Talbert with an open hand.

She pushed it aside and gave him a hug and kiss on the cheek. "Next time you come this way, Mr. French, do bring your wife. I would like to meet her."

Billy smiled. "I'll surely do that, Mrs. Talbert." He turned to Sarah, took her gently by the shoulders, and gave her a small, quick kiss on the cheek. "He'll be all right, Sarah."

She smiled, looking doubtful.

"I've known Wade a long time," he said. "He'll be all right."

She looked into the distant west of clear sky, grasslands, and mountains, wondering where her husband was. "I know all that," she said. "It's him not ever being able to come home that worries me, Billy. What will become of him?"

Billy French had no answer for Sarah. Wade had crossed the line where lawmen aren't supposed to go. But he knew if it were his family, he'd be where Wade is this very minute with no regrets. He kissed her on the cheek once more, said goodbye, and walked down the steps to his horse.

After he climbed up onto his saddle, both men tipped their hats, turned their horses, and rode away from the Circle T and the mystery of Wade Garrison.

Wyoming Territory

Wade slowly opened his sleepy eyes, looking up at the freckled, worried face of Nora Peters as she gently wiped his face with a cold, damp cloth that felt cool and soothing against his fevered face.

She paused and smiled. "About time you woke up." She dipped the cloth into a pan of cold water, rung it out, and continued wiping his face and forehead. "How are you feeling, Mr. Garrison?"

"Not so good," he said lazily.

"Well, I ain't surprised." She gently wiped his face with the damp cloth. "You have a bit of a fever."

"Feels warm," he said just above a whisper. Then he reached up and touched his painful left shoulder, feeling the bandage.

Nora gently pulled his hand away. "Charlie dug the bullets out of your shoulder and side, then stitched you up." She continued wiping his face. "I wrapped them as best I could and put on a remedy an Indian once told me about."

The scene at Friendly's and the long ride back to the Peter's place slowly crawled into Wade's clouded memory. "Could I have some water?"

She stopped with the cloth, leaned toward the nightstand next to the bed, and poured water from a chipped and dented white pitcher into a gray, tin cup. She helped him raise his head as she put the cup to his lips.

"Not too much now. Charlie found you tied to your horse around midnight last night."

Wade slowly closed his eyes and drifted off, not hearing her ask who shot him.

The room was dark when Wade next opened his eyes, and feeling the need to relieve himself, he turned onto his side and tried to get up, but he was too weak. It hurt like hell, but he managed to sit on the side of the bed and call out.

Moments later, Charlie Peters hurried into the room dressed in his long johns, carrying a lantern.

"I gotta go," Wade told him.

Charlie sat the lantern down, picked up an old pitcher that sat on the floor beside the bed for that purpose, and when Wade finished, he helped him back into bed. "You're sweating," said Charlie as he put the covers back over him then felt his forehead. "You got a fever." Then he asked, "Who shot ya?"

Shivering, Wade pulled the covers up to his chin, looking like he was going to pass out. "I'm cold."

"I'm sure you are," replied Peters. "Let me take a quick look at them bandages."

Nora hurried into the room dressed in an old, faded, faded pink robe.

Charlie turned to her, looking worried. "He's got a fever, and his wounds are oozing a bit."

Wade was shivering and saying things that didn't make much sense about a dog, a fire, and an Indian.

Nora felt his forehead. "He's delirious," she said, looking worried. "He's burning with fever Charlie." Then she stepped backward, filled with worry. "We got to break this fever." Then she pulled the chair next to the bed away, felt his forehead, and looked at her husband. "Help me get him on the floor, then get me a bucket of cold water."

He looked at Wade and then at her. "What ya got in mind?"

"Just help me get him on the floor," she said.

They managed to get Wade on the cold, wooden, floor then Charlie headed for the kitchen and the water. When he returned moments later, Nora had Wade covered in an old sheet. Curious about what she was doing, he set the water bucket next to her on the floor. "Maybe I should ride for a doctor."

"By the time you rode to Rawlins and back," she said. "His fever will either have broken, or he'll be dead." She looked up. "I need you here. I'll try some of the herbs and plants we have, and then first thing in the morning, you kill me a chicken, and I'll boil some chicken broth. If he makes it through the night, he'll be needing something to get his strength up." She took the sheet off of Wade, dipped it into the bucket of cold water, and without ringing it out, she laid it over Wade and then wet another cloth and wiped his face. "You go on to bed and get some sleep," she told Charlie. "I'll stay with Mr. Garrison."

Charlie picked up the pitcher Wade had used and headed for the door. "I'll go dump this."

Charlie walked into the bedroom around three in the morning, finding Nora sitting on the floor resting against the side of the bed with her head and arms on it sleeping. Worried about her, he gently touched her shoulder.

Opening her eyes, she looked at Charlie, then she moved toward Wade and felt his face. "Still a little warm, but he's resting easier."

"You come on to bed," Charlie told her. "He'll be all right. It looks like you broke the fever. It'll be light in a couple of hours."

She felt his face again. "Let's get him back into bed. I think his fever has broken."

Wade opened his eyes to the unfamiliar, dim room of closed window with curtains drawn. He could see the daylight through the crack between the heavy cloth curtains, and in the dim light of the room, he saw his holster and Colt hanging on the wall next to the door. Realizing he was naked under the covers, he lifted his head to look for his clothes finding only his black, wide-brimmed hat on top of a dresser across the room. He lifted the covers, looked at the bandage wrapped around his midsection and then the one on his shoulder. Both were clean and looked recently changed. As he lowered the covers and his head returned to the pillow, Friendly's came back to him. The vision of Nora Peters sitting next to him wiping his face came to mind, but not much else. A rooster somewhere outside crowed

330

proudly, a horse neighed, and a few calves bawled for their mothers. Hearing sounds in the next room, he called out. "Anyone out there?"

Nora Peters opened the door and hurried into the room, carrying a dishtowel, looking tired as well as worried. "You all right, Mr. Garrison?"

"I need to go to the bathroom, but I ain't find my clothes."

She glanced around, then bent down, picked up a metal pitcher from under the bed, and handed it to him.

He looked up at her. "I may need some help, Mrs. Peters. I'm pretty weak." She nodded once. "I'll get Charlie," and hurried out of the room.

After Charlie helped him with the pitcher and then back into bed, Wade looked up at him. "Sorry for the bother, but I ain't got much strength for some reason."

Charlie bent down to pick up the pitcher. "You lost an awful lot of blood." He turned to walk out with the pitcher just as Nora walked in.

She felt Wade's forehead. "I think you'll live, Marshal." She smiled, then sat down and took the cloth out of the pan of water, rung it, and gently patted his face with it. "You sure had us worried."

He was tired, and the cold, damp cloth felt good against his skin. "How long have I been here?"

"About two days," replied Charlie, still holding the pitcher. "Me and the missus were in bed sleeping when that mare of yours woke me. I lit a lantern and went outside, finding you tied to your saddle."

Wade closed his eyes, remembering that he put the rope around himself in case he passed out. Then he closed his eyes and drifted off to sleep.

"Who shot you, Marshal?" asked Charlie

"He can't hear you, Charlie," said Nora.

Charlie frowned, looking disappointed. "Sure would like to know what the hell happened out there."

"Gonna have to wait to find that out, Charlie," offered Nora.

Mrs. Peters was standing over Wade, feeling his forehead the next time he opened his eyes. "Fever's gone," she said, looking relieved. "Now that you're awake, we need to get some broth down you."

"Sorry, Mrs. Peters, but I ain't hungry."

She frowned, looking strong-minded. "You need to eat, even if it ain't much." She gestured toward the door. "I made a pot of chicken broth, and it's been waiting for you to wake up." She started toward the door talking over her shoulder. "I know when a man is hurt, they don't feel like eating, but the broth is good for you and will give you strength and help rebuild the blood you lost. So you'll eat like I tell you."

He watched her disappear through the doorway, hearing her tell her husband that he was awake.

A moment later, Charlie walked in, pulled a chair next to the bed, sat down, and combed his sandy hair back with his right hand looking curious. "Who shot you, Marshal?"

Wade looked into Charlie's blue, curious eyes. "I found myself in a gunfight with Ed Reese and his brother, Jethro."

Charlie looked surprised. "You got shot by Ed Reese?"

"Him and his brother, Jethro."

"So it was Ed's little brother you were after?"

Wade nodded. "That's right. He opened up on me right after I walked in the place. I shot him, and when I turned to see what Ed Reese was doing, he fired, hitting me in the shoulder. I got off a shot and killed him." Wade looked puzzled. "What I don't understand is why Ed Reese shot me? I wasn't after him."

Charlie considered that with a puzzled look and then shrugged. "Maybe he just got scared or was trying to protect his brother."

"Maybe," replied Wade thoughtfully. "How well did you know the Reese's?"

"Not all that well," he said, frowning. "I recall that Jethro rode out of the territory ten or twelve years back." Silence filled the room, then he asked, "Who was it Jethro tried to kill?"

"My wife and son."

Charlie's face lit up with surprise, and his next question was interrupted by Mrs. Peters walking into the room with a bowl of chicken broth and a spoon. Her husband stood so she could sit down next to the bed. He stared at Wade for several moments thinking about Friendly's while Nora spoon-fed him. "Jethro Reese tried to kill the Marshal's wife and son," he told her.

Nora's face filled with disbelief. "Why on earth would he try and do a horrible thing like that?"

332

Wade took a little broth and swallowed. "It's a long story, and I'd like to tell it some other time."

Seeing that Wade was getting tired, Charlie said, "Well, I've chores to do." He walked out of the room, wondering how much of this was law and how much was vengeance.

Mrs. Peters' red hair wasn't in its usual braid but hung loosely over one shoulder, and Wade was surprised at its length. Her freckled face held a kind smile as she dipped the spoon in the bowl and put it to his lips.

Wade took a small sip of broth, thinking it tasted good, and managed to eat about a quarter of the bowl. Finally, he motioned he'd had enough, saying he was tired.

She put the spoon in the bowl, set the bowl down on the nightstand, got up, and walked to the window. She was wearing a plain, gray housedress and apron. "Your clothes are full of blood and holes from getting shot, Mr. Garrison," she said, sounding apologetic. "I tried to clean them, but the blood had set, and your shirt and underwear had bullet holes in them." She turned. "My brother was about your size, I believe. You can wear some of his clothes." She gestured to a trunk in the corner. "You'll find what you need in that trunk when you're up to it."

He glanced at it. "What happened to your brother?"

Sadness came over her as she pulled the curtains back, letting in the daylight. She looked out the window in thought. "Ralph passed away two winters ago with the sickness." She turned with a sad smile. "He's buried up on the bluff with our three children."

Still weak, Wade fought the sleep that hunted him and thought about the three children she lost, feeling sorry for her. This is a rough country for women, he told himself, and then he thought about Sarah and the baby she lost from the accident and how she cried afterward.

Nora smiled warmly in memory of her brother as she looked out the window. "I still miss him." She turned from the window to say something to Wade, but his eyes were closed, and he was sleeping. She walked to the table beside the bed, looked down at him a moment, touched his forehead to make sure he had no fever, picked up the bowl and spoon, and walked out of the room.

Light from the other room spilled through the open doorway of the bedroom when Wade opened his eyes. He lay listening to the muffled voices of Charlie and Nora in the other room. His shoulder and side still hurt, but he managed to push himself up against the headboard of the bed and hollered, "Hello."

Moments later, Charlie walked into the room, followed by Nora, asking Wade if he was alright. He said he was, but he needed to go to the bathroom. Charlie turned to Nora, saying he'd help Wade, and as she turned to leave, Charlie lit the lantern, picked up the pitcher, helped Wade, and then helped him back to bed. "You hungry?" asked Charlie.

Wade nodded. "Some."

"I'll have the missus see if there's anything leftover from supper."

"What time is it?"

He stopped at the door and turned, looking curious. "Close to eight o'clock, I imagine. Why?"

Wade shrugged. "Just curious."

"Maybe after you eat, we can talk." Then Mr. Peters turned, walked out of the room, and told his wife that Mr. Garrison was hungry.

After eating a meal of warmed-over stew and bread, Wade drank the last of the coffee and placed his cup on the nightstand next to the bed. He settled back against the pillow and headboard and worried over his wife and son, knowing that George Hoskins was still alive.

Nora walked into the bedroom and was surprised to see that he had eaten everything. "Nothing wrong with your appetite." She smiled. "That's a good sign."

"I was hungry, and the stew was really good, Mrs. Peters."

She smiled appreciatively as she picked up the empty plate and coffee cup.

As she turned to leave, Mr. Peters walked into the room. "Get enough to eat?"

Wade smiled. "Sure did, thanks to your misses."

Charlie moved the chair closer to the bed, sat down, and looked at Wade. "Sheriff Bob Finch and a posse from Rawlins rode in late today while you were sleeping."

Wade's heart skipped a beat.

Charlie smiled. "Don't worry. I didn't tell him you were here." He paused and then continued. "The sheriff asked if we'd seen any strangers around. I told him, no, and when I asked why, he said that Friendly's had burned to the ground, and they recovered two bodies inside one they believed to be Ed Reese."

Nora walked into the room, sat on the edge of the bed, and folded her hands in her lap.

Mr. Peters glanced at his wife and then looked at Wade. "I hold no secrets from my missus, Marshal, and if what happened between you and the Reese's could cause us harm with the law, we have a right to know."

Wade could find no argument with that.

Charlie's eyes narrowed. "You told me earlier that Jethro tried to kill your family. Mind explaining that?"

Wade drew in a deep breath and let out a long, soft sigh knowing it was time to tell them. "It's a long story."

"We got time," said Charlie Peters.

Wade's eyes went from Charlie to his wife and then back to Charlie's questioning, blue eyes. Wade shifted, trying to get comfortable, and began. "It started back in July while I was in Santa Fe." They listened as he told the story of the killings in Sisters, the accident, the warrants, and the jailbreak of Pete Hoskins. Then he told them about George Hoskins paying each one of his men one hundred dollars to burn down the Double J Ranch and kill his family, but leaving out the burning of the Hoskins ranch. When he finished, silence fell in the room while Charlie and Nora digested what he told them.

Moments passed, and then Charlie sighed and looked at his wife with a perplexed look and then at Wade. "Sounds like you and your family have had a bad time of it with this Hoskins fellah." He paused. "What are your plans now?"

Wade sighed, thinking he needed to find George Hoskins and kill him, but he couldn't tell that to the Peters. Worried about the local law, he looked at Peters. "What about the sheriff?"

Charlie shrugged. "What about him?"

"He may come back," said Wade. "And if he does, he may find me here, and we'll both have a lot of explaining to do."

Mr. Peters glanced at his wife and then looked at Wade. "I doubt he'll be back, but I guess he could." He glanced at Wade's bandaged shoulder. "I hate to rush you, but you need to ride out as soon as you're able."

Silence covered the room while Wade thought about leaving. "I don't think the sheriff will come back for a day or two, if at all." His eyes went from one to the other. "I don't want to cause you, nice folks, any trouble." He paused. "I'll leave in the morning if that's agreeable."

Nora Peters' face filled with worry as she looked at her husband. "He can't leave now, Charlie. He could bleed to death."

Charlie looked at her and nodded in agreement. "That's a fact." Then he looked at Wade. "Stay until the day after. We'll keep you and your horse hid in case the sheriff or some of his men should come by."

Wade looked relieved but worried. "I'd appreciate it."

Mrs. Peters gently slapped her knees and sighed, sounding relieved. "Well, that's settled." She stood and looked at Wade. "You rest and get your strength back." Then she smiled. "You need to go and take your family back to Santa Fe, Marshal, where they'll be safe."

Knowing his family was safe for the time being with Tolliver Grimes and his men, Wade knew they would never be safe as long as George Hoskins was alive.

"You look tired," she said. Then she looked at her husband. "Time, we all got a good night's sleep."

Circle T Ranch

A calm breeze smelling of wildflowers mixed with ranch smells made its way across the front porch where Sarah was sitting in a white, wooden chair. She was darning a pair of Emmett's socks and wondering where her husband was and if he were alive. Her mother was in the kitchen, baking to the displeasure of Tolliver's Indian housekeeper, Bertha, and Emmett was playing a few yards away. Hearing the neigh of a horse, Sarah sat up and looked over the railing of the porch at two men riding their horses at a walk past the barn and bunkhouse toward the big house. Curious who they were and if they brought news of Wade, she stood holding the socks she was darning, walked to the porch railing, and called to Emmett. "Come up to the porch Emmett."

Seeing the two men as he stood, Emmett shielded his eyes from the afternoon sun, looked at them, and then walked toward the porch. "Who are they, Ma?"

"I don't know, now go inside." Sarah opened the door, put one hand on his shoulder, and gently pushed him inside. Seeing Tolliver walk out of his office, she said, "Someone's coming."

Tolliver Grimes took a quick look through the lace curtains of one of the living room windows, reached above the front door for his Winchester, and then joined Sarah on the porch. "Might be best if you waited inside. I don't know who these men are or who sent them."

Hesitantly, she turned and started into the house.

"Sarah," Tolliver said softly. "There's a pistol in the top drawer of that little cabinet next to the dining-room door. I think you know how to use it."

She stepped inside, took the pistol from the drawer, held it at her side in the fold of her dress. Leaving the door ajar so she could hear what the two men had to say, she waited.

Wanting the riders to see the Winchester Mr. Grimes was holding, he stepped to the edge of the porch holding the rifle across his midsection and cocked the hammer.

Taking notice of the Winchester, the two riders stopped a few yards from the porch steps. "I'm the United States Marshal Wayne Lewis from Denver," said one, then gestured to the man next to him. "This is my deputy, Brad Aikins." Then he looked at Grimes. "You must be Tolliver Grimes?"

Tolliver nodded. "I am. What can I do you, Marshal?"

The two men nudged their horses closer to the porch, and then the marshal leaned forward, resting his hands on the saddle horn. "We're looking for Wade Garrison, Mr. Grimes. We thought he might be here, or you may know where we can find him."

To Tolliver's surprise, Sarah stepped out of the house onto the front porch. "What is it you want with my husband?"

Marshal Lewis was not a very big man and looked even smaller in the saddle next to his taller deputy. His light brown hair bulged from under his tan, wide-brimmed Stetson, and his black suit coat bulged on his left side, where he wore his Colt pistol. He was clean-shaven and looked at Sarah through brown, narrowed eyes. "We'd just like to talk to him, that's all."

"About what?" she asked.

Marshal Lewis stared at Sarah for a moment. "That's something we'd prefer talking to your husband about, Mrs. Garrison."

She stepped closer to the edge of the porch standing next to Tolliver. "I don't dare suppose it'd be about my pa getting shot in the back."

Surprise held Lewis. "I wouldn't know anything about that, Mrs. …"

"Or the loss of my unborn infant child?" said Sarah cutting him off.

Lewis fidgeted in his saddle, looking nervous. "Ma'am, as I was…"

"Or my son having a broken leg," said Sarah cutting him off again. "Or me a concussion at the hands of your employer, George Hoskins?"

"Now hold on, Mrs. Garrison. I ain't on Mr. Hoskins' payroll, and if you'd let me finish, we'd just like to talk to Mr. Garrison about what happened out at the Hoskins' Ranch a while back?"

Sarah gave him a look as she stepped forward. "Why aren't you asking about what happened at the Double J when it was burned to the ground? Why aren't you asking about one of the Double J men getting murdered? That bastard Hoskins and his men tried to kill my son and me twice, but you wouldn't care about that now, would you, Mr. United States Marshal?"

Lewis was getting angry as he stared at her. "I don't know anything about that, Ma'am."

She took another step to the edge of the porch. "I suppose not, Marshal Lewis. You say you're not paid by George Hoskins, but I'm telling you to go back and tell that bastard that the next time he comes near my son," she paused while taking the gun from the folds of her dress. "I'll use this on him, and I'm a damn good shot."

Shocked at Sarah's language, Lewis looked at the pistol. "Making empty threats won't do you any good, Mrs. Garrison."

Tolliver chuckled. "You're misunderstanding if you think Sarah Garrison's making empty threats Marshal." Silence fell on the porch, and Tolliver chuckled as he stepped next to her. "Wade's not here, Marshal

338

Lewis." Then he shrugged. "We don't know where he is. No one here's seen him for several days, and none of us knows anything about what happened out at the Hoskins place."

"Very well," said Lewis, then he looked from Tolliver to Sarah, tipped his hat, and the two men turned their horses and rode away.

Tolliver watched the two men as they rode away. "Hoskins ain't about to let this thing end, Sarah. He'll hound Wade 'til his death, and I fear he still has his eyes on you and Emmett. I don't want you straying too far from the house. From now on, there'll be a couple of armed men about."

Sarah looked worried. "Do you think they'll arrest Wade?"

He considered that. "Maybe, but so far, no one's saying they saw him. The only man pressing the issue is George Hoskins, and he's safe up in Denver."

"Too bad," said Sarah in a soft, thoughtful voice.

Tolliver reached down and took the gun from her hand.

Letting go, she looked into his soft eyes. "I never wished a man dead before, Mr. Grimes."

He grinned. "Well, I have, and there ain't no shame in it when it's deserved."

Charlie Peters Ranch

Wade got dressed in a blue shirt and pants that once belonged to Mrs. Peters' brother, put the red bandana around his neck that Sarah had given him, tied it, and walked out of the bedroom carrying his wide-brimmed, black hat in one hand, his gun belt with the Colt in the other.

Mrs. Peters looked up from the stove and stared at him for a long moment in memory. "Like seeing a ghost Marshal, you wearing Ralph's clothes and all." She smiled. "They look good on you." She motioned to a chair at the table. "Now, sit yourself down and have some breakfast."

Accepting the compliment in silence, Wade eased into a chair at the table while she set a plate of eggs, potatoes, and ham in front of him. Thinking everything smelled good, he took a drink of hot coffee

Charlie walked in the door and looked at Wade. "Horse is saddled and waiting outside, Marshal." Then he sat down at the table. Watching

Wade eat, he looked regretful. "Hate to push you out like this before you're completely healed, Marshal, but we don't want no trouble with the law."

Wade smiled. "I understand Charlie, and I hold no hard feelings. I appreciate all that you and" he looked at Nora, "your wife has done. If it weren't for the two of you, I wouldn't be alive today.

Nora smiled as she poured her husband a cup of coffee, "Couldn't let you die now could we Marshal." Then she returned to her chores in the kitchen.

Wade smiled at that, and then he and Charlie made small talk while he ate, and when he finished, he pushed his chair back and slowly stood with the help of the table. He smiled at Nora. "Thanks for everything, Mrs. Peters."

She smiled warmly, "You're most welcome, Mr. Garrison."

He picked up his hat and gun belt from a nearby chair as he glanced around to burn the memory of this place, Charlie and Nora, into his mind. He smiled at Nora a final time then followed Charlie Peters outside. Standing at the edge of the porch, he put on his hat, his gun belt, and holster strapping it to his thigh. He looked at the mare, standing at the hitching rail, and thought of the long ride ahead of him. Thanking Charlie for putting the Sharps in its scabbard, and the bandolier over the saddle horn, he stepped off the porch, took the mare's reins, and with Charlie's help eased up into the saddle.

The door opened, and Mrs. Peters stepped onto the porch. "I packed you something to take along," she said, smiling.

He took the bag and shoved it into his saddlebag, and thanked her. "Bye, Mrs. Peters."

"Goodbye," she said with a big smile. "Be careful, Mr. Garrison. I'll pray that you get home safely."

"Thank you, Mrs. Peters. "He turned to Charlie Peters. "Take care, Charlie."

Peters nodded. "Mind them wounds, Marshal."

Wade looked at the two a final time. "I'll not forget your kindness." Then he turned the mare away from the house and nudged her into a walk, and never looked back.

Thirty-One

Harper

It was dark when Wade rode up to the big doors of Levi Wagner's Livery. He pulled up, slowly dismounted, feeling the stitches pull, and looked back along the main street of Harper. Soft, orange light flowed from the windows and doors, leaving their images in the street. It was a quiet Sunday night besides a few horses outside the two saloons and a single rider riding down the dirt street. Soft piano music and laughter from the Blue Sky and Sundowner Saloons found one another in the center of the dirt street. Turning from the familiar scene, he knocked on one of the big doors.

"Who's there?" asked Levi.

Wade glance over his shoulder back along Main Street and softly said, "Levi, it's Wade Garrison."

The sound of the heavy board lifting away from the livery doors broke the stillness, and as the door slowly opened, Levi stuck his head out and quickly glanced around. "That marshal from Denver and a deputy were here a few days back, asking about you." He pushed the door open. "Better get inside."

Wade led his horse into the livery, where he gestured to a vacant stall. "That one all right?"

Levi glanced out the doors along the main street, making sure no one saw Wade, closed them, and put the board back over the two livery doors. "That'll do fine," he said, then watching Wade as he led the mare into the stall, he asked, "Didn't ya hear what I said about the marshal?"

Wade gently pushed the mare to one side of the stall. "I heard." After taking the Sharps and its scabbard off the saddle, followed by the saddlebags, he lifted the stirrup and started on the saddle cinch. "Hear anything from the Circle T?"

Wagner shrugged. "They're all okay if that's your worry." Then his eyes narrowed. "George Hoskins is in Harper."

As if he hadn't heard what Levi said, Wade grabbed the saddle and started to lift it off with a jerk but grimaced in pain and stopped. Feeling faint as sweat filled his forehead; he closed his eyes, leaned against the mare, and took off his hat.

"You all right?" asked Levi, looking worried.

Wade wiped his forehead with his shirt sleeve and stepped back, looking a little pale. "Could you give me a hand with the saddle, Levi?"

Levi looked worried and wondered what was wrong with the marshal. "Sure." He hung the lantern he held over a hook and walked into the stall, keeping an eye on Wade. "You don't look so good. You ain't shot, are you?" And when Wade didn't answer, he motioned to a stool. "You have yourself a seat, and I'll unsaddle your horse."

Wade sat down on the stool and watched as Levi unsaddled the mare. "I need a place to stay the night, Levi."

Looking puzzled, Levi tossed the saddle on the top railing, walked out of the stall. "You're welcome to sleep here." Then he shrugged. "All I got's the loft." Then he remembered the days when Wade and his friend Emmett Spears would get drunk and spend the night in the loft. "That old cot is still up there, and I can give you a blanket or two."

Wade wiped his forehead, looked up, and smiled. "Sounds good, Levi, thanks."

Levi took a closer look at Wade. "You sure you're all right?"

"Could I bother you for a feed bag for the mare? It's been a long ride."

Wagner nodded quickly. "I'll get one for her." Then he headed into another stall for a bag he filled with oats, all the time keeping a curious eye on his guest.

Wade stood, took his canteen from the saddle Levi had placed on the railing, and took a long drink of water. After he put the canteen back, he sat down, opened his coat, looked at his bloody shirt, and softly said, "Shit."

Levi walked past with the bag of oats, and upon seeing the blood, asked, "What the hell happened?"

"Long story. You got anything I can use for bandages?"

Levi put the feed bag on the mare and then knelt and looked at the blood. "I have some clean wraps that I use on my horse's legs when they get sore."

Wade considered that. "That'd do, I think."

"Mind telling me what the hell happened, Marshal?"

Wade knew Levi wasn't going to let it go. "Got shot."

"Who by?"

Wade needed a drink of whiskey, and he needed the dressings changed. "You have any whiskey?"

Levi nodded. "About half of a small bottle is all."

Wade reached into his pocket and gave him some of the money he took off of Jethro Reese and the others. "Run down to the Blue Sky and buy two big bottles. We need to clean these wounds before we put on clean bandages."

"Maybe I should get the doc?"

Wade looked worried. "No. I don't want anyone knowing I'm in town."

Levi raised his brow and nodded. "Gotcha." Then he took the money and headed for the side door. "I'll be right back."

As the door closed, Wade sat down on the livery floor, rested against a stall post, closed his eyes, and waited.

Twenty minutes passed before Levi returned with the two bottles of whiskey and handed them to Wade. "Sorry, it took so long."

Wade took them and set them on the livery floor. "I'm gonna need your help."

Curiously, Levi looked on. "Whatever you want."

Wade thought of Nora Peterson as he began unbuttoning his shirt. "I don't want my clothes smelling like cheap, rotgut whiskey, so you're going to have to be careful cleaning me up.

Levi nodded. "I'll bring what wraps I have from the tack room." He headed for the rear of the livery, and when he returned several minutes later, he had several bandages under his arm and a pan of fresh water. He set everything down, helped Wade take off his shirt, get out of the top of his long underwear, and lower his pants. After he removed the bloody bandages, he paused to look at the wound. "Looks more like someone knifed you. Who did this?"

"He wasn't a doctor, if that's what your wondering," replied Wade.

Levi looked at Wade and then at the wound. "I guess not."

"Said he had to cut the bullet out."

Levi looked worried. "I guess he did the best he could." He picked up a bottle of whiskey, uncorked it, and handed it to Wade, and said, "Pour some of that over my hands." After Levi washed his hands with whiskey, he poured some of it on a clean cloth, gently cleaned the blood from Wade's wounds, and examined the stitches. "Yep, you got some pulled stitches, all right." He sat back, shaking his head. "You need a Doctor. You need to be stitched up again."

"No, doctor."

Wagner figured he could do it and gestured toward the back of the livery. "I got a needle and stuff in the backroom I've used to sew up cuts on horses and mules."

Wade thought on that for a minute. "Think you can sew me up?"

Levi nodded as he stood. "What choice we got?"

Wade considered that. "None, I guess."

"I'll get my stuff."

Wade watched him walk toward the back, knowing it would hurt like hell, but the wounds had to be closed.

Minutes later, Levi returned with a small, metal box of medical supplies, set it down on the ground next to Wade, and carefully examined both wounds once again.

Wade looked concerned. "You ever sew up anything but a horse or mule?"

He looked at Wade. "A time or two over the years." Then he lifted his pant leg showing a scar of seven inches just below the knee. "Had to do my leg once, and it hurt like hell." He grinned. "Same as this is going to."

Wade failed to see the humor as he watched Levi pour whiskey over a long, thin-bladed knife and an ugly curved needle. "When did that happen?" he asked, referring to Levi's leg.

"When I was a foolish young man." Levi took a drink of whiskey, knelt next to him, and examined the wound. "Mind me asking who shot you?"

"Jethro Reese shot me in the side, and his brother shot me in the shoulder."

Levi started cutting the stitches that had pulled away with the sharp, thin knife, leaving those in that had not pulled away. "Didn't know Jethro had a brother. But then, we weren't exactly friends."

"Yeah, we weren't either," replied Wade in an attempt at humor. Looking away, he tensed up while Levi cut the old stitches out, hoping the old man knew what the hell he was doing.

When Levi finished, he put the knife down, pulled each stitch out with a quick jerk, poured a little whiskey on a cloth, and patted the wound. He took a drink of whiskey and picked up the needle, and looked up at Wade. "Might be a good idea if you were to take hold of that post there."

Wade's side hurt like hell and kept him up most of the night, and it seemed he had just drifted off when Levi's rooster began crowing. Wade opened his eyes to the tiny slits of light pouring through the spaces between the boards of the eastern wall of the livery and then slowly sat up so he wouldn't pull at the stitches. After letting the pain subside for a few moments, he gathered his blanket, pistol, and hat then slowly climbed down the ladder from the loft.

"Good morning," greeted Levi as he walked out of the backroom, pulling his suspenders up over his shoulders. "How's the side?"

Wade stepped off the last step. "Kept me awake most of the night." He looked at Levi. "Ever think about killing that rooster?"

Wagner looked in the direction of the coop. "Thought about it a time or two, but then the hens probably wouldn't lay any eggs." He grinned at Wade. "I'm was just about to fry myself a couple. You hungry?"

Wade nodded that he was then wiped the sweat from his forehead with the sleeve of his blue shirt, hoping he wouldn't pass out.

After a breakfast of fried eggs and strong coffee fixed by Levi, Wade walked to the front of the livery, stood in the shadows of the open doorway, took a drink of his strong coffee, and looked down the main street of Harper in memory. Ed Mason was busy sweeping off the steps leading up to the boardwalk in front of his store. Sam Carney's hired man was doing the same in front of the saloon as were other business owners. Smoke poured out of the chimney of the restaurant where he and Sheriff Block ate breakfast, and it all seemed like it was years ago. Other than a person here and there, the street was empty.

Levi walked up, stood in the doorway next to him, and spit tobacco juice on the ground. "He's staying at the Hoskins Hotel around the corner. Heard tell he has the whole top floor."

Wade glanced down at the gob of dark spit and then at the corner of the street, picturing George Hoskins in his elegant room eating a breakfast prepared by others.

"Has three men with him," said Levi in a soft voice. "All look like they know what they're doing, and one's always in the lobby."

As if not caring, Wade stared down the street. "Harry still sheriff?"

Levi nodded. "No deputies yet. Guess after Lee and Booth Fox, the sheriff's doing the hiring instead of the town council."

Wade grinned. "Can't much blame Harry for that." Then he turned and walked back to the stall where the mare was.

Levi watched him for a moment, then followed, stopped at the end of the stall.

Wade took his gun belt off the wall, strapped it on, and took the Colt out of the holster. He spun the cylinder, making sure each had a cartridge, holstered the Colt, and turned to Levi. "I'd appreciate you saddling my horse for me, Levi. I'd do it myself, but I'm afraid I'd rip these stitches out again."

Stepping into the stall, Levi asked, "You leaving?"

Wade walked out of the stall, making room for Levi to saddle the mare. "Time I left Harper, Levi. I don't want to cause you any trouble." He smiled. "You've been a good friend."

Levi tossed the saddle on the mare, wondering if maybe Wade Garrison was trying to say goodbye. "You headed out to see your family?"

"Not just yet." Wade picked up the Sharps leaning against the stall and the bandoleer of cartridges draped over the railing.

The cinch of the saddle tightened, Levi backed the mare out of the stall

Wade shoved the Sharps into the sheath on the front of the saddle, hung the bandoleer over the saddle horn

Levi handed Wade the reins. "There ya are, Marshal."

Wade took the reins and led the mare out of the livery into the warm, early morning sun. He stopped and shook Levi's hand firmly. "Thanks for patching me up, the cot, and breakfast." He smiled in memory. "Takes me back a few years."

Knowing Wade talked about the days when he and Emmett slept off a night on the town in the livery, Levi grinned. "Sure does at that."

Wade put one foot in the stirrup, then slowly and carefully climbed up, settling into the saddle and waited for the pain to subside. "Take care of yourself, Levi." Then he nudged the mare into a walk, turning her west and away from town.

Worried about the marshal's wound, hoping the stitches he put in last night held, Levi watched as Wade guided his horse at a walk across the yard, past the pile of firewood, chicken coop, and outhouse west toward the mountains. Wondering why he was heading west instead of east toward his wife and son, Levi hoped him a safe journey no matter where he went. Filled with curiosity and a little sadness, he watched the man named Wade Garrison a moment longer, then turned and walked back into the livery to tend to a horse that needed a new shoe.

The Wade Garrison Saga continues in the next book of the series 'Atonement.'

347

Other books by Richard Greene

Death of Innocence

The book Death of Innocence is a story about five families of my ancestors who lived during the Civil War. The story is based on fact, along with fiction and family lore. What happened to each of these families, for the most part, is true, but I also added in some fiction to fill in the gaps. Joseph Samuel Greene, the main character, was my great grandfather. I think you will find the story interesting as well as entertaining.

Befriended by a slave and the captain of a riverboat, a young Joseph Greene found adventure on the river and the love of a young Mary McAlexander. The Civil War would not only test their love for one

348

another, but the faith of the McAlexander, Chrisman, and Patterson families as each endured the war's death and destruction.

Death rode across the South in the guise of the southern home guard, taking the innocent without hesitation or regret. The sorrow they left, as well as the war, would last forever as each proud family endured while losing their innocence.

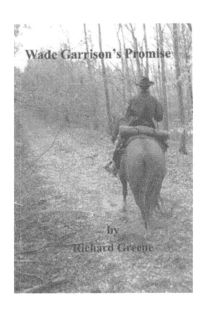

Wade Garrison's Promise

Wade Garrison was a simple man who, as a young man, came west chasing the stories he had read about in cheap western novels while growing up on a farm in South Carolina. He was not a violent man, and like most men of humble beginnings, he held his name and promises in high regard.

Watching the pine coffin containing Emmett Spears's lifeless body lowered into the dark grave, Wade made a silent promise of revenge. It was a promise that would take him far from the girl he loved and the Circle T Ranch in eastern Colorado.

As young Wade Garrison trailed the four men responsible for his friend's death, he would soon find himself unprepared for the death and violence he would find. He was unaware that in fulfilling his promise to avenge Emmett Spears, he would lose himself in the process.

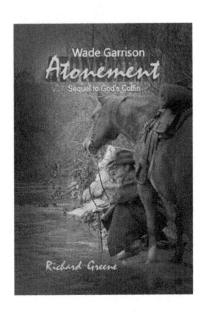

Atonement

In August 1878, Wade Garrison took his vengeance against the men who took the life of his unborn daughter and tried to kill his wife and son to settle a score. When the last man was dead from Wade's Sharps Rifle, he rode out of Harper, Colorado, a wanted man, and disappeared into the Montana Territory.

Morgan Hunter was a forty-eight-year-old gunman from west Texas wanted for killing a sheriff and his deputy. Fleeing from those killings and riding away from the sorrow that caused them, he rode into the Montana Territory. Unaware of the other, both men rode toward the same destiny.

Sarah looked toward the top of the hill every day, waiting for Wade and his red sorrel mare to come home. The days turned into weeks, and then into months, and still no word of him or from him.

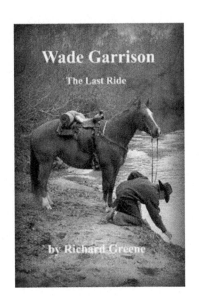

The Last Ride

It has been a year since Wade was shot and nearly died after being found innocent of murder at his trial in Harper, Colorado. Keeping his promise to God and Sarah, his Colt pistol lies tucked away in the bottom drawer of a chest in his bedroom, and the Sharps rifle covered in the rawhide sheath stands in a corner behind the chest. While he misses the life of a United States Deputy Marshal, he is content being with his wife Sarah, son Emmett, and daughter Mary Louise on their ranch.

Unknown to Wade and Sarah, he is about to be thrust into a life of violence once again by events that take place in the small town of Harper, Colorado. When the people of Harper seek his help for justice, the old life pulls at him. Resisting those old ways, he fears the town, and his son will think he is a coward. How can he break his promise to not only Sarah but to God?

Feeding the Beast

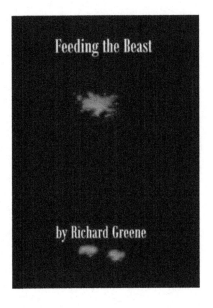

Feeding the Beast

by Richard Greene

1951

The Second World War has been over for six years, and the United States is now involved militarily in Korea, termed a Police Action rather than a war. On April 10, President Harry S. Truman fires General Douglas MacArthur, commander of the United States forces in Korea. This action resulted in the president's lowest approval rating of 23%, which remains the lowest of any serving president.

The Denver Police Department protecting a population of fewer than 415,000 residents was small compared to cities such as Chicago, New York, and Los Angeles.

The use of DNA by the judicial system is far in the future, electrically powered streetcars were the primary source of transportation and soon to be replaced by electric buses. Computers were in their infancy, and while most old newspapers and other public records are on microfilm, thousands of documents are not. Not every home could afford a television, so the radio remained the household's nightly entertainment. The closest thing to a cellular telephone was Dick Tracy's two-way wristwatch found in the comics, so the police had to rely on rotary phones and shortwave radios. Being Mirandized was not an option criminals were given in 1951 and would not be until 1966.

The term 'Serial Killer' would not be coined until 1970 by FBI Special Agent Robert Reesler.

The Last Time I Saw My Dad

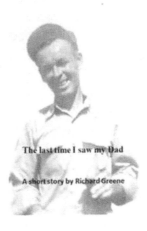

The last time I saw my Dad

A short story by Richard Greene

This short story is of my last trip to Houston, Texas, to visit my Dad and the memories it brought back of the summers I spent in Houston as a young boy.

Made in the USA
Coppell, TX
24 May 2021

56200906R00197